His lips brushed hers.

Her knees buckled at the sweetness of it. As his lips opened into hers, she invited him in. The butterflies in her stomach took full flight, and she felt a passion she'd never felt before. Gray's kiss made Henry seem like a schoolboy.

When the kiss deepened, she surrendered to it completely, letting her free arm drift over his shoulder, and she allowed the moment to absolve fear and fill her with unexpected need. He made her feel wanted, awakening every inch of her feminine body, sending chills all the way to her toes.

Her heart raced and her head spun. The good doctor knew exactly what he was doing, and if he didn't stop soon, she'd be his first patient of the day. . . .

By Lori Copeland
Published by Fawcett Books:

PROMISE ME TODAY
PROMISE ME TOMORROW
PROMISE ME FOREVER
SOMEONE TO LOVE
BRIDAL LACE AND BUCKSKIN
ANGEL FACE AND AMAZING GRACE

ANGEL FACE AND AMAZING GRACE

Lori Copeland

FAWCETT GOLD MEDAL • NEW YORK

A Fawcett Gold Medal Book
Published by Ballantine Books
Copyright © 1997 by Lori Copeland

All rights reserved under International and Pan-American Copyright Conventions. Published in the United States by Ballantine Books, a division of Random House, Inc., New York, and simultaneously in Canada by Random House of Canada Limited, Toronto.

http://www.randomhouse.com

Library of Congress Catalog Card Number: 96-96972

ISBN 0-449-14886-6

Manufactured in the United States of America

First Edition: January 1997

10 9 8 7 6 5 4 3 2 1

"Love never dies of starvation, but often of indigestion."
—NINON DE LENCLOS

Prologue

Show me a man who suffers the monthly miseries, and I'll show you a man hell-bent on finding relief.

Women should show the same gumption when it comes to female complaints. And since April Truitt believed so strongly in her philosophy, she'd made up her mind to do something about it.

Anxiously fingering the printed envelope, she glanced around the general store. It was busy this morning. Faith Lawson was buying fruit jars to put up the remainder of her vegetable garden. Lilly Mason was counting out eggs, the amount to be credited to her account. Lilly had dark circles under her eyes this morning, due to her habitual female problems. Poor Lilly suffered every month with severe depression. And severe cramping.

If only the women of Dignity would listen to Lydia Pinkham, their woes would be over!

Mail the letter, April! Mail it!

Edging the envelope closer to the mail slot, April eyed Ellen Winters, the town postmistress. The silver-haired, robust sixty year old was busy sorting mail, glancing up occasionally to smile at her.

"Nice morning, isn't it?"

"Beautiful."

"I'm always happy to see the heat of August give way to September."

Nodding, April took a deep breath, shoving the letter into the slot. The missive disappeared into the empty receptacle with a soft whoosh!

Elly glanced up. "Sending off for another catalog, dear?"

Pretending she hadn't heard her, April hurried out the front door, closing it firmly behind her. Exhaling a deep breath, she started down the walk at a fast pace.

Of course, once Elly saw who the letter was addressed to she would blab it all over town that Riley Ogden's granddaughter was in cahoots with Lydia Pinkham, but April would deny it as long as she could. Grandpa's heart was wearing out, and she didn't want to upset him. She knew the town thought she was impulsive and didn't think things through properly, but she liked to describe herself as spontaneous, impromptu—blazing a trail of new, exciting discoveries!

She believed in Lydia's vegetable compound. Though no one outside the Pinkham family knew the exact formula, it was said that unicorn root, life root, black cohosh, pleurisy root, and fenugreek seed mashed and combined with alcohol made up the mixture, which percolated like jelly, then it was filtered through cloth and bottled. The compound was touted to be the best thing that had ever happened to women, curing everything from prolapsed uteri to dandruff.

And she intended to help Lydia spread the good news about the miracle tonic. She wanted to encourage women to help themselves with their personal problems. She remembered her mother's distress and tragic death because she listened to unsympathetic doctors.

Grandpa, along with most of the doctors, thought Mrs. Pinkham was a quack, but wasn't that just like a man? *Men* didn't suffer female problems, so they didn't see what all the fuss was about. It was much easier to dismiss the subject with a shrewd wink and the simple explanation, "It's that time of the month."

Women had been getting short shrift for too long by men who had no understanding of women's physical problems, showing little sympathy for complaints of backaches, nervousness, and lack of pep and energy. If a woman was happy, peppy and full of fun, a man would take her places, but if she was cross, lifeless, and always tired out, well, a man just wasn't interested.

Doctors were too quick to offer surgery as a remedy for women's functional disorders, surgical procedures that were inadequate, ill-advised, and often too late and usually creating even larger problems for the woman. Medical men thought that by removing the uterus, the problem would be alleviated.

When faced with irate, hormonal women, physicians argued they were doing everything possible to find better, more acceptable alternatives, but April had her doubts. She was certain there had to be a better way to treat women's medical problems, although other than the painful monthlies, she wasn't personally affected yet. But someday when she needed it, she wanted effective treatment available.

She could have easily told her decision to Mrs. Pinkham in person. After all, the town of Lynn was only five miles from Dignity. But she thought a letter offering her assistance was more appropriate.

It was done. Now all she had to do was wait to hear from Mrs. Pinkham.

Crossing the street, April nodded good morning to John and Harriet Clausen, who were crossing from the opposite side. John tipped his hat pleasantly.

"Morning, Miss Truitt."

April nodded. "Mr. Clausen. Mrs. Clausen."

"How's your grandfather?"

"Very good, Mrs. Clausen. Thank you."

"Give him our best."

"I will."

Wagon teams lined the streets of Dignity, Massachusetts, this hot, August morning. Truckmen loaded the long wagons that were balanced on one axle and pulled by two horses harnessed in tandem. The carters wore long, loose frocks of heavy cloth or leather that were gathered on a string at the neck and fell to the calf, an outfit that dated back to the 1600s.

The men unloaded hogsheads of molasses, flour, and brown sugar from the wagons they'd driven from Boston. They'd haul back produce grown by the local farmers and wood goods carved by artisans.

In the distance, the sun glinted off sparkling blue waters in the harbor. The mercantile and livery were doing a thriving business this morning. The mouthwatering smells of cinnamon and apples drifted from Menson's Bakery. Many a Dignity housewife would forsake her kitchen and buy one of Addy Menson's apple pies for supper.

Striding past Ludwig's Drug Store, April paused long enough to tap on the front window. Beulah Ludwig, known affectionately as Porky, glanced up, smiling when she saw April peering in at her.

Grinning, April mouthed, "I did it."

Shaking her head, Porky made a face that clearly expressed her disapproval.

Dismissing the look with a cheerful wave of hand,

April walked on. She didn't care what anyone thought. When April Truitt believed in something, something as important to womankind, as exciting as Lydia E. Pinkham's Vegetable Compound, then she had to support it.

Period.

She was committed.

"Or should be," she giggled.

Feeling surprisingly confident about the decision, she hurried toward Ogden's Mortuary, sitting on the corner of Main and Fallow Streets. The funeral parlor had become her home when Delane Truitt, her mother, died seven years ago. Riley Ogden had taken his granddaughter in and raised her with stern, but loving, care.

At times he was prone to throw up his hands in despair, stating, "You, young lady, have too much of your father in you!"

But April didn't take offense. She knew he thought the world of his son-in-law, Jack Truitt, and had grieved as hard as his daughter when Jack died in a train derailment at the age of thirty.

Someday she would marry Henry Long, and Grandpa would come and live with them in Boston, which Henry favored. Maybe Henry didn't send delicious ripples down her spine, but he was considered a good catch and they did share the same philosophies about the Compound.

But marriage was in the future.

Right now, she planned to do what she could to improve women's lot in modern society.

And the first step was to tell every woman she could about Mrs. Pinkham's elixir.

Chapter 1

Dignity, Massachusetts—August 1876

"Ladies, Ladies! Please! May I have your attention! There's no need to shove! There's plenty to go around for all!"

As Lydia Pinkham shouted to gain order, April stood behind a long table piled high with bottles of Lydia E. Pinkham's Vegetable Compound, eager to sell to those women brave enough to try the revolutionary new cure-all for female complaints.

"Sickness is as unnecessary as crime," Lydia declared as the women pressed closer, trying to get a better look at the small brown bottles. "And if I may be so bold, no woman should be condemned to suffer 'female problems' when there is a curative readily available!"

Eyes widening, the women drew back as if a snake had bit them.

"Ladies, ladies! Don't be alarmed. The Pinkham Compound is a curative that is a special formula of nature's own elements," Lydia explained.

Women were hesitant to talk about such things, but today's group of women who'd come to hear Mrs. Pinkham's theories on women's health issues seemed eager to hear what the product would do. April was excited by the response and delighted to be part of Pinkham's team.

Rumor had it that Lydia's brew was ninety percent alcohol, but the remedy apparently helped. Mrs. Pinkham brewed her compound on a stove in the cellar of the Pinkham home. Rows of brown bottles with labels detailing all the ailments it could cure, were lined up on the table in front of April, waiting to be sold.

Lydia was usually too busy making the compound and writing advertising copy to conduct a rally herself, but she'd decided to take the campaign on the road to Boston.

April considered today a plus. Since Grandpa was unaware of her involvement with Lydia, she was relieved when the small Pinkham marketing entourage—consisting of her two sons, Dan and Will, Henry Trampas Long, and herself—had left Dignity to conduct sales in Lynn, a small town between Boston and Dignity. She'd been with Lydia a little over two weeks, and she was relieved to discover that Dignity residents chose to overlook her involvement with Mrs. Pinkham in order to keep her activities from an ailing Riley.

The town mortician and cofounder was narrow-minded on the subject of Pinkham's compound.

"The perfect woman," Lydia continued, "should experience no pain, but since that woman would be rare, indeed, the great majority suffer near deathlike anguish during her natural functions."

Lydia Pinkham's sad but compelling eyes met the gaze of every woman in attendance as she walked the length of the table, holding a bottle of her vegetable compound high for all to see. Tall placards held by Dan and Will displayed copies of newspaper advertisements that had run in most papers in Massachusetts. The headlines decried the major complaints of women of the day—I AM NOT WELL ENOUGH TO WORK, one stated, followed by the photo of a contrite woman standing before an angry husband who had no dinner waiting on the table and no clean shirts in the wardrobe due to temporary menstrual impediment. In the descriptive, Lydia E. Pinkham offered her "sympathy and aid" but reminded that there was a ready remedy. Lydia E. Pinkham's Vegetable Compound would, the ad stated, "restore to vigorous health the lives of those previously sorely distressed."

Another claim boldly stated: OPERATIONS AVOIDED; another I'M SIMPLY ALL WORN OUT, then depicted a woman who had collapsed from fatigue.

Yet another touted: SOCIAL TRAGEDY—WOMEN WHO BRAVE DEATH FOR SOCIAL HONORS, detailing how one very socially prominent woman suddenly leaped from her chair with a scream of agony, then fell insensible to the floor. The doctor told the victim's anxious husband that she was suffering from an acute case of nervous prostration brought on by female trouble, and hinted at an operation.

Fortunately, a friend suggested Lydia E. Pinkham's Vegetable Compound.

Surgery was avoided.

The din was getting louder, and Lydia raised her voice to be heard above it. April shifted from one foot to the other, wishing she'd worn more comfortable shoes.

All the pandemonium only verified how badly women needed Lydia's cure.

More than once during the brief time she'd been working for Lydia, she'd wanted to sink right into the ground when a riot broke out. Containers knocked over and broken, women clamoring for a little brown bottle that would change their lives. Selling to women who pushed, shoved, and made it impossible to conduct business in an orderly fashion unnerved April.

But she believed in what Mrs. Pinkham was doing, so she wouldn't think of giving up her job. She not only took pride in her work but was earning her own money for the first time in her life. It gave her a sense of purpose and fulfillment.

As Lydia droned on, Will Pinkham passed out the "Guide for Women" leaflets to ladies who were not as convinced as Mrs. Pinkham that their ailments should be openly discussed in a public forum, even among other females.

The babble was getting louder, and a couple of the women were looking embarrassed.

Lydia continued, "I wish that every woman who feels dissatisfied with her lot would realize that she is sick, and take steps to cure herself.

"Lydia E. Pinkham's Vegetable Compound will make a woman cheerful, happy, eager to meet her husband's wishes. Ladies! Once more you will realize the joys of your home! You will have found your true vocation—to be a devoted wife and loving mother!"

"It's hard to believe that a compound could do all that!" a tall, raw-boned woman shouted from the back of the crowd.

Lydia, thin lips pursed, pale except for the two coins of color high on her cheekbones, leveled a look at the woman who would dare to question her claims. "Have you tried the product, dear lady?"

The woman shrank back. "Not yet."

April readied the copies of the four-page "Helps for Women" that Lydia and her sons had written and had had printed to encourage sales.

Glancing up, she took an involuntary step backward as three women in the crowd voiced their dubious skepticism that the claims were nonsense.

"It just doesn't seem proper to talk about female complaints so boldly in the newspaper for everyone to see," a voice added softly from the front row.

April looked up, mentally groaning when she saw Gray Fuller join the crowd. Having stationed himself conspicuously to her right, he was listening, arms folded, a scowl on his handsome features as he listened to the sales pitch.

Dr. Fuller had made quite a stir when he'd moved to Dignity. Speculation ran rampant about him, and why he'd chosen a small coastal town to establish a practice.

Then there were his looks.

No kind, comfortable country doctor, this man. Tall and lean, wearing his "city clothes" like one of those men in the catalog in Pearl Mason's mercantile. Even Porky said that the rich dark brown hair that the young doctor wore just a shade too long was outrageously attractive. From what she'd heard, every single woman in a twenty-mile radius was making a fool of herself over Dr. Gray Fuller.

What is he doing here? April thought resentfully, squirming at the expectation that he just might recognize her as the woman he'd seen at a distance at the mortuary. He and Grandpa had struck up an instant friendship and for the past week visited nightly on the mortuary side porch. She purposely steered clear of them during the doctor's nocturnal visits, preferring to keep a safe distance between her and any doctor—but still, he could have gotten a close enough look at her to associate her with Riley. . . .

Sinking lower behind the bottles of compound, April prayed he wouldn't recognize her.

* * *

Standing back from the crowd, Gray listened to Lydia Pinkham make her sales pitch with growing skepticism.

The majority of the women present this morning were older, he observed.

His eyes narrowed as he studied the young woman with honey-brown hair and whiskey colored eyes, crouched behind the table stacked high with bottles of elixir. Studying her for a moment, he tried to place her.

He'd seen her before.

But where? She looked a lot like the elusive woman he'd seen in the shadows when he visited Riley at the mortuary.

Since coming to Dignity a month earlier, he'd seen a sea of new faces. But this one . . . yes, he was sure he'd seen her somewhere before.

Focusing on the speaker, Gray listened to Pinkham's outrageous claims. He was relieved that druggists were reluctant to display the Pinkham posters or sell the compound. He was told many women refused to read the pamphlets because the explicit language embarrassed them.

It was a damn good thing. Women in pain, who had seen family members and friends debilitated by health problems related to the reproductive systems, were vulnerable. Open to all kinds of shysters who promised relief.

It was ridiculous the way someone just cooked up a batch of weeds on a stove, bottled it, and peddled it as a "cure." More often than not it worked against normal bodily function.

Still, such snake-oil salesmen were successful. Public trust had dropped so low, women were beginning to abandon doctors in favor of newcomers such as Lydia who promised a non-surgical option.

He regarded Mrs. Pinkham and her kind as over-zealous. Pure and simple. She, and others like her, were a great part of the reason he'd decided to practice in the rural area rather than Boston.

If he could convince people to trust doctors, the well-schooled physicians, then he could save lives. That wasn't always possible, but he was dedicated to eliminating needless death—if he could only educate others.

He suspected that the reason for Mrs. Pinkham's efforts to sell her medicine was not born of a need to help the sick. The Pinkhams were the victims of the financial panic of September 1873. After the banking house of Jay Cooke failed, credit froze, factories shut down, businesses folded, and wage workers had faced a winter of starvation. Isaac Pinkham, Lydia's husband, was one of the thousands who'd seen their speculative ventures fold. When banks started closing, Cooke's foreclosed and threatened to arrest those unable to pay their overdue bills.

Isaac Pinkham collapsed under the pressure of the threat of losing everything he'd spent his life accumulating. When the bank's attorney, who it turned out was a distant relative of the Pinkhams, arrived to serve notice of foreclosure, the family persuaded him to spare Isaac the embarrassment of arrest and jail because of his illness.

Isaac had not improved; Dan, one of the sons, had lost his grocery store and went into bankruptcy; son Will had given up his plans to attend Harvard and was working as a wool-puller.

Charlie, another Pinkham son, was working as a conductor on the horse cars, along with helping the family endeavor. Daughter Aroline, who had just graduated high school, helped support the family by teaching school.

The Pinkhams had given up their grand house in Glenmere and moved to a smaller home on Western Avenue, and recently, with what little resources the Pinkhams possessed, begun their vegetable compound venture. Marketing the elixir was now a family venture. Everyone contributed to the enterprise. Dan and Will provided the brains and sinew. Lydia made the medicine. Charles and Aroline turned over their wages to help pay for alcohol and herbs. And together, Will and Lydia had worked up advertising copy and put out a pamphlet called "Guide for Women." Even Isaac contributed. Sitting in his rocker, he folded and bundled the pamphlets for Dan to hand out.

Gray was told that at first Lydia had made the compound for friends. Before long women were coming from as far away as Salem to purchase it. Now the Pinkham family had expanded the manufacture of the elixir, and Gray was worried. Pinkham's business was growing. More and more women were forsaking a visit to the doctor in favor of self-medicating with the Pinkham compound.

The newspaper was full of ads for remedies like Wright's Indian Vegetable Pills, Oman's Boneset Pills, Vegetine, and Hale's Honey of Horehound and Tar.

Vegetable remedies, botanicals, had gained wide popularity, and Gray wasn't sure how the growing tide could be stemmed.

Today, looking around the crowd, it appeared his worries were well-grounded.

"Just try the compound for thirty days—"

"Excuse me," Gray called out above the growing din, interrupting Mrs. Pinkham's sales pitch. "Ladies—" He tried again.

The sound level lessened enough for him to be heard.

"If you believe in potions, you're placing your health in untrained hands! Your faith is better placed in trained physicians—"

He's just like all the others, April thought, irritated.

A voice from the back interrupted. "My doctor just says I have to 'put up with pain' because it's 'woman's lot,' " she parroted. "Is that fair? Aren't women deserving of more concern?"

That's what Mama should have done, April thought. Just put up with the heavy bleeding until she could find something like Lydia's tonic. The memory of her mother's surgery and ensuing death fed her anger at the situation in which women found themselves.

"Of course you are," Gray started. "But you must be patient! We're looking for remedies—"

"He's as blind as all the others," April murmured, her hands making fists at her sides. This arrogant man was going to be a thorn in her side, she could see that.

"My doctor prefers to talk to my husband, as if I didn't have enough sense to know what he's talking about!"

"And it was one of those 'trained physicians' who let my mother bleed to death," April blurted out, as much to her own surprise as to everyone else's.

When Gray's gaze swung to her, April wished she'd kept her temper in better control. Ordinarily she avoided drawing attention to herself, but today she couldn't help it. He was a rude, boorish . . . *man!* She met his gaze, lifting her chin in defiance.

"I say we take responsibility for our own bodies," a tall heavyset woman declared. "I'm buying two bottles right now."

The women were on the move, and April watched the onslaught coming toward her with growing alarm.

Bracing herself, her gaze darted about for a quick escape if things got out of hand. Boxes of compound were stacked to her right; two bramble bushes to her left. Groaning, her eyes searched feverishly for an out. She'd have to make a break for the middle, and run straight at . . . Him.

She was sure Gray Fuller would recognize her now. Grandpa might look like a genial old Santa Claus without the beard, but when he was riled he didn't have that jolly old person's mild temperament.

Far from it. The rotund octogenarian had a razor-sharp wit and a tongue to match.

April was jolted back to the present as the women bore down on her, attempting to squeeze between the table holding the vegetable compound and the boxes of product stacked to the right.

Aware she wasn't going to be able to get out of their way quickly enough, she braced herself for the onslaught.

A robust matron hit her sideways, knocking her into the heavily laden table. Stumbling, her hand flailed out for support, and she braced herself as she was slammed from the other side. Another hard bump from the rear, and she fell against the table, knocking bottles of compound over in a domino effect.

Grabbing out, she tried to save the batch of tonic from ruin, but the table legs collapsed, and it and the bottles tumbled to the ground in a thunderous sound of breaking glass and splitting boards.

The women kept coming, undaunted.

April was hurtled forward into the splintered table, double-stepping broken bottles of compound that were draining sticky contents onto the earth below. She hit the ground with a thump!

Attempting to get up, she was knocked aside, whacking her head on a piece of the table. Pain shot through her temple and everything went blurry as she fell back, holding her eye.

Silence fell over the crowd as all heads turned to the wilted figure lying on the ground.

"Oh, my!" a shrill voice exclaimed. "She's fainted!"

She hadn't, but she certainly wished she had. Not only had she humiliated herself, she was going to have a whale of a headache.

Moaning, she stirred ever so slightly at the feel of a cool hand on her cheek. She kept her eyes tightly closed, wishing they'd just leave her alone so she could crawl away, unnoticed.

"Is she injured?"

"Oh, my, my." A hand gently fanned her face. "Some-one bring a dipper of water!"

"Stand back!" a voice cried. "This man says he's a doctor!"

April froze when she heard *his* voice coming toward her. Drats. Now she'd really done it. Of course Dr. Fuller would offer his services!

"Someone get this table out of the way." Gray Fuller threaded through the crowd, issuing orders. "One of you ladies loosen her collar. Please, stand back and give her some air."

April felt the pressure of four manly fingers rest casu-ally against her neck for a brief moment. A woodsy scent drifted pleasantly to her, and she wondered why *he* smelled so good when other men smelled like . . . like . . . well, men.

Embarrassed, she groaned in frustration at the situation she'd gotten herself into. Most of the women she knew would give their eyeteeth to have the handsome doctor's attention. She might feel the same way if the circum-stances were different. She'd hoped to be introduced to him at church, or a social function, not while lying on the ground surrounded by broken glass and brown sticky goo.

Pressing his head to her breast, he pretended to listen

for a heartbeat as he whispered, "You're going to have to groan louder. They didn't hear you."

April's left eye flew open, then quickly closed. "Wh . . . what?"

Lifting his head, he grinned.

Cracking one eye open, April looked up into a pair of startling dark green eyes set off by lashes so thick any woman would envy them.

His smile, trained directly on her, was decidedly wicked. The firm set of his jaw excited her. She had never seen that look on Henry's face.

She mentally moaned. If they were handing out awards for good looks, he would take the prize. His practiced masculine gaze ran over her lightly. She shivered, even though it was blazing hot.

She felt a warm wave of breath in her ear just before he repeated, "You'll have to groan louder. They can't hear you."

Embarrassed he had seen through her ruse, she mumbled through closed lips, "Are you sure?"

"Trust me."

Of course. Trust him. The first thing he was sure to do was tell Grandpa that she was helping the controversial Lydia Pinkham sell her medicinal elixir. And when Grandpa heard that, along with what had happened here today, he'd have a fit of apoplexy.

"Moan!" the doctor ordered quietly.

Complying, April rendered a loud, mournful wail.

"Stand back," Dr. Fuller demanded, rising to clear a path through the crowd. The women obediently stepped aside, murmuring approvingly among themselves about the doctor's quick action.

"Is she all right, Doctor?"

"She appears to be coming around."

The women oohed and ahhed, their eyes worriedly

trained on the young woman lying on the ground like a rag doll.

Assisting April to her feet, the doctor led her to a nearby bench. She pretended to be dazed, and if the truth were known, it was the good doctor that sent her head spinning.

Although uneasy at the sudden physical intimacy, she kept up her pretense, wavering convincingly for the women who watched on with obvious concern.

Excitement over, the crowd began to break up. Most refused to leave without purchasing a bottle of Lydia E. Pinkham's Vegetable Compound.

Henry Long rushed to April's side, concern on his babyish features. "April, are you ill, darling?"

Patting Henry's hand consolingly, she assured him she wasn't, only a bit shaken up.

Lydia stepped over to ask if April had sustained any serious injuries. When told she hadn't, she threaded her way back into the crowd, where Will and Dan were selling the compound as fast as they could dole it out.

When the area cleared, Dr. Fuller attempted to conduct a brief examination. "You've got a bump." He touched her forehead. "Should make a nice bruise."

"Wonderful," she muttered, drawing a deep breath to clear her head. Something else to explain to Grandpa.

"Are you experiencing any pain?"

"No, and you've done quite enough, thank you." April felt like a fool! Not only had she drawn undue attention to herself by speaking up like that, she'd created a scene that was sure to get back to Grandpa and all of Dignity before she did. Still, it wasn't all that unpleasant being administered to by Dr. Fuller. The feel of his gentle hand on her forehead lingered, and she reached to touch the spot.

"Ouch!" It had felt much better when the doctor touched the bump.

Studying her for a moment, Gray's forehead wrinkled in a frown. "I'm trying to place you—haven't we met, Miss . . ."

"I have an ordinary face," she excused, standing up.

Regaining her bearings, she straightened her dress, smoothed her fly-away hair, remembered to thank the doctor, and took off in the opposite direction in a hurried gait.

"If you have any pain, be sure and see a doctor . . . Miss?"

She dismissed him with an absent wave.

"I'm fine, really."

He'd remember where he saw her and tell Grandpa. She might as well brace herself for the explosion.

Gray stared after her and watched the sway of her slender hips as she hurried along. He searched his mind trying to recall their meeting. How could he possibly have met such a beautiful woman and not remembered?

One thing for sure, their meeting today would not be forgotten. It would take some doing to forget the surge of delight her softness caused cradled against him when he helped her to the bench, or the intoxicating smell of her hair that wafted through the air when she tossed her head.

No, if he ever saw her again, he'd remember.

Chapter 2

The woman in bed languidly ran her fingers through the thick mat of dark hair coating Gray Fuller's chest. "You fairly steal a woman's breath away, *chéri*."

The irresistible ebony-haired beauty curled against Gray, purring like a kitten full of milk lying on a rug in the warm sun. Her hand drifted across his muscled stomach.

"You're insatiable, Francesca," he murmured sleepily.

Closing his eyes, he waited for his heartbeat to slow. Francesca DuBois was, if anything, inventive. Silently he conceded that their passionate reunions spoiled him. They'd been engaged for nearly a year, but when he'd moved his practice to Dignity, it caused a disruption in the intensity of their relationship. Francesca thought he should practice in Boston.

At first she had argued with his decision, but when it became clear he was going to make the move, she stopped arguing. Gray knew that she thought the forced separation would make him homesick. But, just the opposite had occurred.

Gray had realized his calling. Boston had its share of progressive doctors—and few people who needed, or wanted, them. The rural communities still depended on midwives and herbalists to serve their medical needs—people with no training, who gained what little knowledge they had through information passed down from family members who had learned it from a grandmother or aunt.

No, he wasn't needed in Boston. But he *was* needed in the countryside. Francesca couldn't understand that; couldn't or wouldn't understand it. Her father wasn't much better.

Though he was indebted to Louis DuBois for financing his medical internship, he didn't agree with the man's focus on medicine as merely a means to make money. Somewhere along the way, Louis had forgotten medicine was a service to humanity.

When Gray announced his intentions to take over Joe McFarland's practice in Dignity, Louis hadn't argued with him. Instead, he took the position that it wouldn't take long for Gray to admit his mistake and return to Boston, where he would then be taken into one of DuBois's three clinics as a full partner—a stance Francesca also embraced.

Louis's offer was tempting. Only a fool would refuse it, but Gray had dedicated his skill to treating the ill rather than catering to the privileged.

Now that he had been in Dignity for a little over a month, his convictions were even stronger. He wanted a solid practice, to lay down roots in the small harbor town. Somehow he would make Francesca see this was his mission in life, his destiny.

Personal aspects of his life could be, and were readily, set aside in his ongoing desire for medical knowledge. His wife should support his choice. Obviously Francesca wasn't ready to do that. At least not yet. But if she loved him as much as she said, then she'd come to understand his need to serve rather than conciliate.

He had explained his position to her on a number of occasions, but she refused to listen. It was clear she believed her powers of persuasion were mightier than his ideology.

Admittedly, the past hour had gone a long way to prove her point. She was a beautiful woman, and they were obviously well matched physically. Once she accepted his decision, they could move forward.

"Ooh, poor *chéri*. I have made you tired?" Francesca murmured, feistily nipping his shoulder with small, pearly white teeth.

"Mmmmm."

Sliding astride him, she smiled seductively, her eyes darkening with pleasure. "But, Monsieur Fuller, I remember the long hours we spent together only last month . . . this afternoon has barely begun."

Closing his eyes, Gray held his breath as she eased him inside her. "I hadn't gotten up before dawn to deliver a baby that day, nor been up until midnight the night before with a child who had croup, then travel twenty miles to get to Boston to see you. . . ."

Francesca's throaty laughter floated through the small hotel room. A fan lazily turned overhead, stirring the hot, languid air. Heavy drapes were drawn against the afternoon sun, but the room was stifling. A thin sheen of perspiration coated their heated bodies.

Dotting light kisses across his jaw, she whispered, "Then you should not have moved away, bad boy. It was not necessary. You know Papa would—"

Pulling her mouth back to his, he stilled her arguments. An argument was averted as a month's abstinence overrode his logic.

* * *

Much later, he eased her off him, lying for a moment until his breathing returned to normal.

"Gray," she purred softly, touching his skin that was still moist from lovemaking, "why won't you listen to reason . . . come back to Boston with me—"

"Francesca." Sitting up, he shoved his fingers through his damp hair.

She followed him up, pressing her bare breasts against his back, slick with perspiration, and letting her hands drift over his furred chest.

"I do not understand why you feel you must live in that bumpkin town . . . Destiny. What is there in this Destiny?"

"It's Dignity, and people there need a doctor."

"There are sick people in Boston as well. People who pay for their services with things other than chickens, produce from the garden, and baked offerings from their ovens!"

Rising to her knees, she ran the tip of her tongue across his shoulders. "Give up this crazy idea and come back to Boston. Papa will set you up in practice with Jake Brockman, Lyle Lawyer, and Frank Smith. We can be married within the month."

Drawing a deep breath, Gray pulled back the curtains to look out on the streets of Boston. Dignity wasn't Boston, but that was the attraction that drew him. He liked the town's sleepy lifestyle. He liked its people— good, hardworking, God-fearing farmers, their children and wives, town merchants, and neighboring families who came from miles around to seek his medical advice. His, Gray Fuller's knowledge, not Brockman, Lawyer, Smith, and Fuller's advice, as Francesca would have it.

The area itself drew him. Dignity, like Boston, was on the coast of Massachusetts Bay. Wind-swept land, trees shaped by the wind and the breeze off the ocean, rolling countryside with rounded hills, gentle glens, and glacial deposits. A finger of land called East Point protruded into the ocean. The township itself centered around a common with a white-spired church standing on one side and the town hall directly across.

Families strolled around the common on a cool evening, or brought picnics on Sunday afternoons. Dignity was interesting, compelling, and more to his taste than the Boston Francesca loved.

It was a sense of peace that had drawn him when he first visited there six months earlier. The doctor in him demanded it, the man in him wanted it.

Twirling a lock of his hair around her finger, Francesca pouted. "Papa was talking about you last night. He asked if you had come to your senses—"

Gray cut her off. "How is Louis?"

"Oh, *chéri*," she complained, "someone has stolen your mind in that town! You are surely not thinking clearly!"

Gray was suddenly claustrophobic. Throwing the sheet aside, he got out of bed. Looking bereft, Francesca dropped her head to the pillow, eyeing him sullenly as he began to dress.

"But there is so much more here in Boston," she protested, her hands toying with the thin sheet draped across her breasts. "I am here."

Yes, she was here, he conceded. And he loved her. But he also knew her strengths as well as her weaknesses. Francesca was a beautiful, charming, but spoiled young woman who'd been raised in the lap of luxury; a woman who used her position as leverage to get whatever she wanted. Position her father had earned for her.

Louis DuBois had come to the United States from France shortly before Francesca was born. Starting with little more than ingenuity, he'd built a successful group of medical clinics in Boston. Francesca was his only child, and he wasn't subtle about his desire for his daughter to marry Gray.

Rolling out of bed, Francesca let the tangled sheets fall to the floor. Sauntering to the mirror, she studied her naked reflection, her expression perfecting a small frown as she preened. "Papa is not a patient man," she mused. "I fear he will soon tire of asking you, Gray, and bring someone else into the clinic."

Deep-blue eyes shifted to him as he continued dressing. Gray was aware of her silent invitation. Her confidence in her sexuality was plain, and she used it without shame. Coal-black hair framing a heart-shaped, creamy face and wide blue eyes made a pretty package. Agitated, he felt a renewed stir of passion.

Francesca was a woman any man would be proud to be seen with, and he knew the medical business in Boston was strongly connected with power. What sane man would turn down the offer that had been set before him six months ago? Marry Francesca and be set for life.

Still, something in him refused to make the compromise.

"You could return to Boston and never have to work long hours again. There will be three other men to see to your patients when you have better things to do. Papa will furnish everything we would ever want or need."

She turned ever so slightly to allow him a better view of what he was resisting. Her young, firm body beckoned to him, pleading for reconsideration.

"Gray, this would be the perfect time." Her voice dropped to a husky timbre, mistaking his silence for conformity. "The old Tealson mansion is up for sale—I've always wanted that house. It has been left to molder a bit, but it's such a beautiful house. I will decorate it, make it the showplace it should be. We will throw the biggest, most elaborate Christmas party this city has ever seen! It will be so . . ."

As she droned on about the party, Gray's mind was on Dignity, and Lydia Pinkham's show a few days earlier. The nerve of that woman, claiming her elixir could cure everything from cramps to kidney ailments. And women were listening to the exaggerated claims!

His irritation eased when he thought about that spunky girl who pretended to faint. Surely if she was the girl he had seen at the mortuary, she would have said so. He smiled. The way she had felt in his arms. It was nice. But he wasn't in the market for a woman. Francesca was all the woman he could handle.

"Gray? Gray!"

Francesca's strident tone drew him back.

"Sorry. What were you saying?"

"You're *not* listening to me."

"I'm . . . a bit tired today."

"Oh?" A smile dimpled her cheeks as she provocatively tilted her head at him. "Too tired?"

Chuckling, he looped his tie around his collar. "You're unquenchable, you know that?"

Giggling, she crossed the room to drape her arms around his waist. Pressing her face into his back, she murmured, "You do miss me, don't you?"

"Of course, Francesca, but my work keeps me busy."

"If you would only return to Boston, your life would be so much easier. There is no need—"

"Francesca, we've talked this to death."

"You are entirely too practical, Gray Fuller." She dropped a kiss on his arm, trailing her long nails down the length of his shoulder, "but I can wait. For you I will wait."

"It won't be long. I promise. Six months, a year, and

I'll have a practice established; then we'll talk about buying a house."

She frowned. "In that horrid Destiny?"

"Dignity. And you'll grow to love it, I promise." He dropped a kiss against her lips. "I've got to go."

"So soon?" Francesca pouted, easing to his front. Her tongue slipped between his lips.

The effort was not lost. His hands explored the soft line of her waist, her bare hip, feeling a niggling of regret as he briefly returned the kiss before gently setting her aside. "Give your father my best."

Frowning, she reluctantly stepped back. "You are coming to dinner on the twelfth? You know Papa is entertaining some very prominent businessmen."

"I plan to be here if nothing urgent arises."

He'd have the next installment on his debt to Louis. Though Louis had assured him many times that repayment wasn't necessary, Gray was determined to owe nothing to Louis except gratitude before the year was finished.

"Gray!" she wailed. "You promised!"

"Of course I'll be here, Francesca." He impatiently jammed his arms into his jacket. "I'll instruct all my patients that they are, under no circumstance, to become indisposed on the twelfth." Suddenly he needed fresh air.

"Oh, wait! I have something for you." Reaching for a silk wrap, she tied the sash around her waist before going to the mound of boxes he'd carried in from their morning shopping expedition.

She brought out a small hatbox and opened it with some ceremony. "You're going to adore this."

Gray stared at what he had to assume was a hat, but he'd be damned if he'd call it that himself.

Holding it up for inspection, she grinned. "Isn't it just the most extraordinary thing?"

Extraordinary? Every bit of that.

"Very nice. You'll look lovely in it."

"Me? Oh, you silly goose! It's not for me, it's for you."

Gray's heart sank. Surely she didn't expect him to wear . . . *that*.

"It's marvelous, isn't it?" She turned the hat around for his inspection.

"What is it? Exactly."

"A pillbox hat. It's the latest thing in bicycling attire. You're to wear it with tight-fitting knee breeches, a very tight, military kind of jacket, and when you're cycling down the street, you carry a bugle to warn pedestrians of your approach. I ordered it from France."

"I don't bicycle."

"No?" She frowned. "Well, you should. It's the most amazing thing. Daddy bought me one . . . of course, I've purchased the britches and jacket for you also so we can dress alike when we bicycle."

"I don't have a bicycle."

Her eyes sparked devilishly. "You do now!"

She smiled satisfactorily as she turned the hat round and round in her hand. "Here. Try it on."

Gray let Francesca settle the navy-blue pillbox hat atop his head. He felt stupid. Was this what it would be like married to Francesca? Being manipulated was certainly not to his liking. Between her and her father, he wouldn't stand a chance to be his own man.

But surely their love for one another— He did love Francesca, didn't he? There was certainly strong physical attraction. Was it love or lust? And the lure of her family's standing and money was not to be scoffed at. What was he thinking? Of course, he loved Francesca.

She clapped her hands with delight. "Oh, it is as dashing as I imagined! Look at yourself in the mirror."

Catching a glimpse of his reflection, he mentally grimaced. The hat made him look like an organ grinder's monkey. All he needed was a tin cup.

"Francesca, I don't wear hats." Feelings be damned. He wouldn't be caught dead in this hat.

"Nonsense." Standing on tiptoes, she kissed the end of his nose. "You look splendid, darling. Absolutely splendid."

He looked like a fool. A splendid one.

"I have to go. I have patients to see."

"You work much, much, much too hard, darling," she gushed, hanging possessively to his neck.

"Francesca. Let go. You're choking me."

Relinquishing her hold, she sighed. "When will I see you again?"

"The twelfth. That's the earliest I can be back."

"I will be waiting," she promised. Her hand trailed down the front of his trousers and rested on his manhood. "And you promise to think about returning to Boston to practice?"

"I have thought about it."

"Then think some more." She blew him a kiss as he left the room.

As he walked through the lobby of the hotel, he carried the pillbox hat hidden beneath his jacket.

Eyeing the trash receptacle, he pushed temptation aside and walked out the front door. Francesca had an elephant's memory. She remembered every article of clothing she ever purchased for him.

For now, at least, he was stuck with the damn thing.

Francesca had satisfied his male needs, but she'd done little for his confidence. He knew what he wanted, yet if he listened to her, he would become little more than a puppet, jumping to her every whim.

He needed to get back to Dignity where he could think. He preferred the simple life, the life Francesca could never accept.

Chapter 3

"How much?"

April told her the price, folding brown wrapping paper around a bottle of Lydia Pinkham's Vegetable Compound. "And thank you. You'll be feeling better in no time."

The past week had been successful for the compound. Sales were up, and women were beginning to return for second bottles.

April was starting to relax. Apparently the good doctor hadn't recognized her. At least she assumed he hadn't. Grandpa hadn't blown up, and he would, if he knew.

It was enough that Grandpa wouldn't approve of her involvement with Henry. Learning about her involvement with Lydia Pinkham would do him in.

She worried about his health, but it was his lectures that bothered her as well. Grandpa was stubborn and easily worked into a tizzy when she did something that went against his grain. It was best to just keep things to herself that would cause Grandpa fits.

"Miss?"

April returned to the business at hand. "I'm sorry. How many bottles?"

"Five. I wouldn't start a day without a dose of the elixir."

"Wonderful." April smiled, counting back the woman's change.

By the time the rally was over, April's feet hurt, her back ached, and she was thinking about taking a sip of Lydia's elixir herself. Not a big one, just enough to revive her sagging energy.

"Well, we've had a good day," Lydia commented as she sank onto a chair beside April's table. It was nearing dark now, and the last happy customer had left the meeting hall with a bottle of vegetable compound.

"We made eighteen dollars today."

"Eighteen? That's wonderful."

April put the money into an envelope and handed it to Mrs. Pinkham, then began placing the remaining bottles of elixir into a box. Dan would carry it to the carriage later. She glanced up, smiling when she saw another of Lydia's sons, Will, busily gathering up pamphlets the crowd had left behind.

Rubbing the bridge of her nose, Lydia closed her eyes wearily. "Wouldn't it be wonderful if we could place a bottle of compound in every woman's hand?"

"The way sales are picking up, that might not be so implausible."

"Oh, my dear." Lydia chuckled. "It's a very large world, and there are so many, many women who are trying to cope with female problems. . . . If they only knew there were alternatives."

"Ready to go, Mother?" Will called.

"Coming, dear." Getting up, Lydia smoothed back a stray hair. A tall, striking woman, Lydia was imposing enough to compel people to accept her claims. "We'll not have a meeting tomorrow, dear. Dan is traveling to Boston to look into new market opportunities."

April tried to conceal her relief. Every rally she attended left her anxious and full of guilt. If it wasn't for the community's concern for their kindly old undertaker, Riley would already know what his granddaughter was doing.

Lydia hesitated a moment at the door. "Is Henry coming for you?"

"Yes, he'll be here any moment now." Consulting her pendant watch, she noted the time. Henry was always prompt. If today's meeting hadn't ended early, he would be waiting now.

"I'm glad he's working with us. He and Daniel are quite bright. They have sound ideas for getting the compound into stores in Boston." Lydia shared a tired smile. "Well, there's advertising copy for the newspaper to write yet tonight. Good night."

"Good night."

Henry was going to Boston with Dan again? Why hadn't he told her? April wondered. That made the third trip in as many months, trips he'd failed to mention.

Checking her appearance by feel, April carefully rearranged her hat on curls that had taken her a full hour to fashion. She hoped she looked pleasing to Henry today. She'd worn the princess-style dress he favored, recalling how he swore its warm sherry color exactly matched her eyes. The dress was outrageously overpriced, but Grandpa was good about letting her purchase whatever she wanted from the mail-order catalog.

Turning slowly, she glanced down, perusing the cut of the dress. The jacket bodice was fashioned with short basques that formed a full overskirt. The buirasse bodice was tight and molded to the hips—an effect, if the look in Henry's eyes was any indication, he appreciated.

Tugging at the close-fitting waist, she wished she could wear the style without a long, tight corset. It was a good thing her job required her to stand, for the skirt of the dress was so tight, she couldn't have hoped to sit with any semblance of grace.

Straightening the tight sleeves, she absently reached for her reticule and turned toward the front door of the small meeting hall to see if Henry had arrived.

He had not, but it was still early. She'd told him seven o'clock, and it was just barely 6:45. Yet, she hoped he would hurry. They had so little time together anymore. His involvement with the compound kept him working long hours, sometimes late into the night.

Henry Trampas Long. Yet another secret she was keeping from Grandpa. One that would most certainly give him an attack if he ever learned of it. Grandpa didn't see Henry as she did. Devilishly handsome, with flaxen hair and bright-blue eyes that seemed to see right through her, Henry was admittedly more a "woman's man" than a "man's man."

Although they'd just begun working together, she'd known Henry all her life. They'd been schoolmates during their growing up years.

Henry was a natural born charmer. He got the nickname "Sweet Talker" after he'd persuaded the teacher to end classes a week early one summer. Miss West, clearly enchanted with her handsome pupil who was a mere two years younger than she, had fallen for his concocted story about the spring fever being counterproductive to learning.

As they grew up, they'd had their spats, but after they left school she began to view him differently—less as former schoolmate and more as the opposite sex.

At first April wasn't sure how she felt about the gradual change in their relationship, but then she realized

how wonderful it was to be courted by a man like Henry. Not only did they know one another well, but also he could charm the petals and thorns off a rose.

Grandpa, of course, still saw Henry as the fool who'd turned over outhouses at Halloween and played pranks on unsuspecting Dignity residents. It was easy for him to consider Henry's occasional appearances at the front door as innocuous.

But April didn't consider anything about Henry innocuous. Their relationship was growing closer every day. In fact, he'd been dropping hints recently that led her to believe he was about to propose any day now.

Hearing Henry's runabout buggy turn the corner, she ran to the doorway, watching him masterfully bring the bay to a halt in front of the building. Smiling, he stepped down, his wry grin hidden beneath a flaxen mustache.

April's heart swelled as she watched him approach. He was indeed a fine figure of a man, resplendent in a navy-blue double-breasted cutaway coat over a matching vest with trimly cut trousers in an imperceptible check pattern. A patterned tie was just visible beneath the collar of a snow-white shirt.

His hair, thick and full, was tamed somewhat by pomade, his mustache meticulously trimmed. He carried a flat-crowned hat in his left hand and his gaze was pinned directly on her.

"Angel Face," he murmured, reaching for her hand.

"Henry," she whispered, embarrassed that he would utter such an endearment in public, though delighted he would be so daring.

Concern filled his face. "Have I kept you waiting?"

"No, we finished early. You're right on time."

Assisting her into the buggy, Henry climbed aboard, and, with a smile in her direction, gently slapped the reins against the horse's rump.

"I hear we had a very good day," he commented as the buggy rolled away.

"A very good day. No problems, and we sold a number of bottles." Turning in the seat, she looked at him. "Henry, Lydia said you were going to Boston."

Glancing sideways, Henry smiled. "Didn't I mention it to you?"

"No . . . no, you didn't."

"Really? I thought I had. Dan and I will be looking for new marketing possibilities." He glanced her way. "Why?"

"Well, there's the Founders Hall dance next week . . ." The dance was an annual event everyone looked forward to. April had purchased her dress months ago. A frivolous evening-blue silk. Though Grandpa would protest, she intended to go with Henry.

Meeting her troubled gaze, he smiled. He was merely doing his job. There would be other dances, his eyes suggested to her.

"I'm sorry, dearest. It was thoughtless of me not to mention the trip earlier, but I kept hoping it could be delayed until after the Founders Hall dance. Alas, it can't be."

She ignored the awful sense of disappointment, vowing to conceal it. It would only make Henry's business commitments more difficult.

Arching his brows in concerned triangles, he said, "Forgive me, dearest?"

"Of course, Henry, it can't be helped."

"Dan and I will be going to Boston tomorrow. Had I known sooner, I'd have planned something special for us today."

"How long will you be gone?"

"I'm not sure. A few days." His hand reached over to cover hers in her lap. "Miss me?"

"You know I will."

"We'll have a very special supper when I get back."

He smiled down at her and her pulse accelerated. A "special" supper. Had the time finally come? Was he about to ask her to be his wife? Her mind whirled at the implication. Was that what she really wanted? She suddenly felt a trifle ill.

Henry halted the carriage at the side of the mortuary. A large mulberry tree partially hid the area. She insisted Grandpa wouldn't be as likely to see them together here.

"I wish—"

"Don't say it," April interrupted. "I just have to persuade Grandpa that I'm grown up enough to make my own decisions. He still thinks of me as a little girl."

His eyes swept her slender figure. "The man must be blind."

April's cheeks colored. Henry was so bold. So much more exciting than any of the other single men in Dignity or even in Lynn.

"He also still thinks of you as that hooligan who tied my sash to the school seat so my skirt would fall down around my ankles when I stood."

His grin was irresistibly devilish. "It was one of my better pranks."

"I was mortified, you know."

The grin widened. "I know. But your cheeks turned pink and your eyes got so wide with surprise, I was captivated by you from that moment on." Leaning forward, he stole a kiss.

She glanced nervously toward the house. "I need to go."

Henry settled back with a wry smile. "I'll see you when I get back from Boston."

She adored his acts of affection, but in proper surroundings. Not here. Not in public.

For now she contented herself with the tightening of his hand on hers.

Dignity's apothecary was midblock of Main and Fallow Streets. The establishment had been there for over twenty years. The sign over the door was faded, the building comfortably weathered.

Inside there were shelves of medicinal helps, bandages, alcohol for cuts and scrapes, liniment for strained muscles. One corner of the room held potions for farm animals. A long wooden counter stretched along the back, with the pharmacist's desk a step or two higher behind. This was Eldon Ludwig's throne from early morning to nearly twilight, dispensing medicine and opinions on everything from boils to congestion to broken limbs.

At the moment Eldon's seat was vacant, and a squarely built figure dressed in a butternut-brown dress stood behind the long counter, explaining the directions on a bottle of headache powders to Judge Petimount's widow.

April browsed through the store, reading labels on funny-looking bottles while she waited for Porky to finish with her customer.

Mrs. Petimount made her purchase and left shortly.

Wiping her hands on her apron, Porky grinned at April. "I thought you were busy selling Lydia E. Pinkham's Vegetable Compound to the enlightened ladies of Dignity, Boston, and surrounding areas."

"I'll have none of your irreverent sass, Porky Ludwig," April bantered, resting her hands lightly on her hips. "Lydia E. Pinkham's Vegetable Compound will cure what ails ya."

Giggling, Porky came around the counter and grabbed April's hands to pull her into a brief hug.

"Now tell me, how is the sales job going?"

April settled herself on a worn bench near the counter, and Porky sat beside her.

Porky had been her friend forever. The daughter of Eldon Ludwig, she still spoke with the thick German accent of her parents, who had emigrated to the States before she was born. When the other children had teased her, April had defended her, then taught her to speak with the clipped New England accent that made the word vigor less "vi-GOR" and more "vigga."

There was little April could do to protect her friend from the children's other cruel barbs. Beulah Ludwig, unfortunately, was the victim of her mother's good cooking. Her round face and pudgy body had won her the nickname "Porky" in the first grade, and the name had stuck. Even now, at twenty, Porky was never called Beulah. She was Porky.

Little Porky Ludwig.

Little fat Porky Ludwig.

April knew the name hurt, but there was nothing she could do to change it. Over the years Porky had tried cutting down on her food, but somehow the pounds never budged.

In response to April's friendship, Porky had appointed herself April's protector. In grade school Bud Grady had taken a shine to April, but she hadn't shared his feelings. Every recess he waited for her by the swings, trying to grab her for a kiss. Once he'd managed to smear his lips across her cheek and her stomach rolled.

The day before summer vacation, Bud had apparently sensed his opportunity to make his point with April was almost past. He waited for her by the water pump and, when she came out, grabbed her, nearly knocking her to the ground. She managed one shrill screech before Bud planted his lips on hers.

Porky had been waiting for April beneath the big oak

in front of the schoolhouse. When she saw Bud pounce, she started running. Before Bud could get in a second kiss, Porky grabbed him by the collar, whirled him around, and sent him facedown into the dirt.

Turning to April, she dusted her hands triumphantly. "There. We're even."

They'd been inseparable ever since.

Porky had begun helping her father in the apothecary when she was barely old enough to see over the counter. She cleaned the shop at first, then gradually worked her way behind the ledge as soon as she was old enough to make correct change to the clientele. April became mistress of Riley's house. She helped at the funeral parlor when needed—making sure the services moved along smoothly, overwrought family members comforted, even filling in when a vocalist failed to arrive in time.

April's slim, delicate frame and light features were a stark contrast to Porky's dark features and five foot, two-hundred-pound frame.

Porky had inherited her father's stockiness, and April knew it had long ago ceased to concern her. She'd accepted her lot in life, eating cinnamon rolls without apology, while April was still trying to find her purpose.

"So, how's the job?"

"I wasn't sure at first how I was going to like it, but I do. I feel I'm doing something important, and I like that."

"Your grandpa find out what you're doing yet?"

April shrugged lightly. "No. You know he wouldn't understand."

"Your mother was his daughter. He knows she didn't have to die."

"I'll grant you that if men had the same problems as women, there'd be no 'cutting it out' without some very serious deliberation."

"Oh, dash! You're getting radical."

Porky got up and dusted a shelf of medical supplies as they talked. "I do think you ought to tell your grandpa you're selling Mrs. Pinkham's compound. If he finds out what you're doing—"

Not wanting to hear any more about the subject, April abruptly switched topics. "I'm not going to the Founders Hall dance."

Glancing up, Porky frowned. "You're not?"

"No, Henry has to go to Boston on business."

"Oh." Her face fell. "And you bought that lovely evening-blue dress."

"I know, but I can use it another time. Henry's work comes first."

Resuming her dusting, Porky muttered. "Rather thoughtless of him to plan a business trip at this time."

"It couldn't be helped, Porky."

"Mmmmm, maybe."

"Are you going to the dance?" April asked.

"Of course."

"Wonderful . . . with anyone I know?"

"Papa. Mother is still away tending her ailing sister."

"Oh."

"Don't sound so disappointed. You know no man is going to ask me to a dance."

"Beulah Ludwig, you stop that!" Crossing the room, April gently took her by the shoulders and shook her. "Don't ever say that again in my presence. If the men in this town are so blind they can't see anything but a woman's dress size, then I say shame on them! Their loss!"

"Dash it all, I don't care," Porky said as the two hugged each other. "My life is full. I don't need any old man like Henry to boss me around."

"I know you don't like Henry, but you don't know him like I do," April whispered.

"I've known him as long as you have."

"He's so . . . charming, attentive," April argued. "Do you know what he calls me?"

"Slave?"

"No, be serious."

Eyeing her warily, Porky said, "What?"

"Angel Face. Isn't that romantic?"

"Simply ducky."

Just then the bell over the door rang, and aged, nearly deaf Mrs. Faith hobbled in.

"Good day to you, Mrs. Faith," Porky greeted the elderly lady loudly. "What can I do for you?"

"Eh?"

"What can I do for you?"

Mrs. Faith leaned on her cane and waved a piece of paper at Porky.

"Got this paper. That young doctor gave it to me and told me to bring it over here and give it to you."

"Let me see what you have," Porky said, reading the prescription. "Yes, we can fill this for you."

"Eh?"

"We have this!" Porky shouted toward her deaf ear.

"You sure? I wouldn't want to get the wrong thing. Doctor said it would help my gout."

"I'm sure it will. It'll only take a minute."

"Well. Hurry up. It's been paining me something awful lately."

April motioned to Porky, and Porky excused herself from Mrs. Faith, saying she'd be right back.

"Give her some of Mrs. Pinkham's vegetable compound."

"What?" Porky demanded in hushed whisper.

"Give Mrs. Faith some of the compound."

"Are you out of your *mind*? She's got the gout, not the

monthlies!" Glancing at Mrs. Faith, Porky smiled. "Just take a minute, Mrs. Faith!"

"Eh?"

"Some of the *compound*, Porky. Pour some in a bottle and tell her to use it in addition to the prescribed medicine."

"Never. The compound is not going to help her gout, and Papa would kill me. Do you know the consequences of dispensing medicine without the proper authority?"

"It isn't medicine, Porky. It's just a little alcohol and herbs. Mrs. Faith gets more alcohol in that nightly hot toddy she drinks than what she'd get in the compound. But it will really perk her up, you'll see."

It was the perfect answer. April had been trying to think of a way to boost sales and get the word out about the compound, and the answer was right her under her nose!

"The compound is for *female* problems," Porky argued in a quiet tone, glancing at Mrs. Faith again. "Her female parts have probably dried up and blown away by now."

"A woman's female parts don't dry up and blow away, Porky. Now, come on, do Mrs. Faith a good deed and give her some of the compound."

When Mrs. Faith glowered in Porky's direction again, she waved. "Be right with you, Mrs. Faith."

"You do have some, don't you? You didn't pour it out?" April had brought her a sizable jugful a few weeks ago, thinking she might use it.

"I have it," Porky snapped. "I intended to throw it away, but Papa's always around when I think of it."

"Then do it, Porky." April took her arm, urging her toward the back room. Mrs. Faith looked up again glowering.

April and Porky waved, grinning.

"I can't tamper with Papa's prescriptions," Porky whispered.

Taking her by the arm, April made sure she kept

smiling as she led her to the back room. "What tampering? There's nothing in the compound to hurt her. I want to see if it really does what Lydia says it will."

"I can't."

"Come on, Porky! I need to know how good this compound really is."

It would make her decision to help Lydia Pinkham in her endeavor to improve women's health and lying to Grandpa so much easier if she knew for certain the compound worked.

"Then take it yourself."

"I don't have any problems—except the wicked monthlies."

"Mrs. Faith doesn't even have the wicked monthlies. She's got the gout!"

"*And* female problems, I bet. She has to. She's old as dirt. At least offer her some, and see if she agrees to take it."

Dragging a chair to the shelf, Porky climbed on it, balancing her jolly bulk as she reached for a gallon jug well hidden behind a row of bottles. "If Papa ever gets wind of this he'll take a belt to me."

"Just tell him the truth. In addition to filling Mrs. Faith's prescription, you suggested a mild tonic that one of your customers makes and uses herself." April helped lower the gallon jug. "That isn't a lie."

"Well . . . we do sell a lot of nettle tea to Mrs. Pinkham."

Reaching for a funnel, Porky poured some of the compound into a small brown medicinal bottle. "See what you're making me do?"

"You'll be glad you did it when you see how perky Mrs. Faith will be."

When the bottle was full, Porky stuck a cork in it and hurriedly shoved the jug of compound back on the shelf.

The two young women emerged from the back room, smiling. "I'll fill your prescription now, Mrs. Faith."

April browsed the small pharmacy, keeping an eye on Porky as she attended her duties.

"Here you are, Mrs. Faith," Porky said a few moments later as she came down the steps carrying the medicine.

"Hrrrmpt—and high time," Mrs. Faith grumbled. She dug in he purse for a coin. "How much?"

"Twenty five cents."

"*Twenty five cents!* Where's your gun? Does that young whippersnapper doctor think I'm made out of money!"

"Papa's working hard to get the prices down."

"Does he think money grows on trees?"

"I don't think so."

Handing Porky the coins, Mrs. Faith turned to leave.

Shooting Porky a warning look, April motioned to the bottle of compound Porky was still holding.

Porky's face screwed into a stubborn mask.

April stared back, daring her to back down.

"Oh, Mrs. Faith?"

Mrs. Faith stopped in the doorway. "What is it?"

Clearing her throat, Porky grinned. "Would you like to try some tonic?"

The old woman frowned. "Some what?"

"Some tonic. It's supposed to give you get up and go."

The old woman frowned. "Are you saying I don't have get up and go?"

"No, of course not. You're a fine old woman . . ." Porky's voice trailed off, "for your age. . . ."

Mrs. Faith's frown turned menacing.

April quickly stepped in. "Oh, you mean that *wonderful* tonic everyone is talking about? Do you have some?"

Porky nodded half-heartedly. April could see she wasn't in the spirit of the ruse.

"Well, I'd *love* to try some. Wouldn't you, Mrs. Faith?"

"Don't need it." Mrs. Faith started out the door again.

"Wait!" April hurried over to take the bottle out of Porky's apron pocket. Handing it to Mrs. Faith, she smiled. "Just take a couple of spoonfuls a day for the next week and see if you can tell any difference in how you feel."

"I feel fine."

"I know, but you'll feel even better." April confidently tucked the bottle into the small basket the woman habitually carried on her left arm.

Mrs. Faith studied the bottle suspiciously. "Don't think you're going to charge me for it."

"Certainly *not*—you wouldn't think of charging her for it, would you Porky?"

Shaking her head, Porky busied herself dusting the foot powders.

"Well, guess it can't hurt." The old woman eyed the two girls sternly. "Porky Ludwig, does your papa know you lollygag around whispering and giggling when he's not here?"

"Yes, ma'am, he does, and he's warned me about it," Porky assured her. April held the front door open as the old lady hobbled out.

When the door closed, Porky flew into her. "I hope you know what you're doing, April Truitt!"

April laughed. "She'll be swinging from the rafters this time next week."

Returning to her dusting, Porky fretted. "Dr. Fuller will kill me if he ever finds out I gave her Lydia Pinkham's compound."

"He won't know it's Lydia's compound."

"Dr. Fuller better not find out, either. He caters to Mrs. Faith, you know. Tells her she's beautiful. She laps it up—but then, most of the unmarried women in town and half the married women suddenly have a 'problem' now. Have you noticed?"

"That he's single?"

"That he's handsome, silly."

"I've noticed." April knocked an imaginary speck of dust off the counter.

"Now, there's a man I'd like to kidnap for a couple of weeks."

"Well, he is nice looking, but he isn't my type."

"Meaning he doesn't agree with your opinion of Mrs. Pinkham's compound?"

"You should have seen him at the rally the other day. Standing there in the middle of all those women, arms crossed, looking as if he couldn't believe what he was hearing. Spoke right up about how women should trust doctors. Started a near riot. He saw me, and if looks could kill, I'd be lying in Grandpa's front parlor right now."

"Golly." Porky's eyes widened. "Does he know who you are?"

"No. He visits on the porch with Grandpa every night, but I've never met him. I sneak peeks at him from behind the curtain." She grinned.

"Boy—if the compound's everything Mrs. Pinkham claims it is, he'd be out of business in a week."

April snorted. "I don't think he's threatened by either the compound or me."

Porky paused, her dust cloth suspended in midair. "You didn't make a scene."

"No . . . well, sort of. I fell over my table of elixir."

"Accidentally?'

"No, on purpose. The crowd was out of control,

coming at me. I backed up, fell over the table, cracked my head, then pretended to be knocked out."

"And it worked?"

She blushed, recalling how Gray Fuller had seen right through her little ruse. Undoubtedly he had had a good laugh at her expense.

"You should have seen me, Pork. It was humiliating. The table collapsed to the floor, making a horrendous scene. I would've been smarter to let the crowd trample me."

Porky laughed at the picture her mind painted. "And Dr. Fuller saw you?"

"Saw me? He rushed over to see if I was all right. Naturally, I pretended to faint, but he knew what I was doing."

Porky's hand flew to her mouth. "He knew?"

"Without a doubt, but he went along with me. Actually, he was rather charming about the whole thing."

April knew his kind. All charm, certain his diploma gave him all kinds of rights—including meddling, if he could.

"I don't know, April, eventually he'll know who you are. Maybe you should go to him and explain about your grandpa's heart, and why you don't want him to know you're working with Lydia."

"No. It's none of his business."

"After your mother's unfortunate death, your grandpa might understand why you're working to help save other women from the same fate," Porky mused.

"Grandpa refuses to talk about Mama."

The loss of his only daughter during a routine hysterectomy seven years earlier had traumatized him. Riley never fully recovered. When Delane's name was mentioned, he refused to discuss her.

"Any man who takes in a fourteen-year-old girl to

raise—a pig-headed fourteen-year-old girl, I might add—can't be as close minded as you paint him to be."

Sighing, April moved to look out the pharmacy window. "I saw Mama die, Porky. And she didn't *need* to die. If that doctor had known more, if he'd had something like Lydia's vegetable compound to at least try before surgery, my mother might still be alive. That's why I do what I do—not to torment Grandpa, but in the hope someone else won't lose their mother or daughter to needless medical procedures."

"Then why wouldn't your grandpa encourage you to sell a product intended to help women?"

"He thinks the compound is nonsense, and it wouldn't help anyone."

"He told you this?"

"He doesn't have to. I've heard him talking. He thinks women are silly for taking it."

"Still, I think you should tell Riley what you're doing."

"Well, you're entitled to your own opinion. Just make sure you don't let it slip when Grandpa comes in to buy tobacco."

"Don't worry about me," Porky told her as April opened the door to leave.

"And you don't have to worry about me. I'll see you later."

Chapter 4

Datha Gower had kept house for Riley Ogden for over five years. Since she was eleven years old she'd polished floors, hung wash, cooked, and cleaned.

Ogden's Mortuary was a towering, two-story landmark with a large, wrap-around front porch that caught the sun in the morning, and a roomy back porch that caught the cool breeze in the afternoon.

It took a powerful lot of work to keep it all clean.

A screened-in privacy porch on the north side of the house allowed Mr. Ogden to smoke in peace. He was known to sit for hours, drawing on the meerschaum pipe while watching the foot traffic that passed in front of the mortuary, knowing that one day, like as not, he'd be burying every last one of them. Why, he could guess within an inch how tall anyone was and what size coffin it'd take to put them away.

Riley lived with his granddaughter in six big rooms above the main parlor. The rooms had been tastefully decorated by Riley's deceased wife, Effie, who had favored overstuffed chairs, cherry wood, and a passel of worrisome trinkets that needed dusting.

Wisteria vines trailed the length of the white porch railings shaded by large, overhanging elm trees. Datha and Flora Lee, her grandmother, lived in servants' quarters in back of the main house. Flora Lee had been with the Ogden family all her life. Flora Lee's great-granddaddy, Solomon Tobias Gower, had served the Ogden family during the Civil War, refusing to leave them when the Emancipation Proclamation was effected. The Gower family thought themselves lucky to serve such a fine, upstanding family.

When Flora Lee had gotten too crippled to do much around the house, Datha took over. She'd lived with Flora Lee since her mama died in childbirth. On good days Flora Lee still came to the main house to help clean, but like as not, her rheumatism kept her home. Comfortably lodged in nice quarters, the two served the Ogden family with humble gratitude and tireless loyalty, counting their blessings that April and Riley were kind, caring people who were more family than employers.

In Flora Lee's youth, long before the dead were taken to funeral homes for eulogies, long before the Ogdens had turned their private home into a mortuary, Flora Lee had helped Owen Ogden, Riley's papa, to prepare friends and neighbors for burial.

Datha loved to hear stories about how her grandma had cried along with distraught wives and inconsolable mothers as they bathed and dressed their loved ones, then laid them out in the front parlor. Folks would come from miles around to view the body, offering words of comfort. Flora Lee liked to tell how she'd curl up in a corner, pulling her legs up beneath her, out of the way, but there to serve if anyone needed her.

Friends, in an effort to share the grief, brought overflowing baskets of food, arriving throughout the day to mourn the deceased. The yard would fill with buggies and neighbors standing outside visiting as the deceased lay in wake.

Datha hummed as she dusted the mortuary entryway, remembering Flora Lee's stories. Land, how the Gowers owed a debt to the Ogdens!

Neighbors had ridiculed Owen for taking a personal interest in his household help, but anyone who'd known Owen would tell you that he was a good man. Gossip had never bothered Owen Ogden, God rest his soul. He went about his business, serving the citizens of Dignity in their time of need, reading the Good Book and following its teachings.

Never one to judge others, he'd made it clear that he didn't intend to be judged by anyone other than himself and his Maker. When his health began to fail, Owen had turned the funeral business over to Riley, then just up and died.

Just like that.

One minute he was sitting on the porch enjoying his nightly smoke, and the next he just keeled over dead as a doornail.

But things went on like always. Riley had the same goodness in him that Owen did. Datha knew the senior Ogden only by her grandmother's memories, but Flora Lee said that when Owen passed on, Riley hadn't treated them any differently. Told her that this was her home, and Datha's, as long as they wanted it, and that's how it was going to be. Datha could hold her head high, proud as could be because she wasn't ignorant. No sir. Mr. Riley Ogden had seen to it that she was schooled as good as or better than most folks.

Grinning, Datha realized that she had just about everything she wanted, with the exception of Jacel Evans.

Jacel was a fine black man who, because of Riley Ogden's generosity, was about to go off to Boston to attend a university. Harvard, Riley called it. Real fancy school somewhere up there in Cambridge.

Jacel's family was dirt poor. The rich folks the Evans family worked for owned the sawmill, but they didn't share their good fortune with others. Certainly not with their black help.

Ellory Jordan provided meals and shelter for his servants, and that's all. If they needed more, they could just do without.

Most did without.

There was one young man determined to do more than just "make do." He'd decided to pull himself out of that rut, and one man in the community saw potential in him. Jacel Evans, youngest son of Tully Evans, was a tall, powerfully built Negro who did more than his share of work in the sawmill. On his dinner break he read books while other boys his age lay in the shade and dipped cool water over their sweat-drenched bodies.

Pride nearly suffocated Datha when she thought about her man. Why, her Jacel could saw more logs than any other two men put together. Work harder than a team of Kentucky mules.

And he was smart. Real smart. Thought about things most folks never thought about. Things like how it wasn't fair one man should be treated differently than the other just because he had a different color of skin. He'd lie for hours, looking up at the sky and say to her, "Datha, why is it the rich get richer and the poor get poorer?"

Or he'd ponder why some folks were born with good fortune and for others if it wasn't for bad luck, they'd have no luck at all.

Why did some suffer with bad health and others rarely

see a sick day? Why did the good die young and the evil prosper?

Why was death and senseless tragedy deemed to be the will of a loving God?

Why did some work hard only to go to bed at night with a hungry ache in their belly, while others made gluttons of themselves and grew fat and slovenly because of laziness?

Why were innocent children mistreated because of someone else's rage?

All questions to which she didn't know the answers. But Jacel worried them about, turning them over and over in his mind. A fine mind that was hungry to learn and grow.

Her Jacel was going to be a lawyer some day. An upstanding lawyer who wanted to undo some of the injustice he saw in the world. Once his practice was established, they were going to get married.

Datha smiled as she flicked a cloth at a spot of dust she'd missed on the foyer table. Yes, someday she was going to be Mrs. Jacel Evans. Her heart nearly burst from the joy of it. She and Jacel, holding hands, would "jump over the broom." What a fine day that would be!

Once Jacel had his law office, they could have their own place. But until then Datha planned to stay right here, taking care of Riley, April, and Flora Lee for as long as they needed her. Jacel said that that was only right, seeing as how good the Ogdens had been to him and her.

Young April would marry someday, and not far off, if Datha was guessing. She was bound to hook a man soon, pretty as she was. Chances were it'd be that Henry Trampas Long, the handsome, no-good swain she'd had a crush on lately.

Riley had never liked the young scamp, and he would

be having a fit if he knew April was still interested in Henry. It wasn't her place to say anything, but rumor had it that April was seeing Henry more than socially.

Of course, Mr. Ogden was blind as a post when it came to April. Any time Henry's name was mentioned, he'd change the subject, saying he had better things to talk about. Datha didn't have any trouble seeing that Miss April had a powerful crush on Henry Trampas Long, why couldn't he?

The gossip mill predicted Henry would be asking her to marry him soon; then he'd whisk her off to some high-falutin city, and they wouldn't see much of her after that.

Datha could either take Henry or leave him. He was too smooth for her liking, but she could see why April would be caught up in his youthful good looks. Words just poured out of him like honey, words that sounded nice but didn't make a whole lot of sense.

But Datha knew her place, and she kept it. If April wanted to waste her life on the likes of Henry Long, it was hers to waste. She only worried for Mr. Ogden's sake. What with his heart acting up, she sure didn't want him finding out that April was selling Pinkham's vege-table compound with Henry. Law sakes, it would be like waking up a nest of snakes, and no one wanted to do that. Certainly not her.

Humming to herself, Datha dusted around a lamp. The interior of Ogden Mortuary was a tribute to Flora Lee and Datha's devotion. The shiny wooden floors were spotless and the rug beaten until no dust would dare remain. The dimly lit interior of the fine old establish-ment smelled faintly of flowers and lemon furniture polish. Though barely sixteen, Datha worked tirelessly to provide a comfortable, pleasant surrounding for Riley and his granddaughter.

When she heard April coming in the front door, Datha

hurriedly stuffed the dust rag in her pocket and called out.

"Supper'll be on the table in ten minutes, April girl."

"Thanks, Datha. I'll tell Grandpa."

The cloying scent of gladioli permeated the air as April passed the open parlor doors. Clarence Deeds was laid out in his best blue suit, awaiting services in the morning.

It was sure to be a big funeral.

Clarence was town mayor, and friends and business associates from neighboring communities would turn out in droves to pay their final respects.

Proceeding to the side porch, she found Riley sitting in his rocking chair, staring off into space. He'd been sitting like that when she left the house early this morning, and she was starting to get concerned. It wasn't like Grandpa to just sit and stare at nothing.

"Grandpa?" When Riley didn't respond, she pushed open the screen door. "Are you all right?"

"Right enough," he said.

"Supper's ready."

Riley got slowly to his feet and followed April to the dining room table set with fresh flowers and white china. Taking his place at the head of the table, he reached for the butter, still not saying anything.

Shaking out her napkin, April noticed his hand was trembling as he buttered a piece of corn bread. Perusing his pale features, she frowned. He hadn't had a spell with his heart for weeks now. Was he ill again and not telling her?

Picking up a dish of Datha's watermelon pickles, she offered it to him. "You're awfully quiet today. Don't you feel well?"

He was bad about not telling her when he felt poorly, thinking to spare her unnecessary worry. But she worried anyway. Grandpa wasn't young anymore, though the way he worked like a harvest hand around the mortuary, lifting bodies and moving heavy pine caskets, you'd never guess it.

"I feel fine, thank you." Riley's face heightened with color as he snapped open his napkin.

"You look odd. Is the heat bothering you?"

It was insufferably hot for fall. Muggy, as if a storm was waiting just off the coast. A good rain to settle the dust and cool dispositions would be appreciated.

"Nothing wrong that a little dinner won't take care of. Pass the preserves, please."

They waited in silence for Datha to bring the main course.

"Clarence looks nice. I'm sure Edith is pleased."

"Hummm," Riley muttered, taking a sip of coffee.

Datha carried in a large platter of roast beef, boiled potatoes, and carrots. A bowl of cooked cabbage, brown beans, plump ears of corn, festive red beets, and thick brown gravy followed.

April's distraught gaze swept the heavily burdened table and she sighed. Datha cooked enough to feed an army of foot soldiers, but she had given up complaining. It didn't matter what she said. Having learned at her mother's side, it seemed Datha couldn't cook meals for any less than twelve people.

Now they just let her cook to her heart's content, resigned to share leftovers with neighboring shut-ins.

Serving herself potatoes and meat, April smiled. "This looks delicious."

"Thank you, April girl." Smiling, Datha returned to the kitchen for the string beans.

They ate in silence until Riley suddenly cleared his throat and laid the butter knife aside.

April, knowing some kind of pronouncement was forthcoming put down her fork.

"April Delane, I've mulled this over all afternoon."

April's pulse jumped. Grandpa never called her by her full name unless he was upset with her. By the thunder-cloud forming on his face, he was more than upset. He was furious—

Oh, no! He knew she was working with Lydia Pinkham. Someone—some blabbermouth doctor—told him! Dr. Fuller had recognized her after all!

Casually dabbing the corners of her mouth with her napkin, she steeled herself. Riley Ogden was a patient man, but when he was angry, he was just like Great-grandfather Owen. Impossible to reason with.

Managing to keep her tone light, she asked. "Is something wrong?"

"April," Riley's voice held a rarely used hint of authority as his faded blue eyes pinned her to the chair.

Swallowing, April feigned unusual interest in the bowl of potatoes. "Yes, Grandpa?"

"Young lady, you're old enough to do what you want, but how can you think of selling that Pinkham woman's poison!"

April's knife clattered to her plate. "Who told you!"

"Never mind who told me!"

"I know who it was! That snoopy doctor told you, didn't he! That interfering, sanctimonious—"

"Never mind who told me!" Riley thundered. "Doctoring's best left to doctors! No silly brew concocted by that Pinkham woman is going to fix women's ills. No vegetable compound is going to cure what ails them. People get sick and die, April. Living in a mortuary, you should know this. Mrs. Grimes died in childbirth. Mrs. Wazinski from influenza. Bertha Dickens from a burst appendix. Why, I've buried a half dozen women just this year—"

"Not from taking the compound!" April interrupted. "And if Ginny Grimes, Mary Wazinski, and Bertha Dickens hadn't listened to some overzealous doctor and tried to find other ways to treat their problems, they just might be alive today!"

"Hogwash! Not one of those women died from a doctor's neglect!" Riley's face was as red as the bowl of beets he was holding. "Young lady, you are to resign from the Pinkham 'circus' first thing tomorrow morning! Do you hear me?"

"Grandpa—"

"Tomorrow morning, April Delane!" A vein in his temple throbbed.

She knew better than to argue with him. It was like barking at a knothole. He was just a stubborn old man!

Shoving her chair back, she pitched her napkin on the table and stormed out of the room.

Riley got to his feet, his hand automatically going to the left side of his chest.

"April Delane Truitt! You come back here, young lady! I'm not through talking to you!"

Entering her bedroom, April threw herself across the bed. Flipping onto her back, she stared at the ceiling, cursing the fates that had brought Gray Fuller to Dignity. It had been a nice, quiet town until *he* got here.

Darn his busybody hide.

Lydia Pinkham was helping women, and instead of working hand in hand to find solutions to problems, Gray and other doctors like him were doing everything they could to hinder her progress.

Women needed Lydia Pinkham's Vegetable Compound. Why, Henry had told her that a Connecticut preacher was actually murdered by his wife after she'd suffered for sixteen years with female complaints. That could have been averted if the poor woman had only had the elixir!

It was a crime the way doctors routinely removed healthy ovaries, like they had done to her mother, to treat heavy bleeding. It was absurd for anyone to think that monthly discomfort, no matter how severe, warranted the removal of ovaries! Far too many women were dying from the process.

Rolling over, she buried her face in the pillow, recalling how her mother had died an untimely, unnecessary death.

Delane Truitt had been in the prime of her life when she was beset by female problems. A heavy menstrual flow put her to bed two out of four weeks a month. She'd gotten to the point where she couldn't appear in public for fear an "accident" would leave her red-faced with shame. In desperation she finally consented to let the doctor remove her ovaries and uterus. The procedure had taken her life.

April was glad her father had not been around to witness the tragedy. He had died three years before Delane's death in a train derailment as he was returning from New York. "Dignity doesn't have anything good enough for my wife and daughter," he'd say, so off he'd go every December in search of the perfect gift.

That December, he never came back.

April was obsessed by the thought that Mrs. Pinkham's compound might, just might, have saved her mother's life, although there wasn't firm proof it would have.

Yet, that hope was what fired her crusade.

If she could spare one woman Delane's fate, then her cause was justified, no matter what Grandpa thought.

Lydia Pinkham, far from being the quack Dr. Fuller

called her, was truly a pioneer. She hadn't come by her trade easily. One of twelve children, her father had been a cordwainer and farmer. Twice married, he was a Quaker but left the Friends because of a conflict over the slavery issue.

Lydia had graduated from Lynn Academy, then served as secretary of the Freeman's Institute. She was a school-teacher when she married Isaac Pinkham, who had a daughter by a previous marriage. Their union produced five more children—Charles, Dan, Will, Aroline, and a baby who died.

Lydia confided that Isaac was a dreamer. Though he'd tried various real estate promotions and other business ventures, nothing had worked out. That's when the money problems began.

Lydia, unable to stand idly by and watch everything they had be taken from them, decided to market her elixir. She chose botanical bases for the compound because she had so little faith in orthodox practitioners. She considered their medical treatment to be far too harsh.

And over and over again her skepticism proved to be sound.

Rolling onto her back, April stared at the ceiling, blinking back hot tears.

Grandpa had forbade her to sell the compound. All because of Dr. Fuller.

April beat the sun up the next morning, anxious to tell Porky about the doctor's betrayal.

Adjusting her hat as she entered the kitchen, she smiled at Datha, who was turning hot cakes at the stove.

"April girl! What are you doing up so early?"

Helping herself to a piece of sausage, April licked her fingers. "I wanted to get an early start."

"Well, breakfast is ready." Datha dished up three steaming hotcakes on a plate. "Sit down; I'll pour the milk."

It was just past seven when April left the house. On her way to Ludwig's Pharmacy she smiled at Fred Loyal, who was busily sweeping the sidewalk in front of his store and called a greeting to Miss Thompson, the dressmaker and milliner.

Neldene Anderson was just unlocking the schoolhouse as Reverend Brown meandered slowly down the sidewalk, obviously rehearsing his Sunday sermon.

Crossing the street, she spotted Gray Fuller's office and started a slow burn.

DR. GRAYSON FULLER, GENERAL PRACTITIONER, the sign said.

It should have read: DOCTOR BUSYBODY.

The name was printed in large script on the window of his office. A pulled shade prevented curious passersby from looking in to see who might be seeking the doctor's advice.

April hurried past the office, determined to avoid a confrontation with Mr. Butter Inner.

It was early, and chances were he wasn't up yet.

Righteous indignation bloomed on her cheeks when she thought of what he'd done. The nerve of the man going straight to Grandpa, as if what she did were any of his concern!

Walking faster, she told herself to settle down. If his actions at the women's meeting were any indication, he'd *want* her to confront him so he could tell her how foolish and misguided she was for working with the Pinkhams.

Well, just let him try to tell her anything. She walked faster. She'd give him a well-deserved piece of her mind!

Prompted by a sudden urge to throttle him, she stopped

dead in her tracks, whirled around and started back. She could not let him get away with this. Other women might overlook his antagonistic attitude, but not her.

To her surprise, the door of his office opened easily, and she stepped inside.

The interior was freshly painted, but the furnishings were deplorable. A wooden coatrack stood in the corner. Hanging on it was the strangest hat she'd ever seen.

The scent of alcohol and some other substance she couldn't identify was strong in the air.

The door to the doctor's examining room was closed, so she sat down on one of the half dozen straight-back wooden chairs scattered throughout the room.

Tapping her fingers, she waited.

She wasn't at all certain what she was going to say to him, but she would give him a piece of her mind. Someone needed to put him in his place, so it might as well be her. If he thought his good looks and arrogant manner intimidated her, he was wrong.

The moments stretched. There were no sounds coming from behind the closed door.

He's probably in there asleep, she thought and considered getting up and slamming the door again, loudly.

Drumming her fingers, her gaze drifted to the strange looking hat hanging on the coatrack.

Pfft, she thought. *His, no doubt.*

She studied the odd hat a moment or two, then curiosity drove her to get up to examine it more closely.

Silliest looking hat she'd ever seen in her life. No brim. No shape to the crown. Just round and flat. What would possess a man to buy such a frivolous contraption? She picked it up, turning it over and over in her hands. Why, it looked like a navy-blue felt oversized pillbox!

Glancing up, she focused on the closed door of the examining room. Maybe it belonged to his patient.

No.

No self-respecting man in Dignity would be caught dead in this atrocity, nor anyone from Lynn, for that matter.

On impulse, she stepped in front of the small gilt-framed mirror on the wall and removed her own hat. Perching the foolish-looking thing on her head, she peered back at herself. The hat teetered atop her curls like a loose cap on a medicine bottle.

Pfft.

Utterly ridiculous.

Turning it first one way, then the other, she laughed out loud at the picture she presented. Wouldn't you know that he'd wear something this absurd? Why, if the local men saw him, he'd be run out of town on a rail—

"Can I help you?"

"Oh!" She jumped, sending the ludicrous hat flying off her head.

Dr. Fuller stood in the doorway staring at her as she scrambled to pick the hat off the floor.

"Sorry," she murmured.

His gaze slowly traveled the length of her sprigged cotton dress, lingering on the soft swell of her bodice. For some insane reason, she was glad she had worn blue this morning. Henry said it was most becoming to her complexion.

"It's you—the woman who sells Pinkham's compound?"

"You know very well who I am, *Doctor*." How dare he play innocent with her! Did he think he could tell Grandpa about her activities and expect her to roll over and play dead?

His implacable expression showed no indication of betrayal. "Do you want something?"

She did, but his unexpected appearance startled all thoughts from her mind.

Oh, he was arrogant. Leaning against the doorframe as if he'd been there all the while observing her. His jacket was off, his shirt stretched across his broad shoulders in a distracting fashion. Hair mussed as if he'd run his fingers through it.

Studying her with heavy-lidded eyes, he waited.

What was it about this man that made rational women lose their minds! It was infuriating, that's what it was. Simply infuriating.

When she realized he was waiting for her to state her business, she blurted out the first thing that came to mind.

"Is this your hat?"

His gaze was unwavering. "Yes."

A smug smile twitched at the corner of her mouth. "I thought so."

She hooked the hat back on the rack, embarrassed he'd caught her making fun of it. Now what she had to say to him wouldn't carry the same impact.

"Is there something you wanted?" His eyes refused to leave her, bringing a rush of color to her cheeks. "Other than to make fun of my hat?"

"Actually, I'm here on a personal matter." She adjusted her dress, repositioned her own hat on her head, then smoothed the sides of her hair, trying to bolster her courage. She hated confrontations, but this man *inspired* them. She could not, would not, allow him to think he could interfere in her life and get away with it.

Awareness dawned in his eyes, and he straightened. "Oh . . . I see. Step into the examining room, please."

She didn't have all day, and this wasn't a social visit. She could say what she had come to say out here just as easily. And she was about to say it when he took her by the arm and ushered her into a small room lined with cabinets and reeking of alcohol.

Wrinkling her nose, April glanced around the room, uneasy with his close proximity. "Aren't you with another patient?"

"No, just catching up on paperwork. Are you in pain?"

She met his gaze curiously. *Do I look like I'm in pain? If I am, Mister, you're the cause of it!*

Reaching for a chart, he cleared his throat. "I'll step out while you disrobe."

Her gaze darted around the room to see who he was talking to.

They were the only two people in the room.

"Disrobe?"

"Yes. Take off your clothes, cover yourself with that white sheet, and I'll be back in a moment."

Her eyes narrowed. Disrobe? Why the knave!

"You're not only a blabbermouth, you're disgusting!"

Already halfway out the door, he stopped and turned. "I beg your pardon, miss?"

"Disrobe?"

"Before I can examine you, you'll have to take off your clothes."

She stiffened. "I did not come in here to take off my clothes."

"If you have a female complaint, I'll have to—"

"Female complaint?!" She stopped. Oh, yes, a *female complaint*. She couldn't have a simple ache or pain, no, it had to be a "female complaint."

"Yes, I do have a complaint and I am female, but the last thing I would do is disrobe for *you*."

Calmly closing the door, Gray returned to his desk and sat down. "Let's start over. Exactly what is your 'personal' problem?"

Planting both hands on the edge of his desk, she leaned

close, glaring at him as she clearly enunciated each word in clipped tone. "What I do with my life, or what I take up as a profession, is absolutely *none of your business*!"

Leaning back in his chair to keep space between them, Gray frowned.

"And I'll thank you to keep your opinions to yourself, *Mr. Butter Inner*."

It was his turn to look over his shoulder to make sure she wasn't speaking to someone else.

There were still only two people in the room.

"It's bad enough," April continued, "that I have to contend with your *archaic* views on the female population, but now you've really done it." Her tone dropped menacingly. "You've dragged Grandpa into this, and I cannot *emphasize* strongly enough that it is not *your* place to be telling *Grandpa* what I do, *just* because we do not see eye to eye on certain subjects!"

Pulling herself up to her full height, she felt weak with relief. This hadn't been as bad as she'd expected.

Readjusting her hat, she expelled a deep breath. "I believe I've made myself clear."

That said, she headed for the door and slammed it soundly behind her.

Gray's framed medical certificate fell to the floor amid shattering glass.

He stared at the rubble, mystified. Getting slowly to his feet, he walked to the outer office in time to see the tail end of her skirt whipping out the front door.

Gray opened the door and watched her flounce down the sidewalk and enter Ludwig's Pharmacy, slamming that door as well.

What in the hell was that all about?

Stepping onto the sidewalk, he peered at the closed door of the pharmacy, still muttering under his breath.

More to the point, who in the hell was her grandpa?

The woman was an infuriating mystery, one he wasn't sure he wanted to unravel. She had a temper, his shattered medical certificate was proof. But she was angry because he'd told her grandpa what she was doing with Lydia. The question still hung in his brain. Who was her grandpa?

Gray narrowed it down to three possibilities, with Riley at the top of the list. Could she be the "April" Riley talked about? It was more than possible since he described her as stubborn, but beautiful, and if she *were* April, he couldn't argue with either description. In fact, if it weren't for Francesca, he might be interested . . . What was he thinking? There was *always* Francesca!

"A man, Porky. That's what he is! A pigheaded, obstinate, *man*! Doesn't that say it all?"

April was still fuming over Gray Fuller. The fact that she hadn't let him get away with it didn't help. The nerve of that man to expound about "modern medicine" at Lydia's rallies when so many doctors still inflicted their obsolete opinions on women just galled her!

"A most good-looking man," Porky mused. "But not good enough for you to break the glass out of Papa's front door."

"Handsome? I hadn't noticed."

"Better have your eyes checked."

"Not all women are blinded by meaningless appearances," April reminded her. "There are some of us who judge a man for his character, which, if you recall, Dr. Fuller is sadly lacking."

"Not me. I judge a man by how tight he can wear his pants and still look decent."

"I'll simply pretend you didn't say that."

"Dr. Fuller really gets under your skin, doesn't he?" Porky carefully counted out fifteen pills before taking a knife and scooping them into a bottle. Plastering a label on the bottle, she placed it on the shelf. "I don't see what all the fuss is about. From what I can see, the women in Dignity don't take every word the doctor says as gospel. If you ask me, they seem open enough for alternative help to their problems. Mrs. Pinkham is garnering her share of their attention when it comes to health issues. Our laudanum sales have dropped off since she started selling her compound."

"Mrs. Pinkham cares about women," April said. "That's why she's so believable."

"Believable, well, I didn't say that." Porky set aside a bottle. "I just hope she knows what she's doing. I am, after all, taking my life into my own hands for you, you know. If Papa finds out I'm handing out Lydia Pinkham's Vegetable Compound to women customers, I'll be lying in your grandpa's parlor, April Truitt, inhaling baskets of stinking gladioli."

Turning around, April sobered. "How is you father feeling? I haven't seen him in the pharmacy this week."

"Papa has a frightful cold, and I made him stay home."

"I'm sorry. I'll have Datha bake him one of her chocolate cakes. That should have him feeling better in no time."

"He'd love that," Porky agreed.

April's eyes lit with interest as she edged closer to the counter. "Has anyone said how the compound is working?"

"I haven't had any complaints, but of course the women I've handed it to don't know that's what they're taking. They think it's just a tonic. So," Porky leaned closer, "are you going to stop?"

"Selling the compound?"

"Isn't that what Riley told you to do? Stop working for Mrs. Pinkham immediately?"

April frowned, hating the thought. "Yes . . . that's what he told me to do."

"Are you going to do it?"

"I guess."

"April," Porky warned, "are you going to quit selling it or not?"

"Selling it, yes. Helping Mrs. Pinkham, no. I'm going to see if there isn't something I can do to promote the compound without blatantly going against Grandpa's wishes." She couldn't give up her cause on such a flimsy excuse. Grandpa might not believe in the tonic, but she did, and she had to help some way.

"Oh, brother," Porky groaned. "Knowing you, this means trouble."

"I can't stop helping now, Porky, not when Lydia is on the brink of success. Dan and Henry are this moment in the Boston area, trying to expand the market."

"When are they coming home?"

"A couple of days," April said with a sigh. "I miss him."

"Dan?"

April swatted Porky playfully. "You have no reverence at all for love."

"For love I do. It's infatuation I have no patience for. And I, simpleminded cretin that I am, can clearly see that what you feel for Henry is nothing more than infatuation, pure and simple."

"No, it isn't. I care deeply for him. Besides, isn't it 'infatuation' you have for Dr. Fuller?"

Porky ignored the question. "You've clearly lost your mind. You know what kind of man Henry T. Long is? He'll steal a woman's heart, then run like a rabbit. It escapes me why, all of a sudden, you think that you're in love with him. You've known the knave since childhood and until six months ago hadn't given him a serious thought. What happened?"

"I've recognized how charming, how utterly caring, he really is."

"Dash. Double dash! He'll break your heart then wonder why you're angry with him."

"Porky, your swearing is atrocious! He's wonderful, and I think he's on the verge of asking me to marry him."

"Deliver us all." Porky stepped down, pulling her apron off. "You're worried that Riley will discover you're selling the compound and have another heart episode. What do you think it will do to him when he finds out you are actually entertaining the idea of marrying Henry Long—not that I think Henry will ever ask you to marry him, mind you. Henry isn't husband material. Never has been and never will be."

"Henry respects women," April defended.

"I know Henry likes women. *All* women, April, my dense but lovable friend. *All* women. Open your eyes and be *healed*!"

"Henry enjoys the fairer sex, yes, but I know he's falling in love with me. And Grandpa will just have to adjust to the fact, and he will once he gets to know Henry, really know him."

"April Truitt," Porky chided as she picked up her dust-cloth. "If you believe *that*, and Lydia's compound cures insanity, you, dearest, should drink a full bottle of the stuff."

Chapter 5

The marketplace was bustling with activity this morning. April and Porky got there early, filling their shopping baskets as they sorted through fruits and vegetables.

"Better take advantage of the eggplant; it's the last of my garden," Mr. Portland said, adding several more of the plump vegetables to the display on the wooden tables outside the market.

"What a shame," April said, choosing one, sniffing, then holding it for Porky to smell. The aroma of warm sunshine and green vines still clung to the shiny purple skin. "I'll take three, two of the peppers, four tomatoes, and—"

The rumble of heavy wagons interrupted her list of purchases. Turning to investigate the racket, April saw three ox-drawn wagons lumbering into town. The weary, dust-covered animals plodded down the main street, heads low, straining against the load. Leading the entourage was a shiny black carriage with fringe around the top, drawn by two beautiful black mares high-stepping prettily.

Porky, holding a large melon in the palm of her right

hand, paused to look at the strange cavalcade. "What is that?"

April studied the fashionably attired young woman sitting beside the carriage driver. The woman, more beautiful than April had ever seen in a magazine, smiled and waved at a passerby while twirling a black satin-lace parasol.

"Mercy," Porky breathed. "Whoever it is, I hope she doesn't stay long."

"Perhaps she's a street vendor." April's gaze traveled the length of the bizarre entourage. "Or a circus." The wagons creaked beneath the heavy cargo.

Squinting, Porky shaded her eyes against the sun. "She doesn't look like any merchandiser I've ever seen."

The sound of a door slamming caught their attention. They glanced across the street to see Gray Fuller hurriedly coming down the outside staircase leading from the living quarters above his office.

"Oooh," Porky mused. "Must be someone he knows." They stood elbow to elbow to watch.

The woman spied the doctor and stood up to wave. "Oh, Gray! Yoo-hoo! Gray, darling!"

"Gray," the girls mouthed to each other as the parade came to a halt in front of the doctor's office.

Dr. Fuller stopped on the bottom step, his eyes scrutinizing the wagons. "What is all this?" Stepping off the sidewalk, he approached the lead wagon.

April and Porky watched as the driver assisted the raven-haired beauty out of the carriage. Snapping her parasol closed, the woman rose on tiptoe and kissed Gray flush on the mouth.

Looking at one another again, the young girls' eyebrows lifted in question.

* * *

"Hello, darling." Francesca brushed Gray's lips with her fingertip. "Surprised?"

"Very. I wasn't expecting you."

"Of course you weren't, darling. It wouldn't be a surprise otherwise."

Walking around the overburdened rigs, he frowned. "To what do I owe the pleasure?"

"If you insist on living here in this . . . this . . . town, then you must at least have decent quarters." She smiled up at him, "Darling? Don't I get a better welcome than this?"

As he rounded the wagon, he brushed a quick kiss across her pouting lips. To anyone looking, the gesture might have appeared one born more of necessity than affection. The woman was blocking his path.

Gray glanced up and down the street.

"Shy, darling?"

"I'm new in town, Francesca. I don't need any gossip—"

"Ha!" Her laughter floated through the air. "I'm sure this town could stand some stirring up. Besides, I am your fiancée. I'm entitled to kiss you," her voice dropped, "and more."

Taking her arm, he steered her toward the office door. "Let's go inside."

"Just wait until you see what I've brought you."

His gaze warily assessed the canvas-covered wagon beds.

"What have you done now, Francesca?"

"Something to help your career."

He frowned. "My career doesn't need help."

"Ah, but it does, because you're so . . . rural, darling. A successful doctor must look successful. That's what Papa says." She swept a finely manicured hand along the line of waiting wagons. "I've brought you beautiful things to look as successful as you're going to be."

"Francesca—"

"Shush! I won't hear a word of gratitude. It's what I want to do"—she stood on tiptoe and kissed him again—"for you. Now, wait until you see—Charles, start unloading the first wagon, please." She turned back to continue. "We'll unload the furniture for your office. . . ." Perusing the steep outside stairway, she said, "Do you live up there? I thought you had a house."

"No, Francesca. I told you, I live above my office. The living quarters are quite comfortable and convenient—"

"Well," she waved a lace handkerchief dismissively. "No matter. I'll have it looking so lovely, you'll think it's a mansion."

Gray felt himself losing patience with her, something he did often lately. When she was around, he lost his ability to say anything other than her first name!

But she didn't notice. Pressing closer, she puckered her full lips in a kissing motion. "Tonight darling, you can thank me . . . meaningfully. *Oui?* Now, show me your office so I can instruct the men where to place the furniture."

Obstinacy set Gray's handsome features. "I don't want new furniture."

"Nonsense, darling." She smiled back at him, squeezing his arm. "Since when does a man know what will best suit an office? Besides, this is my gift to you."

Spying his name on the office door, Francesca started in that direction, leaving Gray and Charles to follow in her wake.

When the drivers drew the canvas covers off the wagons, April saw that they were heavily loaded with large pieces of expensive-looking furniture. Massive pieces of dark, polished, ornately carved oak more suitable for a palace than Gray Fuller's tiny office. If she was any judge, the wagonloads of furniture had cost a small fortune.

"What's the accent?" Porky asked, clearly awed by the display of opulence.

"French, I think. Who do you suppose she is?"

Leaning closer, Porky whispered. "His mistress, of course. Who else would arrive unexpectedly to decorate his office and living quarters with wagonloads of expensive furniture? Who else would think she had the right? A shameless hussy," she grinned, answering her own question.

"You don't know that," April chided.

"Ten to one they break in that fancy bed tonight."

Embarrassed at Porky's bluntness and irritated that she found the idea was more annoying than funny, April returned to her shopping. Porky continued to watch the lavish spectacle of furniture being unloaded, unable to take her eyes off the public display.

"My, my, my, she's pretty sure of herself."

"Have you seen the McIntoshes today? They look wonderful."

The shiny red apples were far more tempting than silly goings-on with Gray Fuller.

"And did you see that dress? Fifty dollars if it cost a cent. Look at that bed!"

"Look at this! String beans, and so late in the season!"

Porky absently dropped a couple of apples into her basket. "Did you see the way she took charge of him? I'd say Miss Frenchie is fairly aching to sink her hooks into our doctor."

" 'Our doctor'? Really, Porky. What difference does it make what he does or who it's with?" April stuffed a melon into her own receptacle.

But she did happen to glance across the street to where

heavy chairs were now lining the sidewalk. A crowd was gathering to watch the activity.

"Wonder if they are engaged or just being outrageously indiscreet?" Porky mused. "Do you think—"

"Porky," April cautioned, turning her attention to the pile of rutabagas, "you can be sure it makes no difference to me what Dr. Fuller is doing with that woman."

"Who said you should be interested?" Porky asked. "But I, for one, am curious."

"You and every other single woman in town," April said dryly, then smiled as she turned to the waiting clerk. "I'll take a head of lettuce, also."

What Dr. Fuller and his fancy French coquette, who obviously had more money than common sense, did was of no interest to her.

She suddenly frowned.

But if that were true, why was she experiencing a feeling of nausea in the pit of her stomach.

"Francesca, I can't accept this."

Gray saw the look Mrs. Perkins gave him as the wagons stopped in front of his office. He was concerned mere curiosity would quickly turn to antagonism when the town saw the extravagantly expensive furniture being unloaded.

"*Oui, chéri*, you can and will." Francesca sauntered around the sparsely furnished waiting room, her finger laying pensively against her cheek. "This is not the waiting room of a successful doctor. This is the waiting room of . . . apology, a pauper. It is obvious you spent your funds on equipment."

That and repaying your father.

"I must have equipment to treat my patients."

"That may be true," she admitted, "but now you will have a waiting room befitting a successful physician."

Gray's eyes swept over the sparse, purely functional furniture. The chairs were old but serviceable. Nicked by countless kicks of children's feet, dulled by age, he felt they had character. Joe McFarland had used them for over forty years before he retired. If they were good enough for Joe, they were good enough for him. Besides, the people of Dignity accepted the room as it was. Seeing the old furniture made them more comfortable with a new doctor.

"There's nothing wrong with this furniture."

"Darling, there is no need to discuss it further—"

"Dr. Fuller!" A breathless young boy nearly fell inside the door. "You've got to come quick! My pa, he's cut his foot real bad!"

Gray grabbed his medical bag and started after the youngster.

"Gray . . . darling?" Francesca frowned.

"Just as well," Francesca murmured as the door closed behind him. "Ah, the lovely, lovely table. Here, gentlemen. Put it here. Just so. And arrange the chairs . . . there, I think. Oh, my! The coatrack must go. Oh, wait. The hat. Gray would never forgive me if I misplaced it!"

When Gray returned from stitching up George Daton's foot, which the man had accidentally sliced open while cutting wood, he found his office had undergone a full-blown transformation.

He stood in the center of the room, in near shock. Where once there had been straight-backed wooden chairs and a small, wobbly, wooden table there were now finely carved oak chairs with padded seats. A large, round, low table held a stack of the latest journals.

The front window was stripped bare, awaiting, Francesca said, a heavy fabric in a similar version of the navy blue satin that covered the windows of her father's private office.

A sculpture of a naked female figure stood on a tall stand, taking up valuable space. Two vibrantly colored landscapes hung on the nailhole-pitted wall. A wool rectangular rug with bright jewellike colors of navy, wine, and green covered the center of the tobacco juice-stained floor.

"Oh, there you are, darling," Francesca cooed as she came out of his personal office. "I'm nearly finished down here. Now for the upstairs."

He silently followed her out the door and around the side of the building. She was in her element, directing three burly men as they maneuvered a heavy chest up the narrow stairway on the far end of the building.

"Careful . . . *careful*!" she screeched. "I paid a fortune for that!"

His living quarters were simple—a small living room with a chair and a table he used as a desk, a scarred kitchen table and two cane-bottomed chairs made up the eating area.

An alcove served as a bedroom with a sagging double bed and a four-drawer chest. A smoky mirror over the washstand stood next to the window overlooking the back alley. The furnishings weren't fancy, but they were comfortable, and he'd grown accustomed to them.

Unfortunately, Francesca had already begun her reconstruction campaign. "Take that and . . . give them to . . . someone," she directed, waving a hand in the air. "Push that aside," she ordered two men struggling to manipulate a satin-covered settee through the doorway.

Wrinkling her nose, she pointed to the bed. "And for heaven's sake take *that* away immediately so there's room for the new one."

"Francesca," Gray said. He *liked* his bed, sagging

though it was. It was oversized with a soft ticking mattress. Warm in the winter. Cool in the summer.

Busy directing the men on where to place the new chest, Francesca ignored him. Gray was shoved aside, forced to watch the parade of gaudy furnishings, already hating every new piece, and they hadn't been in the room an hour yet.

Whirling in a circle, Francesca clasped her hands together in delight, obviously satisfied with the morning's work. "Oh, my, there's so much to do! There is a restaurant nearby, isn't there?"

"The hotel, but I have patients—"

"Gray." The pout resurfaced. "I've come all this way and brought you all these lovely things, and you can't spare a moment to have dinner with me? You are a selfish man."

Oh, hell, he recognized the tone. When she was in this mood, there was no distracting her. She was trying to please him, and he wasn't being grateful. Whether he liked the gifts or not, he would, if it killed him, act as if he was pleased.

By the time Francesca finished, the sun was standing at high noon.

As the men departed, Francesca consulted the lapel watch pinned to her close-fitting jacket. "Dear me. Is it dinnertime already? Well, something light will do, for appearance' sake, or shall we . . . lunch in?" She smiled at Gray wickedly. "What would you like to do?"

"What I'd like to do, and what I must do, are different matters. I must see the patients that I've neglected this morning."

When she looked at him with her large blue eyes, he momentarily regretted his call to duty. The gleam of invitation in her seductive gaze compelled him to stay, and he felt his body responding.

When she saw his hesitation, she feigned petulance. Sighing softly, she said, "There is a hotel nearby?"

"A block down the street."

"Then I will take a room." She smiled, returning to her earlier buoyancy. "For appearance' sake."

"I'll be gone until late, Francesca. I have a patient who lives a good distance outside of town."

"Very well," she said. "I'll content myself with a long, hot soak in the tub until you're finished." Sighing as if very sad, she rose on tiptoe and gave him a promissory kiss.

As she reluctantly stepped back, she touched the tip of one finger against his cleanly shaven cheek. "Don't be long. I'm anxious to see if the new mattress is half as comfortable as the salesman assured me it is."

A moment later the door closed.

Hitting the wall with a balled up fist, Gray swore. Anger suffused his face. Hell. A moment ago he wanted to throw her on the bed and keep her there, but when she turned manipulative he wanted nothing better than to send her packing. He was tired of her showing up unexpectedly and demanding his undivided attention.

And one more load of furniture and the wedding was off!

Punching the wall again, he left the room, slamming the door behind him.

"I don't know about you," Porky said as she and April strolled toward the pharmacy—after the market, they shopped for dresses, then had tea at the hotel—"but I'd say the good doctor doesn't make those trips to Boston simply for medicines."

"I fail to see what the doctor does in Boston, or here, for that matter, is any of our business."

April had tried to get Porky's mind off the subject of Gray Fuller for the past four hours, but she was obsessed with the new doctor's personal life.

"You're not disappointed that he's taken? Don't you think he's incredibly handsome?"

"Of course he's handsome. He probably knows exactly how good looking he is and uses it to his full advantage. Just like that woman uses her beauty to wrap him around her little finger."

"Who? Frenchie?"

"Frenchie. You wouldn't want a man like that."

"Oh, yes I would. In fact, I'd take any man I could get."

"You would not."

"I would, too."

"Henry says—"

"Oh, Henry, Smenry. Henry isn't nearly as smart, or as handsome, as Dr. Fuller."

"Or as *talkative*." Her tone rang with implication.

"True, he shouldn't have told on you," Porky agreed. "But . . . did you notice the way his trousers hug his firm little—"

"Porky, that's enough about Dr. Fuller." She did notice, but Porky wasn't going to know.

Glancing over her shoulder, Porky frowned. "It's obvious they're lovers, don't you think? I mean, did you see the way she walked up to him and kissed him on the lips, right in broad daylight? Brushing against him that way. . . . Now that's a woman who knows a man well, if you understand what I'm saying."

"I understand clearly," April said, "and I wish you'd stop saying it." The subject of Gray Fuller and his "mistress" was wearing thin.

"She is gorgeous, isn't she? Did you see that dress she was wearing? Some outrageous price or I'll eat my hat."

"Far too self-assured, I'd say. A hussy."

"Hussy?" Porky laughed. "Hussy, indeed. Poor Rachel

Brown won't like hearing our fine doctor has a lady friend in Boston."

"Why should Rachel care?"

"Because she's set her sights on him but good. Are you working this afternoon?"

April was relieved Porky had finally changed the subject, albeit suddenly. "I have a meeting with Mrs. Pinkham at two."

"Was she disappointed when you told her you'll have to be less conspicuous in your work?"

"She understood my concern for Grandpa's health."

Consulting her locket watch, Porky sighed. "I have to cover again for Papa in the pharmacy this afternoon"—she grinned wickedly—"though I doubt the good doctor will be writing any prescriptions."

"Porky, you're incorrigible. You don't know anything about that woman. She could be his . . . sister."

Porky hooted. "Sister? With that dress and French accent? Besides, whose sister kisses them like that?"

April's expression firmed. "Anything's possible."

Porky grimaced. "Anything but that."

"We don't know anything about Gray Fuller."

"Nothing except he's partial to French ladies who bring him *beds*."

Women who bring him beds. April fumed as she sauntered toward home. How forward . . . how desperate can a woman be?

Granted, Gray Fuller was infuriatingly attractive. The puzzling paradox made him that much more intriguing.

He may have come from Boston, but she had to admit that he'd settled into Dignity as if he'd been there all his life. The residents seemed to like him, especially Grandpa, and Riley was usually a good judge of character.

The suits he wore were good—not new, but comfortably broken in. Nora Stonehouse washed and ironed his white shirts, and he always looked fresh . . . nice. She remembered how good he smelled that day in his office. As if he'd just stepped out of a hot tub, scrubbed fresh, and smelling nicer than a warm rain.

Datha told her that every single woman and their mothers were making fools of themselves over him, bringing endless baked offerings to attract his attention.

Judith Hawthorn had taken him an entire baked turkey last week.

A baked turkey!

Had the woman no shame?

It seemed that everyone in town, women especially, thought the doctor was next to God, and that every word he spoke was gospel. It was exactly the sort of distorted thinking Lydia was trying to discourage.

April stopped in a couple of stores on the way home, once to look at a hat, another to consider a pair of brown shoes that would go well with her new heavy cloak.

By the time she reached home, it was well past noon and she was hungry. The house was strangely quiet this afternoon. Thinking Grandpa was asleep, or in the mortuary working, she put the fresh vegetables in a pan for Datha to wash, then went in search of him.

"Grandpa?" she called. Pushing open the screen door she stepped onto the side porch. "Grandpa?"

The smoking porch was empty.

Going back through the house by way of the kitchen, she checked the mortuary office, even went into the dressing room. No one. Now she was concerned.

Just as she was walking back through the house, Datha burst in through the front door.

"Miss April!"

The girl's hair was coming loose from tight braids, and her eyes were as big as saucers.

"Datha—what's wrong?"

"It's Mr. Ogden. He got sick—" She panted. "I didn't know what to do. I took him down to Dr. Fuller. He said to come get you."

"Dr. Fuller?"

"Yes'um. He said for you to come right *now*."

April followed the young woman out the back door, her heart pounding in fear. Sick? How sick? Was it his heart, or something else?

By the time they reached the doctor's office, she was out of breath. Going past two women in the waiting room, she entered the examining room after a brief knock.

Riley was lying on the examining table, his face pale and damp. Dr. Fuller bent over him, listening to his heart with a stethoscope.

"Grandpa?"

Riley raised a hand in greeting, and April took it between her own.

"He's doing fine," Gray said. His eyes darkened as he glanced up and recognized her.

Glowering at him, her eyes warned him to not to make a scene.

"What happened, Grandpa?"

Giving her a feeble wave, Riley smiled. "Law, they won't let an old man rest."

Leaning over him, April took in his ashen features. His eyes drifted shut, his mouth went slack, and his breathing was shallow.

"The heat . . . must be getting to me today," he whispered weakly.

Pressing her hand to his forehead, she said quietly. "Was it another spell?"

"I . . . just a . . . weak spell," he managed. "I'll be fine. Just need to lay down a bit. Datha got scared—"

"I'm glad she acted quickly."

"I brought him here fast as I could," Datha said, hovering nearby in the corner.

"You did well, Datha. Thank you."

Stepping back, she cleared her throat, then said, "Doctor, may I have a moment, please?"

"It's too blasted hot for October, that's all that's the matter," Riley complained. "I'll be fine. I need to be home—Sadie Finley is only half done. . . ."

"Doctor, may we speak?"

Laying the stethoscope aside, Gray ushered her to the small dressing alcove at the other end of the examining room.

"All right, what's happened to my grandfather?"

"First, I'd suggest you calm down—"

"I'll calm down when I know what's wrong with Grandpa!"

He studied her a moment as if prudently weighing his answers.

"I didn't think you liked doctors. We're quacks, remember, unethical fools who don't know the difference between a scalpel and a butter knife."

"You don't, as far as I'm concerned. If I had been home, I would have dosed Grandpa with herbs and put him to bed, but I wasn't there, and Datha was, so here we are. I can hardly jerk him off the examining table and take him home, so we'll just pretend I go along with your diagnosis."

Crossing his arms, he stared at her. "But you don't. You know more than I do when it comes to the heart."

"Not more, but probably as much."

"Fortunately, most sane people don't agree with you."

"Are you saying I'm not sane?"

"I'm not saying anything."

"That's wise, because most people haven't had the experience I have with the godlike egos of the medical community."

He stiffened. "Miss. . . ?"

"Truitt. April Truitt. Riley's granddaughter."

"I *knew* I'd seen you somewhere before."

Stepping closer, she hissed. "You know perfectly well who I am. You told Grandpa about me selling the compound with Mrs. Pinkham, and don't deny it. Because of you, I can't sell it anymore!"

His eyes turned glacial. "I don't know where you got that idea, but I haven't said a word to your grandpa about your activities with the Pinkham woman. How could I? I didn't know who the hell you were until five minutes ago!"

She rolled her eyes in disbelief. "Oh, really, Dr. Fuller."

He met her defiant tone and matched it. "Yes, really, Miss Truitt. I don't give a damn what you do—got that?"

"Dr. Fuller." She drew herself upright, facing him. "I may not like it that my grandfather is here, but I trust you to do the best you know how—"

"Meaning you think someone else could do better?"

"Meaning that I want to know what's wrong with him."

"Then what?"

"Then I'll determine what course of action to take."

Shooting her an angry glance, he studied his notes. "Your grandfather has a heart problem. Today's episode may have been an attack, or it may have just been a warning. In any event, he needs rest. I'll want to observe him."

"For how long?"

"At least through the afternoon."

April was against leaving him here, but she supposed she must. If she caused a scene, it would upset Riley more. The extra time would give her the opportunity to consult with Mrs. Pinkham and old Mrs. Blake as to what herbal treatment would be most beneficial for him.

Meeting his eyes, she whispered ominously, "I'll be back for him late this afternoon."

Gray's face tightened. "And I'll release him as soon as I feel confident it's safe."

"Oh, really?" Did he actually think he could take that tone with her?

"Really."

Apparently he did.

He walked off before she could get him back.

Datha was waiting for her when she stepped outside.

"Is Mr. Ogden all right?"

"He'll be fine," April reassured her. "I'm glad you were home to take care of him."

"I was so scared," Datha admitted, her shoulders slumping in relief.

"The doctor wants to observe him for a little while, but he'll be back home by this evening."

"I'm so glad."

It was nearing four o'clock when April returned. Gray was standing in the doorway of the examining room studying the tall vase that Francesca said should stand on the floor in the corner. Something just didn't fit. No matter where he put it, it didn't look right.

When he heard the door open, he turned to greet the new arrival. His smile faded when he saw who it was.

"How is he?"

Setting the vase back in the corner, he said calmly, "He's doing very well. Color is good. He had a little soup to eat."

"I'm doing just fine," Riley grumbled, pulling his suspenders up over his shoulders as he emerged from the examining room.

"I see you've met April. My granddaughter worries too much."

"Why, Dr. Fuller knows every woman in town, isn't that right, Doctor," April goaded.

"If you say so, Miss Truitt."

Riley laughed lightly. "So, that's where that delicious pie came from."

"Pie?" April glanced at Gray.

He shrugged, looking guilty. "He was hungry. It was less stressful to feed him than to enforce his new diet at the time."

"He's trying to starve me," Riley groused.

"Don't get in a hurry to leave," Gray said, directing Riley back into the examining room. "I want to listen to your heart one more time."

April started to follow, but Gray closed the door in her face.

Sitting down in one of the padded chairs, she leafed through a magazine, listening to the muffled sound of men's voices behind the closed door. That was just like a doctor, thinking women didn't "need" to be involved in medical discussions.

When she heard Riley's laughter over some story the doctor was telling, she almost envied them their camaraderie. Dr. Fuller didn't find anything amusing when he was with her.

Tossing the magazine aside, she studied the new waiting room. The colors were nice, but the furniture spoiled the effect.

Large pieces, and too many of them, eliminated space to move around. Where the room had been stark and totally functional, now it was colorful and far too ostentatious for Dignity, Massachusetts.

"Wonder what she did to his personal quarters?" she murmured, then clamped her lips shut. She felt warmth move up her neck and over her face. What the doctor's living quarters looked like was none of her business.

Straightening, she sighed, wishing Henry would get back. Obviously she had too much time on her hands if she was thinking about Gray Fuller's personal life.

Her gaze returned to the closed door of the examining room as the sound of laughter drifted out. What could Riley and the doctor find to laugh about?

Getting up, she started to pace. Finally the door of the examining room opened. Riley came out, buttoning his shirt, followed by Gray.

"Well?" April demanded, trying to decide if the flush on Riley's face was from exertion or too much laughter.

"Your grandfather should rest for a few days. Don't let him do anything strenuous."

"I have a business to run," Riley reminded him.

"Let someone else do it for a few days. Your health is far more important."

"Well, that's nice, but I don't have anyone who can do it. Most folks are skittish about letting someone new take care of their loved ones. I'll be just fine," Riley said.

"Grandpa, the doctor said *rest*. And that's what you'll do," April said. "Beginning now. Thank you, Doctor. What do I owe you?"

His gaze swept over her and she flushed. His eyes were the most unusual shade of green; like pictures of the ocean she'd seen—just before a storm.

"A dollar."

She paid him, then steered Riley toward the door.

"I like that young man," Riley said, as they started down the sidewalk. The spring was out of his step this afternoon. "Seems to know his business. Nice office. Fancy."

"Yes. Fancy and crowded."

Dr. Fuller might be a barrel of laughs, but he hadn't given her a diagnosis of Riley's condition. It occurred to her that he'd not said anything definitive about it, and she wondered why.

Her heart nearly stopped with fright. Was there something seriously wrong? So wrong he didn't want to frighten Riley?

Rushing her grandfather down the sidewalk, April knew she had to go back and talk to that infuriating man alone. Her gaze fell on the fancy buggy parked in front of the hotel.

If he could spare the time.

"Where's the fire?" Riley blustered, trying to keep up with her.

"Sorry, Grandpa," April murmured. "I just want to get you home so you can rest."

Chapter 6

After breakfast the next morning, Riley went straight to the side porch with a stack of journals and stayed there throughout the morning. Apparently he was taking the doctor's order to rest seriously. Jimmy Peters, a neighboring teenager, agreed to help with the heavy work. Other than Sadie Finley's service that afternoon, business was quiet.

The nagging suspicion that Dr. Fuller hadn't told her everything wore on April's mind. Midmorning she gave up trying to concentrate. She simply had to know if Gray Fuller thought Riley's weak spells were getting worse. Being a doctor, his opinion wasn't of much value to her, but if she were to treat Grandpa effectively with herbal medicine, then she needed to know what she was fighting.

Dropping what she was doing, she changed into a pretty, lavender cotton dress with matching hat and gloves. The change wasn't intended for Dr. Fuller's approval, she assured herself as she checked her hair once again in the downstairs hall mirror. She had just made it a practice to look her best when she conducted business.

"I'm going out for a while," April called as she passed the door to the side porch. "You stay right where you are until I get back."

"What am I, a child?"

"Yes, and you're being punished." She laughed at his indignant growl.

"Jimmy's here if you need him."

"I'll be fine. Stop your fussing."

He seemed to be himself this morning, and April was relieved. Still, she was concerned about him, and Dr. Fuller was the only person who had, at least for now, the answers she needed.

A brisk wind rolled off the ocean as April walked toward the center of town. The weather was nippy this morning. A distinct touch of fall was in the air. Low, pewter colored clouds building in the west promised rain by evening.

Walking along the cobbled street, April breathed in the smells of burning leaves and fresh bread from the bakery.

Tall ships crowded the small harbor. Casks of whale oil and bundles of whalebone were piled high on the bustling piers. Not many big ships came into the small harbor, but enough to create a good business for everyone in town.

Near the waterfront, sailmakers, blacksmiths, carpenters, candle makers, and coopers conducted business. A few blocks away, she could hear the sounds of hammering as wealthy merchants built stately mansions surrounded by large lawns and lush summer flower gardens.

Weathered houses originally built seventy-five to a hundred years earlier lined the routes that intersected the main thoroughfare coming inland from the wharf. The houses were small and unassuming. One room for cooking and dining, living and sleeping quarters adjacent for the husband and wife; children and servants made do with a loft above the main room.

The unadorned houses would never blend with that overbearing Doctor Fuller's new ostentatious office.

Toward the center of town, near the square, shop windows sparkled with intricate jewel-colored glassware, copper pans, drapes of fabric, ready-made dresses, and millinery. Wonderful aromas drifted from a spice shop, exotic scents that came to Dignity from faraway places. Larger cargo ships passed by and put in at the Boston harbor, but many smaller ones stopped here first.

April paused at the shoemaker's window to look at a pair of red-leather boots. Henry didn't like red—but Gray and his Frenchie lover obviously would. What better reason for her to pass on the boots?

Stepping around fresh mounds left by a flock of sheep being herded down the street in front of her, she heard the schoolhouse bell ring and quickly stepped out of the way of a young boy who was in a desperate race to make it to his seat before the last peal.

"Milk, cheese, butter. Get your fresh milk, cheese, butter churned fresh this morning."

A wooden cart, pushed by a ruddy-faced farmer, made morning rounds, hawking farm goods. More than likely the woman of the house had been up before dawn to help her husband milk, churn butter, and wrap cheese for him to sell to the grocer and then peddle what was left on the street.

April felt lucky. Her grandfather's profession provided a comfortable income, and when she married Henry, he, too, would provide for them well.

The sight of the approaching doctor's office set her heart to racing. Oh how she dreaded facing his piercing gaze and his holier-than-thou attitude. She hated it even more the way he could start her stomach fluttering with one careless look. What did she care if the new town physician *was* the best looking man in town? Henry wasn't a troll.

Porky's earlier words suddenly colored the pleasant walk. *Henry will never ask you to marry him.*

Porky was wrong. She wasn't a fool. She knew Henry had faults, but who didn't? True, she'd never paid particular attention to him growing up. He'd favored the girls too much, preferring to play one against the other. But he was different now. Just as she was older and more appreciative of Henry's outgoing nature. At least he didn't kiss women on Main Street in broad daylight.

Admittedly, he had taken her by storm when he decided to court her. Unaccustomed to his undivided concentration, she was caught up in the excitement of having a man like Henry openly vying for her attention. Like Porky, she wouldn't have thought that she would be magnetized by a man with Henry's propensity to flatter, but she was.

Too much so, she was afraid.

Dr. Fuller's waiting room was empty when she opened the door. Once again her gaze focused on the massive heavy furniture, and she couldn't suppress a giggle. It was so grotesquely ostentatious that she almost felt sorry for him. The French woman must really have an influence over him for the doctor to allow her to do this to him. A picture of Hans Stenzel sitting on a fancy, upholstered chair, cramming his six-feet-six-inch frame between the chair and table, tucking his long legs and huge feet beneath the chair, was almost comical.

Amazing. The doctor's lady love, for all her beauty and lovely clothes and all her obvious money, had no taste. None at all. The room would have to be twice its size to accommodate the furniture she'd crammed into it.

April's lips quivered with amusement again. She'd forfeit a new dress to see what the Frenchie had done with the doctor's small living quarters.

Frowning at the naked sculpture sitting in the corner, she was glad the office was empty so she wouldn't have to wait in the vulgar looking waiting room.

Hoping her cheeks would cool before Dr. Fuller came out of his examining room, she moved on around the room. Dignity people were used to simple things. She doubted they would take to the doctor's fancy new furnishings, or the lewd sculpture.

The vase Gray had been worrying with the day before was in the corner, but somehow it looked out of place.

Curious, April bent to study it. Three feet tall, an intricate pattern of crouched figures in purple and blue, entwined with ropy green and brown vines that depicted both the ground and overhanging tree branches, spilled around the bell. Noticing it was already dusty, April extracted a handkerchief from her bag and wiped the vase clean, looking closely at the small, intricate drawings that made up the design circling the vase.

When the bell over the door rang, she turned, expecting to find a neighbor. Instead, "Frenchie" swept in on a cloud of expensive smelling perfumed air.

Snapping blue eyes in a pale heart-shaped face framed by a cloud of sooty black hair glanced over April imperiously.

Whoever she is, April decided, *she's absolutely gorgeous. And rich. Extremely rich, if those stones in her earrings are real.* The dress she was wearing had to have cost a fortune, and the pin on her bodice had a number of rubies that were nothing less than first-grade stones.

"Oh, good. I'm glad you're here."

April lifted an eyebrow questioningly.

Closing the door, the woman crossed the room to run a

gloved finger over the mahogany table. "I expect these fine pieces to be dusted properly every day and oiled once a month. The carpet is to be taken out and beaten at least once a week. And that vase. You do realize what it is?"

"I believe I do," April said hesitantly, aware the woman had her confused with the cleaning lady.

"It's of the Ming dynasty. It must be handled very carefully. It's museum quality, you understand. Of course, I'm sure even you do understand. Is the doctor in?"

"I believe he's with a patient," she said, not bothering to correct Frenchie.

"Well, remember what I've told you about caring for the wood." The door opened again. "Oh, excellent!"

Two men came in, one carrying more framed pictures, the other two potted plants.

"Put them down by—" Laying her fingertip on her cheek, she frowned. "Oh, dear, it is a bit crowded, isn't it?"

The door to the examining room opened, and Gray emerged ahead of a young boy and his mother.

"Don't be putting anything else up your nose, young man," he admonished the boy, ruffling his hair affectionately.

"Thank you, Doctor," Freeda Brown said gratefully. "Come, Robert, you'll not be missing school because of this." Freeda ushered her young son out of the office in a flurry.

"Francesca," Gray acknowledged, closing the door behind the pair.

"Good morning, darling."

Glancing at April, his expression tightened. "Is your grandfather feeling worse this morning?"

Ignoring Francesca, who was suddenly busy directing the men on where and how to hang the new pictures and where to position the plants, April raised her voice above the racket they were making. "He seems more like himself today, but I—" She glanced at Francesca, who was dragging a chair across the floor. "I'm concerned about him. You didn't say what you thought—" She gave up trying to talk above the noise of the men hammering nails into the walls.

Gray regarded her quizzically, waiting for her to continue.

Suddenly feeling awkward and out of place, April wished she'd waited to talk to him. Apparently this wasn't the best time to garner his concentration.

"I—I noticed yesterday that you didn't actually say what you thought about grandfather's condition."

Gray suddenly shouted. "Francesca, can't that wait?"

The hammering temporarily ceased. Her eyes wide, Francesca blinked back at Gray. "Sorry, darling. Go right on with whatever you're doing. You won't bother us."

Turning back to April, Gray indicated for her to go on. "You were saying about your grandfather?"

"Just . . . is there a reason why you didn't elaborate on his condition?" She found herself extremely conscious of how handsome he looked this morning. And he had this special way of looking at her as if she were the only person in the room. No wonder single women found any excuse to visit him. Why, if she didn't have Henry, she might be tempted—but she *did* have Henry, and Gray Fuller was a doctor, the last man she would be interested in.

"As I indicated yesterday, your grandfather needs to take it easier. Rest. Eat more vegetables and fruit. Take a long walk every day." Gray leaned closer, lowering his voice to a whisper. She detected a faint whiff of soap and water—French soap, no doubt. "And have him stay away from that elixir you're selling."

April's eyes flashed with anger. "Because of you, *that*

won't be a problem. Grandpa has forbidden me to sell the compound."

"Good."

When she stiffened with resentment, he continued. "Joe McFarland's diagnosis, in my opinion, was correct. Your grandfather isn't a young man. He needs to slow down."

"I've told him that, but he won't listen."

The workmen were making so much noise it was practically impossible to carry on a normal conversation.

"Do the best you can," Gray said, smiling at her with candor, the corners of his eyes crinkling with amusement.

She was stunned by her reaction. Her heart thumped like a foolish schoolgirl in the midst of her first crush. Why, she was no different than the other besotted single women. The thought was terribly irritating.

"Thank you, Doctor."

"You're most welcome, Miss Truitt."

He smiled again, as if he knew the effect his smile had on her.

"Gray, darling, come tell me what you think about putting this plant here—"

Turning on her heel, April strode quickly out the office and closed the door firmly behind her. The giggle that had been threatening burst into full-blown laughter. Frenchie, you might be a fancy Boston lady, but you have no idea what it takes to be accepted in Dignity. And Gray Fuller's an even bigger fool if he thinks fancy furniture will make him a respected doctor.

April giggled again, and Mrs. Handleman gawked at her as she walked past the bank.

Remembering her manners, April forced a straight face. "Morning, Mrs. Handleman."

The banker's wife nodded, looking as if she thought April had lost her mind.

Swallowing a giggle, April set off for the pharmacy, anxious to tell Porky about Dr. Fuller's lady friend who seemed bent on making him the laughingstock of town!

Riley was playing checkers with Jimmy on the side porch when April arrived home. Realizing she hadn't spoken with Lydia in a couple of days, and wanting to know how Will and Henry were doing with their work in Boston, she decided to take a trip to Lynn that afternoon, if Riley was feeling better. Henry had promised to write, but so far she hadn't even received a note from him.

Satisfied Riley would be fine for a few hours, she told Datha she'd be back by supper.

"He wouldn't eat his fruit at lunch," Datha complained. "Says it gives him the runs."

"I'll talk to him."

"Yes, April girl. That would sure help."

Jimmy hitched up the small carriage April used, and she drove through town on the way to Lynn, which was about forty-five minutes away at a fast clip with a good horse. As she passed Dr. Fuller's office for the second time that day, she noticed the Ming vase that had been of such concern to Francesca was now sitting on the sidewalk in front of the office.

Slowing the carriage, she wondered how the vase had gotten out there. Had a young patient played a prank on the new doctor? She hoped not.

Not with a Ming vase.

The vase sat outside the doctor's office, conspicuous by its shape and color. Just then she noticed Jackson Myers coming down the sidewalk, hands in his pockets as he swaggered, whistling a tuneless ditty. As he reached the doctor's office he leaned over and spat.

In the Ming vase.

April winced. Jackson had used the vase as a spittoon. Francesca would have apoplexy.

As Jackson continued on down the walk, April climbed out of the carriage. Gingerly picking up the vase, she carried it into the doctor's office. The door to his private office was open, and he was bent over a ledger. He glanced up as she entered, frowning when he saw the vase in her hands.

Leaning back in his chair, lacing his fingers behind his head, he regarded her with a half smile, his gaze sweeping over her carelessly. It wasn't hard to see she wasn't making any points with him today.

"Forget something?"

"Fancy spittoon you have here, Doctor."

"Spittoon?" His gaze moved to the vase. "That's not a spittoon. That's Francesca's vase."

Shaking her head, April tilted the vase away from her and peered inside.

"No. Jackson Myers just walked by. It's definitely a spittoon now."

Gray paled as he straightened, his feet thudding against the wooden floor. "Francesca will have my head on a platter."

"Ooooooh, is the doctor scared of the mean ol' woman?"

Ignoring her goad, he got up to circle the desk and take the vase.

"I'd suggest, Doctor, that you make a place for the vase inside. Have you any idea what this 'spittoon' is worth? Your lady friend informed me it's museum quality."

"Her name is Francesca DuBois."

"How fancy."

He shot her a disgusted look and carried the vase back

into the waiting room, looking as if he didn't know what to do with it.

Trailing behind him, April realized that she was enjoying this. Frenchie had the poor man in a hapless dither. "I understand you were having difficulty fitting it into the waiting room, but I don't suggest leaving it outside. It makes a terrible spittoon, and I have very specific directions from 'Francesca' on how it, and your other furniture, should be cared for."

He turned, a scowl on his face. "I beg your pardon?"

"You should." Her eyes hardened. "Francesca thought I was the cleaning woman."

"I'm sorry. Francesca—" He appeared to search for the proper term.

"Is presumptuous?" April supplied.

"That, too," he agreed, still standing in the middle of the room uncertainly.

"Use it as an umbrella stand," she suggested. Then, curiosity overcoming manners, she blurted out, "Exactly how presumptuous is she?"

Gray's mouth curved in a smile, the corners of his eyes crinkling in that distressingly attractive way.

"Sorry," April murmured. "I guess that makes two of us, being presumptuous, I mean. I apologize." She studied the vase again. "I think I know a place it would fit in."

"There's actually a spot left?"

His smile was captivating, and she found herself smiling back. She hadn't meant to smile but he looked so appealing with his shirt sleeves rolled up. And she had to admit Porky was right about the way he filled out his trousers. A woman would have to be blind not to find him attractive.

"Over there," she pointed to a tiny alcove beneath the

nude sculpture. Color dotted her cheeks as she started for the door.

"Does Riley use refined sugar on his morning oatmeal?"

"Yes"—she turned back—"he does. Why?"

"Does he use jam and jelly on his biscuits?"

"Of course."

"And he favors biscuits and gravy?"

"Yes." Her pulse jumped. "Why? Is there something wrong with that?"

"Well, it's just that that sort of eating habit isn't healthy for him."

"But he's eaten those things all his life."

"I know, but let me put it this way. Your heart is the engine, you might say, for the body. It's what makes everything work. The heart needs the proper nourishment to work efficiently. Refined sugar, gravy, biscuits all clog the working parts of the body and slow it down, until one day it stops altogether."

Moving back to the desk, she waited for him to go on. "Are you saying Grandpa is about to die?"

What would she do without him? She'd lost nearly everyone she loved. He was so important to her, and she loved him so much. Sagging against the desk, she let the frightening possibility sink in.

He stepped toward her, his hand closing around her arm as if he was afraid she was going to faint. "Are you all right?"

"I—I'm fine. What about Grandpa—"

She forgot to breathe. He was so close, his concern potent, and the warmth of his hand burned through her sleeve! Her stomach started to flutter, and she dismissed it to his warning about Riley, but deep down she couldn't deny it was him. There was a softness in his dark eyes that made her melt.

Gray stepped back as if realizing she was about to pull away from him.

"I'm saying that your grandfather needs to eat more vegetables, use honey instead of the sugar. And walk. In fact, get him to take two teaspoons of honey with each meal, and walk a couple of miles a day. You'll find he feels better, sleeps better, and has fewer stomach complaints."

April was skeptical. "They," whoever "they" were, thought Lydia's ideas were far-fetched. What would "they" say about this? "What good is honey, other than it tastes good?"

Moving to a metal cabinet, he filed a document he'd left on the desk. "Back to nature. I've done quite a lot of study in that area."

She tilted her head to one side, deciding that while he was an adversary, he was a well-educated one. Her admiration was grudging.

"Yet you charge Mrs. Pinkham with being a quack?"

He smiled. "Honey is pure, untouched. The body assimilates it easily, and uses it well. The 'elixir' that Mrs. Pinkham puts in those bottles is more than half alcohol and you know it. People feel good when they take it because they're half drunk by the end of the day."

April straightened, crossing her arms as she faced him smugly. "You, good doctor, are jealous of her results."

He laughed. "You, dear woman—"

The outer door suddenly burst open, and they turned in unison.

"There you are, Doctor!"

Two wide-eyed young women, assisting a third who leaned heavily on them, came into the office. April recognized the Gibson twins, Marilyn and Carolyn.

Manhunters.

Molly Nelson was the injured party.

"What's the problem?" the doctor asked.

April could tell him the problem, but he'd know soon enough himself. The Gibson twins wanted a husband. They'd even sniffed around Henry when it was plain he was courting her. Marilyn and Carolyn each supported Molly with one hand and a freshly baked pie with the other.

Their intent was evident. It was hunting season.

"Why, we don't know, Doctor." Marilyn handed him her gooseberry pie. "We were just walking by when Molly suddenly felt faint. We thought perhaps we should bring her in here to rest and . . . perhaps you could look after her?"

Gray glanced at April, and she couldn't help grinning at his discomfort. "Why, Marilyn, the doctor was just saying how he was trying to cut down on sugar and lard. Good diet, you know, is very important to the digestion."

"Let's get your friend into the examining room," Gray suggested, sending April a look that was both censure and amusement.

April was still grinning as the women led Molly into the other room.

Pies, she thought. *How transparent.*

She spent the afternoon with Lydia Pinkham. Together they wrote advertising copy for the newspaper and assembled new flyers for Will and Henry to use in their sales efforts in Boston.

On the way back home she stopped by the pharmacy to tell Porky about Marilyn and Carolyn's outrageous behavior. Pies. She wondered who'd made them. Everyone in Dignity knew the twins couldn't peel potatoes.

"A couple of teaspoons a day, now. You'll be feeling like a new woman before you know it," Porky was explaining to a woman with four young children tugging at her skirts. "One in the morning, and one after supper."

"Well, I guess it won't hurt to try it." The woman held up the small brown bottle to inspect it. "Just two teaspoons a day, you say?"

"Just two."

April held the door open as the woman shooed her rowdy brood out the door.

"Was that Mrs. Pinkham's compound you gave her?" April asked as she closed the door.

"Isn't that what I'm supposed to do? Give the women a sample and tell them it'll solve all their problems?"

"Yes, but you could be more enthusiastic about it."

Porky shook her head. "All that poor woman needs is a rest. Four children in five years, and she hasn't recovered from the last one two years ago. How's your grandpa today?"

"Dr. Fuller says he needs to change what he's eating, and take a long walk every day. I don't know how Grandpa is going to take to that. He loves his biscuits and gravy every morning, along with all the rest Datha insists on cooking. She cooks enough to feed a milling crew."

"Speaking of Datha, people are saying that she and Jacel are seeing a lot of one another lately."

"Let's hope Flora Lee doesn't hear anyone saying it. But, Datha's awfully crazy about that boy."

"You think she's too crazy? You know, do you think she knows how babies are made?"

"She's sixteen—and the last of twelve children. I'm sure she knows. Why?"

"I was just wondering." Porky absently straightened a row of salves. "Jacel comes in once in a while. He's been buying Stoneseed root lately."

Stoneseed root? April had heard the herbal remedy

was used by Narragansett women to cause permanent sterility. What use did Jacel have for it?

"That's odd. Do you think I should say something to her?"

"No. It's probably . . . nothing. It just seems to me that Datha's awfully young to be so serious over a boy. Knowing how Flora Lee is so dead set against the relationship, I just worry about her."

"Jacel's hardly a boy. He's what? Seventeen now?"

Coming around the counter, Porky wiped her hands on her apron. "Eighteen actually. And Datha being sixteen really isn't too young. You know, more girls in this town are married before they're seventeen than wait as long as we have—though it hasn't been exactly our choice," she finished with a grimace.

The news was disturbing. Jacel and Datha were terribly close. "I know Datha's loyal. Once she gives her heart, nothing sways her."

"Well, let's just hope Jacel is mature enough to know the consequences of . . . well, you know."

"Yes, let's hope," April said pensively.

"Back to Dr. Fuller," Porky said, "I hear half the ladies in town have suddenly developed fainting spells." She grinned. "Seems they could at least be creative."

"Umhum, that was Molly's ploy this morning."

Porky laughed as she pulled down the "closed" shade on the door of the pharmacy.

"Have you heard what the doctor's fancy lady did with his living quarters?"

"Her name is Francesca," April supplied. "Francesca DuBois."

Porky looked mildly impressed. "How do you know that?"

"Dr. Fuller told me."

"Dr. Fullller told meeee," Porky mocked. "Did you have a 'fainting' spell, too?"

"No, you witch. I was on the way to meet Mrs. Pinkham when I noticed Miss DuBois's Ming vase setting out in front of the doctor's office. It was being used as a spittoon at the time."

"A spittoon?"

"Jackson Myers initiated it, and I nicely took it back inside. I don't think the doctor has any idea what a vase like that costs. I found a place for it in his office, and in the course of the conversation he told me that the lady's name is Miss Francesca DuBois from Boston. And while I was there, the lady in question brought in yet more paintings and plants. You can hardly get a live body in that waiting room now."

Removing her apron, Porky hung it on a hook. "Wouldn't you just love to know what she's done to his personal quarters?"

"No."

"Would, too."

"I would not, Porky. Stop being so nosy."

"She went back to Boston this afternoon."

"Who did?"

"Miss DuBois."

"How do you know that?"

"Thought you weren't interested."

"I'm not. Just idle curiosity."

"Umhum. You know what curiosity did."

"Killed the cat. How do you know the lady left today?"

"I saw her. She rode out of town in her fine black buggy, preening like a peacock. Want to know what she did to his bedroom?"

"Absolutely not."

"Do, too," Porky challenged.

"Do not."

"Liar."

"All right," April surrendered. "What is the *new* decor?"

"No. You're not interested, and far be it from me to bore you with the details. Ready to go?"

"Porky!"

Porky laughed. "Well, since you've twisted my arm. The rumor is, and it's from a very reliable source, that the doctor's fine lady has redone his bedroom in a shocking lavender! Can you imagine? Little frilly curtains at the windows. The bed coverlet is lavender with matching lacy pillow covers. And, I understand his collection of fine furniture now includes a dressing table complete with silver brushes and a 'charming' little chair with a lavender seat cushion. Can you just imagine Gray Fuller perched on that tiny chair?"

They broke out in giggles and April felt foolish. They were acting like schoolgirls. She cringed when she thought about what Porky would say if she knew how she'd reacted to a mere touch by the doctor. Of course she wouldn't admit acting like an adolescent and give Porky more fuel for her fire.

"And," Porky continued, "he has a fine table with matching bone china. China, I'm told, with silver plate silverware. There's also a magnificent china hutch, the bottom of which now holds the finest linens money can buy. Irish linen, it's suggested."

"You can't be serious."

"I am! Crystal candle holders with store-bought candles! A carpet, similar to the one in his new waiting room. I'm told the upstairs of that old building looks like a palace now."

"It's shameless the way Dr. Fuller is letting her take over." April was sure Henry would never permit such a thing, and if Gray Fuller had any gumption about him, he wouldn't either.

"I suspect Dr. Fuller appreciates the effort Miss Francesca DuBois has put into making him . . . comfortable," Porky winked. "If you know what I mean."

"Why, Miss Porky! How you do go on," April drawled dramatically, laughing while ignoring a sudden, irrational spurt of jealousy.

"She is a beautiful woman," Porky commented. "Beautiful, rich, sure of herself." She leaned against the counter, dreaming again.

"Yes," April concurred, sobering. "Perfect."

Porky sighed. "Almost too perfect."

Chapter 7

Fall was in the air. That crispness that made a person feel alive. But the promise of rain was yet to be fulfilled; a rain that would wash everything clean and fresh by morning.

A round, golden moon, a harvest moon, bathed the woodshed as Datha paced back and forth, worrying that Jacel couldn't get away to meet her, and praying he wouldn't come around about the time Flora Lee woke from her evening nap and came looking for her.

Peeking between the cracks in the door, she nervously chewed her fingernail as she looked out. Mama would tan her hide if she knew she was meeting Jacel almost every night. The mere mention of his name and Flora Lee flew into a tirade, preaching her sermon about "uppity folk" and how they ought to have enough sense to know their place.

Jacel wasn't uppity. He just had big dreams—dreams of being a lawyer someday and helping people who needed him. Why was that so hard for Mama to understand and respect?

It wasn't as if Jacel hadn't already done more than most men his age—black *or* white. He'd read every book in town and ordered books from Boston whenever he had enough money.

Mr. Ogden loaned him books from his own library and even promised to get Jacel into law school and pay his tuition when he was accepted. But that hadn't convinced Mama that Jacel wasn't uppity.

Datha had learned to ignore it when Flora Lee's aches and pains made her unreasonable, but sometimes it made her downright mad that her own mama disapproved so much of the man she loved.

"Uppity, he is," Flora Lee said far too often. "And ain't no good gonna come of it. He'll hurt you, girl. Hurt you powerful bad with his fancy ideas."

Datha was plain tired of hearing Mama complain about Jacel and his dreams. Jacel had a right to dream; what eighteen-year-old didn't?

It wasn't much comfort to know Jacel's folks weren't too happy about the situation, either. While Flora Lee had her strong opinions about Jacel, the idea that Jacel's parents might have bad thoughts about Datha didn't set well with her.

Truth was, the Evanses thought Flora Lee had lived with rich white folks too long.

"Nothin' good will come of you two seein' one another," Flora Lee said again and again. "Mark my words, girl, that boy's gonna get you in trouble some day."

Well, she loved Jacel, and he'd die before he saw her hurt. Why, she loved him more than life itself, and she'd do anything to see that he got a chance to go to law school. Even if it meant they couldn't think about marrying for years.

A rap on the shed door pulled her from her litany of worry and she hurried to open it.

"Hi, baby," she whispered.

"Datha, darling," Jacel whispered back, his dark gaze hungrily drinking in her nubile curves.

"I missed you, baby," she whispered.

The hunger was there tonight, just like all the others.

Eager for the other's young, strong body, they quickly disposed of clothing. Their snatches of intimacy were brief, and there was no time for foreplay.

"Oh, Datha, woman, I love you," Jacel whispered as their bare flesh touched, igniting a hotter flame.

Nipping his shoulder, she whispered. "I love you so much, Jacel."

They wanted each other now. Passion throbbed, urging to be appeased.

"You will be careful, won't you, Jacel?" She peered up at him, anxious, but oh so needy. The ache between her legs was unbearable.

"Don't worry, baby, I'll be careful."

The thought was lost, scattered to the wind as he bore into her, his mouth swallowing her muffled cry.

It was all right to let him love her, Datha told herself as she opened to him in a volley of blinding pleasure. They would be careful, and once they were married, they'd never have to worry about making love again.

Riley lingered at the supper table as April finished putting away the remains. They'd decided to eat in the kitchen tonight. For the past week, Datha had cooked fresh vegetables and roast chicken for their evening meal. Grandpa complained that the chicken wasn't fried and the creamed gravy was missing, but April noticed the bland fare hadn't affected his appetite. He ate like a harvest hand.

"I'm glad to see you're adjusting without a lot of fuss," April said.

"My belly thinks my throat's been cut, but I guess I'll live." Striking a match, Riley lit his pipe. "I'm surprised at you, though. You're not putting up a fuss over the doctor's orders. Why not?"

"I don't disagree that it's a sounder way of eating. It doesn't take a doctor to know all that grease and sugar isn't good for you." Dipping a skillet in hot water, she added, "Even an occasional doctor can come up with sound advice."

Chuckling, Riley pushed back from the table to smoke. "What have you done all day?"

"Oh, visited with Porky."

Drawing on his pipe, he grunted. "Don't know why that woman can't use her real name."

"Everybody's called her Porky so long, she thinks that *is* her real name."

"She'll never get a husband if she doesn't put a stop to it. What man wants a woman called 'Porky'?"

"A smart one. Someday the right man will come along for her, and he won't care about her dress size. He'll see how her eyes shine like black agates and he'll notice the way she lights up like a Christmas tree when she laughs and makes you just feel good all over."

"Hummpt. How many men want a Christmas tree for a wife?"

"Well, obviously not many," April conceded, thinking of her friend's noticeable lack of male companionship. The last man Porky had walked out with was married now and had two children.

A smile touched the corners of her eyes when she thought about Porky's crush on Dr. Fuller. April purposely hadn't teased her about it. Not much, anyway, because she hoped the infatuation would pass. And, she didn't want to hurt her feelings. Gray Fuller had his pick of every single woman in Dignity, not to mention Francesca DuBois from Boston. Speculation about that relationship ran rampant after the woman redecorated the doctor's office and living quarters. Were they engaged or not? If not, just what was going on there?

To Gray's credit, he did nothing to encourage Porky's affections, or any of the other women's, but the last thing she wanted was for Porky to be hurt. She was good as gold. There wasn't another woman in Dignity as caring or as giving as Porky Ludwig, but she wouldn't stand a snowball's chance in hell against Dr. Fuller's wealthy Bostonian.

Grandpa glanced around the empty kitchen. "Where'd Datha disappear to?"

"She asked to be excused early tonight. I told her I'd clean up."

Smoke formed a wreath around his head as Riley chuckled. "She off with Jacel again?"

Storing a tin of flour in the pantry, April answered over her shoulder, "I didn't ask."

When the kitchen work was finished, April retired to the back porch, taking her book with her.

Lying back in her favorite chair, she breathed deeply of the brisk night air. Fall was her favorite time of year. The vivid shades of red maples and golden oak against the crystal blue of the harbor and the sharp rocks of the rough shoreline made a perfect picture. The pungent smell of wood smoke hung in the air as she settled deeper into the chair.

Loneliness filled her when she thought about Henry. She missed him, but his work was important, as was hers, although she couldn't be as open about it as he could.

Her visit this afternoon with Mrs. Pinkham had been inspiring. She felt useful and productive in Lydia's company. Advancing the cause of something she believed in so completely was gratifying.

Resting her head against the back of the chair, she thought about the new flyers they'd designed this afternoon: bright blue paper printed in black ink. The message touted:

> *A Sure Cure for prolapsed uteri or falling of the womb, and all FEMALE WEAKNESSES, including Leucorrhea, Painful Menstruation, Inflammation, and Ulceration of the Womb, Irregularities, Floodings, etc. Pleasant to the taste, efficacious and immediate in its effect, it is a great help in pregnancy, and relieves pain during labor. For All Weaknesses of the generative organs of either Sex, it is second to no remedy that has ever been before the public; and for all diseases of the Kidneys it is the Greatest Remedy in the World.*

Well, maybe not the "greatest remedy in the world," April silently admitted, but it did help women in a variety of ways.

She was still troubled over what Lydia had told her this afternoon. Doctors were actually *closing* the vagina to treat the prolapsed uterus.

Neither the fact that the treatment had poor results, nor the fact that the procedure ended sexual intercourse and childbearing seemed to matter.

"Coping" appeared to be the prescribed treatment for female complaints. That and soap, proper diet, and exercise.

Opening her eyes, she stared at the darkening sky thinking about how Dr. Fuller prescribed a proper diet and exercise for Grandpa.

She wondered if he recognized the similarity between his advice to men and that usually tossed off to women, no matter what their complaint. A man like Gray Fuller wouldn't appreciate the comparison, she decided.

Lydia had explained to April that the very nature of her compound added a sexual dimension to the sales and distribution effort, which elicited an undue amount of lewd winking and ribald laughter.

It happened not only when the compound was mentioned, but also when Mrs. Pinkham's name was uttered. Society, Lydia had said, was not progressing very swiftly in recognition of women's rights.

Women were still considered sentimental creatures, spiritual, sexless, and far too often referred to as "the opposite sex" rather than as women or female. "We are considered only in conjunction with our reproductive function," Lydia stated angrily, "rather than as persons."

Lydia, however, claimed that her vegetable compound acted as a "specific" for female ailments—a claim that doctors generally called a blatant lie.

But despite her claims and proof that her compound produced amazing results, sales were not good. Lydia was expanding the advertising campaign. In order to create a consumer demand and to convince Boston druggists to carry the compound, Dan, Will, and Henry were sent to distribute the hundreds of thousands of pamphlets to potential customers as well as druggists.

Newspaper ads were taken to equate demand and supply. Daily journals, hungry for advertising, often accepted merchandise in payment for advertising space. Many a periodical had a good supply of Lydia's compound lying around their offices. The newspaper publishers acted as a sales force. They took the product and turned it over to local wholesalers and druggists, who accepted it because they could count on a retail demand stimulated by the newspaper ads. With Henry's marketing ability, the next few months should prove equally successful.

Voices from the side porch interrupted her thoughts. Frowning, April sat up as Gray Fuller's voice drifted to her. He and Grandpa were playing checkers.

Opening her book, she took out the letter she'd received from Henry the day before. Spreading it on her. lap she reread the untidy script. Henry, charming rake that he was, had handwriting that would do credit to a physician. Henry wrote:

It has been raining and we've been forced to stay in our room. I am anxious to get out and start selling again. We are in a back room and little air circulates, even when we can open the one window. Also, Will snores.

Money is short. If you could, put in a word to Lydia. We have not been extravagant. We've spent less than $2.00 a day. Fortunately, I have a few dollars of my own put aside or I would not have the funds to buy a stamp to send you this letter. We've even cut back on our laundry bills, wearing a shirt two weeks, which I thoroughly despise. Dan is sewing his shoes together every night and is trying to keep his one suit clean so he can continue to make successful contacts for us.

But, I'm convinced that we're going to make a fortune, once we are able to get out the word that Mrs. Pinkham's Compound is "the thing" for women today.

Boston is most exciting. There's something about the town that is invigorating. It makes me know we'll be successful.

But, enough of this business talk. I miss you, my love. I miss your smiling face, your gentle laughter. You are sunshine to my soul. The days cannot pass quickly enough until I hold you in my arms again—or am I too bold?

We have mùch to discuss when I return. Meanwhile, think of me fondly, and often.

With love,
Henry

With love. Closing her eyes, April rested her head on the back of the chair. What, she mused, did Henry want to discuss with her when he returned? Matrimony perhaps?

Spreading the letter on her lap, she caressed the pages as if touching them would bring her closer to him.

"Letter from an admirer?"

She jumped, her eyes flying open in surprise. "Oh! I didn't—" She sat up in concern. "Is something wrong?"

Gray Fuller stood in the doorway, frowning. "Wrong?"

He had taken her completely by surprise. She thought he was on the side porch with Riley. "With Grandpa?"

"No, Riley's fine." His gaze moved questioningly to an adjoining chair. "Mind if I sit a moment?"

Why would he want to sit with me? she wondered, but politely nodded her consent.

"Riley says you're starving him to death. Vegetables, fruit, baked chicken. Says he'd really like a plate of biscuits and gravy."

She shrugged, relaxing. "He complains too much. I assure you, he still has a healthy appetite."

"Good. Has he been walking?"

"No, I'm not a miracle worker."

Gray glanced at the letter in her lap. "Mail?"

Refolding the letter, she put it back in her pocket. "A note from a friend."

His presence unnerved her. She'd been deep in thought about Henry, but since he'd sat down she couldn't even picture Henry's face.

"Someone special?"

He had the hands of a doctor, long fingers, nails carefully

trimmed. Manly looking hands. She was inexplicably drawn to his virility. Was that it? Was it that Henry lacked in the raw masculinity Gray so easily exuded? She couldn't remember a time when Henry induced goose-bumpely shivers she was suddenly having.

"Why do you ask?"

"The way your hand is laying on it."

Embarrassment warmed her cheeks. "Well, he is . . . rather special."

"Someone from here?"

"Yes."

"Serious?"

"I don't think that's any of your business."

"It is, if it affects my patient."

April frowned. "Your patient? Grandpa? Why would my relationships affect him?"

"Because he worries about you."

She studied the doctor's face a long moment. "He's discussed something with you? Something about me?"

Leaning back in the chair, he studied the sky. She thought he looked tired tonight, as if he'd worked long hours. "He was very upset when he learned you were selling the tonic."

"That's your fault."

"I did not tell your grandfather you were selling the tonic." His tone was testy now.

"Then who told him?"

"Have you asked him?"

She had and he said never mind who told him. "What's that got to do with my relationship with—"

"Everything you do affects him. He takes his responsibility for you seriously."

"He shouldn't. I'm a grown woman."

"Well"—Dr. Fuller smiled slightly—"apparently he thinks he does need to worry about you, for whatever reason. I'm just suggesting that you try not to worry him overly much."

Anger flooded April at the doctor's audacity. "Dr. Fuller, you take care of your own business, and I'll take care of my grandfather—"

"Your grandfather *is* my business," he interrupted. "He's a patient. I worry about my patients—"

"Then stick to worrying about Grandpa, and leave me alone."

Gray stood up. "I assure you, nothing would suit me better. But, remember what I said. At this point I'd rather Riley wasn't under any undue stress. That includes worrying about you, and any man you might be involved—"

"Doctor," April said, standing also, "good night!"

"Good night—but I suggest you and I call a truce."

"I wasn't aware we were engaged in a war."

"Neither was I, but since we can't carry on a conversation without firing a shot, apparently we are."

Turning her back to him, she studied the moonlit sky. Clouds skittered across the moon, darkening the porch. "What are you suggesting?"

"Let's agree to disagree. I believe modern medicine is what people need most—"

"And I believe the natural way to health is better. Did you know there are herbs that—"

"Let's not argue."

His smile was charming, and she felt her temper begin to cool. "You're right. We're not going to agree, and we do have to live in the same town. A small town at that."

He seemed relieved with her acquiescence. "You're right. It is a small town."

She stepped to the porch railing and leaned against it, watching the moon slide in and out of the clouds. "Why did you come here? I mean, after all, Boston has so much more to offer a doctor."

"I didn't want that. I like Dignity."

"How does your lady friend like Dignity?"

Gray shrugged.

"I hear she, ah, helped decorate your living quarters as well as your office."

"That's gotten around town already?"

"Umhum. It doesn't take long in Dignity—one of the negative aspects of living in a small town."

Joining her at the railing, he stood for a moment, looking at the sky. "There seems to be an epidemic of fainting going on."

"Lightheadedness, that sort of thing?"

Closing his eyes, he smiled faintly as if a little embarrassed. "Yes . . ."

Grinning, she rested her head against a post. "Must be something in the water."

"Yes, very puzzling. Half the eligible women in town seem to be coming down with it."

"Really, now."

She met his smile.

"I don't suppose there's going to be a box supper or a bake sale around any time soon?"

"Not that I know of. Why? Planning to make a bid on someone's box?"

"No, planning to contribute. It appears the mothers of Dignity are under the impression that a single man lives on baked goods alone. I've got a wagonload of pies going to waste, at least a half dozen cakes, and I haven't bothered to count the tins of cookies."

April chuckled at his consternation. When he smiled, his green eyes crinkled at the corners and shone with boyish mischief.

"There must be something about a medical license hanging on a man's wall that makes him nearly irresistible."

"Speaking of Mrs. Pinkham—"

April couldn't help laughing. As much as she hated to admit it, he could be charming when he wanted to be. "I didn't know we were."

"I wanted to. Not too subtle?"

"Not nearly enough. I warn you, Dr. Fuller, I like Mrs. Pinkham very much, and I believe in what she's doing."

"I would think a woman with your intelligence might have reservations about a product that promises to be a cure-all for women's ills."

April stiffened. "Then you've misjudged me."

"The compound isn't proven to be effective. Aren't you concerned that you will mislead a woman into thinking she can cure something she can't?"

"No. I believe women are astute enough about their bodies to know when something is working and when it isn't. The compound works, Doctor. You and your colleagues refuse to admit it."

"It's a lie, Miss Truitt."

"It's an alternative, Dr. Fuller. A very good one. If you suffered with monthly cramps and other painful problems during and after childbirth, you'd be singing the elixir's praises."

"There's nothing in that elixir that can do what she claims it will."

"Then why does it work?"

"It doesn't," he said. "At least not the way you're saying it does. It's mostly alcohol. That relaxes the body. That's what works."

"Then—"

"It's addictive, Miss Truitt."

"No, it isn't, Dr. Fuller," April retorted. "You just don't want anyone to have information you, and other doctors, don't spoon-feed us."

"You're letting your prejudice against men color your thinking."

"You're thinking like a typical man, Doctor."

Leaning closer, his eyes met hers as he spoke in a low, almost suggestive tone. "Well, you're right for once. I'm very much a man, Miss Truitt."

"Really, now. I'm sure Miss DuBois is thrilled about that."

His contemplative gaze measured her with practiced ease. "Feisty little wench, aren't you?"

What was there about him that made her so angry, she would gladly shoot him where he stood one minute, and the next make her pray that he wasn't able to see the way he affected her. At that moment she knew what the women of Dignity saw in Dr. Fuller, and it made her wary. He was engaged to a beautiful woman from Boston. The women of Dignity were wasting their time, and she certainly wasn't about to join their ranks.

"Feisty enough to keep on helping Mrs. Pinkham make her elixir available to women who need it."

"Then we still agree to disagree?"

"Yes. We certainly do," she retorted, lifting her chin in defiance.

"Good evening, Miss Truitt. Remember what I said about keeping Riley calm."

"I'll try to do that."

With a nod, he stepped off the porch and disappeared around the corner of the house. His unique scent was left hanging lightly in the air.

Sighing, April rubbed goose bumps that had suddenly cropped up on her arms.

Oh, yes, Dr. Fuller, she conceded. *You are very much a man.*

That's what bothered her.

Chapter 8

Porky was dusting the shelves of the pharmacy when April came in the next morning. She was clearly annoyed with someone, and that someone was Doctor Fuller unless Porky missed her bet.

"What's wrong?"

"Dr. Fuller, that's what. The gall of that man."

"What's he done now?" Porky stuffed her dustrag into the pocket of the large apron she wore to cover her dress while in the store.

"He was playing checkers with Grandpa again last night."

"So? He does that at least three times a week. It's never bothered you before."

"Well, this time he cornered me on the back porch and warned me—*warned* me, mind you—that I should make sure Grandpa isn't upset about anything!"

Porky frowned. "Warned you? What does that mean?"

"It means that he's sticking his nose into my business! He told me to make sure that what I do doesn't upset

Grandpa. That includes working for Mrs. Pinkham as well as my relationship with Henry."

"He knows about your relationship with Henry?"

"I'm not sure, but he saw Henry's letter laying in my lap."

"Well, you know how Riley feels about Mrs. Pinkham, and you also know how he feels about Henry." Porky flicked her dustrag over a line of bottles. "Why all the fuss when the doctor says something about it?"

"What's wrong," April enunciated clearly, "is that he told me to be careful of my 'relationships' so Grandpa wouldn't be upset. It's not his place to tell me what to do."

"I suppose he thinks that anything to do with his patient is his concern."

April paced the crowded aisle. "Then he's mistaken. What I do is none of his concern. I might have expected you to defend him. You're like every other woman in town. Gray Fuller walks on water. Well, he doesn't, and he'd better keep his nose out of my affairs. My 'relationships' are none of his business."

April took a deep breath to stay her temper. She'd fumed over that man all night, trying to come up with a way to prove to him that Mrs. Pinkham's elixir *was* a "miracle," but she'd failed. Nothing she thought of was overwhelmingly conclusive.

"Have you been getting comments from women you've given the elixir to? Are they feeling better?"

"Well, maybe they are. I'm not sure how much of it is due to Dr. Fuller's prescriptions, and how much to the elixir. But three of them have specifically mentioned they have more energy."

Rubbing her hands together smugly, April grinned. "Good. Now, if I could only get the doctor to try it himself—"

"Beulah, it's time to get busy."

"Yes, Papa," Porky called out to her father who was settling onto the high stool behind his counter. "Dash, his cold is better," she whispered to April. "He insisted on coming in today even though he's still feeling poorly."

"Maybe you should give him the elixir," April suggested softly. She laughed at Porky's shocked expression. "I'll talk to you later." She smothered another laugh. "Good morning, Mr. Ludwig," she called out as she opened the door.

"Humph," Mr. Ludwig grunted, sparing her a brief glance.

Porky spent the morning filling prescriptions and advising young mothers on how to treat the first colds of the season. When young Mary Benson left the store, she was toting the obligatory bottle of tonic.

While Porky didn't completely agree with what April was doing, she suspected there was something in the elixir that did make women feel better.

Now, if only she could find a way to recommend the elixir to the doctor. If it worked, then perhaps he would consider using it all the time.

Aware that nearly every woman in town was trying to make an impression on Dr. Fuller, she would have to use a different approach. She didn't want to make an idiot of herself. Gray Fuller would not be attracted to an idiot—No, wait—there was Francesca.

The solution came to her that afternoon.

Gefüllte Klösse. It was a safe assumption Dr. Fuller had never tasted her grandmother's recipe for this German delicacy. Nor *Brombeerkuchen*, the blackberry cakes her father loved. Though not sweet like dessert, it went wonderfully with coffee at breakfast. Not one other woman in Dignity could offer the doctor such a wonderful treat, and, while she was plying the good doctor with *gefüllte Klösse* and *Brombeerkuchen* she could casually mention the elixir.

Sometimes her brilliance shocked her.

That afternoon she opened a jar of blackberries, and mixed up a batch of dough. That evening she made the desserts for her father, with extra portions for Dr. Fuller.

The next morning she dressed with care, wrapped the dumplings and cake in a new cloth and put them in a basket, along with a bottle of the elixir. Then, gathering her courage, she strode quickly down the sidewalk toward Dr. Fuller's office.

The waiting room was full, and from the assortment of boxes and towel-covered items held securely on laps, few of the women were patients.

Porky felt a little foolish carrying her shopping basket, fearing she would be counted among those enamored of the doctor. Even if she was, she didn't have a chance with someone like him. But if she could get him to dispense the tonic for April, that would be appeasement enough for her hard work.

Locating a chair in the corner, she perched on the edge, hoping she wouldn't have to wait long. The young man seated in a corner of the room nodded at her, before letting his gaze shift back to the picture hanging on the wall behind her. She hadn't seen him before, but he was nice looking. Brown hair, round face, kind blue eyes. She studied him a moment, until he glanced at her again, and she quickly looked away.

The examining-room door opened and Mrs. Greenwood came out, followed by Dr. Fuller. As one body, fully half the women in the office stood up and advanced on him.

"Doctor—"

"Dr. Gray—"

"Dr. Fuller—"

"Just a moment, please." He walked to the door with Mrs. Greenwood, bent close to finish his instructions, then gave her a reassuring pat on her shoulder.

As the door closed, he confronted the sea of anxious faces awaiting his attention. "Who was next?"

Chairs scraped noisily as he was set upon like a plague of locust.

Ten minutes later he was staggering under the weight of pies, cakes, and bread fresh from the oven, looking awfully stressed. Only Porky and the young gentleman remained seated.

"Uh, who's next?" He sounded a little dazed, balancing a stack of pies and cakes as best he could.

"He was here first," Porky said, nodding toward the quiet young man.

"I'm here as a representative of Claxton Medical Supplies," the young man said quickly, as if afraid the doctor would think he was involved with the madness he'd just witnessed.

"Sorry, I buy my supplies from—"

"I'm aware you may have an established supplier," the young man inserted, "but I'd like the opportunity to show you what I have, give you a few prices, and if you like something—or, if not," he swallowed, "then just keep my card in case there is something you need in the future. I'm through here every three weeks."

Gray took the card, balancing the baked goods on one arm. "Thank you, Mr. Grimes. I'm busy at the moment, but perhaps next time you're through town we can talk."

"I'd appreciate that. I'll let you get back to work now. I'll be back in three weeks."

"Thank you," Gray said, tucking the card into his mouth as he shifted a chocolate cake to his left hand.

Mr. Grimes nodded at Porky, then left the office.

"Now, Miss Ludwig, what can I do for you?"

Clearing her throat, Porky got up. "Can I help you with those pies?"

The consternation on his face turned to relief. "Thanks . . . just put them in there." They carried the offerings into his office, and he kicked the door closed behind him. He glanced at her basket.

She laughed. "Well, it looks like my thoughts aren't original," she began. "I do have more than a pie for you, though." She helped him heap the baked goods on his desk.

"What is it?"

"April said you left this on their porch last night."

He took the pillbox hat she offered, smiling at the look of chagrin on his face.

"It is yours?"

"Yes, unfortunately it is. Something Francesca bought. I carry it with me so I won't have to lie when she asks if I use it."

Porky hid a smile. "Sort of hard to get rid of, huh?"

"Well, guess I'll hang it up." He pitched the hat toward the coatrack, hooking it expertly on a wooden prong.

"You're good at that."

"I've had a lot of practice."

"Oh, I have something else for you."

"What is it?"

"Some of Mrs. Pinkham's vegetable compound."

He frowned, and she could see he was going to be a hard sell.

"I know your objections, but I think you will find the tonic is useful." She set the jug on his desk. "You can't say it doesn't work when you've never used it, now, can you?"

"I don't prescribe anything I don't have faith in."

"And I say you can't form an opinion without ever using it."

"You're a friend of April Truitt's," he guessed.

"Yes. Did she tell you?"

"No, you're just alike. You're suggesting I try the compound?"

Porky studied him a moment. "If I tell you something, will you keep it in confidence?"

"If I can."

"I've given it to several women as a tonic only. Not prescribing it for anything other than as a tonic. Three out of four women have said they felt better after trying it."

He looked surprised, but not convinced. "Does your father know about this?"

"Heaven's no, and if you tell him, he'll tan my hide."

"Well, I appreciate your generosity, but I don't want the tonic."

"The women really do feel better. I can tell by the way they act. Addy Menson is actually singing in the choir again."

Gray studied her a moment, amusement lighting his eyes. "You and Miss Truitt think the elixir is a 'miracle'?"

"I don't know whether it's a miracle, but it works."

"But it doesn't cure anything."

"I don't know. I'm just suggesting you try it." She edged the jug closer to him. "Just . . . think about it. All right?"

Shrugging, Gray walked to the medicine cabinet. "I don't think so, but thank you."

"Well." She thought about not leaving the *gefüllte Klösse*. It was her favorite and if he wasn't going to cooperate . . . "Oh, here." Taking the *gefüllte Klösse* and *Brombeerkuchen* out of the basket, she made a place for them on his desk.

"Not more desserts," he muttered.

"Certainly not." She straightened, refolding the cloth and putting it back in the basket. "It's German delicacy."

"Oh." He sat down, giving up. "Good day, Miss Ludwig."

"Good day, Doctor."

After the door closed behind Porky, Gray stuck the bottle of Mrs. Pinkham's elixir on a shelf behind his office door.

There was no way in hell he was going to prescribe the elixir to his patients.

No way in hell.

Henry, Will, and Dan returned from Boston on Friday, disgruntled about their experience but still dedicated to the mission.

"I missed you," Henry said, drawing April into his arms. "It's been the longest two weeks I've ever spent."

April gazed up into his face, resting her fingertips against his lapel. "What a wonderful surprise! Lydia didn't expect you back until Sunday."

They were at the Pinkham house, where she had gone to help fold pamphlets when the three men arrived unexpectedly. After greeting Mrs. Pinkham, Henry had pulled April onto the back porch where they could be alone for a few minutes.

"The rain never let up, and we didn't see the sense of staying another two days crowded into a room together." He smiled charmingly. "But more than that, I couldn't wait to get back to you. Dinner tonight?"

"Of course." She frowned. "Are you limping? Have you hurt yourself?"

He looked a little chagrined. "No. Just a . . . well, my toe is a little sore. Probably all that walking we did handing out pamphlets."

Going back into his arms, she embraced him fondly. "I will look at it if you like."

"It's nothing, really." Consulting his watch, Henry frowned. "I really must run now. I promised to meet a business contact shortly after noon."

"So soon?" She tried to conceal her disappointment. They hadn't seen each other in two weeks, and already he had another meeting. They'd barely spent five minutes together.

"Will seven be convenient for you?"

Nodding, she absently leaned forward to receive a brushed kiss across her lips. He hesitated as if the nearly public display of affection might compromise them.

"Seven," she agreed.

That evening they ate in the dining room just off the foyer of the Kingston Hotel. The menu was limited, but it didn't matter. Henry's company was all that mattered to her.

Henry dominated the conversation with stories of his recent adventures in Boston. April was determined to make a trip there soon herself, thinking a woman could make inroads in placing the vegetable compound where the three men had failed.

When Henry suddenly paused, lifting the tablecloth to look under the table at his foot, April frowned. "Is your toe still bothering you?"

He grimaced. "Somewhat."

"I can recommend a herbal treatment . . . or—" She couldn't believe she was going to say this. "Perhaps you should see Dr. Fuller."

Glancing up, Henry grimaced. "Fuller?"

"The new doctor."

"Oh, yes. Would you care for dessert?"

"No, thank you. Grandpa and I have been doing

without pastry and sugars. Dr. Fuller won't let him eat refined sugar, so I've been doing without, too."

Henry frowned. "You've been discussing health issues with Dr. Fuller? You haven't been ill have you?"

"No, Grandpa had another one of his dizzy spells. A bad one. Datha was frightened, and she took him to see Dr. Fuller."

"Ah, yes, Dignity's new doctor. I recall seeing him on occasion at the meetings." He quirked his eyebrow questioningly. "Is your grandfather all right?"

"Yes, but I worry about him. Dr. Fuller suggested a change in diet and a walk every day. Surprisingly, Grandpa's stuck with the diet, though he complains a lot. I haven't been able to persuade him to walk yet."

Henry tilted his head to one side to study her. "I can't believe you're trusting your grandfather's care to a doctor. He must be extremely persuasive."

April smiled. "If it had been my choice, Dr. Fuller wouldn't have seen Grandpa. But, he seems to be doing well with the doctor's supervision, though I have had a tonic made up for him."

"It sounds as if the good doctor is doing well."

"If the daily parade of eligible women marching through his office with baked goods is any indication, the doctor is doing *very* well."

Henry laughed. "He's single?" He leaned forward, his smile teasing but confident. "Dare I ask if he's made an impression upon you?"

"Only a bad one," she parried. "He's all for 'modern medicine' and says prescribing the elixir is the same as calling in a witch doctor."

"But Riley likes him?"

"Unfortunately, yes. They visit on the side porch every night."

*   *   *

Emerging from the hotel an hour later, Henry glanced up at the sky. Clouds scudded swiftly overhead. "Are you in the mood for a stroll?"

"I'd like that."

They walked slowly around the town square, arm in arm, enjoying the beautiful night. A large harvest moon sat in the night sky like a huge dish, bathing the town with a white glow.

"Ah, what a lovely sight," Henry said, patting her hand.

Breathing deeply of the crisp air, she smiled. "It is a lovely evening."

"I was referring to the lady on my arm," Henry said, stopping and turning her into his embrace.

His kiss was warm, persuasive. Comfortable. He didn't stir the butterflies like Gray. His touch didn't burn her skin and threaten to set off some mysterious explosion deep inside her. Was comfortable what she wanted? Or the excitement of Gray?

The voices of others strolling in the square floated to them, making April feel uneasy. They were in a public area, making a spectacle of themselves.

"Henry, we shouldn't," she whispered.

"I know, but I can scarcely contain myself," he murmured against her ear.

She wanted his embrace, but it wasn't seemly. If Grandpa were to hear she was encouraging the attention of a suitor in the public square, he would be angry. Gray Fuller's voice, repeating his earlier warning about upsetting Riley, sounded in her ear. Reluctantly removing herself from Henry's arms, she sighed. "It's late, I must be getting home."

"I'd rather take another turn around the square."

"That would be nice, but I really must go. Grandpa is waiting for me. He worries if I'm out too late."

By the time they arrived back at the mortuary, Henry was limping again.

"I do think you should have the doctor look at that toe," April said as he kissed her good night.

"If it's not better in the morning, I'll stop by and meet your new doctor."

"He's not *my* doctor," April retorted.

"Only teasing," Henry laughed. "I know I'm the man in your life."

"You are," April confessed, unable to shake the feeling that Riley was watching from the upstairs window.

"Ah, my love." Henry pressed her tightly to his wool jacket. She breathed in the faint smell of tobacco, the lingering scent of his cologne. He smelled nothing like Gray . . . nothing at all.

"I don't want to leave you. I thought about you every waking moment while I was in Boston. There in that room, listening to Will and Dan snore—"

"How flattering."

"I didn't mean—" Holding her away from him, his gaze captured hers affectionately. "You're teasing me."

"I am, but I do appreciate that you were thinking of me."

"I merely meant—"

She lay her fingertip across his prickly mustache. "I know what you meant, and I love it."

"I'd rather you loved me."

"I'd better say good night," she whispered.

"Will I see you at Lydia's tomorrow?"

"Yes, I promised I'd help with the pamphlets."

Taking both her small gloved hands into his, Henry held them tightly. "The hours that separate us are endless."

She smiled up at him. "Good night, Henry—you're not in too much pain, are you?"

"I barely notice it, darling. Just a little sore to the touch."

"But you will see the doctor first thing tomorrow morning?"

"If I think of it, dearest."

"Good night, Henry."

"Good night, my love."

"Damn! Holy shit! *Son-of-a-bitch*!"

Upon entering his room, Henry threw his shoe half way across the room and yanked his foot up on his knee so he could look at the toe that felt like someone had seared it with a branding iron.

You could bet he planned to be on Dr. Fuller's door step.

At dawn.

Rolling out of bed the next morning, Henry examined his toe. Overnight it had increased to double in size, and it hurt like a knot passing through an artery!

"How am I going to get my shoe back on?" he murmured, staring at the pulsating extremity.

After spreading the laces of his shoe as wide as possible, he gritted his teeth and gingerly edged his foot inside, at the last moment clamping his eyes shut and jamming it in the last inch. Groaning, he fell prostrate back across the bed, sweat rolling off his forehead.

Several minutes passed before he could muster up enough gumption to sit up and lace the shoe. Making his way slowly down the stairs of the boardinghouse, he straightened his coat and attempted to stride naturally down the street.

As he entered the doctor's office, he smiled at the long row of women all packing baskets of fresh baked goods. The women looked him over like a piece of meat, and he remembered what April had said about them setting their sights on the single doctor. He could almost feel sorry for the man.

Nodding to the ladies, he hung his hat on the coatrack and sat down.

The waiting room was not what he expected. Rich colors in the carpet and drapes, upholstered chairs, and very nice paintings on the walls. A bit crowded—very crowded, but nice. He liked nice things. One day he was going to own fine things himself.

The door to the examining room opened, and the doctor appeared. "Next?"

Glancing at the women, Henry waited for someone to get up. When, one by one they smiled at him and said, "You go on; we're waiting to see the doctor on a personal matter," he didn't quibble. He needed relief, and he needed it fast.

Getting up, he moaned, straightened, and limped behind the doctor into the examining room.

Closing the door, Gray asked. "What can I do for you today?"

"My toe is killing me. You've got to do something."

Gray smiled. He hated to think this about his own gender, but there was nothing worse than a male patient. "Let's have a look at it."

Henry noticed the examining room was small, but the equipment was new.

"Sit on the table, and remove your shoe, Mr. . . . ?"

"Long. Henry Trampas Long." Henry climbed on the table and untied his left shoe. After a slight hesitation, he yanked it off.

"Aghhhhhhhhhhhh!"

"Sock?"

Henry carefully pulled off his sock and let it join the shoe on the floor.

"Prop your foot up here, Mr. Long, and I'll have a look at it."

Henry gingerly rested his foot on the towel across the doctor's knee. "You got to do something, Doctor. It's killing me."

"How long has it been this way?"

"Two . . . three days."

"Ummm, angry looking."

"Scares the hell out of me. What's wrong with it?"

"Ingrown toenail. Been doing a lot of walking lately?"

"Nothing but. Can you fix it?"

"Yes, a little minor surgery, a little trimming; then we'll need to treat it for a few days, and you'll be good as new."

Fear flooded Henry's face. Hell. He fainted at the sight of blood.

Gray smiled, moving to the glass-fronted medicine cabinet. "It'll be a little uncomfortable for a few minutes."

"Can you give me anything for the pain?"

The doctor laughed. "I'll heat some water and let you soak it before we start."

Henry met the doctor's eyes expectantly. "This is going to hurt, isn't it."

"Like hell," Gray admitted. "I'll get the water."

A few minutes later Henry's foot was soaking in a tub of hot water while Gray laid out his instruments.

"How are you liking Dignity?"

"I like it fine. It's a nice town, and I'm settling in comfortably."

"Folks treating you all right?" Henry asked, trying to get his mind off the upcoming surgery.

"The people are very accommodating. You from around here?"

"Lived here all my life."

"Mmmm." Gray selected a small scalpel.

"Miss Boston?"

"No, can't say that I do."

"Really?" Henry said. "I'd think you'd miss the conveniences, the theater, the restaurants."

"Perhaps, but I don't miss the traffic, people in too big a hurry, rude. No, I like Dignity. I plan to make it my home."

"Not me." Henry winced as Gray probed the distended toe. "I've been in Boston the last couple of weeks. I'm looking forward to working there full time one day."

Gray bent over Henry's toe, blocking his view. Henry was relieved. He would just as soon not see what the doctor was doing.

"Dignity too familiar?" Gray guessed.

"Boring," Henry returned, wincing as Gray's probing became sharper.

"Odd, I haven't found it to be so."

"Hooolllly!" Henry shot up from the table. *"What* are you doing?" Gritting his teeth, he gripped the edge of the table harder.

"Just looking. Relax," Gray murmured. "It'll be over in a few minutes."

Lying back, Henry clamped his eyes shut. Sweat beaded his forehead. "You haven't lived in Dignity long enough. You'll see I'm right. In a year you'll be wishing you'd never left Boston."

"Perhaps . . . this might hurt a little."

Henry groaned, getting a firmer grip on the sides of the table. That meant it would be excruciating. . . . *SHIT!*

Gray straightened, tossing a wad of cotton aside. "That should do it."

Henry closed his eyes. "Are you finished?"

"I'm finished."

Swiping his forearm across his shiny forehead, Henry whispered in a croak, "April said you knew your business."

"April?" Gray was wrapping Henry's toe with a piece of white gauze.

"April Truitt. She said you'd treated her grandpa."

"Mmmmm," Gray murmured. "I'd suggest you stay off the foot for the next few days, keep it elevated. Come back in a couple of days and let me check it again."

"Sure thing, Doc."

Both men looked up as the door of the examining room burst open. "Gray, darling!"

The woman framed in the doorway wore a tiny hat perched over her forehead atop a mass of hair that formed an enormous cloud of curls. Her Dolly Varden dress was fashioned of a brightly patterned fabric in colors of blues and maroon that fit closely in the bodice and waist, with rows of lace-trimmed fabric down the front of the skirt.

On anyone else the bright colors would have been overwhelming, but on Francesca DuBois the effect was smashing.

"Francesca?"

"It is I!" Gliding across the room, she planted her hand on the front of Gray's coat and looked up into his face demurely. "Have you missed me?"

"I didn't expect you until the weekend."

"I couldn't wait." Her gaze swept the man on the table who was openly ogling her and gave him a withering look. "I was hoping to whisk you away for a while, for an early lunch perhaps?"

Sitting up, Henry straightened his jacket, grinning at her as he tried to hide his big toe under the towel.

"Sorry." Gray walked over to close the door. The waiting room was crowded this morning.

"Ohhh, Gray! I've come *all* the way from Boston and you can't even spare a moment to have lunch with me?"

Impatience tinged Gray's features. "Francesca, I have

an office full of patients. Why don't you wait for me upstairs? I'll try to get away shortly after noon."

She reluctantly agreed, after eliciting his promise to hurry.

"My goodness," Henry said when the door closed behind her. "Now, *that's* a woman!"

"You like her?" Gray offered. "You can have her."

Stomach ailments involving adults and children, a broken arm, a badly cut hand, four women who were having babies within the month, and an infant with the croup occupied Gray's time until late afternoon.

The stream of patients paraded through the office in a steady flow. Lunch was a hastily eaten piece of pie brought to the office by Madelyn Lewis and her mother. Inventing an excuse as to why he couldn't come to dinner Sunday, he treated Madelyn's sore throat and ushered the two fawning women out the front door.

It was close to four before he realized the time. Letting the last patient out of the office, he locked the door and pulled down the shade on the front window.

"Damn," he muttered, looking at his watch again. Francesca would be in a fine temper.

"I'm sorry," he apologized as soon as he entered the small living quarters and closed the door. "I had no idea it was so late."

Francesca, arms folded beneath her breasts, was pacing the floor like a caged tiger. Whirling to confront him, she shouted, "*Where* have you been?"

"Working." Loosening his tie, he stripped it off. She knew a doctor's time wasn't his own. His eyes searched for the brandy. He needed a drink—and peace and quiet.

He doubted he'd get either one.

Tears welled in Francesca's eyes. "You left me alone in this . . . this horrid place all day—"

"I had patients to take care of." Relenting, he attempted to draw her stiff body into his arms, hoping to make amends. Every visit they had lately ended in a row. "I'm sorry. . . ."

Jerking free, she avoided his embrace. "You could have told them to come back tomorrow."

"I'm a doctor, Francesca. I'm building a practice. I can't neglect my patients at your whim."

"You could treat patients in Boston. That's where you should be, working with Papa. Then you would have time for me."

"I'm tired, Francesca. Let's not waste time arguing."

"Waste time? I am the one who has *wasted* time! I came to see you because *you* have not come to see me. And do you appreciate it? No! You leave me here, alone, in this . . . this rathole that I have tried to make more comfortable for you. And do you appreciate it? No. Not one word of thank you. Not one." Reaching for her cloak, she slung it over her shoulders angrily.

"Are you staying at the hotel?"

"No."

"Do you want to stay here tonight?" He'd prefer she didn't. Tongues wagged easily in Dignity.

"I'm going home."

"Return to Boston? Tonight?"

"I'll hire a driver. I won't be treated this way, Gray Fuller. I won't permit it."

"Francesca, this is insane. It's too late to go back to Boston tonight—"

But he was talking to thin air. She was gone. The door slammed, and he could hear her running down the stairway.

Sitting down on the side of the bed, he ran his hand through his hair wearily.

Hell. He should have made her stay, but he was just too damn tired to argue with her.

Was he feeling guilty, or was he worried he wasn't treating her right?

Was he relieved he didn't have to make love to her?

Did he hope she was mad enough stay away for good?

Lying back, he stared at the ceiling, fearing it was the latter.

Even more troublesome was the knowledge he didn't know what he was going to do about it.

Chapter 9

The sun-dried scent of grass surrounded the young couple, prickling their sweat-drenched skin.

Gazing up at the sky, they listened to the wind moving through the trees. A hint of the winter to come was behind the warm breeze. A sense of anticipation was in the air; a time of celebration for the hot summer and impending knowledge of winter closing in on them. Datha loved fall, but then, any time was good as long as she was with Jacel.

They lay on their backs, side by side, arm touching arm, too spent with the past hour and a half of loving to speak.

"Are you my woman, Datha?"

"I'm your woman, Jacel Evans."

Rolling over, Jacel propped his chin on his elbow, gazing into her face. A half smile curved his lips.

Datha let her hand drift over his bare shoulder. Jacel was powerfully handsome. And he was strong. He could move more raw lumber than the most seasoned worker.

Problem was, Mr. Jordan didn't appreciate Jacel's work, or his loyalty.

But, before too long Jacel would be going off to school. Mr. Ogden had contacted Harvard in Cambridge, Massachusetts, and arranged for Jacel to attend. He'd paid for a year's schooling, a sum Datha could only imagine. When Jacel described the school to her, she felt small and insignificant. When he told her Harvard had been established not long after the Pilgrims landed at Plymouth Rock, why, she just couldn't comprehend anything being that old and still serviceable.

Already it was over two hundred years old, turning out lawyers and doctors and scientists who made a difference in the world. And Jacel would be one of those who made a difference in people's lives in just a few years. Just thinking about it gave her goose bumps.

"I love you, Datha Gower." He kissed her, his lips hovering above hers until the heat inside started to build again. "I'm sure going to miss you when I go off to Harvard."

"I'll miss you, too, but it'll be worth the wait," she told him.

"One of these days we won't have to sneak out to be together. One day we'll be married. I don't like sneaking around this way."

"I don't, either," she whispered, letting her fingertips drift over his shoulder and down his muscled biceps.

"In a few weeks I'll be leaving, and before you know it I'll have a law degree."

"And you'll be the finest lawyer around," she stated emphatically.

"And I'll be making lots of money, and we'll get married, have lots of fat little babies, and live like rich folks."

They laughed at the extravagant thought. Them? Rich? That was pretty funny, all right.

"I don't want to live like rich folks," she whispered. "I just want to have your fat babies and not have to worry about whether somebody thinks we're being 'uppity.' "

He frowned. "Has your mama been talking again?"

Datha shrugged. "No more than usual. She says . . . she says we're going to get in trouble if we keep seeing each another."

A frown put a crease between his brows. "What kind of trouble?"

Worried that concern for her would make Jacel rethink his plans for school, Datha tried to sit up, but Jacel wouldn't let her escape that easily.

"What kind of trouble, Datha?"

"Babies," she admitted. "I'm scared I'll have a baby before . . . before we get married. It would ruin everything."

He pulled her into his arms, laughing away her fears. Nuzzling her neck, he whispered, "Don't you be worrying your pretty head about that. I'm real careful. I wouldn't ruin our future by doing something crazy. When I'm finally a lawyer, nobody can say anything about what we do. We'll get married, buy us a place for ourselves, and have all the fat babies you want."

Datha rested her head against his shoulder, her eyes closed, as she tried not to cry. It seemed such a long time before Jacel would have his law degree, before they had that home they dreamed about, before she could have all those babies she wanted. Such a long time—

"Don't you worry, Datha. I'll take care of you. And someday no one will tell us what to do. No one."

"You . . . you really know how to keep me from getting pregnant?"

Lowering his mouth to hers, he said softly. "A man knows how to do these things, Datha. Now, stop your worrying, girl. We have better ways to spend our time than worrying. . . ."

She felt his manhood grow hard again, and she prayed he was right. If she was ever to get pregnant . . . why, it would nearly kill Mama. . . .

Early Monday morning, Henry limped into Dr. Fuller's office, nodding to two women already seated in the waiting room.

Sitting where he could stretch his foot out in front of him, he settled down for a wait. This was his fifth visit for treatment, and he'd yet to come in when the waiting room was empty.

No doubt about it, Gray Fuller was carving a nice little niche for himself in this town.

Well, that was just fine. He planned to carve a niche for himself—only it wasn't going to be in Dignity.

The door of the examining room opened, and Gray followed Mary Rider out.

"Remember, Mary. Rest. Get some exercise, and I want to see you in two weeks."

"All right, Doctor."

Gray watched Mary leave, then turned to the waiting patients.

Grinning, Henry stood up. "Good morning, Doctor."

"Henry. How's the toe?"

"Better, I think."

Gray smiled. "Let's take a look at it."

Glancing around the crowded waiting room, Henry frowned. "I think there are others ahead of me."

Gray grimly assessed the baskets resting on the women's laps. Smells of beef roast and dumplings, unless his sense of smell had failed him entirely, wafted from beneath the checkered cloths. The scent was a nice change from baked goods, at least. "I'm sure they won't mind a small delay."

Henry followed Gray into the examining room. "How are things going, Doc? I see the ladies are still flocking in to see you."

"I'm not going hungry," Gray admitted as he unwrapped the toe. He paused a moment, examining it. "Seems to be coming along fine."

"It's better," Henry agreed. "Looks like you have your share of women fawning over you."

Smiling, Gray cleaned and dressed the injury.

"Heard you live upstairs." That wasn't all Henry had heard. He'd heard that that fancy French woman came to see him on a regular basis. Henry winced as the doctor worked. "You live overhead, don't you?"

When Gray didn't immediately respond, Henry chuckled. "Heard that French woman redecorated your bedroom." Nudging Gray knowingly, he grinned. "What is it about us professional men that attracts women like flies?"

"I don't know—what do you think it is?"

"It's the aura of success—that's been my experience."

"You don't say."

"Women are easily influenced. A man with the determination to succeed draws them like honey."

"You've experienced this personally?"

Henry laughed. "Man to man? I have found women fascinated by success. The look of success is a fine aphrodisiac. Oh hell . . . careful, Doc. It's still tender."

He winced as Gray rebandaged the toe.

"When Will and Dan and I were in Boston I was in a cafe, just having a cup of coffee, and a woman came over to my table and invited me out. I must say, she was a pleasant diversion—know what I mean?"

"Humm," Gray said noncommittally.

"I find women in the city more adventurous, don't you? This woman in Boston is something. Very . . . sure of herself. More worldly than the woman I'm seeing here. The one here's a beautiful woman, gentle, genuinely caring, but innocent." He punched Gray. "Know what I mean?"

Gray straightened and reached for a brown bottle of medication. "You're seeing a woman in Boston, and one here in Dignity?"

"Ungentlemanly of me, and"—Henry shrugged—"foolish. If one should ever learn of the other . . . Well, you know what I mean."

"I believe I do."

"I don't like to think about it," Henry conceded. He was playing with fire, no doubt. "I shouldn't be seeing this woman in Boston, but when I'm with Grace—I call her my Amazing Grace, well, you know." He winked. "My best intentions fly right out the window."

"What about the woman you're seeing here?"

"An angel. Sweet innocence. I call her Angel Face."

"Isn't that dangerous? Seeing two women at a time?"

"Ah, that's the problem. Yes, it is foolhardy, but I find myself overly fond of both. I've known one all my life. She's been the flower in my life in this otherwise colorless garden. But, she isn't Amazing Grace."

"She's Angel Face."

"Yes, she's my Angel Face."

Who also happens to be April Truitt, Riley's granddaughter. Gray wished his patients would keep their dirty laundry to themselves.

"April is a wonderfully bright woman. And just as lovely as Grace. But Grace . . . Grace makes me feel alive, good. I find myself in quite a dilemma."

Gray finished wrapping the toe and indicated he could sit up.

Henry pulled on his sock and reached for his shoe. "Think the toe will be healed in time for me to return to Boston next week?"

"I don't see any reason it shouldn't. Just wear comfortable shoes, and allow plenty of air to the wound."

"Good, I'm looking forward to getting back to Boston." He winked slyly. "And not just for fun. The Pinkham formula is finally taking off." Henry raised a hand, palm toward the doctor. "I know your opinion of the elixir. April's been very clear about your position. But your opposition doesn't stifle our enterprising spirit."

Henry preceded Gray from the examining room. "Thank you, Gray—You don't mind that I call you Gray? You seem more like a peer than a doctor."

Gray's expression sobered. "A friendly word of advice, Henry. I'd be careful I didn't find myself caught between two very angry women."

Henry laughed. "That would be awful, wouldn't it?" Laughing, he clasped the doctor on the shoulder warmly. "See you when I get back."

Henry Long was an ass.

Leaning back in his chair, Gray relished one of the few quiet moments he'd had lately. His mind kept turning over Henry's troubling revelation of that morning, trying to absorb the ramifications.

The man was seeing a woman in Boston, Amazing Grace, and Riley's granddaughter, April. Angel Face.

Angel Face and Amazing Grace.

Henry was playing with a loaded gun. It was evident that neither of the women knew about the other.

April was enamored of Henry Long. Gray had seen that the night he found her on the porch with Henry's letter in her lap.

It was shabby, not to mention foolish, of Henry to

court two women at the same time. But it wasn't his place to inform Riley's spirited granddaughter of what Henry was doing.

God knew she didn't want his opinion about anything.

His previous encounters with "Angel Face" had been confrontational, and he didn't intend to goad her further by butting into her business. Her grandfather's health was too important for him to push her into feeding Riley her herbal remedies and refusing his help. She'd made it clear what he thought didn't matter.

Her and her blasted "vegetable compound."

Angel Face had called him a quack. Far be it from him to put himself in her way again by telling her she was involved with a skunk.

Picking up a chart, he turned to the more pressing problem of Mary Rader. Studying his notes, he shook his head.

Mary Rader had been one of his first patients. In her late twenties, married, she suffered with cramps so severe that she was reduced to bed nearly two weeks out of the month.

The situation was even more frustrating in that Mary's husband had no understanding of the difficulties she was experiencing. Severn Rader was getting more belligerent that his wife had not conceived.

This situation had worn Mary down. She walked like an old woman, slightly bent as if to protect her abdomen. Her face often had a waxen look, a look of despair. He never concluded a situation was hopeless, but he was beginning to suspect this one might be.

Gray leaned back in his chair, his gaze passing over the large bottle of Pinkham's Vegetable Compound. It sat there on the shelf where he'd left it earlier. He had intended to dispose of it but had never gotten around to it.

Leaning forward, he reached for the jug and uncorked the bottle. He sniffed it. His eyebrows lifted. Definitely a high alcohol content, but Pinkham claimed there was nothing in it to harm a person.

Still, he knew the mind was a strong influence. If the brain were convinced the elixir was helpful, then the body often believed it. He'd tried everything he could think of to treat Mary's problems outside of surgery to remove the uterus, which he didn't want to do.

Studying the jug of compound, he toyed with an idea. True, it wasn't his first choice, but he wasn't as closed-minded as April Truitt thought him to be.

Lacing his fingers behind his head, he leaned back in his chair and studied the bottle pensively. She accused him of being headstrong and narrow-minded about women's problems.

Was he?

His gaze focused on the jug of amber liquid.

Why not prove Miss Truitt wrong? Why not conduct his own studies on the effectiveness, or lack of effectiveness, of Pinkham's elixir? A couple of spoonfuls a day couldn't hurt Mary and might even convince her she was being effectively treated, which, in turn, would allow her to relax.

If she was relaxed, her situation might alleviate itself.

Reaching for the jug, Gray took a small brown bottle from a lower shelf and filled it with compound. Printing Mary's name and the dosage on a label, he affixed it to the bottle and set it on his desk to await Mary's next appointment.

Leaning back in his chair, he crossed his arms, grinning.

There, Angel Face.

Now who's the bigoted one?

* * *

"Honestly, Porky, I don't know what to do." April took off her gloves and deposited them into her reticule. "I'd never thought I'd say this, but women are *afraid* to try anything new. Unless a doctor tells them to take the elixir, most won't. It's just so frustrating."

"I thought Dan, Will, and Henry were making progress in Boston."

"They are. And in the next few days they'll be going to Brooklyn, New York. Henry says, and Dan agrees, there's a world of new possibilities there."

Frowning, Porky rearranged a display of smelling salts. "Are they going to be there long?"

"I'm afraid so. I hate it when Henry's away so long." April moved to the window to look out. "I just wish women would see the value of the compound."

"Well, I'm doing everything I can to promote it. Papa overheard me discussing it with Mrs. Finnaman the other day. When he later asked what I was talking about, I had to do some pretty inventive thinking."

"Did you fib to him?"

Nodding, Porky took an angry final swipe at the salts with her dust cloth. "Pretty much so, and I have to tell you I don't feel good about it."

"I'm grateful for everything you've done—and so is Lydia."

"Well, I'm not getting any complaints," Porky admitted.

"And you won't."

Glancing around the nearly empty pharmacy, Porky leaned closer. "I told Faith Lawson that the compound not only helps women, but it's effective for treating male impotency."

April's mouth dropped open.

"I know." Porky's look of guilt was almost comical. "I don't know what made me do it, but she's always complaining that Fred is lifeless. She told me the other day that he'd be dead a week before she'd ever notice."

Eyes narrowing, April whispered, "Porky, how could you tell her something like that? Lydia has never claimed her compound was an effective treatment for . . . for *that*!"

"I know, I know. Then I overheard Mrs. Garrison telling Mrs. Gillis at the market yesterday." Porky's eyes darted away remorsefully. "I think I might have created a problem."

Grasping Porky's hand, April tried to think. "Don't panic. We can't panic. Maybe it's just false expectations that'll pass in a few days."

"I don't think so." Porky glanced toward the store-room, lowering her voice so Eldon Ludwig couldn't hear. "Mrs. Gillis said she went right home and put her Daniel on the compound."

April's eyes widened. "And?"

Edging closer, Porky whispered. "She said Daniel needed some perking up."

"Oh, Porky! What have you done?"

She was trying to conduct a private, unscientific study! How would they ever keep it quiet that it was Pinkham's compound Porky was doling out if every woman in town thought it would improve her love life?

Of course she *wanted* the compound sales to rise, but she hardly thought Lydia would be elated to know Porky was selling it under the guise that it would cure male impotency!

"I don't know," Porky admitted. "She was back first thing this morning for another bottle. I gathered Daniel . . . you know . . . the South was starting to rise again?"

"Oh, dear," April breathed pensively. "Lydia will be appalled."

"Not only that, but the women have been raving about

the tonic so much lately, I was afraid if I didn't tell Papa what I was doing, he would find out soon enough."

Groaning, April started to pace. "You told him?"

"I had to, but I just said it was a mild tonic that one of our customers was making. That wasn't a fib—Lydia comes into the store occasionally. But don't worry. Papa didn't make the connection. He just said to make it clear to the customer that we weren't responsible for the product or its claims."

"Male problems?" The absurdity of the news suddenly hit her, and she started to laugh. Wait until she told Henry! She sobered fast when she realized what Henry would say when he learned she was responsible for marketing the compound through Porky without his knowledge.

Porky stood back, eyeing her suspiciously. "Laugh if you want, but this has got to be an exciting development."

"Maybe, but how does Mrs. Pinkham advertise this marvelous side effect, if it is true? It's not something she can put in a newspaper ad or on a bottle label."

"Seems to me that word of mouth advertising may be enough."

This time April couldn't smother her amusement.

"Hush," Porky hissed. "Papa will hear you."

"Wonder what our Dr. Fuller would think about this little discovery?"

Porky's eyebrows rose. "Perhaps he'd try it himself. Seems to me his lady friend is the, um, the lusty sort."

April's smile faded. "I doubt that Dr. Fuller is in need of any tonic."

"Jealous?" Porky teased.

"Certainly not."

"Well," Porky was more somber now. "I am. I'd give my eye teeth to be in Francesca DuBois's shoes—or more pointedly, out of them."

* * *

"How are you feeling this week, Mary?"

Gray's hopes that Mary Rader was feeling better faded the moment she came into his office two weeks later. If possible, she looked paler than before.

Tears pooled in Mary's eyes. "I don't know anymore, Doctor. I've forgotten what 'feeling good' is like."

They were sitting in Gray's office, he behind his desk, she sitting in front of it, twisting a lace handkerchief into a tight knot.

Gray knew there was no need to examine her. He'd done so, from head to toe, and found nothing that he could fix as a definitive problem. Mary had female problems, and other than surgery that would dissolve all hopes of having a family, there wasn't a damned thing he could do about it. He had never felt so frustrated by a medical problem in his nearly ten-year career.

"Well, Mary, I know we both hoped to avoid surgery, but it looks as if that's our only alternative."

Twisting the handkerchief, Mary stared back at him, frightened, near tears again. "When?"

"As soon as I get you built up a little." Reaching for the small brown bottle of Pinkham's compound sitting on his desk, he smiled reassuringly at her. "There's something I'd like you to try, Mary. A tonic. Frankly I don't know how much it will help, but I know it won't hurt."

He wasn't going to hold out false hope to her. If it helped in any measure, it would enhance her physical condition for the surgery. Handing her the bottle, he instructed her on the dosage.

She viewed the bottle with lifeless eyes. "Will this stop the flooding?"

"No, Mary. I'm only trying to get you stronger before I perform the surgery. Take a couple of teaspoons a day for the next couple of weeks, and then come back. We'll set up a time."

Wiping tears from her eyes, she got up and followed him to the door.

"Two teaspoons a day?"

"Three, if you like." Hell, it couldn't hurt.

"Thank you, Doctor."

Taking her hand, he held it momentarily. "I know you're frightened."

Tears rolled down her cheeks. "I wish there was another way."

"I've done all I know to do, Mary. I'm as frustrated as you are, but there's no alternative."

"Severn is going to be angry. He wants children."

Patting her shoulder, Gray said quietly. "I'm sure he's more concerned about your health. If he wants to talk to me, have him stop by the office. I'm here every night until late."

"Ah, indeed, we're leaving first thing in the morning," Henry confessed as he and April ate dinner that evening. The hotel dining room was quiet tonight, affording them much needed privacy. "Dan and Will want to get in a full day, if they can."

"I wish you didn't have to leave so soon," April admitted.

Taking her hand, he stroked it gently. "We must make progress on marketing the compound soon, or I'll be out of a job."

"I know, I was just hoping the trip to Boston would be more successful. I hate the times we're apart."

Henry's forehead furrowed with his frown. "As I do, dearest. We're doing everything possible, but women are reluctant to try something new. You know that."

"Lydia and I have written more advertising copy and pamphlets. Poor Isaac, sick as he is, helps fold the pamphlets and pack them. He's so supportive of Lydia's work."

"He should be," Henry muttered. "If the compound isn't successful, the Pinkhams will meet financial ruin."

"You will faithfully write, won't you?"

"Of course, darling. Have I ever failed?"

She hated to be critical, but yes. He always said he'd write, but he rarely did. It was almost as if he forgot about her the moment he left Dignity.

Later, as Henry walked April home, he drew her close to his side. "I wish you were going with me," he whispered.

Warmth flooded April's cheeks. "So do I . . . I was thinking. Perhaps I can come for a visit—"

"No!" Henry concluded quickly. Too quickly, almost as if he was hiding something. "No," he repeated more gently when he noted her shocked countenance. "I won't hear of it. Brooklyn is too far, and traveling is unsafe for a woman alone."

"I wouldn't be traveling alone. I can get Porky, and we can come for a few days, do some shopping—"

"I *won't* hear of it, darling. I'll only be gone a short while, and I promise to write every day."

As they approached the mortuary, he aimed another benign kiss on her forehead, whispering, "How I am tempted to linger, but we'd best part quickly, my love. I wouldn't want to upset Riley."

"You'll be so lonely—perhaps I could travel to Boston and take a train to . . ."

"Such a lovely thought, but I will cloak myself in loneliness and count the moments until we are together once more."

He was right. It was a lovely thought, but foolish. Besides, leaving Riley for more than a few hours at a time was risky. "You promise to write?"

"Of course, dearest. Every day."

*   *   *

April stopped by the pharmacy late the next afternoon. With Henry gone, she had time on her hands.

The smells of herbs and liniment filled the shop. April always liked coming here. The creaky wooden floors, whitewashed walls, and plain shelves were friendly. Porky had hung plants in the windows, the southern light and her green thumb keeping them healthy as their trailing vines framed the wide windows. Over the years many a homemaker had pinched a start from Porky's plants.

"Hi, Pork. Doing anything later?"

"Me? Nothing, why?"

"Oh, I'm just lonely."

"Henry off again?"

"Yes," she sighed. "He left for Brooklyn this morning."

"Well, I've got a remedy for your melancholy. Just let me finish up; then we'll eat dinner out tonight."

"We should go to the quilting bee. We haven't been in a while."

"I don't want to go sew on some old quilt. Let's splurge and eat at the hotel."

"I don't know, Pork, I haven't had dinner with Grandpa hardly at all lately."

"He doesn't mind, does he?"

Actually, he didn't. April knew he would eat quickly and retire to the porch to play checkers with Jimmy.

As the two women walked home after a late supper, April filled Porky in on her day.

"Will and Dan accompany Henry this morning?"

"Yes. I hope they're successful in Brooklyn. We can't afford many more setbacks."

"Speaking of Dan Pinkham, what do you think about him?"

April shrugged. "He's nice—he has some political ambitions."

"Umhmm."

"Why?"

"Just wondering." Porky sighed.

"I think Will is much nicer. He has kind eyes, though I don't much care for the long muttonchops."

"Dan's beard is nice."

April laughed lightly. "I don't know why our opinion matters. Both men are married."

Porky released another long sigh. "All the good ones are, except Dr. Fuller, of course. But, I did notice a nice young man in the doctor's waiting room a few weeks ago. A medical equipment and supplies salesman."

"Oh? And did you just happen to notice whether he was married and what his name was?"

"I might have, but since you're being so snippy, I don't think I'll share it with you. I did notice that *woman* was back to visit Dr. Fuller the other day. They disappeared up to his living quarters and stayed there a loooong time."

April's eyes rolled toward the sky with exasperation. "Porky, haven't you anything better to do than spy on people?"

"Not really. Aren't you the least bit curious about what *she's* done to his living quarters?"

April stopped short. "No, nor should you be. You're becoming obsessed with Gray, Porky, and it has to stop."

Porky wasn't listening. "I wonder if she did redo everything in lavender."

"I would find that extremely disturbing. Surely Gray—"

Porky stepped in front of April and stopped. " 'Gray'? He's 'Gray' now?"

April realized that some time in the past month she'd ceased thinking of him as Dr. Fuller and referred to him as Gray. Oddly enough, she no longer thought of him as an adversary. He had been helpful with Riley, and she couldn't deny he was intelligent and informative to talk to. But so what? That didn't mean she thought of him in a personal nature, even if he was the most attractive man she'd ever seen. And so what if her heart skipped a beat at the very sound of his voice. Yes, so what?

"He comes by the house nearly every evening to see Grandpa, you know."

"But you call him 'Gray'?"

"Don't try to make something of it. He's Grandpa's friend, not mine."

Falling back into step, Porky laughed. "Wouldn't it be funny if she *has* decorated his room in purple?"

April looked disgusted. "Personally, I think it would serve him right, if he stood idly by and let her do it."

"I'd kill to see it," Porky admitted.

"I wouldn't waste my time."

"I can't stand it—let's go have a look!"

April suddenly halted, leaving Porky to walk on for several steps before she turned and looked back at her. "What's wrong?"

"You're not serious."

"Of course I'm serious. Why not?" She glanced in the direction of his office. "No lamp on upstairs. This would be the perfect time."

"To *break* into his office?"

"Certainly not," Porky stated, lifting her chin in indignation. "To *look* into his living quarters. Come on. Enis Matthews keeps a ladder behind his store. We can use it."

"Definitely not," April said, intent on walking right past the doctor's office.

"It'll only take a minute. Come on. What happened to your spunky spirit?"

"It left at the mention of window peeking."

"Well, I'm going to look." Porky started toward the narrow alley in back of the doctor's office.

"Porky!" April hissed.

"It'll only take a minute," she hissed back. "Who's to know? It's obvious he's not there. Come on, scaredy cat!"

"Porky, no—"

Ignoring the warning, Porky's eyes darted down the alleyway. Enis's ladder was propped against the mercantile's back wall. "See, there's the ladder."

"Leave it alone, Porky. I refuse to take part in this—this idiocy!" Sneaking around in alleyways, staring into men's bedrooms! It was shameful. Sure she was curious, but Porky was going too far.

"We can lean the ladder against the back wall, climb up, sneak a peek in the window, and leave."

"Porky," April whispered, "it's pitch dark. How are we going to see in his bedroom?"

"I've got a match in my pocket. One strike and I can see enough to satisfy my curiosity."

"You have lost your mind—" April found herself talking to thin air as Porky disappeared down the alleyway. Cringing, she listened to faint bumps and scrapes as Porky dragged the ladder into place.

"For heaven's sake! You're going to hit the window and break it," April censured in a harsh whisper. Stealing a second glance at the alleyway entrance, she dropped her reticule on the ground and hurried to help Porky balance the ladder.

"This thing must be fifty feet long!"

"Stop complaining. It's worth the effort."

"We're going to look ridiculous, not to mention be put in jail, if we get caught."

"There. Put it right next to the upstairs window. We

can peek in . . . See? He's left the curtain open. How thoughtful of him."

April closed her eyes with frustration. "I must be *mad* to let you talk me into this."

"Not mad, merely curious. I'll go first."

April held the ladder while Porky hiked her skirts up to her knees. Holding the material with one hand, she clasped the rung with the other, slowly making her way up the steps.

The climb took forever. April's eyes darted to the entrance of the alleyway to make sure they weren't attracting attention. Stubborn, pigheaded Gray Fuller was not worth the fuss!

Glancing to her left, she spotted a round, black shape lying on the woodpile next to the building. Standing on tiptoe, she peered at it more closely.

Why, that was his hat!

The hat Francesca had brought him from Paris! What was it doing lying on the woodpile?

Steadying the ladder with one hand, April leaned to the side and reached for it. She felt the ladder move beneath her hand and glanced up just in time to see Porky lean out to the far side so she could get a better look.

The ladder began to wobble, then tip.

"Porky!" she hissed.

But it was too late. Porky leaned too far out and, before April could do anything, the ladder tilted grotesquely to one side.

Porky grabbed for the window ledge, her hands flailing.

Grunting, April tried to shove the ladder back into place. It wavered, wobbled, moved out from the window, then fell away with a loud thud, leaving Porky hanging between the ladder and the building.

"*Now* what do we do, smarty?" April rebuked in a harsh whisper.

A lamp sprang to life in the window, and she mentally groaned.

Oh, wonderful.

Forgetting Porky's predicament, April bolted to the corner of the alleyway as the door to Gray's personal quarters burst open and the half-naked doctor descended the stairs two at a time.

April knew her presence in the alleyway at this time of night was not going to be easy to explain. Leaving Porky hanging, she quickly stepped around the corner to confront Gray just as he reached the bottom of the stairs.

His eyes clouded with confusion when he saw her. "April?"

Taking a deep breath, she grinned, motioning behind her back for Porky to stifle her screams. Beulah Ludwig was dangling from the ledge beneath the doctor's window like a broken puppet.

"Good evening, Dr. Fuller. What are you doing out this time of night—" She paused, her eyes running over his bare torso. It seemed he'd only taken time to drape a large white towel around his hips before starting down the stairs to investigate the noise.

April's gaze swept over him from head to toe. Her breath caught in her throat. He was magnificent. Shoulders that she'd sensed were large beneath the finely cut jackets he usually wore, seemed indecently broad now. His chest, covered in light-brown swirls of hair, was firm and well muscled. The doctor obviously didn't spend all his time in an office. His eyes skimmed her lightly, eyes that were dangerously provocative.

"What are you doing in the alleyway at this time of night?"

"Me? Nothing." She smiled, aware that a decent man would cover himself.

He didn't make any pretense of decency.

Swallowing her pride, she stepped forward to take his arm. Steering him out of the alleyway, she silently cringed as she heard Porky fall to the ground with a soft thud.

"Lovely night, isn't it?"

"It's cold as hell—what are you doing here? Is Riley ill?"

"No, Grandpa's fine. In fact, I've talked him into taking Mrs. Pinkham's tonic—although he doesn't know it's Mrs. Pinkham's tonic—a couple of times a day and he's feeling much better, thank you."

Clutching the towel around his middle, Gray allowed himself to be propelled along, staring at her as if she'd lost her mind.

"I was just walking by when I heard you coming down the stairs," she explained. Her gaze deliberately swept over his near-naked state as she cocked her head to one side. "I hope I didn't disturb you."

"You were just walking by in the alley at ten o'clock at night and you wanted to say hello?"

"Yes. Here." She handed him the hat. "I found this on the woodpile. What, may I ask, is it doing out here?"

"I put the damn thing there."

Shaking her head, she smiled and shook her finger at him. "Francesca would be upset if she knew you were treating your hat this way."

Giving his arm an indulgent pat, she pointed him toward the steps and made herself stroll slowly on down the sidewalk. Good heavens! No wonder the female population in Dignity was salivating over this man! And as much as she hated to admit it, so was she.

Glancing over her shoulder, she saw the expression of

disbelief on his face. So, she'd surprised him. Good. He was far too full of himself, in her opinion.

Walking faster, April prayed Porky hadn't broken every bone in her body, but it would serve her right for being so nosy!

Chapter 10

"Well, that looks to be it," Gray said, rechecking his medication list. "Thanks, Ray. Your coming by every three weeks has been a tremendous help to me."

"Glad to do it," Ray Grimes said, repacking his sample case and closing it.

"It's late. Are you staying in town tonight?" Gray closed the door of his medicine cabinet.

"I'd planned on it. It looks a bit like snow out there. How's the hotel?"

"Nice enough. We're having a dance tonight, kind of a preholiday celebration. If you're not busy, drop by. I'll introduce you to the people, and you'll get to know the town."

Francesca had refused to come for the activities, so Gray would be spending the night alone.

Raymond Grimes smiled and nodded his head. "I'd like that. Being on the road all the time I don't get to meet many people, except doctors like you."

"Good. You get your room, and I'll come by for you around seven."

168

"Thanks."

In the two months since Ray began calling on Gray, the two men had formed a friendship. Gray was glad to have Ray as a supplier. His list of available medications and medical equipment was very good, and was more convenient than traveling to Boston every two weeks. But best of all it afforded him the opportunity to make the break with Louis DuBois.

It wasn't that he didn't like Louis. He owed him a debt of gratitude. Without the prominent doctor's help, Gray wouldn't have been able to study in Boston.

But, he didn't like his life planned for him. He didn't want to be obligated to Louis any longer. He'd mailed another hundred dollars today as payment on the funds Louis had advanced on expenses for his education. Soon the debt would be paid, and he could stop saving every penny and use his funds toward expanding his practice. That was the day he looked forward to.

Gray knocked on Ray's door precisely at seven o'clock that evening.

"I can see why you favor Dignity," Ray commented as they strode across the town square.

A cold wind came up, a portent of the winter ahead. Both men pulled up their collars against its chill.

"I've fallen in love," Gray admitted.

"Oh? You're referring to your fiancée, I assume?"

Chuckling, Gray reconstructed the statement. "With the town and its residents. They're good, hardworking people."

"Ah, then they have accepted you. That speaks well for you."

"They've accepted me too much," he laughed. "The women have taken me under their wing, determined to keep me fed. I've had enough cookies, cakes, pies, and pot roasts to feed two armies."

"Guess that's the way with friendly towns."

"Yes." Gray smiled. "That appears to be their way."

The windows of the town hall spilled light onto the square. The decorating committee had removed most of the benches and shoved chairs back to the walls. Already the room was full. A fiddler was tuning up, and two guitar players plucked at the strings of their flat tops.

The refreshment committee put the last tray of cookies on a table that held a variety of food along with lemonade. Gray was sure that by the end of the evening, at least one tub of drink would have the added ingredient of hundred-proof whiskey.

"Dr. Fuller!" Mazie Bennett hurried over with a wide smile on her face.

"Mrs. Bennett. How nice you look tonight. I'd like you to meet a friend of mine. Raymond Grimes."

Mazie looked the stranger up and down. "Pleased to meet you, Mr. Grimes."

"Mrs. Bennett is in charge of the celebration tonight."

"Quite an undertaking."

"Oh, I enjoyed doing it. The festivities are in honor of our new doctor, don't you know. We feel so privileged to have him in our small town."

"I'm sure you do." Ray's gaze drifted to the door where the young woman he'd seen in Gray's office the first time he called on him had just come in. "I appreciate being invited tonight."

"Any friend of the doctor's is a friend of ours. You just make yourself at home. I've got to greet these new folks coming in."

With that, Mazie Bennett bustled off to spread cheer and good will.

"Lemonade?"

"Thank you," Ray said, keeping an eye on the young

woman who was now making her rounds through the room.

The two men stood to one side, sipping their drinks as the musicians began the first song. Soon the floor was full of couples reeling to the quick tunes that began melting one into the other.

Gray saw April arrive on Riley's arm. She was breathtakingly beautiful tonight.

"I think I'll meander around a little," Ray said.

"Of course . . . and the girl you've got your eyes on is Beulah Ludwig. Her father's the pharmacist."

Blushing, Ray set his cup of lemonade on the table. "Thanks." He threaded his way through the crowd to where Porky was standing.

Gray's eyes lingered on April as she slipped off her shawl and hung it on a hook beside the door. Riley wandered off to join some of his cronies while she spoke to friends.

Lamplight shone in her hair. The dark-green dress she wore made her look older. He thought she was the most beautiful woman in the room, and he found his body responding to her. She was one woman who didn't need a pie to catch his attention. Every time he saw her, he felt that all too familiar urge to pull her into his arms.

The next song began and couples formed a reel. He knew he had to dance with her.

He slowly made his way across the room to where she was standing with friends. He had almost reached her when James Nelson swung her into his arms and joined the couples on the floor. Stepping back, he accepted a dance with Meredith Nelson instead.

When the dance ended, James returned April to her friends. Snapping open her ivory and lace fan, she laughed at something someone said.

Excusing himself, Gray made his way over to her.

"I believe this is our dance."

April turned in midlaugh, her brows lifting when she saw him.

"Why, Dr. Fuller, I didn't notice you here."

His eyes played with hers. Both knew she was lying.

"May I have this dance?"

"Why, of course."

As they approached the floor, the music changed to a slow waltz. April's hand rested lightly on the front of his jacket. He held her loosely, aware that she was conscious of his hand resting at her waist, the warm clasp of his hand around hers.

"I wasn't sure you'd dance with me," he noted as they slowly fell into step.

"Why not?"

"I have the distinct feeling you don't like me, Miss Truitt."

Smiling up at him, she made a face. "Why, why ever would you think that? If we disagree, we disagree on how to treat sick women, not on dancing."

"Where's Henry tonight?"

"He's away on business."

"He's gone a lot, isn't he?" His gaze skimmed her flushed features. Couldn't she see the fool Long was playing her for?

Her smile faded, and she didn't look gullible, just lonely. "Yes, far too often, I'm afraid."

He grinned. "Let's be civil to each other tonight, all right?"

"I say that would be lovely, Doctor. Please keep that in mind when I say something that annoys you."

"Miss Ludwig?"

Porky turned at the soft voice. "Yes?"

"My name is Raymond Grimes. I'm a friend of Dr. Fuller's."

Porky's heart shot to her throat. "Yes, I've seen you in his office, haven't I?"

"I'm a salesman, medical supplies and equipment. Dr. Fuller was nice enough to invite me to the celebration tonight."

Porky's gaze covered the young man from head to foot. Brown hair brushed back from a wide forehead, kind blue eyes, white shirt and brown suit, his boots freshly polished. He wasn't outstandingly handsome; but he looked nice.

"Could I have this dance?"

She hesitated. Seldom did she dance at these affairs. She usually spent her time behind the refreshment table.

"I—I shouldn't leave my post."

He looked disappointed. "Couldn't someone watch it for you a moment?"

Glancing around, Porky spotted Mrs. Steel. Smiling and nodding her permission, Thelma's eyes urged Porky to enjoy herself.

"Well, I guess it won't hurt," she finally said, taking the hand he offered.

She was glad the dance was a waltz. She didn't trust her legs to hold her up through a fast dance. A nice-looking young man had actually sought her out to dance!

Her, Porky Ludwig!

Trying to find her voice, she smiled, hoping to make pleasant conversation. "Do you travel through town often?"

"About every two to three weeks, depending on how things go."

Oh, dear. Did he feel how thick her waist was? Did it matter to him? Why hadn't she worn a corset! Drats! She would have suffered through the atrocity if she'd had any idea a man would ask her to dance!

"This your hometown?"

She nodded. She wasn't good at small talk. Never had been.

"It's a nice town."

"I think so."

They danced, saying nothing, and she didn't mind. This was comfortable. Good. Of course, he was a stranger in town and probably taking pity on her, but she didn't mind. It was worth it to see the look on Janie Anderson's face.

"Gray tells me your father has the pharmacy."

"Umhum. I work there with him."

Oh. That was it. He saw her as a potential account. But, it didn't matter. For now, she was actually dancing with a man, swirling around the floor, smiling.

"You do? What do you find to be the fastest selling medications?"

For the next two dances they talked about medicines, over-the-counter treatments, and even Pinkham's elixir. Ray didn't agree that it was a miracle cure, but he did say for some people it seemed beneficial.

"Would you like some refreshment?"

"Yes," she said, though reluctant to stop dancing. It didn't happen that often, and she wanted to make it last as long as possible.

Ray handed her a cup of lemonade and they stood at the edge of the crowd while they sipped the tart drink.

"Hello, Porky."

"Hello, Melinda."

When the young woman lingered, Porky remembered her manners. "Melinda Barnes, this is Raymond Grimes."

"Raymond, I'm glad to meet you." Melinda's greedy little eyes devoured the young man, but it didn't matter.

He would be gone in the morning. "Are you new in town?"

"Just passing through."

"I see." She smiled, ever so charmingly. "Well, I certainly do hope you'll come back soon."

Melinda's attention was caught by a friend, and she hurried off.

"Did she call you . . . Porky?"

Porky blushed. "That's my name."

"Surely not."

"Well, it's a nickname that's stuck since I was a little . . . since I was a child." She'd never been a 'little' anything.

"Why?"

"Why?"

"Yes." His eyes softened. "I don't see that it fits."

Porky blinked in surprise; then her eyes suddenly welled with tears. That was the nicest thing anyone had ever said to her. He didn't mean it—she looked like a cow in this dress—but it was still a nice thing to say. "You're serious?"

"Yes."

"You're really serious?"

"Miss Ludwig, I—"

"It's because I'm a large woman, Mr. Grimes, or are you blind?" He was making fun of her. Of course. And she had almost fallen for it.

"I assure you, I'm not blind. Do you mind if I call you Beulah? You can call me Ray."

"I do not appreciate being made fun of, Mr. Grimes." Taking her skirt in her hand, she started to walk off, but he reached out and stopped her.

"I wasn't making fun of you, Miss Ludwig." His eyes met hers, and she was hopelessly caught by their sincerity. "Forgive me, if you thought I was."

Now she felt stupid. The first man who'd ever shown an inkling of interest in her, and she'd accused him of poking fun at her.

Hanging her head, she said softly. "Do you mind if we dance again?"

"I'd be delighted, Beulah."

"How did you know my name?"

"The doctor told me."

They spent the entire evening dancing, talking, and by the time the musicians took their break, Porky was sure that the angels in heaven had finally smiled on her. Even if she never saw Ray Grimes again, she'd have this night to remember for the rest of her life.

On the other side of the room, Gray was now spending the evening dancing with one young woman after another, propelled his way by hopeful mothers.

It seemed the women of Dignity had despaired of earning his favor through culinary bribes and had turned to charm on the dance floor to gain his attention.

As he tried to make small talk, his gaze kept drifting to April. Henry was absent, but she had more than her share of suitors.

Around ten, he excused himself from a young girl of seventeen and made his way quickly across the room.

"Miss Ludwig, may I have the pleasure of this dance?"

Porky smiled up at Gray. It was a dream, she knew it. First Ray, now Dr. Fuller. "Me?"

"You, Miss Ludwig."

"Bring her back to me," Ray called with a friendly grin.

Oh, Lord. May she never wake up.

Taking her into his arms, Gray swung her out onto the dance floor. The music swirled around her, and Porky felt like Cinderella. Who else lived such a charmed life? Two wonderfully handsome men vying for her attention.

"You look lovely tonight, Miss Ludwig."

Porky's smile widened. "I'm having a marvelous time."

They danced in silence as Porky racked her brain. What should she say? Gray Fuller was dancing with her, and her mind was a total blank.

"Want a cookie?" she finally blurted.

"A cookie?"

She smiled. "Actually, I'm supposed to be tending the refreshment table, but Mrs. Steel said she'd watch it for me."

"Thank you, no cookies."

Gray swung her around and saw that Ray had centered his eyes on them.

Smiling down at her flushed face, he commented casually, "I see you have an admirer."

Porky's gaze traveled to Ray standing on the sidelines. "He's taking pity on me. What do you know about him? He's new to the area, isn't he?"

She told herself to just enjoy the attention, but her interest was piqued by this kind, wonderful stranger who'd actually danced the entire evening with her.

"Just what he's told me. He has no family to speak of. Got into the sales business in Boston about five years ago. Likes to travel because he likes people, but hates staying out on the road all the time. Seems to be an honest man. Sells good equipment, doesn't try to take advantage. I like him."

"Yeah," she said wistfully. Her eyes returned to the medical equipment salesman and she sighed. "Me, too." If only she didn't. She would hate herself in the morning.

Other than Gray Fuller, there wasn't a man in the room she liked better.

The evening lasted well into the night, but no one noticed the late hour . . . especially Porky, who had her eyes on Ray, and April, who only had eyes for the good doctor.

"Mary?"

The woman who stood before Gray the following week was luminous. She had bright color in her cheeks, and she was smiling.

Actually smiling.

"Dr. Fuller! Look at me! I feel wonderful!"

Gray walked across the room to greet her.

"You *look* wonderful!" His dark eyes assessed her healthy glow. "What have you done to yourself, Mary?"

Mary practically floated into the examining room. "It's that elixir you gave me. It . . . well, I haven't felt so good in I don't know when. I have such . . . *energy*! Why, I'm cleaning my house again, doing laundry. And, well, Severn says he's got his wife back again." Grasping his hand, she smiled up at him. "How can I ever thank you, Doctor? I feel like a new woman!"

"The heavy flow?"

"Much lighter, Doctor. So much so, I don't think surgery will be necessary."

Gray sat back and just stared at her. The change was miraculous. Surely Pinkham's compound wasn't responsible for the change. "Well, I can't say I'm anything but happy that we finally found something that works for you. You look radiant."

Mary leaned forward anxiously. "I need more of the tonic."

"Well . . . yes, certainly. I'll get another bottle for you."

"Oh, good. Severn says I'm never to be without it ever again."

Gray moved to the shelf and poured more of the elixir

into a smaller bottle and printed Mary's name on the label. With a slight hesitation, he handed the vial to her.

She looked at the tonic as if it was nectar from heaven. "Oh, thank you, Dr. Fuller! You don't know what this means to me."

"Just stay healthy, Mary. The diet we discussed, as well as the . . . tonic."

"You want to see me again in two weeks?"

"That's up to you—"

She suddenly looked frightened. "What about my tonic? I'll need more by then?"

"Whenever you run out, come back."

Clasping the compound to her breast, Mary danced out of the office.

Dropping into his chair, Gray watched her skip through the front door, singing.

Singing!

His eyes focused on the jar of compound, and he swore under his breath. Surely not . . . there was no way Pinkham's tonic had produced this wonder.

Was there?

Two days later Charley Black sidled in the door of the waiting room just as Gray was about to pull down the shade and lock up for the night.

"Doc?"

"Charley. Something I can do for you?"

Charley was the town blacksmith, a great burly man who moved slowly and deliberately. Riley had laughingly commented once that he suspected Charley fell asleep between strikes of his hammer against a horseshoe.

"My Delilah says you gave Mary Rader some elixir that cured her. She says I should come and get some from you."

Gray's brow lifted with concern. "Are you ill?"

"Well, not so pert. I work long hours, you know. Just like Severn Rader."

"Severn Rader?"

Charley nodded. "Yeah . . . you know." He winked. "Severn."

"Are you saying you're tired? Too tired to—"

"Delilah says so," Charley inserted, his skin flushing crimson beneath its deep bronze tone. Gray was aware a man didn't like to discuss his personal life.

Gray hesitated, then decided there'd be no harm in giving Charley some of the elixir. The change in Mary was miraculous; maybe it would give Charley a needed boost.

"Wait here. I'll get a bottle for you."

Charley shifted from one foot to the other, making the floor creak beneath his considerable bulk. Gray poured more of the elixir into a smaller bottle and printed Charley's name and instructions on the label.

"This should help. One spoonful, twice a day. Come back in a week and let me take a look at you. All right?"

"I work long hours. Just like Severn," he reiterated.

Gray assumed Charley, like most men in Dignity, didn't want to be seen coming into the office.

"Tell you what. My horse is favoring the right front. I'll bring him by later this week to have you take a look at him."

Relief flooded Charley's face. "Sure thing, Doc. Thanks."

Charley nodded his way out of the office, and Gray wearily rotated his head and shoulders. What made a man choose medicine as a vocation? His day started at first light and rarely ended before dark. At least once a week he was called out in the middle of the night, and often didn't get back home and to bed before dawn.

And now he was handing out elixir to men to improve their sex lives.

Damn!

Maybe tonight he'd get to sleep all night . . . in that lavender bedroom.

"Is that a letter from Henry?"

Porky caught up with April as she emerged from the post office Friday morning.

"Finally." She could hardly contain herself. Henry had been in New York three weeks, and this was only the second letter she'd received. Her eyes scanned it quickly as they walked along the street.

"How's the work going?"

"They've taken a room on Willoughby Street in Brooklyn." April glanced up. "Things are going so well that Dan has written home to persuade the family to move to Brooklyn."

"Brooklyn. What does that mean?"

"It means I'm out of a job, and Henry will want to move to Brooklyn, too."

"Do you think the Pinkhams will actually move?"

"I'm sure Lydia won't want to."

"Henry really likes living in a big city?"

"Well, he's doing all right with it." She read on. "It's exciting, I guess. He went to hear Henry Ward Beecher preach at Plymouth Church, he's attended political rallies at Cooper Union. Henry says Dan sees the opportunity to make good contacts with druggists and patent medicine men. He thinks the business could be worth thousands if the family worked together in Brooklyn.

"Henry says they've walked all over New York City and New Jersey as well as Brooklyn. We've sent them a new shipment of pamphlets, as well as a large supply of the compound. I'm so excited, and so is Lydia. It seems that finally we're making progress."

"But, what if *Henry* wants to move to New York, or Boston?"

April was forced to think about that eventuality. "I don't know. I'll just wait to cross that bridge when I get to it."

"Coward."

"Me? What about you?"

"I don't understand."

"That young man you danced with the other night."

"Ray?"

"Ray?" April's eyebrows arched.

"Ray Grimes. A medical salesman. Dr. Fuller says he's a very nice young man."

"Uh-huh. What do you think?"

"I think . . . that I've never had such a wonderful time. He's coming back in two weeks and, well, we're going to have supper together." Her cheeks turned pink. "He . . . he really didn't understand why I have the nickname Porky."

"I'm glad," April said, and she was. It was about time some man appreciated Porky's good qualities. "You just make sure he treats you right."

As she walked home, April thought about the possibility of the Pinkhams moving. What would she do if Henry wanted to move? New York was exciting, but she wasn't sure she'd want to live there. Nor did she like to think about leaving Grandpa, and Dignity, but if Henry were to decide to move to Brooklyn . . .

For some reason, she didn't want to think about it.

Gray glanced out the window of his waiting room late that morning to see April and Porky crossing the square. The sun glinted on April's light hair, and he realized he was ogling her. The unexpected swell in the front of his britches assured him he was no different than other single men in Dignity—with one exception.

He was engaged to be married to another woman.

The door opened and Delilah Black bounced inside.

Turning from the window, he greeted her. "Mrs. Black, how are you?"

"I'm fine. Just fine. Well, I think I'm fine. I don't know . . . for sure. It's my first, you know."

"Whoa," Gray cautioned. "Slow down."

Delilah flushed as prettily as a young girl, though she was well past thirty. "I . . . I . . . well, I want to consult with you—"

"Certainly. I finished with my last patient fifteen minutes ago. Come into the examining room."

Delilah followed him, twisting the strings of her handbag tightly around her fingers.

"Have a seat," Gray invited, pointing to a straight backed chair.

Delilah perched uneasily on the edge of the seat.

"What can I do for you?"

"Well," she flushed a deep red, "it's a little difficult for me."

"Just relax."

"I wish I could. It's just that this is so . . . well, personal." She twisted her bag into a rag.

"How is Charley?" Gray asked, hoping to make Delilah feel more at ease.

"Oh," she practically trilled, "Charley is just *fine!*"

"Good. Then the tonic I gave him—"

"Is *wonderful!*"

Sensing there was something he was missing, Gray paused, trying to form his next question.

"I gather he's feeling better?"

"I've never seen him feeling *better*." She giggled.

Frowning, Gray nodded. "Good . . . good."

"You don't understand, Doctor. Charley has always been a man . . . who takes things . . . slowly. He has . . . well, my father says he has very little ambition."

Gray wasn't following her. "I don't understand."

"So little ambition, Doctor, that . . . well, he . . . could hardly . . . well, get enthused about . . . well, anything," she said, twisting the strings into a tight knot. "Until lately."

Gray could see she was uncomfortable with the subject.

"Are you and Charley having difficulty in the bedroom?"

"Oh, no! Morning sickness."

Gray nodded. "Morning sickness."

"You don't understand. If I am . . . with child, I'd be most happy to spend the entire day with my head in a chamber pot." She flushed a deep crimson.

"So, you think you're with child?" Gray asked.

Delilah grinned. "Yes!"

Understanding suddenly dawned on Gray. Of course! Charley Black mentioned that he was worn down from working so many hours. Obviously, Charlie had perked up, so to speak, and she was trying to thank him for giving Charley the tonic.

She leaned forward in her chair, her face turning solemn. "It's that tonic you gave him. I'd heard that it would cure . . . impotency"—she whispered the word—"but I would never have believed it . . . until . . . I experienced it . . ."—she turned scarlet—"for myself."

For a woman who was not accustomed to discussing a personal subject, she was doing exceedingly well.

"But you're here to—"

"Have you confirm that I am in the family way. You see, Charley and I have been married twelve years, and I've always wanted children. But . . . well, I explained that."

Mentally shaking the cobwebs out of his mind, Gray tried to follow her.

Grinning, she whispered, "I want you to examine me and see if I am truly expecting."

"All right," Gray said. "Let's take a look."

Fifteen minutes later Delilah Black floated out of Gray's office a happy woman. She was, indeed, with child and was rushing over to the livery to tell Charley the good news.

Gray slowly climbed the stairs to his room, shaking his head in disbelief. Delilah was convinced that the compound he'd given Charley had cured his impotency. What it had done, Gray was equally convinced, was give him the energy to make love after a long day's work. The natural result was for his wife to conceive.

Interesting, he thought as he pulled his boots off and lay back across the bed. He hoped Delilah Black would keep the news of Charley's miraculous rebirth to herself, or he would have every man in Dignity flocking to his office for the compound.

His eyes focused on the ceiling.

He had to do something about that damn lavender ribbon Francesca had put on the fan. Lavender. He wondered how April would look in lavender . . . probably good. Just as good as she felt in his arms at the dance.

For the following three days, half the town flocked to Gray for a bottle of elixir. Fully two-thirds of the women boldly expressed their desire that the compound would motivate their husbands to be more aggressive in bed.

It was unbelievable. Knowing that if they believed it would help them, they'd help themselves and give credit to the elixir, he gave them low dosage instructions.

But this morning he had given the last of the compound to Betty Petersen.

Jim Petersen didn't know how fortunate he was.

Now, Gray had to come up with more compound.

He laid his head back on the pillow.

Where in the hell would he get it?

He could buy it from April and possibly win her admiration for seeing things her way. It would also give him an excuse to see her periodically. Disconcerting as it was, she was all he could think about lately.

Chapter 11

Francesca rearranged the china tray on Gray's dresser, then absently toyed with his hairbrush. "You haven't been to Boston in nearly two months."

"Ah, complaints, Francesca? Aren't our times together gratifying enough for you?" he teased, although he wasn't in a teasing mood tonight.

Far from it.

The day had been long and tiring, but Francesca had insisted they eat out tonight. Gazing at his image in the mirror, he knotted the tie, wondering why he didn't break the engagement. Months ago she ceased to interest him, yet he felt compelled to see it through and powerless to say why. Jerking the knot free, he started over.

He attributed his jittery mood to lack of sleep. It seemed he never slept anymore. He'd hoped to go to bed early tonight, but Francesca had pulled another one of her surprises and hired a carriage and driver to bring her to Dignity. She'd arrived around four, bearing more gifts for his office and living quarters.

At the rate she was going, he would be forced to vacate

the office and find other living arrangements. Wouldn't that make him the laughingstock of the town?

People were naturally curious about Francesca. He was aware of the open speculation concerning their relationship. Conversations stopped when they appeared in public, and speculative looks were commonplace.

He should introduce her as his fiancée. A proper introduction wasn't a deliberate oversight, just one he hadn't gotten around to making, or didn't want to make.

"People are beginning to wonder if we are engaged." Francesca walked her fingers up the front of his jacket. "I need you to come to Boston more often. I miss you," she whispered, burying her face against the wall of his chest.

"You're here now," he said, his voice a silken thread.

"Only because your shameless neglect forced me to come. Besides, I'm having a party Friday evening, and I want you to be there."

"Wouldn't a simple note have been easier?"

She looked up, stricken. "Are you not happy to see me?"

"Francesca, I'm delighted to see you." He kissed her, his tongue exploring the sweet recesses of her mouth. When the kiss ended, he whispered, "Now, will you tie this damn tie for me?"

Brushing his hand aside, she finished off the pesky knot. "You will be able to attend the party next week?"

"I can't."

"Gray! Papa is beginning to think there's something wrong. You *never* come to see me anymore."

He hated it when she began this wheedling. No matter how he explained the demands of his work, she refused to understand. Apparently Louis's practice had demanded less time than Gray's when Francesca was growing up.

"I assure him everything is fine, of course, but I can see he's puzzled. Frankly, he's starting to wonder if we're ever going to set a wedding date. I'm running out of excuses, Gray. I don't know what to tell him."

"Tell him the truth, Francesca. I don't intend to marry until my practice is firmly established."

"Oh, pish pash." She tipped her head to one side, flirting with him, yet the determination in her eyes warned him she wasn't going to be swayed. "If you were practicing in Boston, you would already be established. Papa is upset that you're intent on repaying the loan for your education. He says you're sending him money every month—you know that isn't necessary. The loan was a gift from my father because he believes in you, Gray."

Watching her reaction in the mirror, Gray said softly, "Louis knows I intend to pay my debt to him in full within the year."

"That's so silly, but let's not argue." Looping her arms around his neck, she smiled up at him. "Promise you'll come to my party. We'll have breakfast at The Palm Tree; then later you can take a room at the hotel—"

"Francesca, I can't. Next week I have two serious surgeries. I can't leave my patients and come to Boston to attend a party."

"Gray, *tell* me you'll be there." She showered kisses along his neckline and jaw, tasting him, her tongue arousing him. "Please, Gray, please?"

Boston was out of the question, but he knew if he didn't capitulate, she'd beg until the evening was ruined. Once again he would be forced to invent an emergency, explaining his absence. He was tired of making excuses. When would Francesca grow up and realize he had to fulfill his obligations as a man and a doctor?

"I'll do my best, but I can't promise."

Her small, pearly teeth nipped his lower lip seductively. "That's all I ask, *chéri*."

She prattled on about her plans for the "wonderful party" on the walk to the hotel. Something frivolous that didn't interest him. He listened with half an ear, his mind absorbed with a young man who had developed a large growth on his head. Surgery would temporarily alleviate the tumor, but he knew it was only a matter of time before it returned.

"Dr. Fuller," the proprietor greeted as they entered the hotel dining room. "I have a nice window table waiting for you."

Francesca's gaze swept the diners with a haughty air. Gray hated when she cloaked herself in haughtiness, assuming the air that Dignity residents were beneath her. It made him want to defend the town from the scourge of society.

As he settled Francesca into her chair, he noticed April and Riley were dining across the room. Struck by Riley's granddaughter's presence, his left eyebrow rose a fraction. The soft lamplight turned her hair to finely spun gold. She laughed at something Riley said, her face animated, happy. Though he didn't agree with her work with Pinkham, or her outrageous philosophies, he respected her principles. She worked hard for her beliefs, and backed down to no one. That was more than he could say for Francesca.

"Excuse me a moment, Francesca."

Rancor tinged Francesca's voice as she glanced up, and said, "Gray, you are not going to abandon me."

"No, I want to speak to someone."

Her mouth firmed, but Gray ignored the warning that she was on the verge of a temper tantrum.

Pausing to speak with a young couple sitting to their right, he then crossed the room to Riley's table.

"Gray," Riley greeted, getting to his feet when he saw the doctor. "How nice to see you."

Gray shook his hand, his gaze assessing April with a hint of mockery. "Enjoying a special occasion?"

"No, no," Riley said. "Datha was gone tonight, so April and I decided to treat ourselves." He looked about the room. "Are you alone?"

"No, I'm with someone. I just wanted to say good evening." His gaze focused on April. "Miss Truitt."

She glanced toward Francesca sitting at a window table, and her smile was almost Cheshire. "Dr. Fuller."

"I've missed our chess games, but I hear you've been busy," Riley said.

"Very busy, but I hope to see you one night this week."

"Good. I'll look forward to it."

Turning back to April, the doctor smiled. "I trust you are well, Miss Truitt?"

"Never felt better, Doctor. And you?"

"Very well, thank you."

Conspicuously consulting her menu, she parried softly, "Isn't that Miss DuBois with you?"

Gray turned around to look. "Why, yes, I believe it is. You have met, haven't you?"

"We've met." She burrowed her head deeper into the menu.

He was surprised to see the unwanted blush that crept into her cheeks. He should be ashamed of teasing her, but he found an oddly perverse pleasure in it.

"How is Henry—is he still away on business?"

"Yes. He wishes he could be here, but duty calls."

"How distressing—are you expecting him back soon?" He'd never noticed it before, but she was gorgeous when she was furious.

"I'm expecting him back any day now, thank you."

"You and Henry?" Grandpa blustered. "What's this!"

"Grandpa, you know I see Henry on occasion," April murmured, hoping Gray wouldn't notice the discrepancy.

His smile was so transitory, it made her wonder if she'd actually seen it. "Perhaps you and Henry, and Francesca and I can make an evening of it soon?"

"I don't think so, Doctor." She snapped the menu shut. "We're busy."

He smiled, accepting the parry.

"April!" Riley scolded. "Where are your manners?"

With a disarmingly generous surrender, Gray said, "It's all right, Riley. I understand when a person is busy. Please give Henry my regards, Miss Truitt."

She gave him a scornful look.

Chuckling, he clasped Riley on the shoulder warmly, and returned to Francesca.

"What's this about Henry?" Grandpa was saying as Gray walked away.

Sticking a cheroot in his mouth, Gray grinned. That will teach her to lie.

The following week, half the countryside came down with colds and chest congestion. Gray blamed the unstable weather—warm one day, cold the next. By Friday he wanted nothing more than to go to bed and sleep for twenty hours straight. But that wasn't an option. If he failed to attend Francesca's party, she'd never let him forget it. Since no reasonable excuse materialized by Friday, he felt compelled to go, even if it meant postponing two minor surgeries until Monday.

Friday evening found him sitting in his carriage halfway to Boston. The weather was disagreeable, and he longed for a warm fire. It occurred to him he had no idea what sort of party it was, though it didn't matter. When Francesca summoned, he went.

The air had a cold nip in it, perhaps even a hint of

snow. He was going to arrive at the party late, and she wasn't going to be happy. Young Davey Elliot had fallen out of the hayloft this afternoon and broken a leg; it took over two hours to set the injury, but she wouldn't understand that. She expected him to be prompt, regardless.

Carriages lined the street, and light spilled from every window in the house as Gray's vehicle pulled into the circular drive. He grimaced as he recognized several of the conveyances. It appeared Francesca's guest list included every friend and acquaintance she or Louis had ever wanted to impress.

Drawing a deep breath, he squared his shoulders and strode up the walk, carrying a gaily wrapped box—a small gold locket he would present to Francesca as a peace offering.

"Dr. Fuller," the butler said, taking his hat.

"Good evening, James."

"Gray!" Francesca appeared in the arched doorway leading into the massive ballroom. She was a vision of loveliness from her carefully coiffed hair, to her red-velvet ball gown. She ran lightly to him, taking him by the arm and hugging him warmly.

"I'm sorry, but an emergency came up at the last minute."

Stepping back, she inspected him to see if he'd dressed properly for the occasion.

"Where is that marvelous cloak I gave you?"

"I thought this was more serviceable, considering it's extremely cold outside."

A frown shadowed her brows as she took in his conservative black suit and brocade vest. She sighed. "There are some very important people Papa wants you to meet tonight. Please, Gray, don't bore them with talk of that funny little town. Promise?"

"I'll only speak in German. We should be safe with that."

"Oh, silly."

The DuBois house was ostentatious and outrageously affluent. One of the first in Boston to display electric lights. Towering three stories, made of red brick with white trim and white wrought iron around the balconies. Ornate white grills covered the lower windows that looked out on manicured grounds. At the back of the house were award-winning gardens overlooking a small pond. Some thought the house was the pinnacle of elegance; Gray thought it was gaudy.

Francesca's hand was evident in every room, her signature color—lavender—in the French wallpaper on the entry walls of the grand salon. Even in rooms with white walls, the aura of lavender reflected off heavy brocade draperies and fat pillows scattered across uncomfortable couches. Dishes stacked on the buffet were hand-painted china—purple violets trailing around the edge of each plate and cup.

If he never saw the color purple again, he'd be happy.

A quintet played soft music from a raised stage in a corner of the ballroom. The hum of conversation ebbed and flowed. Women flirted. Men milled about the room, shaking hands while trying to gracefully balance fluted wine glasses.

In a whirlwind tour around the overly heated room, Francesca introduced him to a dozen men whose names he wouldn't remember and a bevy of young women whose faces blurred together.

Introductions out of the way, her mind turned to other pursuits. "Darling, shall we eat, or retire to the balcony?" she asked, her hand drifting up the front of his shirt.

He hadn't eaten since dawn, and a tryst on the balcony wasn't particularly to his liking.

"Whatever you'd like, Francesca."

Taking his arm, she led the way to the balcony. Gray hoped the air would serve to clear his mind. Events such as this suffocated him.

The air was bracingly cold as he stepped onto the verandah. The threat of snow hung over the city.

The holiday season would be upon them soon. Thanksgiving, then Christmas. That meant returning to Boston to spend time with Francesca, time he could ill afford. Why didn't he enjoy their times together? They had been pleasurable once.

They settled on an iron bench overlooking the pond. The setting was idyllic for lovers, but Gray's mind wasn't on the view.

Looping her arm through his, Francesca cuddled close. "Papa would have been upset if you hadn't come tonight."

"Then I'm glad I came."

"He wants to talk to you about something."

"Oh?" Gray took out a gold case. Removing a cheroot, he lit it. No doubt Louis wanted to extend another invitation for him to join one of his practices here in Boston, an invitation Gray would refuse.

" 'Oh?' Is that all you can say? 'Oh?' Aren't you the *least* bit curious what he has to say?" Large, luminous eyes pinned him. She reminded him of an animal, savagely beautiful but dangerous. Somewhere in the corner of his mind he knew he should be feeling desire right about now; he felt nothing but the hard seat and cold air.

"I think I can guess. He wants to offer me a partnership."

"Well, that, too, but that isn't what he wants to talk to you about tonight."

"What is it then, Francesca?"

"A wedding date."

"Francesca—"

She hurried on. "Papa has a whole list of people he wants to invite, some from as far away as California, and that takes time, darling. I know your feeling on the subject, but we have to set a date soon. I have so much to do."

Getting up, Gray moved to the low wall overlooking the pond. Drawing on the cheroot, his eyes darkened with resentment. He knew who the "friends" were. Anyone Louis DuBois perceived to be a potential business associate. Louis planned to make his daughter's nuptials a golden business opportunity.

"Let's go inside," he said.

"Oh," Francesca said, disappointment blooming on her face. "Gray, I don't understand you. Why are you so impersonal when we discuss our marriage? It's almost as if you wished you hadn't asked me to be your wife."

Had he asked her? He couldn't remember. One moment she was discussing the possibility of an engagement, and the next he was betrothed.

Not wanting to spoil the evening, he offered her his arm. "The wind is sharp, you'll catch a chill."

Francesca was not pleased, but she allowed him to coax her back into the house where the small ensemble was tuning up for the first waltz of the evening.

"Gray, my boy," Louis boomed from across the room when he saw them. "Come over here, son. There's someone I want you to meet."

Crossing the room with Francesca on his arm, Gray approached the senior physician.

"Hampton, I want you to meet my soon to be son-in-law, Gray Fuller. Gray, Hampton Brinkman. Gray has recently opened a practice in a nearby coastal town. Dignity. Ever hear of it?"

"Can't say that I have."

Louis laughed. "Don't feel bad. Nobody else has, either!"

Gray shook hands with Hampton.

"Hampton is interested in having you join him in his clinic. You two might want to discuss—"

"Not this evening," Gray interrupted Louis in a polite but firm refusal. When Louis frowned his disapproval, he softened his stance. "I've had a long trip, and an even longer week, and I don't wish to discuss business this evening. I'm afraid I would be a poor conversationalist."

Louis looked perturbed but recovered sufficiently enough to give Hampton a jovial slap on the back. "Perhaps tomorrow, at dinner, Hampton. I'm sure Gray can—"

"Sorry, but I'll be leaving before noon."

"Oh, Gray, I've made plans for tomorrow evening," Francesca protested. "Surely you can stay a few days. Adele Mason's having a holiday soiree Sunday evening, and I told her we would attend."

"I'm sorry, Francesca. I have a patient who is running a high fever, and I said I would return no later than late tomorrow morning."

"Gray—"

"Louis. Hampton? Perhaps another time."

Gray threaded his way back across the room. Francesca would be furious with him, but he couldn't do it. He couldn't spend another night in the company of swine who swore to uphold the medical oath based on the principles and ideals of the ancient Greek physician Hippocrates, but thought of nothing more than lining their pockets at the expense of the ill.

"Your hat and coat, sir," the butler said.

"Gray, you were *rude* to Mr. Brinkman," Francesca hissed as she caught up with him.

"It was rude of your father to waylay me like that."

"He just wants the best for us!"

Gray shrugged into his overcoat. "The best according to Louis."

"Gray Fuller, if you walk out of here and embarrass me like this, I will never forgive you."

Gray knew he was wrong. He should stay and be the man Francesca wanted, but he felt smothered.

"Come with me, Francesca. We'll walk in the park and discuss our future, but I can't stay here."

She gazed at him, attractive, special, sure of her power to please. "No. You stay, and we'll discuss our differences later."

"Don't make this more difficult, Francesca. Come with me, now."

With a quick denying glance, she dismissed him. "You know I can't leave. Papa would never forgive me. He has important associates here tonight, Gray. He expects you to mingle and help entertain. Why are you acting this way?"

His gaze was cold and impenetrable. "In the future, I suggest you consult with me before you plan my life." He opened the door. "Are you coming?"

Her eyes were filled with angry humiliation. "No."

"Then I bid you good night."

"Gray!" she called as he strode quickly toward his carriage. "Gray! I will not have you walking out on me like this. What will people think?"

"Frankly, Francesca," he called over his shoulder, "I really don't give a damn."

Gray smiled as he got into his buggy and the horse trotted off. He felt good, no, liberated. He'd finally stood up to Francesca and Louis.

Never again would he allow Francesca to set his social calendar, or Louis his business associates. He'd had enough. It was past time they realized they didn't own him. His debt to Louis would be paid in full, and if he thought his daughter's hand in marriage was part of that debt, he was wrong.

Chapter 12

The wind was sharper than April had anticipated. Drawing her cape tighter, she slapped the reins against the horse's rump. Usually she didn't mind the trip to Boston, but at the moment she wished she'd picked another day to hand out pamphlets for Mrs. Pinkham's elixir.

Riley didn't know she was making the trip. He thought she was shopping, which, of course, she planned to do before the day was over. Too bad Henry was in Washington this week. She grinned, thinking how surprised he'd be if he were still in Boston and she showed up. He would be flabbergasted to see her!

She arrived midtown before nine o'clock and spent the morning handing out pamphlets. The response was good, and she considered the long hours in the cold wind productive.

By noon she was chilled to the bone. Hurrying down the sidewalk, rubbing her hands together, she saw the sign she'd been searching for: CLARA'S CHOCOLATE

SHOPPE. A cup of hot chocolate and a piece of shortbread were exactly what she needed.

A woman in bright taffeta crossed the street and stepped onto the sidewalk in front of April.

The woman, though beautiful, was wearing a dress far too colorful for day wear. The girl, for she was hardly more than a girl, wore heavy makeup—eyes outlined with kohl, rouge too red for her milky skin, her lips rubied like a strumpet's.

"Excuse me," April murmured, stepping around the young woman.

"Oh, Miss Truitt!"

April turned at the sound of her name.

"Yes?"

She recognized the small boy who had loitered around her table. Approaching her, he extended a stack of pamphlets. "You dropped these."

"Thank you." Patting the lad on the head, April stuffed the brochures in her bag and walked on. That young woman's hat was all wrong, too. Dark green with a large plume that dipped over her forehead.

As she stepped inside Clara's, a bell over the door announced her arrival. The warmth felt wonderful. Shivering, she smiled at all the delicious smells. A morsel to eat and a nice warm place to rest after the long, cold morning danced before her.

"Miss?"

"A table for one, please."

"This way."

She followed the server to a table in the center of the room, admiring the crisp white cloths and blue china.

"Thank you. A cup of hot chocolate, please."

Slipping off her gloves, she studied the small room. Dignity had nothing so lavish. She must bring Porky the next time she came; they could drink chocolate and shop to their hearts content. Smiling, she recalled the young woman she'd seen on the sidewalk. Though her makeup had been too heavy, she was quite beautiful. Worldly, unlike any woman April knew. She wished Porky were here to share the adventure.

The server returned with a pot of chocolate. Picking up the menu, April tried to decide whether she wanted a sandwich as well as she listened to the babble of talk around her.

"Here you are, Miss. That will be ten cents."

April handed the girl fifteen cents and received a light curtsy as a thank you. She sipped the chocolate, letting its warmth flow through her.

The bell over the door tinkled again, and a woman sitting behind her gasped.

Turning to look over her shoulder, April was surprised to see it was the heavily made-up young woman she'd encountered on the sidewalk earlier.

"Look at that. Can you believe it," the woman behind her whispered to her friend.

"Isn't that one of *those* women?"

"Well I hope not," the customer complained. "Surely they don't let her kind in here."

"It is, I'm sure of it. She works at Emogene's Pleasure Palace."

"No—why would *she* come in here?"

"Yes, why? How brazen to parade in just as if she owned the place."

"How do you know she's one of Emogene's girls?"

"I saw her coming out of that—that place yesterday. Do you know they dance nearly naked over there, as well as—well, I don't need to tell you what else they do in there." The woman sniffed. "Disgraceful, it is."

Curious, April glanced up as the young woman looked directly at her.

Not knowing where to look, April smiled timidly back.

The girl started in a beeline for her table. Stopping in front of her, she asked. "Are you April Truitt?"

Glancing around, April realized she was speaking to her. "Why . . . yes," she ventured hesitantly, wondering how the young woman knew her name.

"I'm Grace Pruitt."

Nodding, April smiled at the similarity of their names but failed to see how that concerned her.

"Henry Long's intended."

Her smile faded. "Henry's what?"

"Henry's intended." The girl stared at her. "I gather he hasn't mentioned me to you?"

Shaking her head, April searched for her voice. When she found it, she hastened to correct the woman.

"You're mistaken. *I'm* Henry's intended."

"No, you're the one who's made a mistake." Grace slid into the opposite chair, fixing her eyes on her. "*I'm* engaged to marry Henry Trampas Long. We're planning a fall wedding. I've already ordered the invitations."

"See here—"

The girl's face hardened. "*You* see here, sister. You leave him alone. Understand?"

April not only didn't understand, she was thunderstruck by the girl's assertion. Her Henry? Engaged to this woman? Why that was ludicrous. Henry was sheltered . . . he would never associate with a woman from Emogene's Pleasure Palace!

"I don't know who you are, but there must be a mista—"

"The only mistake is yours," Grace whispered urgently. Leaning forward, her fingers gripped the edge of the table. "Henry is *my* intended, and I want you to leave him alone!"

As the allegation started to sink in, April felt ill. The

room was suddenly too hot, and she could feel the eyes of the other patrons on her.

"How do you know who I am?" she whispered, humiliated by the scene the girl was making.

"I heard the boy call your name. It dawned on me you must be April Truitt, and I remembered the picture Henry showed me. The one you had made when the traveling photographer came through Dignity last summer?"

She *had* given Henry a picture made by a traveling photographer. April's heart sank.

"Have I made myself clear? Henry is mine. You leave him alone."

April nodded, numb now.

Grace looked around the café, glaring at the two women sitting behind April who were eavesdropping.

Suddenly unable to breathe, April blindly reached for the bag containing the pamphlets and got up and walked regally out of the café, color high in her cheeks.

As the door closed behind her, she broke into a run, running a full three blocks before slowing to a fast walk. It had to be a mistake. That was it, a silly mistake. The young woman had confused her with somebody else.

No, she said she recognized her by her picture.

Then someone was using Henry's name.

Yes! That was it. Some cad was using Henry's name!

But how had the girl known *her* name? How had the impostor gotten her picture?

"It doesn't make sense," she murmured.

Henry wouldn't dream of seeing another woman. He wasn't the sort of man to trifle with two women's hearts. He worked day and night to make the Pinkham compound a success; he didn't have time to court two women ... even if he did have the inclination, which she knew, absolutely *knew*, he didn't.

She relaxed. He'd told her he loved her, and she believed him.

It was all some horrible mistake.

Glancing over her shoulder, she shuddered. Some big, horrible mistake.

"Porky, what if it's true? What if Henry has been seeing that woman?"

Henry was still in New York, but April wouldn't have discussed the matter with him, anyway. The young woman's claims were just too preposterous! He would be embarrassed and angry with her for even listening to the girl, much less casting doubt on his gentlemanly conduct.

And she didn't believe this Grace Pruitt, whoever she was. It was a mistake, pure and simple, and she was going to put it out of her mind.

"How did she know who you were?" Porky asked.

"She said Henry had shown her a photograph of me. That one I had made last summer." April paced the pharmacy, upset. She hadn't slept all night for thinking about the bizarre turn of events. Henry, a philanderer? Impossible.

In his youth, perhaps, but not now. He was too responsible. Too decent to involve himself with another woman.

"I don't know, perhaps she isn't quite right. Maybe she just picked me out of the crowd—"

"But she knows Henry."

"I don't know what the explanation is, but I'm certain there is one. Henry would never do something like that, Pork. Never."

"Well, it's simple enough to find out."

Pausing, April looked at her warily. When she got that tone in her voice, her brilliance was about to surface. "How?"

Scooping up another bite of ice cream, she grinned. "Make Henry set a wedding date. He's been dallying around far too long. You claim he wants to marry you, so make him officially announce the engagement."

April felt sick at the thought. She wanted Henry's proposal to be romantic and given from the heart, not forced upon him just to prove his loyalty.

No, she couldn't make Henry propose to her. Besides, she didn't necessarily want to get married yet.

"I can't do that."

"Why not? If he intends to ask you anyway, what difference will it make if you hurry the process along?"

"We've talked about it," she admitted, "but it doesn't seem right, Porky. Obviously this Grace Pruitt has me confused with someone else."

But by the end of the week, April's nerves were taut from suspicion. True, Henry hadn't asked her to marry him, but Grace Pruitt concerned her. Was Grace mistaken, or was Henry seeing two women at one time? If Henry was playing games, she intended to find out.

Henry's familiar scrawl started the letter.

My dear April,

Our efforts are finally being rewarded. Dan and I have nearly walked off the soles of our shoes, but we convinced three pharmacists to make the Compound available in their places of business. The weather has been cooperative. Cold, but no rain or snow as yet. I look forward to seeing you soon.

Love,
Henry.

April let the letter fall to her lap. One letter in two weeks.

One measly letter.

They were working hard, and it hadn't snowed yet. Not much to hold her until he got back.

At least he had written.

Gray looked up the following week and saw Henry standing in the doorway to his office.

"Henry, you're just the man I'm wanting to see."

"Me?" Closing the door, Henry limped into the room.

"Toe bothering you again?"

"It hurts like hell," Henry replied, taking off his hat. "What did you want to see me about?"

Gray ushered Henry into the examining room and closed the door. "Can we speak in confidence?"

Frowning, Henry nodded. "Certainly. What's wrong?"

Gray cleared his throat. "I need some Pinkham compound. A good deal of it."

Henry stared at him for a moment, then threw his head back, laughing.

"Did I say something amusing?"

When he finished laughing, Henry just looked at him. "I thought you were adamantly against the elixir."

"I have been, but I've been conducting an experiment on my own regarding the tonic. I must say, it does seem to have limited success among my patients."

Henry broke out laughing again. "I assume you don't want April to know about this."

"I'd rather she didn't," Gray conceded.

"Don't worry, I understand. We men have to stick together." He punched him in the arm. "Know what I mean?"

"Can you provide me with the tonic on a regular basis?" Gray asked.

"I can get you a barn full, but why me? Why not

purchase it from your original source? Was it April? Oh, that's rich. She's been selling you the tonic!"

"Certainly not."

Henry chuckled.

"It was Porky. She brought me some to try, and I said I wouldn't, but I ended up using it. Now I'm out, and my patients are demanding more."

"Why not just tell your patients to buy it from us? It's readily available."

"I can't do that." Gray was at his mercy, much as he hated the thought. "As you might suspect, I would look like a fool in their eyes if they found out I am prescribing a tonic they can purchase not twenty feet outside the office."

"Yes." Henry grinned. "I see your problem. Well, don't worry, I can supply you with all the tonic you want—unfortunately, our prices have recently gone up." He climbed onto the examining table.

Gray calmly removed Henry's shoe. "How recently, Henry?"

Grinning from ear to ear, Henry said, "About sixty seconds ago."

"Well, that is unfortunate timing for me," Gray admitted, removing his patient's sock.

"Careful, Doc . . . it's sore as a boil."

"I can see that."

"You understand about the price raise. A man's got to make a profit when he can."

Gray nodded. "Oh, I understand." Glancing up, he smiled. "As you will understand when I tell you, much as I hate to put you through it, I'm going to have to do some in-depth work on that toe, Henry."

Henry suddenly paled as the implication of the words sank in.

"And unfortunately, it's going to get real nasty." Gray grinned.

Henry emerged from Gray's office a half hour later, obviously shaken.

Spotting April coming out of Ludwig's pharmacy, he called, "April!"

He limped across the cobblestone street and caught her by the hand, his cheeks ruddy from the trials of the past half hour. "I just got back a while earlier and stopped to talk to the doctor. Look at you! You look wonderful!"

April fought the insane desire to snub him and enlighten him at the same time.

"Thank you, Henry. I didn't know you were back. I take it your trip was successful?"

"Extremely so, my love. Lydia is pleased with the progress." He smiled. "I also just picked up a large account right here in town."

"Oh? Who?"

"I'm not at liberty to say, but it's a nice one." Taking her arm, he steered her away from the damp, foul winds coming off the harbor, insisting they spend a private moment having tea at the hotel before he returned to work.

"How have you been, love?" he asked as he gave their order then settled back in his chair to look at her.

They were seated at a window table, overlooking the square. April should have felt elated; Henry was back, and the silly misunderstanding about Grace could readily be cleared up. But the heaviness in her chest was like a millstone.

Taking her hand between his, he gazed at her. "You grow prettier with each passing day."

"When did you get back?"

"Late last night. I believe we made some real progress."

"That's nice." Her mind cast about for the proper word to bring up the subject of weddings in a seemingly casual way.

"Did I mention three apothecaries have agreed to carry the elixir and highly recommend it?"

"Yes, in your . . . brief letter. That should go a long way toward convincing others to carry it, as well."

Tea was brought, and a plate of tiny sugar cookies.

"Did you hear Sylvia Smitts and Ben Logan have set the date for their wedding?" she asked.

"No, I hadn't, " Henry said, munching on a cookie.

April toyed with her spoon. "They're planning a Christmas wedding. Isn't that a romantic time to get married? Christmas. The season of love."

"I suppose so. Did Lydia tell you we needed more pamphlets?"

"Yes. We're having some made up this week." She casually took a sip of tea. "Priscilla and Jeremy have set a date for their wedding, too."

"Have they?" He chose another cookie. "I think we should have a larger printing this time."

"I'll tell Lydia. Priscilla and Jeremy have decided to get married in June. Priscilla wants a garden wedding."

"Uh-huh. Where's our waitress? The tea is cold."

Henry signaled the waitress as April tried to think of a way to catch him in his duplicity—if that was what he was practicing.

"Henry?"

"Hum?"

"Isn't it wonderful when two people care deeply for one another, they marry?"

He smiled at her, his eyes cajoling. "Of course, love. Now, drink your tea before it gets colder."

She wasn't letting him off the hook that easy. "Henry—"

When he merely smiled at her, it looked like a wrinkle with teeth. "You look very lovely today, my dear. Is that a new dress you're wearing?"

"No, Henry, it's old," April whispered miserably, realizing he wasn't taking the bait.

"Henry!" Dan Pinkham crossed the dining room floor, apparently in a big hurry.

Getting to his feet, Henry frowned. "Dan?"

"I've been looking everywhere for you. Mother wants to talk to you—" Glancing at April, Dan said apologetically, "I hope I'm not interrupting."

"Not at all," Henry told him. Kissing April's hand, he smiled, "We weren't discussing anything important, were we, love?"

Later that afternoon, April pushed the door open to Gray's clinic. She was relieved to see the waiting room empty.

Calling, "Dr. Fuller?" she waited.

"In here."

Closing the door, she followed his voice to the office.

"Hello," she said, holding something behind her.

"Miss Truitt?" He dropped an instrument in a drawer. "Slumming this afternoon?"

"No." She gave him a singularly sweet smile. "I have something for you."

"I'm in no mood for games." He frowned. "What is it?"

"This." She held out the pillbox hat. "Funny how you keep misplacing it. Datha found it in our trash this morning. Wonder why?"

"Because I put it there." Slamming the drawer, he muttered, "That damn thing is like a homing pigeon."

Laughing, she tossed Francesca's gift onto a chair in the corner.

"Just stop by to annoy me?"

"Yes. You're on to me, aren't you?"

Why had she stopped by? The hat was a pretense. Datha could have brought it to him.

"Too bad, because, unfortunately, I have you figured out."

"I doubt that." Perching on the edge of his desk, she watched him work. "A man never has a woman figured out—don't you know that yet?"

"Where's Riley today? I stopped by the mortuary this morning, and he was gone."

"You're not going to believe this, but he's walking. Two miles after breakfast every morning."

Surprise dotted Gray's face. "That's good news."

"Yes," April ran a gloved finger lightly around the rim of the desk, frowning when it came up dusty. "I say this with great trepidation, but maybe modern medicine isn't so bad after all."

He looked up, grinning. "This, from the Pinkham camp?"

"No, 'this' from a woman who is open to new ideas, as you should be."

Moving to the window, she heaved a long, pent-up sigh. She was here because she needed a shoulder to cry on, and his was the broadest, most available one in town.

"Is something wrong?"

"No, why do you ask?"

"You just blew my curtains out the window."

"I'm restless, that's all. Now that I can't sell the compound, I don't have enough to keep me busy."

Returning to the desk, he sat down. "I saw Henry this afternoon."

She turned from the window. He was leaning back in his chair, arms crossed, observing her.

"Did you?"

"His toe was giving him trouble again."

"Yes—we had tea earlier."

She stood at the window, watching the fading light shadow the town.

"Is something bothering you? I know you don't find my company that attractive, and you do seem a little distracted this afternoon."

Rubbing her arms, she said softly. "I tried to get him to propose to me."

There was a short silence. "Who? Henry?"

"He wouldn't do it."

Why was she telling him this? It certainly wasn't his "bedside manner" that prompted her to confide in him. She longed to tell him about the woman in Boston who claimed to be engaged to Henry, but he would only laugh at her.

"And that concerns you?"

His dry humor made her laugh. At the moment she wanted so badly to tell him about Henry's infidelity, but how could she when he wasn't taking her seriously. She couldn't talk to Grandpa, and Porky's perception of Henry was slanted. What was she to do?

"He says he doesn't want to get married until he is financially situated."

"Sounds reasonable. What's the big hurry?"

"I just want to make certain he's not playing me for a fool," she murmured, her fingertips resting against her lips as she watched a young couple strolling across the mall.

His tone was somber, more evasive now. "Do you have reason to suspect he's playing you for a fool?"

"No, of course not."

"Then why worry about it."

April turned from the window, embarrassed that she had bothered him with her problems. Francesca would not appreciate another woman crying on his shoulder.

"I'm sorry. I've taken up too much of your time."

She grabbed her bag and swallowed against the lump in her throat. "Take better care of the hat."

Waving good-bye, she walked out to the outer waiting room.

"Miss Truitt!"

She turned to find him standing in the doorway of the examining room.

"Yes?"

"Next time you find my hat?"

Her brows lifted.

"Lose it for me. All right?"

She grinned. "You lose it—properly for once."

She turned to leave, then suddenly turned back. "Dr. Fuller?"

"Yes?"

"Thanks for listening to my blathering."

A secretive smile formed on his lips. "I'm always here, Miss Truitt."

"That's very gracious of you," she admitted. Their eyes met, and she sensed he knew that she was troubled.

"If you change your mind and want to talk, I'll be in the office late tonight."

Late Monday afternoon, a wagon rattled to a halt in front of a tall building in Boston. Gray jumped down and sprang up the steps.

"Hello?" he called out.

"What d'ya want?" a voice called back.

"I'm Dr. Fuller. I'm here to pick up a cabinet I ordered."

"Sure thing."

An old man shuffled from the back of the building. "Got it waitin' out there on the loading dock. You got a wagon?"

"Yes."

"Then come around back and we'll load her up."

The crate was heavy and awkward, but between the two men they got it loaded on the wagon. Then Gray headed toward the DuBois house, where he'd promised to have dinner with the widower Louis and Francesca. In his inside pocket, he carried another payment for Louis. Six more and he'd be out of debt.

Dinner was roast duck with orange sauce. Much too rich for his taste, but Francesca was proud of having planned the sumptuous meal. After dinner Louis disappeared into his office to take care of paperwork. Francesca drew Gray into the parlor and closed the door.

It was a cozy room, with a fire on the hearth. Gray had little opportunity to enjoy its warmth before Francesca distracted him. Wrapping her arms around his neck, she nuzzled his cheek.

"I thought you were angry at me for walking out on your father's party," Gray said.

Pouting, she looked up at him. "I want to plan a party."

"What kind of party?"

"A Dignity party."

He didn't know where she came up with her ideas. Dignity and Francesca? The thought brought a smile to his lips.

"I want your patients to see what a wonderful, supportive wife I will be for you."

He wasn't a fool. Her motive was plain: The party would be to show him how uncultured his patients were.

"It's a nice thought, but not necessary. It doesn't matter what they think of you, as long as I love you."

"But it *is* necessary. When we're married, I'm going to be your helpmate, Gray, not a thorn in your side. I've seen their looks. They want to know the woman who is going to be Mrs. Gray Fuller better."

"Francesca, I know how much energy you devote to your parties, and I'm afraid you'll be disappointed. Dignity is not Boston."

"I know that, darling, and it will still be a grand party. Simply grand. Can I have it?"

"I'd rather you didn't."

"But you won't forbid me to?"

Resigned to the inevitable, Gray sighed. "Have the party if you like, but don't blame me if it isn't your typical Boston fete."

That settled, she snuggled closer to him, taking his hand and placing it on her breast. "No more talk of parties. I'm sure we can find better ways to spend our time."

Giving her a lazy smile, Gray said softly, "I expect there are."

"You haven't made love to me in weeks," she accused petulantly.

"Forgive me, but I've been preoccupied."

Snuggling closer, she kissed him, and he wondered how long he would be able to provide a viable excuse for his fading interest.

Chapter 13

Exactly two weeks later, Francesca descended upon Dignity. The DuBois party was the talk of the town from the day the gold embossed invitations were received. Gray had insisted that no one be left out.

Francesca had been reluctant to invite "everyone in town"—she wanted the riffraff precluded. But Gray said everyone or no one.

She had agreed, though testily, and he reserved the town hall for the event. A Fall Festival, he called it, and she corrected him: a reception. It was a *reception*.

"Didn't I tell you it would be wonderful?" she enthused as they watched the decorations go up.

Gray looked at the ceiling of the large room, draped with bolts of yellow and orange fabric with large paper flowers fastening the ends in each corner. "It's a little . . . colorful."

"No, it isn't. It's perfect."

Perfectly gaudy. But Gray wasn't looking for a fight.

More paper flowers and brilliant leaves filled large pots sitting in corners and dotted throughout the room.

A long table groaning under the weight of finger sandwiches with the crust cut off the bread, tea cookies, cubed fruit in large crystal bowls, and a lavish ice sculpture in the form of the Greek god Eros, complete with bow and quiver. Francesca had brought along a staff of servants to help serve and keep the wine glasses filled.

"It's just as I envisioned it," Francesca exclaimed, her blue-velvet skirt billowing out as she turned, viewing the room with delight. Seldom had Gray seen her so adamant about a project.

"When the guests arrive, you and I will greet them at the door; then Samuel will take their coats, and Suzanne will serve them wine. The music will have begun before anyone arrives. There will be dancing, conversation, and very little business talk." Looping her arm through his, she smiled. "I know how you hate business talk."

"Is Louis coming tonight?"

"No." She pouted. "He had a business meeting, but he sends his regrets and wants me to tell you he expects you for dinner next week."

They moved through the hall, overseeing the frenzied preparations for tonight's events.

"I still think it's too elaborate," Gray told her.

"You worry too much. I *want* it to be special." She tightened her hold on his arm. "I want them to know who I am."

"And who are you?" Gray said softly.

"Why, your fiancée," Francesca said, her gaze daring him to dispute her.

"You've gone to a great deal of trouble and expense; I hope you won't be disappointed."

"I won't, you'll see. They'll be talking about this party for years to come."

Gray didn't doubt that. Unfortunately, it wouldn't be flattering.

* * *

The first guests arrived promptly at seven o'clock. Gray introduced each couple to Francesca, and she gingerly shook their hands. Murmuring a greeting, they timidly entered the lavishly decorated room, eyes wide with curiosity.

Porky and Raymond came in and chatted for a few minutes before moving to the refreshment table.

April arrived with Riley closer to 7:30.

"Francesca, April Truitt and Riley Ogden, her grandfather. Riley regularly beats me at checkers."

"I am so pleased to meet you," Francesca said.

"And we're pleased to meet such a lovely friend of Dr. Fuller's. He's been a godsend to our town."

"I'm sure he has," Francesca said, "though we do miss him terribly in Boston."

Gray noticed Henry was absent again. Bastard! he thought. Was the pompous ass spending his evening with his Amazing Grace, leaving April to make excuses for him?

Murmuring a soft greeting, April brushed passed him, trailing the scent of lily-of-the-valley as she entered the gaily decorated hall. He had a strong urge to follow her, but refrained from doing so.

Disgusted with himself for what he was thinking, he knew he should have never allowed Francesca to hold this party. She didn't understand the citizens of Dignity and would probably end up insulting the very people from whom he'd tried so hard to gain trust.

People were slow to mingle. The four musicians played violin and viola, classical music Francesca favored but few in Dignity enjoyed.

The guests were reluctant to dance. Instead, they stood in small groups, awkwardly holding the china plates Francesca had transported from Boston and staring at the strange sandwiches the white-coated help kept offering. When an hour had passed, and still no one was dancing, Francesca became more and more frustrated.

"What is wrong with them?" she hissed to Gray. "Why aren't they dancing?"

"Perhaps this isn't their kind of music," he suggested, recalling the livelier tunes played at summer picnics and get-togethers.

"How could that be? Well, never mind. We'll show them how to waltz properly."

Leading him onto the dance floor, she looked around, smiling, her eyes encouraging the others to follow.

"Have you ever seen such a flop?" Porky whispered as she and April stood on the sidelines. Ray Grimes was off getting punch.

"I feel rather sorry for her," April admitted as she enviously watched how gracefully Gray guided Francesca around the floor. "Do you think he'll formally announce their engagement tonight?"

April's gaze followed the way Francesca's hand lightly caressed the nape of Gray's neck, her fingers smoothing the hair against his tanned skin. She was looking up into his face as if they were the only two people in the room.

If he ever looked at her that way . . . if Henry ever looked at her that way, she'd be the happiest woman on earth, or would she? Was it Henry she wanted? Or the handsome doctor who appeared to be enamored with the French woman? Something told her that Gray wasn't as happy and devoted as he wanted everyone to think.

"What is *wrong* with these ungrateful people?" Francesca huffed. "They stand around in their dowdy dresses and their shiny suits and stare as if they've never seen a waltz before. Have they no manners? These are the people you want to spend the rest of your life with?"

She was working herself up again. Gray saw the signs and hoped to avoid a scene. Had she listened, she would know Dignity was a simple town with simple ways.

"Just because they're not dancing doesn't mean they're not having a good time. Relax, Francesca, they can see you're upset."

"But they're not even *trying* to mingle, or to talk, or to enjoy the fine things I've brought for them to enjoy."

"You talk as if they're impoverished children. They don't need to be plied with gifts for you to win their favor."

"Nonsense, gifts can achieve anything one wants. I'd hoped to show them the social niceties that aren't available in this boorish town—"

"Show them, or show me?"

"Honestly, Gray. You're so defensive. After all, there's precious little here for you if you'd only admit it. Tell me you don't miss the opera, the symphony, the plays. There's nothing—" her gaze swept the room pitilessly, "of . . . social value here."

Clell Miller picked that time to strip off his coat, unbutton his shirt, cup his hand beneath his armpit and pump, resulting in an obscene noise that sent Missy Parker into peals of mirth.

Francesca looked faint as the room erupted in laughter. Clell's mother swatted him, even though he was full grown.

"Some may be lacking in social graces, but they're warm and giving people," Gray said. "And they need me."

"Hah! Anyone would do. These people aren't picky."

"No, they need me," he insisted, knowing that he needed Dignity, and its people, as much as they needed his doctoring skills.

All in all, the party fell far short of Francesca's expectations.

The crowning blow came when Clarence Cole burst into his rendition of a song he had written, *Rooster in the Hen House, Hidey Ho,* while clicking spoons against his leg in a well-meaning, albeit disastrous, attempt to liven up the party.

Francesca's sour look turned rancid when Clarence asked the string quartet to jump in anytime they felt like it.

Francesca pouted the rest of the evening, leaving the social amenities to Gray. Around nine o'clock the guests started filing out of the hall.

Gray stood at the door, saying good night. They were gracious but unable to stifle their curious looks at Francesca who cloistered herself away in a remote corner.

Gray was embarrassed for her—and by her—but he kept his temper in check. What he'd really like to do was walk away from her. He was tired of constantly bowing to Louis and Francesca. All he wanted to do was be the best doctor he knew how in order to help the people of Dignity. Louis had no more interest in supporting his effort than Francesca.

The evening ended on a sour note. Decorations were stripped and packed into a carriage to be transported back to Boston. Wine and expensive chocolates were put back in boxes and cases to be used at a later time.

Quiver and arrows melted. Eros would not be slinging any love arrows tonight. And, more notably, the expected announcement of Francesca and Gray would not be announced.

"April, could you take the boys more of the elixir? And more pamphlets? They're so busy they don't have time to come get them."

"Of course, Mrs. Pinkham. Did you want me to go today?"

"If you don't mind. I'll have Charlie put the boxes in your carriage."

Within the hour Lydia's son Charlie had loaded the carriage, and April, making up yet another excuse to Riley why she would be gone for the day, was on her way to Boston. The sun was shining through the bare branches of maple trees. Her mind traveled back to the DuBois party the night before. It had been a grand affair, and she felt sorry for Francesca that people hadn't responded to her efforts.

"She obviously wanted to prove something to us," Porky had told her as they got their coats to leave.

"Such as?"

"That she's better than we are."

"Oh, Pork, I don't think so. I think she's only trying to fit in, and the town isn't helping any."

"You're too nice. She was playing queen to the peasants, and when we didn't drop to kiss her feet she got in a snit. I feel sorry for Dr. Fuller. He was embarrassed."

"He was . . . uncomfortable," April had had to admit.

The Fuller-DuBois engagement seemed wobbly at best. The whole alliance was puzzling. Gray and Francesca didn't fit together. They were oil and water, sugar and salt, vinegar and sarsaparilla. They just didn't go together. Some would say the same of her and Henry. Even she was having second thoughts at times. Henry didn't seem eager to commit himself to a wedding date, and she wasn't so sure she was ready either. He was beginning to look like the scoundrel others had warned her about.

April delivered the supplies to Dan and Will at their hotel. The building's interior was sad, dull, faded paper, the hallway poorly lighted. She was disappointed she'd missed Henry, yet strangely relieved. Will said he was out making contacts.

The encounter with Grace refused to leave her. At the oddest times she resented Henry, feeling as if he had betrayed her when in fact she didn't know that. She'd already made up her mind that when Henry returned to Dignity, she was going to come right out and confront him with Grace's strange accusation and let him assure her it was laughable. Perhaps then she could regain her former trust and affection for him.

"Do you need to get back right away?" Will asked.

"No, just as long as I return before dark. Why?"

"Could you take a few of these bottles to the Brown Pharmacy?"

Agreeing to make the delivery, April left the hotel shortly before noon. For the next hour, she window-shopped. It was a treat to be in the big city and not have to buy her clothes from a catalog. Purchasing new gloves and a soft cotton camisole, she left the store feeling good. There was nothing like a shopping trip to take a girl's mind off men.

When she realized it was noon, she went inside The Green Palm to have lunch. As she was being seated, it occurred to her that she was near Clara's, the café where she had encountered Grace three weeks earlier.

Glancing around the room, she was relieved to see she hadn't been followed.

This is silly. The woman made a mistake. Somewhere in the city there was a conniving man by the name of Henry who was toying with two women's affections. That man was not her Henry. *Her* Henry Trampas Long was at this moment walking the streets of Boston, intent on building a secure future for her.

No sooner had the thought left her mind than she sensed someone approaching her table. With a feeling of dread, she looked up to see Grace Pruitt coming toward her with a full head of steam.

"You!" Grace shouted.

Closing her eyes, April sank back in her chair. This was too much. What *was* it with this woman? Did she lurk around Boston eating establishments, waiting to see April pull into town? How did Grace know when she conducted business here? Uncanny luck?

"Please," April murmured, praying she wouldn't make a scene. Dressed the way the girl was, and Emogene's Pleasure Palace a block down the street, it didn't take a clairvoyant to guess her occupation. "You have me confused with somebody else—would you just please move on?"

April opened the large menu to hide behind it as Grace stopped at her table, pointing a bejeweled finger at her. "You conniving hussy!"

The noise in the room ceased, and everyone turned to look in her direction.

"Will you please lower your voice—"

"No! I told you to leave Henry alone, but you didn't listen. You continue to see Henry—and don't try to tell me you haven't because I have contacts—*reliable* contacts—who tell me different."

April stood up reaching for her cloak. The young woman was clearly deranged. She would not sit here and be subject to such humiliation.

"No, you don't, sister!"

Before April realized what was coming, Grace reached out and grabbed a handful of her hair.

Unable to move, April ordered through clenched teeth. "Let *go* of my hair."

Trying to hold on to her cloak and bag, she reached for Grace's arm to break her hold.

"Henry is mine!" Grace yanked April's hair hard,

bringing tears to her eyes and knocking the bag to the floor, spilling brown bottles of Pinkham compound.

Screaming, April wound a fist of Grace's hair in her hand and jerked, hard. The two women rolled to the floor, knocking over tables, skirttails flying.

"You have *obviously* made a mistake! My Henry is Henry Trampas Long!" April grunted, getting Grace around the neck and squeezing.

Grace tightened her grip on April's mane, yanking harder, dislodging her hat. It fell to the floor, pulling strands of loose hair with it.

"Henry Trampas Long is *my* Henry!" Grace gritted through clenched teeth. "And I want *you* to keep your lily-white hands off him!"

Tears spurted in April's eyes, and she saw stars as Grace continued to pull her hair out by the roots.

With her free hand, fingers curved like talons, Grace lunged for her face. Stumbling into a table, April tried to break her hold.

It didn't work. Grace shoved back, sending April sprawling over the bag of broken elixir bottles.

Scrambling to their feet, the women flew into each other engaged in a shrill, high-pitched squealing, hair-pulling fray. April's hat was squashed beneath thrashing feet. By now, the shocked patrons were on their feet, some running for the door; others spurring the antagonists on.

"Ladies! Ladies!" the proprietor shouted. His handlebar mustache stood straight out as he waded in to separate the two women.

"She's no lady!" Grace gasped, pinning April to the floor in a bruising headlock.

"Please—" the man pleaded, trying to pry the two women apart.

"Someone call a constable," April choked out, trying to break Grace's painful hold.

"Ladies, I insist you stop this!"

A couple of men on the sidelines stepped in to help.

Shaking them off, Grace stood like a spitting panther, glaring at April who was trying to pick herself off the floor.

"That woman is seeing my fiancé!"

"I am not! I don't know who your fiancé is!"

"Liar!"

"Idiot!"

Grandpa would *die* if he could see her now, but she wasn't about to let this . . . this trollop scratch her eyes out!

Straightening, Grace struck April across the cheek with a white glove.

April glared back at her, breathing heavily.

"I challenge you to a duel."

"A what?"

"A duel."

The men in the crowd shrank back with muffled oohhhs.

"A *what*?" April repeated, certain she'd misunderstood. Women didn't fight duels. Men did.

"You heard me right. A duel, sister! Saturday. Miller's Glen. Sunrise."

Grace's words refused to register. A duel? A duel?

April stood paralyzed with shock while everyone around her babbled with a mixture of consternation and humor.

Two women.

A duel!

Who'd ever heard of such a thing?

Someone took her by the arm as the constable arrived. Grace lunged again, making another attempt to get at her.

"Stop it! Right now!" the constable insisted.

Order was quickly restored. Overturned tables were set back in place as a couple of stout looking men led a still-spitting Grace out the front door.

"Miller's Glen, Saturday morning! You better be there or I'll come after you!"

"Ha," April muttered, trying to pin trailing strands of hair back into place. "You don't know where I live."

"I heard that! You live in Dignity!"

April hated Henry at that moment. Hated him with every fiber of her body. Wanted to tear his limbs off piece by agonizing piece. The awful truth came tumbling down on her. Henry had deceived her. Grace's Henry *was* her Henry. The same Henry Rotten Trampas Long who'd made her believe there was no other woman in the world but her.

With an apologetic glance at the café owner, the constable marched Grace out the front door. April could see him escort the woman back down the street to Emogene's Pleasure Palace.

"Are you all right, miss?"

Other than a few missing hairs and shattered composure, April wasn't hurt.

Leaving the café—humiliated and angry—April headed straight for Emogene's. Grace might knock her head off, but she wanted this straightened out.

A duel. Because of Henry, she was going to have to participate in a duel!

At the entrance to Emogene's Pleasure Palace, April paused, momentarily stunned by the gaudy wallpaper and brass fixtures in the entryway.

Glancing into the room on the right, her gaze ran disapprovingly over the bright-red pillows scattered across brocade couches and the richly carpeted floor.

She didn't want to think what the room was used for.

The heavy aroma of incense fogged her nose, and she sneezed.

Grace, hair askew, appeared in the doorway. Her eyes glittered dangerously when she saw the new arrival. "Get *out* of here."

"Miss Pruitt, I want to talk with you!"

An older woman appeared, gently pushing Grace aside. "Go on now. I'll take care of this."

April stood her ground. No whorehouse floozy was going to push her around. "I want to talk to Grace Pruitt."

"What do you want? You can't come in here causing trouble—"

"Trouble!" April blustered. "This . . . this woman, this 'person,' has challenged me to a duel!"

The woman's weathered face broke into a grin. "A duel is it? Well, now, that's different."

Grace sulked near the winding stairway, shooting venomous looks at April.

"Is this true, Grace? Did you challenge this lovely little thing to a duel?"

"She's been fooling around with my Henry."

April met her glare with a challenge of her own. "Had I known he was *your* Henry, I would have gladly given him to you."

"Now, ladies," the older woman purred. "Why don't we sit down and talk about this. Grace?"

Grace sat down at the small hallway table, watching April warily.

Turning to April, the older woman smiled politely. "I'm Emogene. Please sit down."

April did so, reluctantly, keeping a close eye on Grace.

"Let's talk about this. Whiskey?"

"I don't drink," April said. All she wanted to do was clear up the misunderstanding and go home. Porky wouldn't believe this in a hundred years.

Emogene was larger than life, three hundred pounds if she was an ounce. She was decked out in a garish floral gown in shades of pink and red that did nothing to hide her bulk. The vivid colors nearly matched her startling flaming-sunset hair.

"I didn't always look like this," Emogene said when she saw April perusing her. "I was a real looker as a girl. Even prettier than Grace here." She laughed, lighting a cheroot.

The smell reminded April of Gray, bringing an ache to her heart. What would he think when he heard of this hooligan encounter? Francesca, with her elegance and genteel social refinement, would never let herself get involved in such a row.

"Well, you might not drink usually, but I think the situation calls for a steady hand," Emogene said, snagging three glasses off a nearby shelf. "Drink up, ladies."

Grace downed her glass in one swallow, Emogene in three.

April sipped the amber liquid, wondering what she was doing sitting in a whorehouse, drinking with two strangers. She was certain that had not been her objective.

The strong drink burned her throat and made her eyes tear. By the time she started on the second glass, the whiskey was going down more easily.

"Now, tell me what this is all about," Emogene suggested.

"She thinks I stole her Henry," April accused.

"I don't think it, I know it," Grace stated, tossing another whiskey down.

"Ah, men. Aren't they wonderful," Emogene mused, pouring another shot in April's glass. "And what say you, April?"

"I say she's nuts."

Grace made a move to throttle her, but Emogene stuck

out a flabby arm. "Calm down, Grace. You know I've warned you about that temper." Emogene looked at April. "Cut off a man's privates one night in a fit of anger."

April didn't blink. "Too bad it wasn't Henry's."

Chuckling, Emogene restrained Grace.

"A duel. Is that right, Grace? Did you challenge this poor little mite to a duel?"

"I did, and she'd better show up."

"She accosted me in a public place," April said.

"In a public place?"

"The Green Palm. She slapped me and pulled my hair."

"Really, now. My lovely Grace did all that? In a public place?"

"And trampled my hat and broke my bottles of Lydia Pinkham's elixir," April added.

"What kind of elixir?"

"Lydia E. Pinkham's vegetable compound."

"Oh, yes, the elixir Henry sells." Emogene glanced up. "I like the stuff—it makes a body feel good."

April looked pleased. "You use it?"

"Yes, Henry keeps us supplied. Works for my girls." Emogene poured more whiskey all around.

"Your girls?" April was feeling better, more relaxed, as the liquid started to course through her veins. The room suddenly lost its garishness, and seemed almost striking, homey, actually.

"The girls—the ones who work here."

"Work here." April was having trouble focusing.

Emogene laughed. "Now, who is this man you're fighting over? Our Henry?"

"Henry Trampas Long," Grace stated. "My intended."

"He's *my* intended," April insisted, though she didn't want him anymore. Not after today. Not ever!

Emogene smiled over the rim of her glass. "If I know men, he's probably *every* woman's intended."

April blinked. "Do you think so?" Her head was spinning like a top.

"Don't you get it?" Grace spit out. "He's asked *both* of us to marry him!"

Comprehension dawned on April. Actually, Henry hadn't asked her—not exactly—but he'd certainly led her to believe he was going to.

She tried to focus on Grace. "Did he ask you?"

"Well—not officially, but he talked about how he was going to once he was established."

"The rat," April muttered, tossing another whiskey down.

"That's a man, my dears," Emogene said, as if she was an authority on the subject.

"He's *my* man," Grace said stubbornly.

"No," April contended, aware the whiskey was talking now. "He was mine first, Grace." She giggled. "We'll just have to share."

"He's a no-good, low-down bastard," Emogene said blithely, sipping her drink. "But he's a man, and, Grace, you've challenged April to a duel. What are you going to do about it?"

"I will meet her Saturday morning at sunrise," Grace said, rising. "Henry is my man, and I intend to fight for him."

April lurched to her feet. "Henry is my man," she slurred. Her tongue felt like it was twice its normal size. "And I'm going to fight for him, too." She didn't want Henry, but she did want to save face. After she shot Grace, she might aim at Henry!

Springing to her feet, Grace shouted. "Saturday morning, sister!"

"Miller's Glen!"

Oozing back down into her seat, April giggled. "Excuse me, I'm fainting now."

FIRST FOR BOSTON. TWO WOMEN TO DUEL OVER THE AFFECTIONS OF A LYDIA PINKHAM PITCHMAN.

April clipped the article out of newspaper, then quickly refolded the paper and lay it beside Riley's breakfast plate. There was no way she could prevent him from knowing about the duel, but she hoped to buy time—time to learn how to shoot. She also had to do everything possible to ward off a possible heart attack should her grandpa discover what she was up to.

Riley entered the dining room, yawning. Dappled rays of mellow sunshine dotted the freshly polished floor. Scents of lemon polish and bread baking permeated the room as he took his seat at the head of the table.

Snapping open the paper, his brows shot up in a puzzled frown.

April busied herself sprinkling brown sugar on her bowl of steaming oatmeal, careful not to look up.

"Dad burn it! Who's been tampering with my newspaper!"

Feigning innocence, she murmured, "What's wrong?"

Shuffling the pages, Riley impatiently searched through the rest of the paper. "Somebody's cut a hole in the front page!"

"No!" April was on her feet, peering over his shoulder indignantly. "Who would do such a thing?"

"I don't know, but when I find out they'll have a piece of my mind! Datha!"

Datha instantly appeared in the doorway. "Yes sir?"

"What the blue blazes happened to the front page of my newspaper?"

Datha frowned. "It's in your hand, sir."

"Someone's cut a hole in it!"

"Cut a hole?" Datha hurried around the table, her dark eyes wide with concern. "Why, sir, I can't imagine how that happened."

"Did Davy bring it to the door as usual?"

"As usual, Mr. Ogden. Said he picked it up shortly after it was delivered to the Emporium."

"Dad-blasted kids." Snapping the paper open, Riley grumbled under his breath as he tried to read around the gaping hole. "You tell Davy to be more careful in the future."

"Yes, sir, I'll do that."

Datha hurried back to the kitchen as April dropped back into her chair. One crisis over.

There weren't many in Dignity who subscribed to the Boston periodical. She only hoped Grandpa would be satisfied he hadn't missed anything important and drop the subject.

April spent the rest of her day in fear that another subscriber had seen the article about her and Grace and would tell Riley.

Once her head cleared, she had sent a note to Grace in an attempt to settle their dispute peacefully and to thank Emogene for hiring someone to drive her home.

By the time she had gotten back to Dignity, she was feeling rational again. She'd hoped the duel would be canceled once they both sobered up, but the note she received Monday from Grace informed her the duel was scheduled for Saturday at sunrise.

There was going to be a duel. If she didn't appear at the appointed hour, Grace would come here to Dignity to confront her.

The embarrassment would kill Riley. How could she face the people she'd known all her life if Grace arrived in Dignity and announced to the town that she was challenging April to a duel. Over a man?

Over Henry Long?

She had lain awake nights, worrying that Riley would find out what she was doing. The fact she'd been involved in a public row in a prominent Boston restaurant, cat fighting on the floor, would put him in a dither, and the thought of a duel, well, she'd rather not think about that.

Shortly after breakfast she cloistered herself away in Riley's library. Unlocking the large, oak gun case, she studied the weapons he'd used when he hunted as a young man.

Her gaze scanned the weapons dismally: a shotgun that was entirely unsuitable; a handgun that was much too large for her to use. Why, she could barely lift it, much less fire it.

After a moment, she realized she needed help—a man's help. The situation called for sensibility and sound mind, neither of which she possessed at the moment.

She could go to Eldon Ludwig, but he would be sure to go to Grandpa and tell him what she was doing. Ed Williams might help her, but Ed was old and his hands shook so badly, he couldn't hit the broad side of a barn. Besides, Willa didn't let Ed out of her sight long enough to tend to necessities, much less teach her how to shoot.

There were Fox Edwards and Layton Ross, but they would expect payment in the form of courtship, and that was unthinkable. She was seeing no one but Henry—

Henry.

An ache squeezed her heart when she thought of his betrayal. How could she have fallen so deeply for a man without morals? Porky had warned her about Henry's philandering ways, but she hadn't listened. Now look where she was. Forced to participate in a duel that might very likely take her life. According to Porky, a woman was as obligated to honor the challenge as a man. Just because participants wore skirts didn't matter.

After considerable thought, she knew the man she wanted to teach her the art of dueling.

Gray Fuller.

Gray, she felt certain, would not care to involve himself in the situation, but he was the only man she knew who had a stake in the outcome. As Riley's physician, he would want to see that she survived. Grandpa would suffer if his only granddaughter was shot and left to die on the battlefield.

Throwing a cloak around her shoulders, April called to Datha that she was going out and started off for the town square.

The cold November wind whipped her cape open, chilling her to the bone. Thanksgiving was approaching, and everywhere she looked, reminders adorned family doors.

Round, fat pumpkins donated by area farmers sat at the foot of shocks of cornstalks, some hollowed out so they could hold ears of dried corn. The aroma of apples cooking over open fires, apples soon to be thick sauce and creamy butter, scented the chilly air.

In November the residents of Dignity joined together to celebrate a bountiful season, to share and give thanks, to enjoy a time of respite from the hard work of their everyday lives. Church bells tolled at noon to offer praise for another year of peace and prosperity.

Ordinarily she would be thinking about a plump turkey, savory chestnut dressing, and sweet potato pie.

Today she was thinking about a duel.

Hers.

And Grace Pruitt's.

The irony of it suddenly hit her. Grace Pruitt and April Truitt.

At least Henry was consistent with his women's names.

Reaching Gray's office door, she hesitated, then, squaring her shoulders, went in.

The waiting room was empty and, for a moment, she feared he might be away on a call or upstairs in his living quarters.

Hoping that he was working and just hadn't heard the bell over the waiting room door, she moved quickly to his private office and rapped softly.

"Come in."

She hesitated, then turned the handle.

He was sitting behind a desk littered with papers and open ledgers. His eyes turned guarded when he saw her.

She'd never met a man who had such wonderful eyes. Sensuous, passionate— That wasn't what she was here for, but she couldn't shake the unmistakable feeling he stirred in the pit of her stomach.

"Do I need a gun?" he asked dryly, turning back to his paperwork.

He had every right to be leery of her, but not for the usual reason. She had to have his help far more than she needed to argue the pros and cons of medicine.

Now that she was here, her confidence plummeted. Standing in Grandpa's library, rationalizing that Gray would help her, was a far cry from actually standing in front of him asking for his help.

Getting to his feet, Gray stepped around her to the filing cabinet. "What brings you here, Miss Truitt?"

A picture of him half naked, clutching a towel around his middle—broad, masculine chest—flashed through her mind. Too bad she'd made such a mess of things. He'd never look at her as a woman now, or even regard her with respect. She should have lined up like all the other women in town vying for his attention instead of wasting her time and affections on Henry, the two-timer.

Shoving the image aside, she took a deep breath and began. "I'm in trouble."

His expression didn't change. "What kind of trouble?"

She felt a blush warm her cheeks. "Really big trouble."

Closing the file drawer, his smile was cool. "Do I need to examine you?"

April's blush deepened, and she realized she shouldn't have come. It was just too embarrassing. She'd insulted his profession, accused him of being thoughtless, uncaring, and a pretentious quack. Now she was here wanting his help.

She'd bungled things with Gray from their first meeting. Why on earth would he be willing to help her now?

"I shouldn't have come," she said, turning away. This was insane. She had no right to involve him in her problems. If she were foolish enough to believe in Henry, then she had to suffer the consequences.

Muttering a salty oath, Gray reached out and caught her hand. "I'm assuming this isn't a physical problem. Are you here to talk about a personal problem?"

"It's just that—"

Motioning toward the chair, he said softly, "Sit down, April. Tell me what you came here for."

He flashed her a smile, and she obediently sank into the chair. Walking around the desk, he sat down and lit a cheroot before leaning back in his chair, eyeing her speculatively. "What's troubling you?"

Swallowing, April studied her hands as she twisted the strings of her purse.

"Come now. April Truitt speechless?" He lifted his eyes, silently mouthing a grateful, "Thank you."

"I'm going to be in a duel Saturday morning," she blurted, ignoring his theatrics.

His lips sagged, wilting the cheroot. "You're *what*?"

"I've been challenged to a duel. Henry's been seeing another woman in Boston, and she's challenged me to a duel."

He simply stared at her, the cheroot drooping comically to one side. At least she knew she had his complete attention for once.

When he continued to just stare, she shifted in her seat, uneasy. "Don't look at me that way. I know it's insane, but it's true, and I need your help."

The legs of his chair hit the floor with a loud smack. "You cannot be serious."

"I assure you, I am. Quite serious." Deadly serious. She again twisted her purse strings. "The problem is, I don't know . . . exactly . . . what this all means."

"Dammit!!" Gray exploded, jumping to his feet to pace. "What have you done now?"

"I'm not sure. It certainly wasn't something I did intentionally. This . . . this Grace person—one of Emogene's girls—accosted me while I was having dinner in Boston two days ago. There I am, enjoying my treat, having passed out pamphlets and delivering compound, and out of the blue, she marches over to me and challenges me to a duel."

Gray stood in the middle of the room, puffing on the cheroot, glaring at her.

She averted her eyes, willing to give him time to adjust. After all, the ramifications hadn't completely sunk in, yet.

"You can't fight a duel—I've never heard of two women fighting a duel!"

He was blustering, but blustering was good. Once a

man blustered his system thoroughly clean, then he thought more clearly.

"You have now," she said.

Striding back and forth, he drew on the cheroot. She could tell he was thinking. Not what he was thinking, but thinking was good.

"Who in the *hell* is this woman in Boston?"

"Her name is Grace Pruitt . . . I remember that only because her name was so near mine. Grace Pruitt, April Truitt?"

He glared at her again.

"Other than that, I don't remember much about that day, other than the fact that she said we were to meet in Miller's Glen at sunrise, Saturday."

He ceased pacing. "*This* Saturday?"

"This Saturday."

"Hell." Removing the cheroot from his mouth, he asked. "Does Lydia know about this?"

April sat up straighter. "Lydia had nothing to do with this. I was simply standing there minding my own business—"

"When a woman comes over and challenges you to a duel."

"No, a woman came over, announced her name was— *is* Grace Pruitt, said she was Henry's intended and knew I was seeing Henry, and she takes off her gloves and—"

"Slaps you across the left cheek."

She nodded. "She claims to be Henry's fiancée."

"What does Henry claim?"

"I haven't spoken to Henry about the matter. He's away in Brooklyn on business." Or so he said.

She suddenly knew he wasn't on business there, either. If she were to go to Brooklyn, she'd probably have another duel to fight. The thought made her ill. To think she once trusted the snake.

"She demanded I stop seeing Henry immediately. When I told her she had no right to demand anything of me, she, well . . . hit me."

"Hit you?"

"Yes, and I hit her back." Her hand absently touched the slight discoloration on her right cheek. "And pulled her hair."

Gray leaned forward slightly to examine the injury. "This is ludicrous, you know that."

"I know." What was more ludicrous was the way goose bumps suddenly showed themselves when he bent close to her.

Why, she was no better than Grace!

Here she was, getting gooseflesh over a man engaged to another woman. It was disgraceful, and she should be ashamed of herself.

"I'm not sorry for what I did," she said.

"Well, you should be." He jammed the cheroot back into his mouth.

"I'm afraid we got into a brawl. A constable was called, and we had to be separated." She covered her face with both hands. "It was humiliating." She wasn't going to mention she got drunk in a whorehouse and had to be driven back to Dignity.

"Hell." He sank into his chair, drawing on the cigar. "What about Riley?"

"He'll know. There's no way he can't, but for now he isn't aware of the situation."

It broke April's heart to think Henry frequented the establishment, but he had. And far more often than she wanted to consider.

Leaning back in his chair, Gray stared at the ceiling. He had warned Henry that he was playing a dangerous game. Now it seemed Henry had sold both women short.

If there was anything Gray had learned about women in his nearly thirty years it was that they never fit a pattern. Just when you were certain they would do something, they did something entirely different.

Witness the situation now before him with April.

Somehow "Amazing Grace" had discovered "Angel Face" and decided to take out the competition. It would be thoroughly amusing if it wasn't a matter of life and death. April had no idea what this all meant. It was easy to see she was nervous and confused, and he knew how naive she was when it came to men. He'd pegged Henry as a gutless slime when he came in whining about his toe, bragging about stringing two women along.

Gray cringed. He'd been stringing Francesca along, but he'd also kept his hands off other women. Except at the dance. Not Francesca's fiasco, but the one where he'd held April in his arms on the dance floor and liked it all too well. Still, he hadn't led her to believe it was more than a dance, even though he wished he could.

The relationship with Francesca was over, all except telling her—that part he dreaded, knowing the fit of rage she'd fly into, not to mention her denial. She never knew when something was over.

Right now April needed him in a way Francesca never would, and the idea appealed to him. He knew he'd help her.

But a duel?

Only April could get herself in such a fix. She was stubborn. He'd seen it all too often, and he knew with him, or without him, she'd meet the challenge. She had no choice, but he did.

Bringing the legs of his chair back to the floor, Gray's brows raised. "All right, what do you want me to do?"

Her heart fluttered when she realized he was offering

to help without her having to beg. She felt something very close to warmth—closer to love, seep through her.

"I'll have to do it. It's a matter of honor, isn't it?"

"With a man it is."

"It's the same with a woman. Porky's been looking into it for me. I have to do it. The problem is, I don't know how."

"To duel?"

"I don't know what's involved, how that sort of thing works."

"Hell—April, surely you aren't seriously thinking about going through with it?"

April blinked in surprise. "I don't have a choice."

"Of course you do!"

"You mean, back out? Just not show up? That would be cowardly in a man, wouldn't it?"

"Back out, just don't show up—run like hell. Dammit, you're a woman, you're not a man."

Stubbornness glinted in her eyes. "I can't do that."

"Why not?"

"It would be a disgrace. Porky said so."

"Porky's now an authority on duels?"

"No, but she's been studying the subject. I didn't even know what a duel was. Of course, I'd heard of them, but I never paid any real attention to the procedure. But after the front page article in the Boston paper this morning, I knew this matter wasn't just going away as I'd hoped—"

"It's in the *paper*?"

April winced at his tone. He was angry with her, as he should be. She, at the moment, was angry at herself. "It isn't as if she challenged *you*. She challenged me."

"You've lost your mind! You can't participate in a duel! You'll get yourself killed, Miss Truitt. Shot. Dead." He took an impatient puff of the cigar. "Even the compound won't bring you back."

"Very funny."

"I'm serious; you'd better listen to me."

"Well, at the moment, I can't. I don't know how to shoot a gun. That's why I'm here. I'd hoped you'd teach me." She looked up, swallowed, then glanced away. "Before Saturday."

Shock registered on his handsome features. "You don't know how to shoot a gun?"

She nodded miserably. "I don't. Not even an inkling. Never had an occasion to use one."

Not even an inkling? That came as a surprise. She'd gotten herself into a real mess this time.

If Grace Pruitt was one of Emogene's girls, she knew how to shoot a gun. She would be damn good with one! He'd heard all of those girls were good with a gun. But he couldn't shatter what little confidence April had by telling her she was out-matched. It would take all he could do to teach her how to shoot, but it might do her some good to stew about his decision for a while.

"I'm sorry, I know I shouldn't involve you in my problems, but you're the only one I can trust with this . . . rather weighty matter."

Circling the desk, Gray drew on the cigar. She could see he was sorting through his options: throw her out on her ear, refuse to help, go straight to Riley and inform him of his granddaughter's lunacy, shoot her himself, or agree to help.

In the end, he did what any red-blooded man would do. He told her he had to think about it.

Getting to her feet, she prepared to leave. She could see there was no use appealing to his protective nature. He had none when it came to her. She could only hope his friendship with Riley would tip the scales in her favor.

"You will let me know as soon as your decision's

made?" Wincing, she added, "Saturday's only a few days away."

Walking to the window, he angrily drew on the cheroot. Great puffs of white rose like cumulus clouds around his head as he stared broodingly outside.

She took his silence to mean he was thinking.

For a man, it was a good sign.

"One more thing," April said, her hand on the door. "Grace said if I didn't show up at Miller's Glen, she'd come to Dignity and hunt me down."

Chapter 14

By noon the following day, Gray searched her out. She was embarrassed he'd found her in yet another peculiar situation.

Her predicament this morning could be explained quite simply, were he to ask, which she was reasonably sure he wouldn't.

She'd been crawling around on the floor in the sanctuary, brushing stray daisy petals into a dustpan from around the base of Jefferson Teal's casket. The florist was careless when he delivered the elaborate floral display, and she was left to tidy up.

As she'd maneuvered around the wooden coffin, she suddenly stood up, inadvertently snagging the sleeve of her dress on the corner of the coffin.

Yanking lightly at the fabric, she gasped as the sudden, jerking motion sent the lid slamming down in poor deceased Jefferson's face.

Sinking to her knees. she tried to loosen the sleeve pinned inside the casket without tearing it. The lid·had her staked to the floor like a wrestler.

She was behind the coffin, partially hidden by a large bouquet of yellow mums, when Gray appeared in the parlor doorway looking for her.

As his gaze searched the empty parlor, she stooped lower, hoping he wouldn't see her.

"April?"

Crouching lower, she listened to the sound of her own breathing.

"Datha, she isn't in the parlor," Gray called. "Do you know where she is?"

"She was there a moment ago," Datha called from the kitchen. "Maybe she went outside. She'll be back; just sit down and keep Jefferson company."

April could hear Datha's good-natured laugh as she went out the back door to hang wash.

Gray took a seat in the front row of chairs, crossing his hands in his lap as he waited, his eyes casually roaming around the room.

The moments ticked by and April realized he wasn't going to leave. Not soon, anyway, and her leg was starting to cramp from the position she was in. She was going to have to speak up and just be embarrassed that he'd caught her in yet another foolish circumstance.

Taking a deep breath, she gritted her teeth and said in a small voice. "Help me?"

Gray's eyes snapped to the casket.

When he didn't immediately get up, she repeated more loudly. "Don't just sit there, help me. I can't get up!"

The way she was pinned, it was impossible for her to move without toppling the casket—something, she was sure, he wouldn't want her to do.

When the silence stretched, she wondered if he had possibly mistook her voice for Jefferson's.

The idea made her giggle. With a little thought, she could have some fun with the stuffy doctor.

"Hey, Doc, open the blasted lid!" she parroted in a gruff voice. Then in her best grumpy "Jefferson" voice, "It's hot as blue blazes in here—oh, wait—maybe I'm not in here—maybe I'm in blue blazes!"

Suddenly aware of censuring eyes on her, she glanced up. Gray was leaning over the casket, staring at her.

"Hi." She grinned, pointing at her sleeve. "Snagged it." He stared at her.

"Can you . . . open the lid?"

"I suppose I'm capable of that."

When he didn't, she looked up again, irritated. "Today?"

Unlatching the lid, he lifted it. Hurriedly releasing her sleeve, she slipped around the casket, jerking free the scarf she'd worn to protect her hair. A mass of gold colored hair tumbled down her back, reaching nearly to her waist. Quickly pinching color into her cheeks, she turned around. "What brings you here?" When he looked as if he was about to ask her how she'd gotten herself in that position, she rushed on, "I hope you've come to . . ."

Her voice trailed off as they heard Riley coming in the back way.

Moving quickly to the parlor doors, she drew them shut. Turning back, she whispered, "I hope this means you've decided to help me."

"I've thought about it."

"And?" She held her breath. If he refused to help her, she didn't know what she would do.

"If you insist on going through with this, I'll help you."

She closed her eyes, lightheaded with relief. "What do you want me to do?"

"Nothing. A duel requires two weapons alike so each opponent has an equal chance. Since Grace challenged you, you have your choice of weapons. In this case, guns. You'll need a second."

"Second?" The term was new to her.

He drew a deep breath and stared at the ceiling a long moment as if he couldn't believe she was doing this.

"In a duel, it is customary for the two principals to have 'seconds.' Someone they trust, and someone who is willing to stand in for them in case something should happen. If the opponent doesn't show up, the second must stand in."

"As long as I show up, the second is in no danger?"

Gray sobered. "The danger will be all yours."

Good, she thought, because the only person she'd ever really trusted was Porky, but she would never put Porky at risk. She laughed to herself when she thought how Porky reacted to her story. Once Porky had finished her lecture on Henry and how stupid she'd been by not listening to her advice, Porky had become excited!

Well, Porky was Porky. She was worried, of course, but to be personally involved in the scandal really tickled her. She'd tried to tell Porky she wasn't personally involved, but Porky said whatever involved her best friend, involved her as well.

Porky was her friend; she vowed to see April through it. And April knew she couldn't keep Porky away from Miller's Glen Saturday if her life depended on it. And her life did.

"We'll begin shooting lessons immediately."

"Good . . . when?"

"Before dawn tomorrow morning, behind the livery stable. Joe will let us practice on the back side of his land. We shouldn't draw attention there."

"And you'll bring the gun?"

"I'll bring the gun. You just show up."

She turned to reopen the parlor doors, then suddenly

turned back again. "Thank you . . . I don't know what I would have done if you had refused to help me."

A suggestion of annoyance hovered in his eyes. "Riley would never forgive me if I let something happen to you."

Riley. Of course. That was the only reason he was willing to help her.

She reached for the handle on the doors.

"April?"

"Yes?"

"What about Henry?"

She didn't turn around. "What *about* Henry?"

"Apparently this woman in Boston believes she's engaged to him. What does he say about this sticky matter?"

"I haven't spoken to Henry about it. I don't care if I ever speak to him again."

"What if this woman's accusations are false?"

Still not meeting his eyes, she said softly, "I don't think they are. She knows too much about me for them not to be true."

"Well, not everything in life is candy. Sometimes we find out the hard way."

Turning around, she leaned against the door, meeting his gaze. "Henry and I grew up together. I didn't really care for him that much in school. We played tag, swung on swings behind the school, shared our dinner pails, but never once did I look at Henry romantically.

"Porky, on the other hand, never liked him, but I thought he was just different." She smiled. "How could I not? He read poems to me, he was always careful about how he spoke in my presence, how he dressed. He made trips to Boston, but I thought it was—" She shrugged, wishing she'd listened to Porky. "I believed him. Work, buying books, that's what he told me his life consisted of when he went out of town. Instead, he was seeing other women."

Gray's voice, deep and sensual, sent a ripple of awareness through her. "He calls her 'Amazing Grace.' "

His words hurt, but the pain gradually eased into resigned acceptance. "I didn't know that." She glanced up. "How did you?"

"He told me. Weeks ago when he came to me for treatment."

Her eyes saddened. "You knew he was seeing someone else?"

"I wanted to tell you, but I didn't know how."

"Oh." She thought about it and realized it would be a difficult subject to address. "He called me Angel Face."

He pulled her gently to him and held her for a moment. She felt his gaze, which was as sensitive and powerful as he was. Resting her cheek against his chest, she thought how nice it was to be in his arms. He felt good, warm and strong, exactly what she needed. She hoped Francesca appreciated him.

"You're not the first woman to be deceived by a man."

"It's the first time for me."

His hand tenderly moved up and down her back in a comforting motion while tears rolled unchecked down her cheeks. She wished she could stay like this forever. Gray made her feel safe and secure, as if he would always protect her and make everything all right. His heart beat against her ear, and she relished the warmth of his embrace. If he were available, she'd never let him go.

She left his arms only when she heard Riley approaching the parlor.

"I'll see you in the morning," he said.

"I'll certainly be there."

* * *

April was up before five o'clock. Dressing warmly, she slipped out the back door and hurried through town. She refused to let herself think. If she did, she wouldn't go through with the duel.

Because the sun wasn't up yet, Dignity was still asleep. A lone wagon rattled across the square on its way out of town.

She reached the livery and walked way to the back of the property. Gray was already there, positioning bottles in a long, straight row on an old log.

"Good morning," she called.

She'd laid awake half the night, worrying about the duel, afraid Riley would hear about it and discover she was one of the two "fools" involved.

She was extremely worried about Grandpa, and losing her life to the "Painted Lady," but she couldn't shake the feelings she was having about Gray. His embrace said he cared, his eyes had reflected sympathy. Was she reading more into this, or did he have feelings for her?

With Gray it was hard to tell, but he was here ready to help, which was more than she deserved.

Barely glancing in her direction, he continued working. "I see you still intend to do this."

"Yes."

"You're likely to get yourself killed. At the very least, seriously hurt," he warned.

April swallowed against the tight knot in her throat. "I know."

He paused, his gaze skimming her lightly. "It would be far wiser to be made a fool of than killed."

"I've thought of that." She'd thought of little else, but she wouldn't back down now. Her honor was at stake, and Lord knew she had little left. Henry had seen to that.

"Then think again, carefully," he prodded with an odd gentleness in his voice.

"I've thought of nothing else, but I haven't changed my mind. I have to do this—for myself."

His gaze rested on her for several moments. How glorious his eyes were, so compelling, so penetrating, as if he could see to the bottom of her soul. He had a manner that encouraged confidence and hope. How many wanted to be held in his arms as he'd held her yesterday?

"Then permit me to explain what you've gotten yourself into. It will give you some idea of how important it is that you learn how to handle a pistol well."

April settled herself primly on a log and adjusted her bonnet. "I'm listening."

"In the first place, dueling is against the law. It has been since 1839. Anyone found dueling, and surviving, can be tried for murder or manslaughter. Do you understand that? If you happen to win, you could be imprisoned for murder or executed."

"I understand," she whispered, hoping she got that far. "Go on."

"A duel is generally to draw blood. I can't speak for Grace's intent, so we will be prepared for any occurrence. The French used to be satisfied with a wound to end a duel, but the Americans tend to duel to the death. I want you to think about that."

Squirming, she smoothed her dress. To the death. It was so far-fetched, she couldn't associate herself as a participant. It was as if he were talking about someone else.

"Is that your understanding of a duel?"

"I—I didn't think about it." She straightened her shoulders. "I wasn't the one who did the challenging. If I don't show up Saturday morning, Grace has assured me she'll come here to Dignity and call me out. If she does, then Grandpa will hear about it and . . . well, then I might as well be dead."

"You'd rather die than embarrass your grandfather?"

"Aren't you listening? Grace will come here after *me*. It's to my advantage to face her in Boston, rather than have her come here and shoot at me in front of Grandpa."

Gray shook his head. "This is insane."

"Men have it easier," she pointed out. "When they're challenged to a duel, you don't see them making a big fuss over it. They just do it. That's how I intend to handle this situation."

"Just do it."

A cold knot formed in her stomach at the thought. "That's right. Just do it."

Impatient green eyes pierced the distance between them. "I have two pistols. They are as much alike as I could find. When you meet Grace, she'll have first choice of the weapon. Her second will examine the pistol to make sure it's loaded and not tampered with."

She pressed her lips together, waiting.

"When you meet Grace, you will both hold your choice of pistols, stand back to back, then march a specified number of paces. The seconds drop a handkerchief, the two of you turn quickly, and fire at one another. To seize the advantage, you must be calm and steady, don't flinch, hold your pistol evenly and pull the trigger, not jerk it. Understand?"

April nodded, though her thoughts were still on the notion she could die as a result of this foolishness.

"These are breech-loading pistols. Safer than most. Smith and Wesson developed a brass cartridge a few years ago that makes firing them safer. Now, this is the barrel, this is the chamber that holds the bullets. When you fire, hold the pistol at arm's length"—he demonstrated—"but don't lock your elbow. Keep it slightly bent to absorb the shock. That way you'll be more likely to hit what you're shooting at. Close one eye and aim down the barrel. See that nib at the end? That's how you sight in your target."

Sight in? Nib?

"I warn you, when you're dueling, you don't have time to think about doing all that. It has to be second nature for you. Like breathing. Now, let's see how you handle the gun, then we'll try a little target practice."

She stood and he handed the gun to her. She almost dropped it.

"Careful!"

"It's heavier than I thought."

"Get used to the feel of it. Rule one, never point a gun at anyone, never assume a gun is unloaded, and never walk with your finger on the trigger. Unless you're in a duel. Then walk off your paces with your finger on the trigger. It may give you a hairsbreadth of advantage."

"All right. I understand."

"Now, lift it, keeping your arm straight."

Gray stepped behind her. She could feel the warmth of his body pressed against her as she lifted the gun, keeping her arm straight.

"Don't lock your elbow. Keep it slightly bent."

"Like this," she breathed, aware of the unbelievable touch of his fingers against her arm to indicate how she should bend her elbow.

"Sight down the barrel. Move it around, keeping your right eye on the nib. Forget this is a metal object. Make the gun an extension of your arm."

His warm breath caressed her cheek, and she struggled to concentrate. She hadn't counted on body contact or smelling that scent of his that made her head swim.

"A part of your arm," he reminded her. "Point at the bottom limb on the tree. See it?"

"Yes."

"See that knothole to the right of it?"

"Yes."

"Now, point at one of those bottles on the log over there."

"All right."

"Got it?"

Gray sighted down her arm, his chin nearly resting on her shoulder. He stood very close, his body fitted tightly against her, his arm stretched along hers until his hand folded over her hand on the grip of the pistol.

"Ready?"

She nodded. "Won't someone hear the shots, and wonder what's going on?"

"Don't worry. I left word at the livery that I would be target shooting."

His hand was large and warm as it enveloped hers, his finger wrapped around the trigger guard.

"Squeeze the trigger, slowly."

April pulled the trigger.

The morning shattered with a resounding crack that made her jump, the kick against her hand throwing her arm straight up. She would have fallen back a step if Gray wasn't there to catch her.

"Oh, Lordy!" She clapped a hand to her ear.

"Now you know what it sounds and feels like."

"Did I hit anything?"

He laughed. "No, but you will."

A flush warmed her cheeks. At least he had faith in her.

"Now we'll learn to hit an object and not jerk your arm when you fire."

For the next two hours Gray made her fire the gun over and over and over, until her head rang with the sound of pistol shot.

Again and again he taught her how to stay limber, her

arm straight but not tense, how to squeeze the trigger and not jerk it.

"Ready to hit a real object?"

"I'm ready to hit *anything*, but I can hardly pick up the gun," she protested, the muscles in her arm aching.

"Try hitting that bottle over there."

Very carefully, April sighted down her arm, lined up the nib on the barrel, and slowly squeezed the trigger.

Unfortunately, she hadn't mastered the technique of adjusting for the kick of the gun and her arm shot up again—and a squirrel fell out of the tree, knocking over two of the bottles.

She stood with her mouth gaping in shock.

Gray suddenly bent over laughing.

"Squirrel stew for dinner tonight," she murmured, half laughing, half wanting to cry.

To her relief, he put the matter aside with good humor. "Watch your aim. I want to be able to eat my stew tonight."

"I've had enough," she pleaded, sinking onto a log. Her arm ached, her hand hurt, she was half deaf, and her nose burned from the stench of sulfur.

"We'll take a short break," Gray conceded. "I brought cold meat and biscuits."

She wanted to go home, take a bath, put on fresh clothes, and forget this whole thing, but it seemed Gray was taking his job seriously.

"You went to all the trouble to cook?"

Giving her a caustic glance, he muttered. "I have enough food in my kitchen on any one day to never cook again."

"Ah, the single women in Dignity still pursuing you?"

He didn't answer as he dug into a satchel.

Stretching, she yawned. "I'm exhausted."

"If you don't learn this by Saturday, you'll be more than tired."

She took the biscuit he handed her and nibbled on it. For someone about to face death, her appetite was small.

Gray took two cups and dipped fresh, cold water from the stream that marked the limit of Joe's property.

"Shooting always looked so easy."

Sitting down next to her on the log, he started to eat. She tried not to stare at him, but he looked unusually handsome this morning. The suit was missing, his legs were encased in twill trousers, his feet in well-worn boots, his white broadcloth shirt open at the neck. Sometime during the morning he'd thrown aside his coat, though the breeze was chilly. She liked him this way, casual and rugged.

"Nothing's ever easy."

"You make it look easy," she said, fighting the tight swelling in her throat. The last thing she wanted to do was cry in front of him. The decision to go ahead with the duel was her choice; he was only trying to help.

"Only because a man considers a gun as part of himself."

She looked up into the gray sky that resisted the efforts of an early winter sun to break through. "I don't think I can do it."

"Yes, you can. Just remember, if you fire the first shot, you'll more than likely get the only shot. Aim for a shoulder, or Grace's shooting arm."

The thought of shooting someone—actually firing a bullet at another living being—made her queasy. Laying the biscuit aside, she took a drink from her cup.

When the meal was over, Gray reloaded the pistol.

"Remember what I've told you—"

"Aim straight, elbow slightly bent, firm grip but not tense, sight, squeeze."

His eyes swept her approvingly. "Good. You're a quick learner."

She did as told, but again the pistol kicked straight upward and, this time, hit a tree. Splinters of wood showered down upon them as a dead limb separated from the trunk and fell at her feet.

"Well," Gray grinned, "you wounded a limb."

After a moment, she got the joke and scowled at him. Striking out with her left hand, she planted a fist in the middle of his chest.

"Stop making fun of me."

He grabbed her arm. "I'm not making fun of you. I'm trying to save your life, pretty lady."

Pretty lady? His words sang through her veins like warm honey. He sounded like Henry, plying her with pretty words and provocative smiles to win favors, but he was much more handsome, his voice more sincere. But she'd never allow herself to be played for a fool again.

Tilting her chin up with the tip of his finger, he said quietly, "It's not too late to back out."

April refused to look at him, afraid she'd melt and lose what self-restraint she had left. "I want to, I honestly do, but I can't."

Something perversely headstrong deep inside told her if she didn't go through with it, she would always feel as if she'd failed herself. She wouldn't be Grandpa's granddaughter if she didn't want to do things right.

"If Riley were to find out what you're planning, he would forbid you to do it."

She lifted her eyes, meeting his. A deep understanding passed between them, and she hoped her trust in him was not misplaced.

"I'm asking you not to say anything to him. It would only upset him, and it wouldn't change anything."

"That's your decision, then. You're going to do what

you must. You'll be there, fully prepared Saturday morning, and you'll face your enemy."

Her confidence wavered again. "I don't think I can—"

"Yes," he whispered gently, gazing deep into her eyes, "you can."

When he bent slightly, his lips brushed hers. Her knees buckled at the sweetness of it. As his lips opened into hers, she invited him in. The butterflies in her stomach took full flight, and she felt a passion she'd never felt before. Gray's kiss made Henry seem like a schoolboy.

When the kiss deepened, she surrendered to it completely, letting her free arm drift over his shoulder, and she allowed the moment to absolve fear and fill her with unexpected need. He made her feel wanted, awakening every inch of her feminine body, sending chills all the way to her toes.

Her hand roamed his muscled back and she heard a low, muffled groan, then felt his hand press tighter against the small of her back. Her heart raced and her head spun. The good doctor knew exactly what he was doing . . . and if he didn't stop soon, she'd be his first patient of the day.

Ever so slowly, he ended the kiss and straightened.

As her eyes slowly drifted open, she saw he'd been as affected by the moment as she. His breathing was a bit irregular, his eyes soft and admiring. No, he wasn't playing with her, he wanted her. A shiver of pride swept through her. The handsome Doctor Gray, talk of the town, wanted April Truitt?

No, she must be mistaken. He had his fancy "Frenchie," and she had slimy Henry who was about to get her killed. Whatever his kiss meant, she'd enjoyed it, but she wasn't about to fall for the man. If Francesca found out he'd kissed her, she'd have a second duel to fight, and she could only die once!

Clearing his throat, he stepped back. "Let's work on your aim again."

"Yes," she managed. His kiss had reached depths of her that she hadn't known existed, but it was time to get serious. She'd come to shoot, not to start another disastrous relationship with a man she couldn't have.

They spent the next hour ignoring the nagging attraction. Try as she might, April couldn't hit the target bottles, and it wasn't because she kept forgetting to compensate for the gun's kick. Gray's presence was distracting. The ground around her was littered with shell casings, the stench of powder hung heavy in the air. Even when he spoke directly into her ear, she could barely hear him.

For the next three mornings, they worked on her aim.

Her back ached with tension, her arm with the weight of the gun, her hand stung from its kick, and her ears had a constant ring from the sound of gunfire. She had managed not to kill any more squirrels, or knock down any more tree limbs, but she had yet to hit three bottles in a row.

While Gray still stood close behind her to support her or to direct her aim, they were careful to keep their touches brief and impersonal—though she found herself hoping there would be more, then angry with herself for hoping.

Why was her thinking so irrational? Gray was her friend, a good, steady friend, one who was helping her meet the biggest challenge of her life.

He was engaged to be married to another woman. It was frivolous of her to wish for more. At times she longed for the days when she didn't like him. They'd been easier.

*   *   *

On the fourth morning, when she'd managed to hit three bottles in a row, Gray looked at his pocket watch and said regretfully. "I think I've done all I can." He took the gun out of her limp hand. "It's been a good practice."

He commented on her accuracy, but there wasn't the sense of celebration she'd expected. Somehow she felt disappointed.

"I'm sorry, I realize how much time you're taking away from your patients. Is there anything I can do to help you catch up?"

"No, but thank you for the offer. I was due a few hours off. I've been seeing patients afternoons and evenings."

She recalled seeing the light on in his office late Tuesday night when she and Porky had walked home from choir practice. Because of her, he had to work long hours to compensate for his absence during the day.

He picked up the spent shells, and she helped. "I don't know how to thank you, Gray. If I make it through this . . . well, we both know it will be a miracle, but I wouldn't have a chance if it weren't for you."

"I wish you would reconsider, April."

"I can't, but thank you for caring."

Their gazes met, and she felt a sense of peace wash over her. No matter what happened, it would be worth it for the hours she'd had with him.

"I'll walk you back home."

Silence fell between them. Talk wasn't necessary. They'd said a lot in the four days, nothing earthshaking or substantial, just nice, easy conversation. So much different than her stilted, superficial discussions with Henry.

When they reached Main Street, she suddenly paused, staring at the black surrey with the matching team of black horses coming down the street.

Francesca. She was back for her monthly visit.

Steeling herself against the spurt of jealousy she didn't want to feel, she casually let her hand drop from his.

"I have to go. Grandpa will be wondering where I am."

"Tell Riley I'll stop by the mortuary later," he murmured.

April followed Gray's gaze to the vehicle, which had drawn to a stop in front of his office. Francesca, wrapped in a dark cloak—probably cashmere, stepped delicately down with the help of her driver.

"Gray . . . Francesca is your fiancée . . . isn't she?"

"That's what they tell me," he said curtly.

Smiling, she squeezed his hand. "You can't believe everything you hear."

"Chéri," Francesca enthused as Gray approached her. "I have come to invite you to a party!"

"Another party? Couldn't you have asked when I come to Boston next week?"

"Ah," she said, linking her arm with his as he unlocked the door to his waiting room, "it is so much nicer issuing an invitation in person, *oui*? Besides, this is a most important party." As they entered the waiting room, she sighed with pleasure. "I do like this room now—but I like upstairs so much better."

"I wish you would let me know when you're coming." He removed her hand from his arm. "I am so far behind, I can't spare time for a party."

"Seeing you is never wasted, darling."

How many times had they discussed this before? A dozen? Two dozen? She refused to respect his work.

"Oui, darling, you are in a most foul temper." Affecting a flirtatious pout, she urged him toward the door, to the outside staircase, leading to his room.

"Come now, let Francesca make it better." Smiling,

she leaned closer, the scent of her French perfume
provocative.

"Francesca will make you very happy, *mon chéri*—so
very very happy."

Chapter 15

Datha stared out the kitchen window, biting her knuckles until she tasted blood. A cold rain pelted the windowpane, but she was oblivious to the weather change.

Jacel had said he was careful, said he knew how to keep things like this from happening.

What had gone wrong?

She was two weeks late. *Two* weeks late with her monthlies. Every morning she woke up with dread in her heart, praying—oh, God, praying so hard!—for that telltale ache in her belly, but it wouldn't come. Thinking she might be mistaken, she'd hurry to the necessary and clean herself over and over, hoping to find blood.

But this morning she had given up hoping. The awful truth was the awful truth. She didn't know much about babies, but she knew the symptoms, and she sure enough had them. She was pregnant.

A rap sounded at the door, and she jumped. Angrily swiping at hot tears, she went to answer. Her face crumpled when she saw Jacel standing before her, all smiles, like his world wasn't just about to come crashing in on him.

Grinning broadly, he handed her a basket filled with the last of the vegetables from his garden. "Hello, Datha, darling."

He frowned when he saw she'd been crying.

"What's the matter?" His eyes anxiously darted around, looking for Flora Lee.

"Jace . . ." A lump the size of a hedge apple clogged her throat. How was she ever going to tell him? As careful as he'd been, the worst had happened. She couldn't be pregnant! Not when he was about to go off to college and be somebody!

All his dreams, all his hopes of becoming a fine lawyer someday would be gone—disappeared in the blink of an eye. Because of her, he'd be forced to abandon his plans for Harvard, disappointing Mr. Ogden, who had so much faith in him. The knowledge broke her heart.

She was having his baby, and he'd think he'd have to stay here and take care of her. He'd insist on owning up to his responsibility, and she was proud he was such a man, but it was unfair.

So unfair!

And Mama? Dear Lord, what would Mama say when she found out she was carrying his baby? Fear constricted her throat, nearly suffocating her. She caught back a sob. Her life was hopeless, over.

Extending the basket to her, Jacel's dark eyes searched her face anxiously. "I thought Miss April would like these this morning. What's wrong, Datha? Are you feeling poorly?"

Oh, if only she were! What she wouldn't give for the agonizing monthlies that hurt so bad sometimes, she had to crawl into bed with a hot cloth wrapped around her middle to ease the pain.

Accepting the basket, Datha held it as if she didn't know what to do with it. She didn't trust her voice to speak.

"Put that on the table and come with me," Jacel said.

Now she'd done it. He realized something more than Flora Lee was bothering her.

When she just stood there, staring at the doorstep, he took the basket from her and set it on the kitchen table. Taking her by the arm, he led her out to the woodshed.

Closing and latching the door, he took her into his arms and held her tightly as tears damped the front of his work shirt.

"What is it, baby?" he whispered against her hair, gently massaging her back. "Have you and your mama been fussing again?"

"Oh, Jace," she said, weeping softly.

"Shhhh, now, it's all right. Whatever it is, Jace will take care of it."

She knew he would if he could, but there were some things he couldn't fix.

"You can't," she whimpered, clinging tighter to the front of his shirt. The coarse fabric felt smooth against her roughened fingertips.

"Tell me about it . . . it can't be that bad . . . it's your mama, isn't it? Has she been after you about us again?"

"No," she sobbed.

He set her back from him so he could look at her. Biting her lip, she gazed up at him. He was so strong, so *good*. He could take care of most anything—most anything but this. For as long as she could remember, she'd run to him with all her problems and he had fixed them.

"Then what? Tell me what it is that has my Datha upset."

"I'm late."

He frowned, not understanding. "For what?"

She suddenly couldn't look at him. "My monthly . . . hasn't come."

"Monthly—" Suddenly comprehension clouded his face. His demeanor changed, turned sober. "How long?"

"Tw—two weeks."

"Two weeks?" Alarm flicked briefly in his eyes. She reached out, touching him, letting him know it would be all right. No sacrifice was too large. Whatever she had to do, she'd do it. For him.

"Are you sure, Datha, girl?"

Nodding, she brought her handkerchief up to her nose to stem the tide. "I keep hoping, but . . ."

Gently pulling her back into his arms, he kissed the top of her head, holding her tighter as she broke into a fresh round of tears. For a long time they held each other, trying to make sense of it.

"Two weeks," he whispered. "That isn't so much. Anything could have happened. It doesn't mean—"

"I've never been two *hours* late with my monthlies, Jace, let alone two weeks," she said in a muffled voice, her face buried against his chest.

"I was careful. I know how—you *can't* be pregnant." Easing her gently away from him, he gazed into her tear-stained face. "Don't worry. This is all a mistake. Tomorrow, or next day for sure, we'll both have a good laugh about this." He tipped her chin up and kissed her full on the lips. "You'll see. Now, dry your tears, and give Jace one of those special smiles that'll carry him through the long day."

Feeling somewhat mollified—because he said it was a mistake, and because she never doubted him, not ever—she complied.

"I guess . . . guess I am being pretty silly. I love you, Jace," she said. "With all my heart."

"I love you too, Datha, girl." They kissed, pouring

their love into every flick of their tongues, every sweet
nuance of passion. When their lips parted, Jacel just held
her for a moment. Just held her, letting his love completely inundate her.

"Datha."

"Yes?"

"You know . . . even if it were to be true, I'd stand by
you. I'd never let you go through this alone. I'd marry
you in a minute, and I'd stay right here in Dignity and
saw lumber for old man Jordan till the day I died, and
never look back."

Tears choked Datha's throat. "I know you would,
Jace."

All his dreams, his hopes, his future, he would give up
for her if she asked. Trouble was, she'd never ask. She
loved him too much to make him give up his future
for her.

"Then why you still crying, baby?"

"Because, I love you so much, Jace. That's why. I
know you love me more than anything, and it doesn't
seem fair."

Squeezing her tightly, he grinned. "I'd die for you,
Datha. I'd lie right down in front of a train and let its big
old wheels run right over me if you were ever to ask. I'd
stand in front of a firing squad and let them blow a big
old hole clean through my chest if that's what'd make
you happy."

Giggling, she tried to stem the tears for his sake. "That
wouldn't make me happy, silly."

She got the weeps sometimes, and she knew it troubled
him. Mama said weeps was just part of being a woman,
and men would never understand it, so she tried not to
get them too often around him.

"Well, I don't think anyone's going to be giving up
any dreams," he told her. Patting her on the bottom, he

turned her to face the shed door. "Now, you get on back inside and wash that pretty face and stop worrying. If there's any worrying to be done, I'll do it."

Smiling, she stole another kiss, then waited while he silently slipped from the woodshed and disappeared beyond the tall hedge marking the back boundary of the Ogden yard.

Wiping her face with the hem of her apron, she told herself that everything *was* all right. There was nothing to worry about. Mother Nature had just forgotten to look at her clock.

She went inside the kitchen and carried the vegetables to the pantry. Jacel was a good man. A kind and loving man. A man who would someday be very important.

Leaning against a shelf, Datha closed her eyes.

Oh God, please let him be right.
We didn't mean to do anything wrong.
Don't let my mistake ruin his life.

April had dinner with Porky and her father Thursday night. Nadine Ludwig was staying with an ill sister and wasn't expected back for months.

April realized she wasn't doing a very good job of holding up her end of the conversation. As Mr. Ludwig left the table, April helped Porky put food away and clear the plates.

"Okay, what's bothering you?" Porky wanted to know as she stored a cherry pie in the pantry.

"Nothing," April said, carrying dishes through to the kitchen.

"Might as well tell me now. I won't let up. You've been distracted all evening. Aren't the shooting lessons going well?"

Too well, April thought, remembering the growing

attraction she felt toward Gray. "They're going well. Squirrels call for a priest when they see me."

Porky wasn't amused. "It's not too late to call it off."

"We've been over this Porky. I know it's foolish, but I have to go through with it."

Pausing with her hands full, Porky looked at her. "Well, at least you admit it's foolish."

"I never denied that it wasn't, I just had no idea of what a 'duel' really meant. I know I could die, Porky."

"I refuse to think that way, but you could, at the very least, be seriously injured. I don't know why you think you have to go through with it. Forget pride. I couldn't bear it if anything happened to you, April. That's why I agreed to be your second. Someone has to look out for you and . . . well . . . you know how I feel."

April dropped what she was doing and went over to give her a big hug. "Golly, Pork, that's the nicest thing you've ever said to me."

The two friends hugged a minute before parting.

"If I'm not there Saturday morning, you know what will happen," April told her. "Grace will come to Dignity and challenge me here. Grandpa will be disgraced, and I'll still run the danger of her out-shooting me."

"I wouldn't put it past the floozy to ambush you," Porky grumbled.

"Well, she does work in a bawdy house, and you know what kind of women work there. They undoubtedly know how to defend themselves."

"What are you going to do if you win? You don't want Henry after this, do you?"

"Of course not. I don't want to ever see him again. Grace is welcome to him, regardless how the duel turns out."

Porky gathered the silverware as April poured hot water into the dishpan.

"You must be grateful to Gray for helping you."

"Mmm." April scrubbed a dinner plate. "His lady friend is in town again."

"The French woman? Francesca?"

"Uh-huh. He was preoccupied today, and on the way home I discovered why. Francesca was coming down the street in that fancy surrey of hers. You should have seen the look on his face when he saw her."

It wasn't a pleased look, at least not the sort she would have expected him to have when his lover came to visit.

"You have to wonder if a man really wants a woman like her running his life."

April silently conceded she'd wondered that, too. Gray never spoke about her. She thought that was odd, considering he was engaged to marry the woman.

"You think he'll actually marry her?"

"I think it's obvious that she does, don't you?"

"I don't know. Somehow, I can't see those two together—at least not permanently." Porky carefully dried glasses. "What do you think?"

April shrugged.

"Come on, how do you feel about Gray marrying her? You two have spent a lot of time together lately."

"On a purely business matter."

"Maybe, but you get this funny wistful note in your voice when you talk about him."

"For heaven's sake, Porky. You're going to have to do something about your imagination."

"Answer the question."

"I forgot what it was," she lied.

"I've seen how you look at him, April. Gray is a handsome man. You're an attractive woman. He's a man. You're a woman. That's an explosive combination for . . . well, something. Are you going to tell me that you've spent days together and you haven't noticed?"

"Remember Francesca? He's *engaged* to her."

"So? He isn't *married* to her, yet. Technically, he's still fair game."

"Gray isn't like that."

Porky hesitated a moment, then said quietly, "You thought Henry was trustworthy, too."

April closed her eyes, letting the painful reminder sink in. It wasn't pleasant, but Porky was right. "You never believed Henry was anything but an impostor. I believed he was wonderful. Apparently I'm not a very good judge of character."

"Stop being so hard on yourself. That's not what I meant," Porky said, putting clean glasses into the cabinet. "I didn't mean to hurt you. Henry's a rat and we both know it, and now you can move on."

"The truth hurts, Pork. You're right. About Henry being a rat, anyway. But not about me having any designs on Gray. That's your department."

Porky shrugged. "Not anymore. I had a crush on him for a while, but that's over now—although I did enjoy dancing with him at the social given in his honor."

April scrubbed a pan, thinking how much she had enjoyed her own dance with him. He was a charmer, all right. Too bad the duel Saturday wasn't over him. She might be more inspired.

"How's Raymond?" she asked, changing the subject.

Porky's cheeks pinked to a high color. "Who?"

"Raymond Grimes. Haven't I seen him coming out of the pharmacy quite a few times in the last several weeks? He isn't ill, is he?"

"No—" Porky began, then stopped. "He . . . just stops by to say hello. You know. Just polite. We've had supper together once or twice."

"Uh-huh," April said, glad to have finally distracted her friend. The last thing she wanted to discuss was her feelings about Gray. They were difficult enough for her to understand without trying to explain to Porky.

"He is just being polite," Porky insisted.

"Raymond is a nice man. Quiet, but nice."

Porky's cheeks grew even pinker. "My, will you look at the time. It's getting late!"

They finished the dishes; then April walked the short distance to the mortuary, her mind not so much on Porky and what seemed to be a blossoming love between her and Raymond Grimes as on Gray and Francesca.

She had no right to resent Gray for entertaining Francesca, though it wasn't sociably acceptable the way that woman kept showing up. Apparently she wasn't worried about propriety.

Where were her mother and father? Did they approve of her lack of decorum? Grandpa said the world was going to hell, but had it gone so far that well-bred young women now shamelessly pursued eligible men?

April slipped in the back way, not wanting to wake Riley, who had been sleeping poorly lately. Datha had her hands full recently, what with Flora Lee complaining more and more about her aching bones.

The door squeaked as it closed shut. April stepped into the small kitchen. The smells of Riley's supper still hung in the air—meatloaf, potatoes, string beans from Jacel's garden this summer that Datha had canned.

She was so familiar with the household that she didn't bother lighting the lamp. She was halfway across the kitchen when she heard a sound that stopped her in mid-step. Her heart thumped, then raced like a windmill.

What was it?

A mouse?

Oh, she hoped not! She'd told Datha to set traps at night!

There it was again.

Where was it coming from? The pantry?

Not anxious to brave a mouse, she crept closer to the cupboard.

The sound was barely distinguishable, but something was in there. She could hear a faint rustling.

Lighting the lamp, she left it on the table, then eased the pantry door open, hoping to catch the rodent unaware.

As the door opened wider, lamplight spilled into the pantry, reaching into the corners of the narrow room. A piece of gray cloth on the floor caught her attention; then she saw it was part of a skirt.

"Datha?"

The young girl was huddled in the corner, her hands over her face. Her thin shoulders quivered as she choked back sobs.

Kneeling quickly in front of her, April frowned. "Datha? What's the matter?"

When Datha wouldn't answer her, April very gently drew her hands away from the young girl's face. Her eyes were swollen from crying and her cheeks wet with tears.

"Whatever on earth is the matter?" April whispered, trying not to frighten the girl more. "Datha, talk to me. I want to help you."

"Nobody can help me," Datha sobbed brokenly.

"Is it Jacel?" April prodded, certain that something must have happened to the young man. "Has he been hurt? Is that it? Please . . ."

April moved closer, her foot knocking over something that, when she turned to look, appeared to be a bottle of Mrs. Pinkham's vegetable compound. A spoon lay beside the empty bottle, as if Datha had been consuming it.

"What is this?" April picked up the bottle and discovered

it empty. "Are you ill? A stomach ailment? Cramps? Datha, you have to talk to me!"

This brought on a fresh spate of sobs, and April realized Datha was too upset to tell her anything.

"Here, let me help you up. We'll have some tea and—"

She began pulling her to her feet, but even as she made the attempt she saw the widening pool of blood beneath the girl.

"Oh, dear God!" she breathed. So much *blood*. She'd never seen so much *blood*.

"Datha, what have you done." Taking the girl by her thin shoulders, she gently shook her. "Have you done something to yourself? You must tell me!"

"I can't have a baby," Datha sobbed. "I can't, Miss April . . . I just can't."

Baby? April frowned. "You're with child? Does Jacel know?"

"No! He can't know what I've done. Please—I'll tell him I was mistaken, that I started my monthlies just as he said I would—"

"We've got to get you to a doctor," April murmured. Gray. Where was Gray? "You stay right there. Don't move. I'll go get help."

Running faster than she'd ever run in her life, April raced headlong out the back door and down the steps. Her breath came in painful drafts as she ran through the darkened streets.

All she could think about was the blood.

The deep, crimson pool of Datha's lifeblood.

She was so winded by the time she'd reached Gray's office, she had to stop long enough to catch her breath. Bent double, she stood holding to the rail of the outside staircase gasping for breath, trying to think. *Dear God, don't let Datha die before I can get help!* she repeated over and over in a ragged litany.

When she caught her breath, she raced up the staircase and pounded on the door.

"Gray! Gray!"

What if Francesca was with him? It didn't matter. Datha needed him, and she just might have to tear Frenchie's hair out if she gave her any trouble. . . . Stop it! Datha needs help!

"Gray!"

The door flew open and a disheveled Gray looked out. "What is it? Riley?"

"No. Datha. I—I think she's tried to abort a baby. You've got to come!"

"I'll get my bag."

She turned, bolting back down the stairway. Gray followed a moment later, pulling on his trousers with one hand, carrying his medical bag in the other.

Side by side they silently ran toward Fallow and Main Streets, saving their breath for the race against death.

Datha was lying huddled in the corner of the pantry, only half conscious now. She gave no indication she knew they were there.

"I'll get Flora Lee," April whispered as Gray set to work.

"Not yet. She'd only be in the way."

"But if Datha—"

"I'll tell you when to go after her."

"I don't want Grandpa to know." April spoke in hushed tones, hoping that Riley was sleeping soundly on the second floor. "He thinks so much of her. . . ."

Gray unsnapped his bag and removed a stethoscope. "Get some light in here."

April lit two more lamps and carried them into the pantry. Standing back to allow him room, she watched him work for over ten minutes before he impatiently tossed his instruments aside.

"I can't do anything here. I've got to get her over to my office."

"What can I do?"

"I'll carry her. You take my bag."

Lifting Datha's slight weight into his arms, he carried her out of the pantry, her blood soaking the sleeves of his white shirt.

He cradled her to his chest, practically running to his office, with April following behind, taking two steps to his one.

Did Jacel know? April wondered. Had he instigated Datha's decision?

No. April was positive he didn't know. Jacel would be the last person to risk Datha's life.

April reached into Gray's pocket and got the key to the office. Unlocking the door, she lit a lamp as he carried the unconscious girl straight through to the examining room.

"Help me get her undressed."

Grabbing a pair of scissors, April began cutting away Datha's dress. The girl had lost so much blood, April couldn't believe she was still breathing.

"Who would have done this?" Gray cursed under his breath as he laid out surgical instruments that, by the mere sight, made April's skin crawl. Looking at the shiny steel instruments of death brought back painful memories of her mother's death.

"There's a . . . midwife. Mrs. Waterman. She's been . . . helping young women solve their problems for as long as I can remember. She must be nearly as old as Grandpa."

"Where does she live?"

"Up on the hill, at the west end of town. She has a small house up there. She doesn't go out much."

"Damn women like her to hell," Gray muttered.

April shivered. She didn't need the grim look on his face to tell her that Datha was slowing losing the battle.

Standing at the foot of the table, April gently smoothed a lock of coal black hair away from the young girl's face. Datha was a good girl. Her only weakness was Jacel, because she loved too much.

April worked beside Gray, handing him instruments, bandages, towels, wiping the sweat dripping periodically from his brow.

"Damn the butchers!" he cursed blindly, trying to stay the ceaseless flow of blood. "If you and Pinkham are so intent on crusading, this is what it should be about!"

"It is," April said. "This is exactly what we're trying to change. Because women can't find answers, they're forced to do idiotic things like this."

"No doctor worth his salt would do this to a woman."

"I didn't mean women are looking for abortions. They're looking for help, Gray, for answers when they're scared and don't know where to turn. Doctors should be there to give them answers, not just vague reassurances."

When he'd done all he knew to do, he stepped back, wiping his bloody hands on a towel. Datha lay on the table as still as death.

Moving closer, April whispered. "Is she . . . ?"

"No, but she's lost a lot of blood. I don't know, April, maybe you should go for Flora Lee now."

Reaching for Datha's hand, she held it tightly, trying to will strength into her nearly lifeless body. She could feel a weak, weak pulse along the inner index finger on her right hand. It wasn't much, but she knew Datha was strong. She could make it through this if only she wanted to. If she didn't, the shock would kill Flora Lee.

"Could we wait until Datha regains consciousness?"

Gray's features were stern. "I can't promise that will happen."

A moment later, he parted Datha's lips and forced a few drops of laudanum down her throat.

April looked at him, puzzled.

"I don't want her moving around and starting the hemorrhaging again."

Nodding, April scooted a chair next to the table, continuing to hold Datha's hand. "You'll tell me if . . . when there's a change."

Gray nodded gravely. "I'll tell you."

Sometime during the next few hours, April realized that not all doctors were the enemy.

Gray was a doctor. A physician, a healer with true dedication to saving life. This wasn't the kind of man who had butchered her mother. This was not the kind of man she'd vowed to fight with every breath in her. This was a man who fought to save life, not destroy it.

"I'm glad you were here," she said, closing her eyes against weariness.

He was sitting at his desk, cradling his head in his hands. His shoulders didn't look as wide or as imposing tonight. They just looked very tired.

Lifting his head, he offered her a weary smile. "I'm glad you came to me. I hope that means that you and I are making progress."

"I misjudged you, Gray. Please forgive me . . . and thank you for saving her life."

"I didn't save it. If she makes it, the credit will belong to a higher source."

She studied him in the dim light. She'd been wrong to assume he was like other doctors. He wasn't. He was unlike anyone she'd ever known, man or woman. He was uniquely his own person.

"You aren't like most doctors."

"I'm honored by the thought, but I am exactly like

most doctors. There are more physicians who want to save lives than those who use the simplest, and often most cruel, method of solving a problem. I'm sorry about your mother. Sometimes, even our best fought efforts fail. I wish I could tell you why, but I'm not God. I don't have all the answers."

Resting her head on the side of the cold wooden table, she watched the lantern burn lower. It was low on kerosene and needed refilling.

"Thank you."

Yawning, he leaned back in his chair, dragging a hand through his thick hair. The little boy gesture touched her. "I told you, she's not out of the woods."

"I know, but thank you. At first I didn't like you. I judged you by all doctors, and I was wrong. You care . . . you honestly care about your patients."

Staring at the peeling ceiling, he said softly, "Look, April, I'm willing to concede that women do have problems that physicians tend to ignore. I find myself saying, 'Go home, rest, and it will be better in the morning.' I do so not out of indifference, but out of frustration. We do what we can, but medicine is a science. I think of the body as a large, complex map. We follow the recommended routes, but they don't always take us where we want to go. We do what we can, and we guess the rest of the time."

They sat in silence, listening to the ticking of the clock on the wall. Sometime during the night, a shower came up, pelting the glass windowpane, then moved on. The moon came out, illuming the wet streets.

They nodded in and out of sleep, listening to the sound of Datha's barely perceptible breathing. If it were to change, even a fraction, April was prepared to run and get Flora Lee.

Gray stirred, lifting his head to look at her.

"Who's her second?"

Half asleep, April tried to open her eyes. "Who's her second what?"

"Grace. Who's her second?"

It dawned on her he was thinking about the duel.

"I don't know . . . I didn't think to ask."

The admission was so absurd, it broke the tension. They both laughed, temporarily easing the strain.

"I guess I could write and ask," she offered.

Getting out of his chair, he came over to stand beside her. Cradling her head, he held her, stroking her hair. His hands smelled of camphor and soap. He didn't say anything; words weren't necessary. He was there, beside her. That, for the moment, was all the support she needed.

Closing her eyes, she rested her head against his broad chest, overcome by her feelings. Henry had never once made her feel this way, comforted, protected.

At the moment, nothing was pertinent but Datha. Not her feelings toward Gray or Francesca or lavender bedrooms and silly pistol duels over a man unworthy of such theatrical acrimony.

In the overall realm of things, that all seemed petty and self-serving when a young woman lay close to death because she thought she had no other choice.

Chapter 16

The hands on the clock slowly moved to five. Datha was still unconscious. It would be dawn soon, and April knew she had to let Flora Lee know what had happened. When she woke and found her daughter gone, she would be beside herself with worry.

Gray lay back in his chair, his feet propped on the desk, dozing.

Getting up, April stretched, then moved to the window to look out on the deserted streets. In another hour people would be going about their business, unaware of the drama taking place inside the building with DOCTOR GRAY FULLER painted on the window. Many, like her, took his skills for granted. After tonight she would never take anything about him for granted.

She thought he was sleeping until he spoke quietly from the corner where his head rested heavily against the wall.

"Let me ask you something. What in the hell did you see in Henry?"

April kept her gaze trained on the deserted square. "Does it matter?"

"A little. As a man, I can't see the attraction; as a woman—I can't see the attraction."

"You know, I don't even care about Henry anymore. I just want it over and Henry out of my life." Drawing a ragged breath, she let the curtain drop back into place. "Do you have any coffee?"

He motioned toward a battered-looking white metal cabinet. "In there."

"If you'll get some water, I'll make some."

He got the water, and she slid a pot of coffee onto the wood stove.

"Porky says it's like Henry's too big for his britches. More dream than talent to achieve it."

"Henry wouldn't like hearing that. He fancies himself an entrepreneur."

"I know, but it's true. When we were in school, he always had all these grand ideas about life, which is fine, but they weren't doable. Working with the Pinkhams gave him the opportunity to think big. And, it seems, it gave him the opportunity to play me for a fool with Grace. To think he could see two women at the same time, even if they are in different towns, is a little absurd, don't you think?"

"Personally, I think he's the fool."

"And he got away with it for a while, didn't he?" She returned to the window, angry now. "He isn't what I thought he was. I believed he loved me, wanted a life with me. Marriage, children, a home."

"Maybe he does. Men can do some foolish things sometimes."

The tone in his voice puzzled her. He sounded as if he was talking about himself now.

"I was hurt at first, but I soon realized only my pride

was wounded. Had I married him, he would have wanted to move, and I couldn't live in Boston. I like Dignity, it's my home."

Silence fell between them. After a while, April cleared her throat. "He betrayed me for a woman who works in a brothel, for heaven's sake!"

When he didn't say anything, she realized she was being much too forward.

"I'm sorry. I shouldn't be telling you these things. I'm just . . . mad. At Henry. Rotten Henry."

They were both quiet for several minutes.

"Don't worry, I'll be there Saturday morning."

"To bring me home?" She swallowed.

"I'll be there in whatever capacity you need me."

She studied his face in the lamplight, the planes and hollows marked by shadows. "You think I'm going to get shot, don't you?"

"Having witnessed your competence with a gun, I think that's a pretty safe assumption. But I'll be there with you."

Gratitude flooded her. She was *terrified* of what might happen Saturday, but if he was there beside her she felt less petrified.

"Thank you," she whispered.

He rose and poured them each a cup of the just brewed coffee. His gaze met hers over the rim of the cup. "You want me there?"

"It gives me a great deal of comfort to know you'll be there, yes."

As the sun came up, Datha's color improved slightly. Gray bent over her, listening to her heart, gently lifting one eyelid to check that she was not too deeply under with the laudanum.

"How is she?"

"I can't say for certain that she's past the crisis, but there is some improvement. You can go get Flora Lee now."

"Thank you ... I didn't want to bring her here to watch her daughter die."

Gray smiled, absently rubbing the back of his neck. "You know, Miss Truitt, in spite of your prickly nature, you've got a soft heart."

She grinned. "Thank goodness you noticed."

April hurried to the mortuary, wondering just how she was going to tell Flora Lee what had happened to her daughter, and why, and that Datha wasn't out of the woods yet.

The quarters behind the mortuary were quiet, but when she knocked gently at Flora Lee's door, the response was immediate.

"Come in."

April gently pushed open the door. Flora Lee sat on the edge of her bed, dressed and obviously surprised to see her instead of Datha.

"Miss April? It's only dawn. What you doin' up at this hour?"

"I've got some bad news, Flora Lee."

She went to the bed and sat down beside the aged black woman who had practically raised her, taking a wrinkled dry hand in her own two.

Flora Lee looked scared. "What bad news?"

"Datha—"

"Datha? What that girl up to! She run off with that no-count Jacel?"

"No, she hasn't. I'm afraid she's ill. Very ill."

"Sick? What's wrong with her? She was fine last night."

"She . . . I think she went to see old Mrs. Waterman—"

Flora Lee frowned, then her eyes widened with comprehension. "That girl went to get rid of a baby? Is that what you're tellin' me?"

"Yes, I'm afraid so."

"And somethin' went wrong," Flora Lee guessed.

"Yes."

Flora Lee drew a deep breath of resignation, her face seeming to age before April's eyes.

"Is she gone?"

"Gone?" Now it was April's turn to be slow to comprehend. "No, she's alive. But she's gravely ill. She's at Dr. Fuller's. He's been with her all night."

"God bless that man." Flora Lee closed her eyes a moment in prayer. "I know you don't think much of doctors—"

"I've changed my mind, Flora Lee. I know I blamed all doctors for Mother's death, and I know now how wrong that was. Gray worked all night to save Datha. No one could have done more for her. It's because of him that she's still alive."

"I want to go to her."

"I'll tell Grandpa what's happened, then come back for you."

"Go, go. I'll get my cane and start ahead. It takes me a while."

"I'll hurry."

April told Riley what had happened. Still in bed, he shook his head in disbelief.

"Don't know what these young girls think they're doing. You don't worry about me. Take Flora Lee to see about Datha. Do you need some help?"

"No, it's not very far. If we walk, she can get herself under control. Right now she's very shaken."

"I can imagine. I'll come down soon as I get dressed and see what she may need. If I come now, she might think my professional services are needed."

April managed to smile. "I love you." She kissed his round cheek fondly. "I love you a lot, Grandpa."

"And I love you, missy."

April walked Flora Lee slowly down the street, holding the woman's thin arm, talking to her all the while. She told her about how she'd found Datha, how she'd run to get Gray.

The old woman hobbled along stubbornly, heavily leaning on her gnarled cane, listening and nodding as she talked. Shortly, they arrived at the doctor's office, and Flora Lee hesitated at the door as if gathering her courage before going in.

Gray met them at the door of the examining room.

"Good morning, Flora Lee."

"Doctor." Flora Lee nodded. "I understand I have you to thank for savin' my girl. I appreciate that."

"She's doing better," he said, glancing over the woman's head at April. "But she has a way to go, Flora Lee."

"She's all right," April mouthed to him, knowing he was concerned about Flora Lee's fragile state.

April guided Flora Lee toward the wooden table. "Here's a chair so you can sit beside her. She's still unconscious, but touch her, talk to her. I'm convinced that she can hear you. It will comfort her to know you're here."

"I don't know about that," Flora Lee said staunchly. "I don't agree with what she's done. And it's that no-good Jacel Evans's fault she got herself with child and tried to get rid of it. It's his fault my girl nearly died."

"Please, just tell her you're here. Comfort her as best

you can, even if you don't agree with the choices she's made. Deal with those after we have her well. Can you do that?"

"I won't lie, but I won't tell her what I think—not yet, leastwise. Well, let me sit down here and just look at her."

"You sit with her and I'll be right outside with Gray—Dr. Fuller."

Flora Lee fastened her eyes on her daughter's face and sank heavily into the chair. Gray nodded to April, indicating he wanted to see her in the waiting room.

"Who is Jacel?"

"Jacel Evans. He works for the Jordans. He's a fine young man, Gray. My grandfather plans to help him go to law school."

"You better get him over here and find out what he knows about this."

"I doubt he knows what she's done. Datha said she didn't want him to know about the baby because it would ruin his plans for law school."

He looked thoughtful. "So she did it for love."

April nodded.

"Still, you better go get him."

"Flora Lee won't like it."

"He deserves to know the woman he loves is in trouble."

She thought about that for a moment. "Yes, of course he does. I didn't think of it that way." She held his gaze for a long moment. "I'll go get him."

April found Jacel at work, unloading logs from a wagon at the sawmill.

"Miss April! You're up early this morning. How can I help you?"

She hurried to his side. "Jacel, now, I don't want you to react without listening first. I have some disturbing news. . . ."

Jacel frowned. "What's wrong?"

"It's Datha. She's done something very foolish—"

"Oh, my God."

"Jacel, did you encourage her to go to Mrs. Waterman?"

"Waterman? No—oh, God! Where is she?" he demanded.

"She had an abortion. . . . Something went wrong. I found her in the pantry, bleeding to death."

"Oh, God!" Jacel wailed, covering his face with both hands and turning in a circle. "Oh, God, no!"

"Did you encourage her to do this?" It seemed so unlikely, but surely Datha wouldn't do this on her own. She was bright, smart! She would never risk her life for something this foolish.

"No! Miss April, I didn't know for certain she was pregnant! I told her not to worry! I—I have to go to college, to be a lawyer, to support the family, but I told her I would stand by her—Oh, Lord—she's not going to die, is she?"

"She's alive, Jacel, but only because of Gray . . . and God. She's still unconscious, but, for the moment, she's still with us."

"Dear God—her mother?"

"Flora Lee is with Datha."

Burying his hands in his face again, he started to sob. "She won't want me there."

"I know, but I hope the two of you can put animosity aside, because of Datha."

Stiffening, Jacel wiped tears from the corners of his eyes. "I won't stay away because of Flora Lee. Datha needs me—I'm going to her, Miss April."

"I'm just asking that you don't let tempers get in the way of your concern for Datha."

"Take me to my Datha."

Jacel followed April into the doctor's examining room ten minutes later. Flora Lee looked over at him as he walked in, then turned away. Gray came out to the waiting room and greeted them.

"Gray, this is Jacel."

The two men shook hands.

"How is my Datha?"

"Still unconscious, but I have hope that she'll recover."

"Thank you, Doctor," Jacel said softly, his gratefulness clear as he once again shook Gray's hand. "May I see her?"

"Yes."

Jacel followed Gray to where Datha lay with April close behind, bracing for the explosion.

Upon seeing Datha so still, so small, Jacel dropped to his knees beside the table, bursting into tears.

When he regained his composure, he stood up and, careful not to disturb her, lay his arm across her shoulders. Resting his head on the pillow beside her, his body shook with emotion.

The scene brought tears to April's eyes, and she welcomed Gray's embrace when he drew her close to his side.

"Ain't you done enough harm to my girl?" Flora Lee said quietly.

Jacel didn't move for a moment, then he slowly stood.

"I didn't know she was thinking of doing this, Flora Lee. I hope you believe me."

"Didn't know you was puttin' my girl in danger? Didn't know she was in th' family way? Didn't know she'd go to that old woman who'd nearly kill her? You a smart boy. Why didn't you know?"

Jacel turned to her, pain evident in his anguished face. "I love this woman. I wouldn't put her in harm's way. I know you don't like me, but that doesn't change how I feel about her. I *love* her, Flora Lee. We both love her. Can't we set our differences aside for the time being?"

The old woman studied the young man's face for several minutes, then finally nodded.

"Don't mean I changed my mind. I still think you're uppity."

Regaining his spunk, Jacel countered, "That's fine with me, 'cause I think *you're* uppity. But for Datha's sake, let's just keep it to ourselves."

Eyeing him sourly, she shrank back as he moved to the head of the table, cradling Datha's face in his hands.

"She's my girl," she reminded.

"She's my woman."

"Hmph." Flora Lee turned away.

"It's all right, baby, Jacel's here. Nothing's going to hurt my Datha. You'll see, it'll all be just fine." Softly crooning a lullaby, he cradled her face in his hands, tears running down his cheeks. "No, sir, Jacel's not going to let anything happen to you, Datha, girl. You just rest and get well now, baby. I love you."

Looking up, he locked eyes with Flora Lee.

She stared back, then turned away.

April shrugged. It was a start.

Chapter 17

Saturday morning, hours before dawn, Gray arrived at the mortuary. Parking his buggy in the shadows, he trimmed the wick on the lantern, then walked briskly to the back of the house where April was waiting for him.

Shivering in the predawn chill, she whispered, "Well, I guess this is it."

"I'd hoped that sometime during the night you'd changed your mind."

"No. I'm going through with it. How's Datha?"

"Some improvement. Jacel will get me if there's any change."

Glancing at Riley's second story bedroom, he said softly, "Does he suspect anything?"

"No, he thinks I'm going to be with Porky all day."

"Then we'd better go. We'll barely make it as it is."

They walked to the side of the house, and he lifted her into the buggy. He was about to climb aboard when he stopped, gazing at her in the dim lantern light, his expression grave. "I don't want you to do this."

Looking straight ahead, she repeated what she'd

rehearsed in her head during the short night. "Thank you for your concern, but I'm feeling a little incompetent right now. I need your support instead of condemnation."

"That's hard to give at this moment."

"Don't worry. I've left Grandpa a note on my armoire, to be opened in case of my death. In the note, I explain that you were adamantly against this, and you were merely trying to help. He'll only find the note if I don't return. He never goes in my room."

His eyes blazed with a sudden anger. "You think my only concern is Riley?"

"No . . . but I know he's your friend—"

"*I* don't want you to do this, April." Taking her face in his hand, he made her look at him. "You, April. My concerns are for you, not Riley."

Not for the first time, she envied Francesca, envied her from the very depths of her soul.

Drawing a warm woolen shawl around her shoulders, she said, "I'm ready if you are."

After climbing into the buggy, Gray slapped the reins across the horse's rump. He was silent now. She could see by the tight set of his jaw that he would like to turn her over his knee and paddle her like an unruly child. But she wasn't a child. She was a young woman with a mission, albeit a nasty one.

Her hands shook as she straightened the lace on the collar of her pale blue dress. She'd purposely not worn jewelry, but she suddenly wished she had the locket her mother had left her.

The horse's hooves clopped loudly along the deserted streets. Two hours, and she would be . . . What would she be?

Would she be coming back today? Would she ever see Grandpa again? He was unaware that she'd slipped in last night and kissed him good-bye.

"Don't think," Gray said quietly, as if he'd read her thoughts. "Just remember what we've practiced. If you think, you'll waver."

"Don't think, don't waver," she repeated, going over in her mind the endless hours of practice. The proper way to hold the gun: use both hands, good sight picture, squeeze the trigger slowly—*don't jerk!*

Gray pulled the carriage to a stop in front of the only lighted house, Porky's house. He headed for the door, but before he had a chance to knock, the light went out, and he heard her footsteps on the stairs. He quietly waited for her to come out, not wanting to wake her father.

The door opened and Porky stepped outside. "How's April?"

"Scared, really scared. So don't lecture her, just support her."

Porky nodded and got in the buggy beside April.

Gray dropped a blanket over them to cut the chill wind on their legs. It would be the longest, most difficult ride the three of them had ever taken.

Half an hour before dawn, Boston loomed before them. April met the sight with her heart hammering against her ribs. Gray proceeded to the appointed place while Porky squeezed April's hand so tight she thought it would break.

A small glen just outside of town awaited the dueling parties. By the time they approached, the sun, not yet risen, had begun to pink the sky. One other carriage sat beneath the trees when Gray pulled the team to a halt.

"Who's that?" April whispered.

"My guess: the doctor."

April swallowed, her mouth as dry as cotton. "I think I'm going to be sick."

"Take deep breaths."

Gray helped Porky down, then lifted April from the

carriage. They walked toward the glen, his arm strongly supporting April.

"If I kissed you right now, would you read anything into it?" he asked.

She knew he was trying to distract her. "Probably."

"Then I won't."

A tall, excruciatingly thin man in a black suit stood in the center of the glen that was still dark since the sun had yet to reach there.

Their feet crushed the dry, frozen grass, and the man turned at the sound of their approach.

"Miss Truitt?"

"Yes."

He extended a bony hand. "Dr. Reginald Smith at your service. I am here to render my services."

"Th-thank you. This is Dr. Gray Fuller and my second, Miss Ludwig."

"Miss Ludwig." The man tipped his hat. "And, a fellow physician. Pleased to make your acquaintances, but not under these circumstances."

Gray and Porky nodded, sharing the sentiment.

The two men chatted in muted tones as April turned in a circle, memorizing the site. A place where she might soon lose her life. What folly had brought her to this point? Her love of a liar? Had she completely lost her mind?

Porky and April hugged each other tightly, tears springing to their eyes. "You're going to do good, friend," Porky said.

"I'm glad *you* think so."

Porky blew her nose. "You'd better. Just remember, if you get shot, I'll kill you."

April smiled weakly, wiped her eyes and gave Porky one last hug. "I love you, Pork."

* * *

The sound of an arriving conveyance caught April's attention and the knot in her stomach tightened. Grace Pruitt's carriage, with Henry at the reins, Grace and Emogene at his side, bowled into the glen.

Seeing him with his "intended" made April realize how very real this was. Real and terrifying. Tears filled her eyes and blinded her. Somehow, she'd been hoping, praying, Grace wouldn't go through with it. She'd hoped-prayed-implored it was a hoax, a humorless farce. But it wasn't. She felt Porky's hand on her shoulder.

Grace was here. She was here. It was real.

Climbing out of the carriage, Henry spoke briefly with Grace, then turned and walked in her direction. It was the first time she'd seen him since the challenge.

As he approached, his eyes were guarded. "April—I'd like a moment with you."

"I don't want to talk to you, Henry."

"Dearest—if you only knew how sick, absolutely sick, I am about this. I assure you, I can explain—"

"Henry," she interrupted.

He paused. "Yes?"

"Were you seeing Grace at the same time you were seeing me?"

"Well . . . yes, but I can expla—"

April walked away. She'd heard all she needed to hear.

Gray turned as she came to stand by him. His gaze searched hers inquisitively.

"He wants to apologize."

"Did you accept?"

"Pffft."

"I need to speak to the rodent for a moment. Anything you want to tell him?"

"Nothing that Grandpa would let me say."

He nodded, then left.

"Henry's a disgrace to manhood," Porky blurted loud enough for all to hear.

"Enough, Porky. I'm not in the mood."

"Sorry," Porky whispered.

Miller's Glen, in another time, was a lovely site. A place where lovers met to tryst, where promises were given and taken. Hundred-year-old oaks bent to form a splendid canopy.

A light breeze sprang up, fragrant with the smell of fall; the faint hint of wood smoke, pungent dry leaves underfoot, the sky dawning a magnificent blue.

Would she ever embrace this kind of day again? Would she ever sit in her favorite chair on the back porch and watch the sun set, walk in the falling snow, eat one of Datha's wonderful Thanksgiving dinners? She hoped so. That would mean she survived and would have a lot to be thankful for.

Tears clouded April's vision, and she blinked them back. Gray wasn't going to see her cry and neither was Porky, nor the enemy. She'd had every opportunity to call this off, and she hadn't, or rather couldn't.

A stream rippled nearby, a haunting melody to the drama about to take place. As the sun began to peek over the treetops, a mist rose from the glen, shrouding it in privacy.

In a few minutes it would be over.

She watched the sunrise, feeling surreal. This might be the last sunrise she would ever see. Not that she'd seen that many. She was usually asleep.

If she lived, she'd do better. She'd watch every sunrise for the rest of her life, no matter how early.

"April?"

She turned at the sound of Gray's voice. "Yes?"

"It's time," he said, handing the box containing the pistols to Porky.

Nodding, April willed her feet to move. They were heavy with dread. "I'm coming."

She avoided Emogene's and Henry's eyes and steadfastly refused to look at Grace. She kept her eyes toward the ground, allowing Porky to steer her into place in the middle of the glen.

"Ladies, are you ready?" The doctor's voice seemed unusually loud in the silence.

"Seconds? Prepare yourselves."

April looked up into Porky's eyes. Her friend trembled so bad, she almost dropped the guns. She was babbling something about shooting straight and not missing, but her words were a jumble. Everything moved in slow motion, and April felt such despair that she was shaken to the very core of her being.

She glanced at Gray who stood off to the side, a worried expression on his face.

The doctor's hands moved to her shoulders, aligning her against someone's back—Grace, it must be Grace's back. He gave them both a nod.

"Present the weapons."

Porky presented the pistols, letting the doctor examine both to make sure they were alike, properly loaded and in suitable condition.

"Miss Pruitt, make your choice." A rustle of cloth. "Miss Truitt—" The doctor paused, glancing up, as if he'd made a blunder. "That is your name? Truitt?"

Swallowing, April nodded.

He glanced at Grace. "And yours is Pruitt?"

April was relieved to see that even Grace was quaking. Her voice sounded uncertain and far away.

"Yes, sir."

He looked at Henry, his eyes sizing him up. "Truitt and Pruitt. Interesting. Ladies, take your pistols."

The gun felt much heavier than when she'd practiced

with it, but April grasped it with both hands, upright, parallel with her head, as the doctor counted off the paces.

Gray's voice echoed in her head: "Turn quickly on the count of ten and fire." How she wished she were still shooting at bottles and cans.

She felt her knees weaken. Quickly, on the count of ten . . .

"One."

Keep the gun up, squeeze the trigger . . .

"Two."

. . . slowly. Squeeze it slowly . . .

"Three."

Don't jerk. Whatever you do, don't jerk.

"Four."

Why didn't you accept Gray's kiss? So what if you read something into it?

"Five."

"Six."

Wonder what he meant by that? "Would she read anything into it." What was she supposed to read into it?

"Seven."

Back out. Right now. Throw the gun down and run. So what if Grace comes to Dignity and embarrasses the pants off Grandpa? He'd prefer that over her death—

"Eight."

"Nine."

If you're going to do it, do it *now!*

"Ten!"

Whirling, April fired. Two shots rang out, then smoke, mingled with gray mist, engulfed her, muffling Gray's shout of agony.

Closing her eyes, she sank slowly to the ground, waiting for the pain to engulf her. The bullet had caught her straight through the heart, she was certain.

She lay rigid on the ground, afraid to move, afraid to

die, sure blood was pouring from a gaping wound.
Please, God, let me go quick and mercifully. She wasn't
any good at dying, she was reasonably sure of that. If she
died quickly, Gray would be spared the humiliation of
watching her wither in agony, blubbering a coward's
death as the life oozed slowly out of her.

"April . . . April!"

It was Porky kneeling beside her. At least she wouldn't
die alone. "I'll miss you, Pork—"

"April!"

"Don't prolong my suffering, please Por . . ."

"You silly goose, get up. You're not even shot."

"But the bullet . . . it . . ."

"It's lodged in the tree behind you, thank God. But I'm
afraid . . ."

"Doctor!" Henry's voice rang out. "Over here!"

"He's hit," she heard someone say.

April took Porky's hand as she scrambled to her feet.
Numb. She was numb. She couldn't feel anything. No
pain. Lifting her head, she looked around. Grace was still
standing, but Henry was kneeling over a figure on the
ground.

"Gray!" Shock seized her. Gray was lying prone on
the ground, holding his calf while the doctor leaned
over him.

Throwing off her paralysis, she scrambled to her feet,
aware she hadn't been hit. She felt fine! No pain,
nothing!

Apparently, her shot had hit . . . Gray? Racing to
where he lay, she fell to her knees. "Gray! What happened?"

"You shot him," the doctor said gruffly. "Said that all
along. Women should *not* duel. Someone's bound to get
hurt."

"Oh, my goodness—" April bent down, patting his cheek. "What have I done?"

"As a shootist, you stink," Gray choked out. "Help me get up."

"Oh, dear!"

"You fired at the same time you turned," the doctor berated, tearing Gray's pant leg and clapping a pad of cloth against the bleeding hole in his calf. "Fortunately, Miss Pruitt is an even worse shot."

Henry was on the sidelines, comforting an obviously distraught Grace, and Emogene was laughing! April watched as the man she'd thought was the love of her life walked away with his arm around another woman.

"Gray, I'm so sorry! I—I wish I could say something, I'm so sorry—"

"Just get me to the carriage." Gray reached for her hand, struggling to get to his feet. His gaze followed Henry and Grace, who were disappearing beyond the line of trees encircling the glen.

"I'm sorry you lost Henry."

Laughing and crying at the same time, she fell toward him, intending to give him a hug, but knocking him back to the ground.

As he fell to his back, she landed on top of him, giggling.

"I don't see what's so damn funny— Watch the leg!"

"Me," she giggled, her laughter subsiding as she lay on his chest, his big, broad, wonderful chest, gazing at him in wonder. "*I'm* the buffoon. I shot you, but I'm alive. I'm alive!"

His gentle camaraderie and subtle wit managed to come through in spite of his pain. "I'm bleeding, and you're laughing."

Getting to her feet, she held out her hand. "Come on, we need to get that wound taken care of."

"What? No vegetable compound?"

Smiling down at him as if she knew something he didn't, she teased, "No, Dr. Fuller. I'm saving whatever compound I give you for a purely personal reason."

A faint light twinkled from the depths of his eyes. "Are you insinuating Charley Black and I have the same problem?"

She blushed, aware he'd caught her in her shameless thought. "No, I'm quite confident you don't have Charley's problem."

His eyes riveted on her face, then slowly traveled over her. "How would you know that, Miss Truitt?"

"Well, I don't, Dr. Fuller," she admitted, aware of the sensuous spark that passed between them. "Of course, I understand you've been treating Charley and half the men in Dignity with some miraculous tonic, which, I hear, has made new men out of them." Grinning, her gaze playfully locked with his. "That right, Doctor? Where are you getting that wonderful cure-all?"

In a voice that brought shivers to her, he said softly, "Wouldn't you like to know."

"Porky says it's Lydia's tonic, and Henry supplies you with all you want."

Grumbling, he tried to get up. "Porky talks too much."

Porky hurried to the carriage, her face as red as a beet. April and Gray laughed as she busied herself putting the pistols away.

Helping him to his feet, April whispered, "Oh, say. If I kissed you right now, would you read anything into it?"

"You're damn right I will."

"Oh, then I won't."

Chapter 18

The doctor loaded Gray into the carriage. April climbed aboard and picked up the reins.

"Can you drive a buggy?" he asked, grimacing as he maneuvered his injured leg inside.

"Fortunately, I drive better than I shoot," April assured him, relaxed now that she'd survived a duel and hadn't killed anyone in the process.

"Ah, thank God for small favors," Gray said.

"I'll go straight to the doctor's office—"

"No, you'll go directly to Dignity."

"But your leg—"

"Will heal better there. Besides, I've got patients to see. Datha will need attention."

"All right." April grinned, relieved. At the moment all she wanted to do was go home, give Grandpa a grateful hug, and kiss the ground she walked on.

Alive was indeed beautiful!

Flora Lee was sitting beside Datha's cot when April helped Gray into the office.

Seeing the doctor's predicament, she immediately got to her feet. "What happened to you?"

"A little accident," he grumbled, sitting down. "Think you can help me with this?" he asked April.

"If you'll tell me what to do."

"How is Datha?"

"Quiet," Flora Lee said. "She woke up a couple of times, but I'm not sure she knew who I was or what's happened. I tell her she's all right, just like you told me to do, and I talk to her. That uppity Black been here, doin' the same. But she don't seem to know where she is."

Frowning, April came to kneel beside her chair. Rarely would she dispute an elder, but Flora Lee's animosity toward Jacel had to stop—for Datha's sake. "Flora Lee, I know you don't approve of Jacel, but is it necessary to refer to him as that 'uppity Black'?" Jacel and Datha deserved her respect and love.

"Datha loves him, very much, and when she's better she'll resent your sarcasm."

Turning troubled eyes on her, Flora Lee said, "But he *is* an uppity Black. I don't like him."

"I know you feel that way now, but in time you'll have to learn to get along with Jacel or you'll lose Datha. You don't want that, do you?"

"I'll cross that bridge when I come to it—" Her tired eyes rested on her daughter, lying so deathly still on the small cot. "If I come to it."

"Your daughter's young and strong, Flora Lee. She's going to pull through this," Gray told her.

"Yes, my girl's strong," Flora Lee murmured. Turning back to her daughter, she softly hummed the same lullaby Jacel had hummed earlier. A haunting melody April had heard since she was a child, a tune, Flora Lee had told her, she'd sung in the fields as a slave girl.

Gray oversaw April's efforts as she cut one trouser leg off at the knee, cleaned and dressed his wound. She clenched her teeth when he cursed against the sting of antiseptic she poured on it. Somehow she'd managed to shoot him in his left calf, but the bullet had gone completely through, which was good, he told her.

"Wrap it snugly," Gray instructed, holding one end of the wrapping as she maneuvered the other.

When she was through, she saw that his face was pale with a sheen of sweat glistening on his brow. "I think you need to lie down."

"I need to check Datha, first."

"You said yourself that there's nothing more you can do but wait, try to keep her fever down, and rouse her enough to take nourishment. Flora Lee and I can do that. But if something happens to you," she said, taking his arm and urging him out of the chair, "we're all in trouble."

Gray tried to protest, but she could see he didn't have the strength.

"You go on up and rest a spell," Flora Lee said agreeably. "Me and the uppity Black can see to Datha."

Sighing, April realized her efforts had fallen on deaf ears.

Helping Gray up the outside staircase, she unlocked the door to his living quarters with the key he gave her. Her eyes swept the lavender room, and she couldn't resist laughing. "I see you haven't improved the decor."

Gray grimaced. "I haven't had time to throw the damn stuff out."

She helped him across the room, and he sank down onto the bed, attempting to remove his boots.

"Well, when you're married, you'll have to convince Francesca to let you have some say in the decorating," she said, straddling his leg in order to help him. Tossing a boot in a corner, then another, she stood as he fell back across the bed.

"Here," she said, rolling him to one side so she could get the lavender coverlet out from beneath him, "let me help . . . you need to take your trousers off."

He opened one eye to look at her. "You do it. I'm sick."

"My compassion only goes so far," she said dryly. "I'll make you some tea, while you take your trousers off and get beneath the covers."

By the time she returned from the stove with a cup of steaming tea, Gray was undressed and lying beneath the sheet.

Ignoring the rush of heat she experienced when she saw the outline of his manly body beneath the light covering, she lightly touched his shoulder. "Drink this. I put some honey in it."

He managed to push himself upright and take a couple of sips of the hot liquid before lying back. "I'm sorry, I'm suddenly very tired."

"Then rest," she said softly. "If you're needed, I'll wake you."

She stood holding the cup, watching him drift to sleep. Over the weeks his hair had grown long until it nearly covered his ears; his strong jaw was marked by a day-old beard. He was pale, too pale. He'd lost more blood than he wanted to admit.

Lifting the sheet, she checked the bloody bandage. He deserved more than a poorly applied bandage. Guilt ripped through her. Gray was in this condition because of her stupidity. The only doctor in town, and she'd almost killed him. Thank God she hadn't aimed higher.

It was time to get her life together and stop thinking about herself and her problems. She'd made a grave mistake putting her trust in Henry, against the advice of

Grandpa and Porky. Yes, she'd be more sensible in the future—now that she survived the duel—and learn to listen better.

She owed Gray more than a simple "thanks." Until he was fully recovered she would see to his every need and do whatever she could to keep his practice running smoothly. It was the least she could do.

Since he had a fiancée, she couldn't tell him how she really felt. Besides, she didn't fully understand it herself, this compulsion to be near him, to share another kiss . . . to have his arms around her and . . .

"Stop that, April Truitt," she mumbled.

Gently settling the sheet around his leg, she slipped out of the room, closing the door softly behind her.

The following week, April split her time between taking care of Gray and watching over Datha.

When Riley heard Gray had been wounded, he was upset until April explained it had happened in a hunting accident and wasn't thought to be serious. Yet another fib, but she was becoming adept at them lately.

"A hunting accident?" Riley scratched his head. "Didn't know he hunted—when does he find the time?"

"Oh, I don't know," April excused. "You know men— I guess he makes time."

Riley walked off grumbling. "Wish Datha would get back. Flora Lee's making gravy, and I'm not supposed to have it."

By the third day, infection had set into Gray's wound. A fever kept him rambling out of his head, leaving him weak and incapable of arguing with her.

April saw to his needs and even doled out advice to patients who needed it. By now Grandpa had come to see how Gray was feeling. When he found April there, she was forced to lie again, telling him she was working as a nurse's volunteer. Gray was her first patient.

Grandpa went away mumbling under his breath.

When Mary Rader came to the office demanding her tonic, April was stymied.

Mary, almost hysterical when she found out Gray was indisposed, demanded that April wake him.

Running upstairs, she roused Gray out of a deep sleep to ask him what he gave her.

Staring at her wide-eyed, he muttered something that resembled "pinkhamsdamncompound."

Pinkhamsdamncompound. April mulled the garbled words over in her mind.

Pinkhamsdamncompound.

Mmm. Pinkhamsdamncompound?

Pinkham's damn compound.

A light suddenly clicked in her head. He had been doling out Lydia's tonic not only to men, but also to his women patients!

Picking up a pillow, she whacked him soundly over the head.

Grunting, he fell back to the mattress, succumbing to a laudanum induced sleep.

A fourth day passed, and April decided he was not a good patient. He complained incessantly, found fault with every morsel she brought him, and when confronted with the news that she knew he'd been giving Lydia's compound to his women patients, he turned downright surly.

Still, she owed him much.

He'd taught her to shoot, supported her, stood beside her, and what had she done for him? Called him a quack, criticized and shot him.

She'd just settled him for a nap Thursday afternoon

when a knock came at the door. Blowing a strand of hair off her forehead, she ran lightly across the room to answer it so Gray wouldn't be disturbed. Patients came at all hours of the night and day, depriving him of much needed rest. She'd made up her mind she was going to get firm with the incessant disturbances.

They had to stop if Gray was to recover his strength.

"Yes?"

Francesca stood on the small landing, her mouth open in surprise. "Oh . . . you're the . . . mortician's daughter. I've seen you downstairs." A frown creased her perfectly made-up brow. "You are here . . . for what reason?"

"Shhh, Gray's sleeping." April stepped onto the landing and closed the door behind her. This wasn't the ideal person to take a firm stance with, but she had to start somewhere.

"Gray's what?"

"Sleeping."

Francesca's eyes narrowed at the implication. "I think you'd better explain."

Lowering her voice, April explained in hushed tones. "Gray's been injured—not seriously," she added at the stricken look on Francesca's face, "But, none the less, enough that he hasn't been able to work. I've been seeing to his needs."

Her brow lifted. "Seeing to his needs? In what way? Oh. You're cleaning for him. He is very bad at keeping things clean. I have asked him to—"

"No, I'm not his cleaning lady," April said, recalling the woman's autocratic attitude the first time they'd met.

"Then you better explain yourself. Again."

"Gray is ill, and I'm caring for him."

It seemed to April that the woman didn't care one whit for Gray, or anyone else, for that matter. Why else would she insist upon staying in Boston while he was here? She was constantly showing up, unannounced, demanding his attention when he had an office full of sick people!

What kind of love was that?

Francesca's eyes widened. "How hurt is he? Oh, I must see him—"

"No, you don't want to. He's . . . caught something. It might be contagious."

Shame on you April Truitt! Lying was getting to be second nature to her!

"Contagious?" Francesca drew back.

April was ashamed of herself, but her nurturing side was stronger at the moment than her conscience. Besides, Francesca deserved it.

"All kinds of ugly blotches. Ugly."

Cocking her head, Miss DuBois glared at her. "Then why are you here?"

"I've already had . . . it."

"It? What, may I ask, *is* it?"

Disturbed by the commotion outside the door, Gray stirred, opening his eyes. When he recognized Francesca's voice, he groaned.

When the women's voices grew louder, he struggled to the side of the bed, sitting up. Clasping the bedpost, he pulled himself to his feet, slowly inching his way across the room on rubbery legs.

By the time he'd reached the door, the loud voices turned to shouts that half the town was able to hear.

Yanking the door open, he looked out. April and Francesca were face to face on the small landing.

"You will move away from the door!" Francesca told April in a tone colder than January.

April stubbornly held her ground. "Gray is resting. I won't have him disturbed."

Francesca took a threatening step toward her. "Why, how dare you—"

"That's enough, both of you."

April turned at the sound of his voice, her bravado slipping. "Gray—you shouldn't be out of bed."

"What is all the racket out here?"

"She said you were contagious!" Francesca accused, shooting poisonous eye darts at April. "She won't let me in to see you."

"I didn't say ever," April protested mildly.

"You might as well have!" Francesca was worked up now, and getting louder. She stared at Gray. "You don't have any hideous blotches on your face!"

Gray frowned. "What blotches? What in the hell are you talking about?"

"She said you had something terrible!"

"I did not—not exactly."

"Francesca, lower your voice." Motioning for the two warring women to come inside, Gray limped back into the room.

"I will not enter that room with *her* in it."

The ultimatum in Francesca's tone was hard to miss. Gray was being asked—no, ordered—to choose. The mortician's granddaughter, or her.

His choice.

And he'd better make it snappy.

Throwing up his arms in exasperation, he limped back to bed. "Do whatever you want, Francesca."

Francesca stomped her foot, flabbergasted. "Gray Fuller!" she yelled. "You come back here! How dare you walk away from me like that!"

Pushing April aside, she stormed into the apartment, slamming the door behind her.

The lavender curtains covering the door gyrated crazily.

* * *

Leaning against the railing, April suddenly felt weak-kneed. Why had she done that? Francesca was *engaged* to Gray, and she'd been on the verge of a hair-pulling contest with her.

What right did she have to stand between a man and his fiancée? She had made a vow to behave better, but the audacity of that woman sent her into a rage.

From inside she could hear Francesca giving Gray a piece of her mind in a strident voice. An occasional rumble came from Gray, but for the most part Francesca was doing all the talking—or shouting, as it were.

"And you'd better be back on your feet for the Thanksgiving party in three weeks!"

Slamming the door of Gray's apartment behind her, Francesca shot her a withering look and continued down the staircase.

Leaning over the railing, April called, "You should be ashamed of yourself! You don't even care about his illness!"

What kind of love was that!

She barely heard Francesca's cold-blooded, and, if she might say so, impertinent response.

Chapter 19

By the time Thanksgiving arrived, Datha was regaining strength. Flora Lee insisted upon helping April with housework in her daughter's absence. She offered to cook Thanksgiving dinner alone, insisting that cooking kept her young—and besides, the Ogdens were family, and what was family for if they couldn't do something nice for one another.

Flora Lee was slowly coming to terms with Jacel and Datha's relationship, although she openly and frequently expressed her anger at Datha for doing away with her grandbaby.

While Datha had been recovering at the doctor's office, Jacel's attentiveness had shown Flora Lee a new side of the young man. His love for Datha, and his constant devotion to her, gradually persuaded Flora Lee to be less judgmental and more tolerant, although she still called him uppity from time to time.

April looked forward to Thanksgiving season. The holiday held new meaning for her. She'd survived the duel, and she had close friends and family. She had much to be thankful for.

As for Henry, she hoped he'd choke on a turkey bone.

Since the day of the duel, she'd neither seen nor spoken to him, and she planned to keep it that way. Lydia understood when she asked for time off to care for Gray and avoid Henry. Working with Henry on a day-to-day basis would only inflame the situation, and she didn't want to stand in the way of Lydia's long awaited success.

With each new day, she realized her feelings for Gray were the biggest problem in her life. She was no better than Grace Truitt, chasing after a man who was betrothed to another. And she should be suffering from a broken heart over Henry, but she wasn't. She just felt relief, relief that it was over and she didn't have to fool Grandpa anymore.

As Thanksgiving drew closer, her feelings were more mixed than rational, but Gray Fuller, not Henry Long, was responsible for the turmoil. Her almost childlike adoration for Henry was no match for the feelings Gray roused in her.

To her surprise, Gray had no plans for Thanksgiving. She invited him to spend the day with her and Riley, then, afraid she'd been too eager to have him, quickly explained that Porky and her father would be there, as well as Datha, Flora Lee, and Jacel. All in all, eight would be sitting down at the Ogden table to count their blessings.

For three days she planned for the Thanksgiving celebration, wanting it to be more special than any Thanksgiving ever observed at the Ogden home.

"I know I'm forgetting something," she agonized when the day finally arrived. She wiped her hands on her apron, trying to organize her thoughts.

"I can't imagine what it would be," Porky said. "There's enough food here to feed Europe."

Porky had gotten there early to help. With Datha still recovering and Flora Lee busy in the kitchen, April was running around like a chicken with its head cut off.

In the smoking room, Porky's father and Riley visited by the fire. Outside a light snow was falling; there was a huge stuffed turkey in the oven, sweet potatoes boiling on the stove to be mashed with brown sugar and butter, jars of pickles and relish ready to be put into dishes. Two pumpkin pies, a mince-meat pie, and an apple pie were cooling on the kitchen table. She already had the dining room table set, and it wasn't ten o'clock yet.

"Sit down and relax a minute," Porky urged, taking her by the shoulders and lowering her into a chair. "You've worn yourself to a frazzle."

"I can't sit, Porky! Eight people will be eating at my table in two hours!"

"There's nothing left to be done," Porky insisted. "Flora Lee's run us out of the kitchen twice. Besides, I've got something to tell you."

"Can't it wait until later?"

"No, I'm bursting to tell you right now."

"What's so important that you have to tell me right now?"

"Not so fast," Porky said. "I want to savor the moment." Taking a chair opposite her, she leaned back, closing her eyes, grinning from ear to ear. "See what I'm doing?"

"Savoring the moment."

Porky chuckled mysteriously.

Now April's curiosity was piqued. Not only by Porky's strange behavior, but by the nearly wicked smile curving her generous mouth.

"Come on, Pork, what? Don't keep me in suspense."

"I've been seeing Raymond."

April stared at her. "I know that."

"But, I mean, really 'seeing' him."

April absently rearranged a place setting, jumping when Porky swatted her hand.

"I *mean*, he's been coming by every week now."

"I thought his work only brought him to Dignity every two to three weeks?"

"It does, but he's been altering his route so he can come through Dignity more often . . . to see me."

A smile crept into April's eyes. "To see you."

"Yes. To see me."

"And?"

"And, Papa likes him, and he's brought me little gifts like this locket." She held out the enameled heart on a delicate chain around her neck. "I think—oh, dash it all! I'm almost afraid to think. What—what do you think?"

April laughed. "I think he sounds like a man who's seriously infatuated with you, if not in love," April said, laughing again when the pink in Porky's cheeks deepened.

"Do you think so?" Porky whispered, as if saying the words aloud might jinx her.

"I think," April whispered back, "that we'd better start thinking about wedding dresses."

"Oh!" Porky wailed softly in delight, her hands coming up to cover her mouth. "I'm afraid to think of it, but I do like him. So much." She giggled. "So very, very, very much. He . . . he says I'm perfect, just the way I am. He actually said that. I even . . . well, I asked him if he minded me being, well, fat, but he seemed surprised that I'd even ask. And it wasn't an act, he was completely sincere. Do you think . . . do you honestly think he means it?"

April patted her hand. "I honestly think he means it, Pork."

Porky bit her lower lip. "I know I should be so happy—I mean nothing is official yet, and I don't want to make you feel bad."

"Why should it make me feel bad?"

"Well, because of Henry."

"Henry who?"

After a momentary hesitation, Porky laughed, and April joined her. "Indeed, Henry who?"

Gray arrived promptly at 11:30. He brought a large bowl of cranberry sauce and admitted that Frances Marlow and her daughter had brought it by his office earlier. He was also carrying a colorful small bouquet of late fall mums for her.

April wondered why Francesca hadn't descended to spend the holiday with him, but one look at his handsome demeanor, and she didn't care how the fancy French woman was spending her day, not as long as he was here to eat her pumpkin pies.

He looked so handsome in his dark blue suit and tie, his hair slicked back and slightly damp. And he smelled so good she wanted to get closer, as Porky would say, to savor the moment.

"I'm glad you could come."

"Thank you for inviting me." He still favored his left leg, but he was getting back to normal. Stuffing his gloves into a pocket, he handed her the flowers and his hat and muffler.

"Grandpa has the checkerboard set up—"

"Just waiting for somebody to beat," Riley called from the parlor. "Come join us here by the fire."

Gray laughed. "He sounds in rare form, today."

Grinning, April drank in the sight of him. She hadn't seen Gray in over a week, and she missed him.

"You coming or not?" Riley called.

"Anxious to get beat?"

"First time for everything," Riley taunted.

April left the men to their game and went to the kitchen to get on Flora Lee's nerves, asking whether the turkey was going to be ready on time and when to mash the potatoes.

The falling snow had added two more inches to the three already on the ground. April stood at the window, staring out on the town. It was so lovely. A warm feeling spread through her. This was home, and while she wished she had someone to share her life with, she was glad she was here on this day, with friends and family she loved. And Gray.

Around one o'clock they sat down to eat. Holding hands, they bowed their heads and listened as Riley said the blessing.

For once, April was glad she wasn't sitting next to Porky. Aware of Riley's penchant for droning at times, she'd deliberately taken the chair next to Gray. When it had come time for the blessing, her hand had automatically slipped into his, and she prayed Grandpa would be long-winded today.

Flora Lee had outdone herself. The turkey was juicy and tender, the dressing moist, the sweet potatoes toasty brown, the rolls hot, the pickles crunchy. Riley sat at one end of the table with Flora Lee taste-testing every bite.

Datha and Jacel were holding hands beneath the table, as Porky and her father looked on, smiling.

April couldn't have asked for a better holiday.

"Tell me, Jacel," Gray asked, "when are you planning to start law school?"

"Next fall, sir. I've got a lot of reading to do between

now and then to make sure I'm caught up with everyone else entering class."

"Jacel hasn't anything to worry about," Riley said. "He'll graduate at the top of his class."

"I don't know about that, sir," Jacel said, but his grin was wide with hope as he glanced at Datha. "But I'm surely going to try."

"Didn't know they accepted black boys in law school," Flora Lee said.

April glanced at Riley, then at Gray.

"From what I understand," Gray said, casually buttering a hot roll, "Harvard isn't concerned about a man's color, only how good he is at his studies. He could be green and blue for all they care."

A grin tugged at the corner of his mouth as he caught April's eye. Riley laughed out loud.

"Guess he told you, Flora Lee."

"Uppity doctor," Flora Lee sniffed, but April could see she was trying hard not to grin.

"Mama, Jacel's already been accepted for the fall."

The old woman looked surprised. "He has?"

"Yes," Datha said proudly. "And he's already got a place to live in the city. He'll go a couple of weeks early to find a job near school to help pay for his books."

"How'd all that get done?"

"Mr. Ogden wrote him a letter of recommendation, and so did Dr. Fuller and Mrs. Langston, his teacher. She's even offered to tutor him."

"Dr. Fuller found him some law books to read the last time he was in Boston," Porky added.

The last time he was in Boston seeing Francesca, April thought.

"Pestering me all the time, wanting to know about medicine." Mr. Ludwig laughed. "Him and that Grimes boy."

"Raymond?" April asked, glancing at Porky. Seeing the flush rise to her friend's cheeks, she grinned. "Does Raymond know a lot about medicines?"

"Nearly as much as any doctor," Eldon Ludwig nodded, "except for Dr. Fuller."

"Thank you," Gray acknowledged. "You've been a great help to me, getting settled here and all."

April brought them back to the subject. "Tell me what you know about Mr. Grimes."

Porky kicked her under the table, and she kicked back.

Mr. Ludwig paused with fork suspended in midair. "What is there to tell? He's twenty-eight, his parents are gone, only has an aunt he visits from time to time, has a good education, likes selling, doesn't like the traveling. A good boy. Asks a lot of questions."

"Oh? What kinds of questions?" Riley asked.

"He asks many questions about my Beulah. I tell him, ask her yourself."

"Papa!"

April's eyes danced as Porky became even more interested in the food on her plate.

"He does seem the perfect mate for a woman," April said, ignoring Porky's silent plea to let the subject drop. "No doubt he'll be settling down soon."

"He told me he would be coming through town every three weeks or so," Gray said, "but I've noticed he's making his rounds almost every week. I thought it was my stimulating conversation," he winked at April, "but I see I was wrong."

Porky's face was red as a beet from all the teasing. "Really, people, can't you find anything more interesting to discuss?"

"More interesting than Raymond?" April asked.

Everyone burst into laughter, and Porky turned crimson.

* * *

Gray looked down the table, surrounded by the warmth of good friends. People who he'd learned to admire and trust, people who made him feel at home, people who needed him. There sat Riley Ogden, his first friend in Dignity. Mr. Ludwig, though a quiet man, spent hours talking with him about the pros and cons of various remedies and medications.

Porky had saved him from embarrassment many times by filling him in on the quirks of the town's individuals, helpful tidbits that enabled him to form a closer bond with his patients. He found himself hoping Porky and Raymond Grimes would be irreparably drawn together.

His gaze moved around the table and rested on Flora Lee. He tried to imagine this woman and Datha and Jacel being invited to share a meal with Francesca and Louis. The warmth and love around this table was in sharp contrast with the impersonal ritual taking place at the DuBois house. There, a houseful of guests would be seated at an elaborate table, but not one, other than Francesca and Louis, cared about the other. And never would hired help, no matter the color their skin, be allowed with the family.

He'd come to care deeply for the caustic Flora Lee as she sat beside Datha, waiting for some sign of improvement. He'd grown to appreciate Jacel's quiet strength, feeling his anguish as he waited with Flora Lee for Datha to open her eyes and smile. He knew Jacel would make a fine lawyer.

And then there was April. His gaze lingered briefly on her, afraid to stay longer. Her hair was piled atop her head in swirls that ended in tiny curls tucked into a ribbon that matched the green in her dress. Her cheeks were rosy from her work in the kitchen—work that she had probably refused to let Flora Lee do. Her eyes danced with good-natured mischief as she teased Porky about Raymond.

How different April's compassion was from Francesca's self-absorption—April's warm smile and sincerity, Francesca's cold thoughtless ways. Was this where he belonged? By a woman like April, rather than pretending to love a woman he didn't care about?

His reverie was broken when Riley tapped his fork against his glass to gain everyone's attention.

"This is a special day," Riley began. "A day in which we stop to give thanks for the good things sent our way during the past year. I'd like for each of us to share one thing that we're thankful for. I'll start." Lifting his glass, he studied the little bit of wine Gray allowed him. "I'm thankful for my granddaughter. She brings me much joy. And for friends—old and new."

He saluted Gray, and Gray lifted his glass in return.

"I am thankful for new friends and for the acceptance I've found here in Dignity," he said.

"For a good year, and hopes for another good year," Mr. Ludwig intoned, adding his salute to the others.

"For my sweet Datha being returned to me," Flora Lee said. "Thank you God, and Dr. Fuller."

"Part of the thanks goes to April," Gray said. Turning to her, his gaze met hers as he lifted his glass in another toast. "Thank you for showing me that modern medicine can sometimes learn something from old-time ways."

April lifted her glass. "And my thanks goes to your skill and compassion and devotion in helping my grandfather, and Datha . . . and being a good teacher," she praised softly.

They saluted one another, their gazes sharing their secret.

"I'm thankful that . . . the good Lord saw fit to . . . forgive my mistakes, and let me keep my Datha," Jacel said.

"Here here," Riley added softly.

Very slowly, Flora Lee lifted her glass and saluted Jacel, whose slow grin spread across his face.

"And I'm thankful the Lord saw fit to spare me in my foolishness," Datha whispered as tears filled her eyes. "And for my mama who loves me no matter what."

Jacel drew her against him, and Flora Lee patted Datha's hand, and all of them felt the need to search for a hanky as they saw a new family being forged.

"And I'm thankful . . . for snow, and warm fires, good food, and family to share it with—I love you Papa," Porky said, laughing when her father ducked his head, "and—"

"Traveling salesmen?" April said.

"I was going to say I was thankful for good friends!"

Everyone laughed, then lifted their glasses in another salute to one another.

Later, after stuffing themselves with pie, they retreated to the parlor to sit before the fire and recover.

When she felt able to get up again, April went to the kitchen to clear the table and put away the food.

"Let me help," Gray said as he entered the kitchen, taking a platter from her hands.

"Nonsense, you're a guest."

His eyes softened. "Come on. It'll take less time if I help. Besides," he whispered, "Flora Lee told me to."

April laughed and surrendered.

"You don't need to help," April reminded as she tied an apron around his waist. "Porky will be glad to."

"Actually, I'm selfish. I wanted a few minutes alone with you."

She blushed as she picked up the teakettle and poured hot water into the dishpan. If Gray Fuller wanted her undivided attention, he had it. "You wanted something special?"

"No," he admitted. "Where's the dishcloth?"

Tossing him one, she added soap to the pan. "Gray, what did you say to Henry the day of the duel?" She'd wondered, but was always reluctant to ask. Whatever it was, Henry deserved it.

"Just if anything happened to you, I'd shoot him."

Grinning, she looked up. "Really?"

"Really." Picking up a dishcloth, he dried a glass. "What did you say to Francesca the day she popped in?"

"Which day was that?"

"I forgot. There're so many of them they're hard to pin down. The day she came and discovered I'd been shot."

"I don't remember, exactly. Something about you being contagious—I wasn't very nice."

He grinned this time. "Oh?"

"Well, I think she 'pops' in far too often, but then who am I to say?"

"Just the woman who nursed me back to health." For a moment it got very quiet. The murmur of voices drifted to them from the parlor, but it felt as if they were alone. "I didn't see Francesca going out of her way to care for me," he said.

"It wasn't her fault. I wouldn't let her in," April admitted.

"I don't know if I've been remiss in telling you how much I appreciate what you did. I could say I hope to return the favor, but considering the circumstances . . ."

"There's no need to thank me," she murmured. "I wouldn't let anyone else come near you."

Laying the dishcloth aside, Gray approached her. There was an intriguing, dangerous look in his eyes, and for a heartbeat she thought he was going to kiss her.

For a breadth of a second, she wished against hope he would. She didn't care about Francesca. That woman didn't deserve a man like Gray.

Taking her into his arms, he said softly. "You spoil me, April Truitt. You make a man want to wake up to you every morning."

"Would that be so bad?"

His eyes softened. "If I kiss you, we'll both read something into it, won't we."

"Most assuredly," she whispered.

Pulling her closer, he lightly pressed his lips to hers, his tongue tasting, teasing, exploring before he surrendered completely. Whimpering softly, she yielded to his overpowering mastery, knowing nothing would ever be the same between them.

It wasn't right, he was Francesca's, but for this moment he was hers. Tomorrow she would cry and rail against a circumstance that deprived her of the man she loved more than life, but for now she held him tightly, allowing her love to overpower all else.

"April?" Grandpa called from the parlor, shattering the brief intimacy. "Coffee's getting cold. Can you bring more?"

Breaking away, she drew a deep breath, trying to still her trembling. Her emotions were raw.

"April," Gray said as she moved to the stove for the coffee pot.

"Yes?"

"Thank you for letting me come today."

"My pleasure, Gray."

Two days after Thanksgiving, April answered a knock at the door to find Henry standing on the step.

Her temper instantly flared. "What are you doing here?"

Holding a hand playfully in front of his face, he said in a cajoling voice, "I need to talk to you. May I come in?"

"You said everything I need to know the morning of the duel."

"It's cold out here—let me in, April. I can explain my unseemly actions. . . ."

Her eyes were colder than the weather. "If you want to talk to someone, talk to Grace. Amazing Grace, Henry. Angel Face doesn't like you anymore."

"April, you owe me—"

"Nothing, Henry. I owe you nothing. Now, please leave."

He chafed his hands together as he shifted from one foot to another. It was cold outside, the wind whipping around the corner of the house, but she wasn't about to invite him.

"I was a fool."

She folded her arms, hugging warmth to her body, wondering why he no longer meant anything to her. It was nice to see him groveling, but not as nice as she'd pictured it. She felt nothing, actually. Just cold.

"You're being stubborn, April."

"I'm being realistic, Henry. You made a fool of me."

"I don't love her! It was just a small dalliance—you know how men are. We're like that. . . ." His voice dropped to persuasive, adding, "The important thing is that I love *you*, not Grace, and I'm here to make amends. I know you're angry with me, but if you'll only be reasonable, we can work this out."

She stared at him.

"Could I just come in. Please?"

Expelling a sigh, she shook her head no. He looked miserable, and if he caught his death of cold she didn't care.

"I just wanted to, just *had* to tell you, how foolish I've been."

"And just how foolish is that?"

He looked at her as if he didn't recognize her. She

hardly recognized herself. She'd thought she loved this man, and now she just felt pity for him.

"I'm trying to say, April, that I made a mistake."

She recognized frustration in his voice. She knew the sentiment. He should have heard her the morning Gray was driving her to the duel.

"I—I got carried away with—"

"The thrill of having two women in love with you?"

"Well, yes. It was childish, foolish, and I realize that now. I know how shallow Grace is. She's only interested in controlling me. You weren't like that—"

"I don't think I like being compared with Grace, Henry."

"I know that," he waved a hand of apology. "I'm sorry. There is no comparison. You made me believe I could be a success; she was only interested in dominating me." He looked stricken. "You have to forgive me, April. All I think about is you, and what a fool I've been. Please, you have to forgive me."

She stared at him.

"Please just say you'll give me another chance."

She continued to stare, hoping he'd take the hint and leave.

"It doesn't have to be this way. You can be sensible about this. Can't a man make a mistake?"

Still staring, she shifted stances.

"I can make you love me again."

She continued to stare.

He looked completely baffled. April could see that he'd fully expected her to take him back. The old April would have, the new one wouldn't dream of it.

"We'll be working together, and the situation has to be cleared up."

"No, as much as I believe in the compound, I've told Lydia that I can't work with the family any longer."

"Because of me?"

April almost laughed. "Don't flatter yourself, Henry. It's because of Grandpa. I'm tired of lying, and I don't want to jeopardize his health by my actions."

"You're deserting the compound?"

"No, I'll always believe in it, but I've come to realize doctors are invaluable, too. The compound is good, as a supplement to a doctor's skills. Gray even recognizes the value of herbal treatment in relationship with medical skills."

Henry turned petulant. "Gray?"

"Dr. Fuller," April amended, finding it increasingly hard to think of him as just a doctor. He meant so much more to her.

"You've told Lydia your feelings?"

"Yes, and she understands."

"Well, I don't."

"No, a man like you wouldn't understand, and the truth is I don't care."

He left then, reluctantly, and she watched him meander slowly down the walk toward the town square. There was a sadness inside her, not for the death of a love, but for Henry. She had a feeling his life would be an endless succession of Angel Faces and Amazing Graces.

Throwing on her heavy cloak, she left the mortuary, struggling against the blustery wind as she made her way to the pharmacy.

Porky looked up as she entered the store. "April! What are you doing here on a day like this?"

"I needed some air," she said, slipping off her hood and stamping snow off her shoes.

"Well, you should have a bushel basket of it by now. Want some tea?"

"I'd love it," she said, following Porky back to the stove to warm her hands.

As Porky set water on to boil, April told her about Henry's visit.

"The cad."

"The rodent."

"Have you gotten your invitation?"

April frowned. "To the Christmas social? Yes. What are you planning to wear?"

Porky added tea leaves to the pot, avoiding April's gaze. "Raymond Grimes."

April smiled. "What?"

"I'm going to wear Raymond on my arm."

She laughed. "He's invited you to the Christmas social?"

"Just this morning!"

"I'm thrilled!"

"I am, too."

"You're really serious about him, aren't you?"

Porky's cheeks warmed. "I really am. He's shy, rather quiet, but I do like him . . . no, I love him, April." Laying the spoon aside, Porky turned weepy. "I love him so much it hurts."

"Well, then maybe I ought to be thinking about a maid of honor's dress?"

"Oh." She blushed. "I wouldn't get in any hurry, but, well"—she shrugged—"we'll see."

April clasped Porky's hand, squeezing it. "So why the sad face? You're in love with a wonderful man, and for what it's worth, I like Raymond, too."

"But what if he doesn't love me?" The words hung between them like a millstone.

"Why wouldn't he?"

"Well . . . you know."

April quirked an eyebrow questioningly. "I don't know. You're perfect, Pork. What's not to love?" April knew she was waiting for her to mention the weight, but she wouldn't. No matter how many times she told Porky that her weight didn't matter—not to anyone—she wouldn't believe it. It would take years of being adored by a man like Raymond to convince her she'd be loved even if she weighed a ton.

"Oh, I guess I'm just being silly. He probably won't ask me to marry him, anyway, but I can dream, can't I?"

"You sure can. Now, where's that tea?"

For the next half hour the girls huddled in the back room discussing the advantages of a wedding dress with a long train versus a dress without a train, a long veil, satin or taffeta, an empire waist or princess style. By the time April started for home, she felt happier than she had in weeks. Her hopes and dreams of marriage were gone, but Porky's were alive and well, whether Porky believed it or not.

Chapter 20

"Don't you love Christmas?" April asked, as if she hadn't already asked a dozen times. With the holiday only three weeks away, she'd turned her energy to decorating the house, mortuary, a large tree in the front window, and the outside porch railings.

"Yes, ma'am." Datha handed her another ornament for the tree.

"I think I'll go back to the market for more holly."

"You have a house full."

"The parlor needs more."

"Yes, ma'am."

Adding a heavy muffler over her cloak, she set out at a brisk pace toward the square. A cold wind whipped the hem of her cloak. Pewter colored clouds threatened to add more snow to the six inches already on the ground. Laughing, she kicked at the fluffy white blanket, tempted to fall into a drift and make a snow angel.

"I love winter!" she shouted, then quickly ducked her head and walked faster when people turned to stare.

Preparing to cross the square, she saw Gray coming

toward her. Her heart hammered against her ribs as she stood for a moment, just looking at him. He hadn't dropped by the mortuary in over a week. It was almost as if he was avoiding her, and she didn't know why.

He hadn't spotted her yet. Reaching down, she scooped up a handful of snow and formed a ball.

Obviously deep in thought, with his head bent, he didn't see her.

He was too serious. She needed to do something about that.

With an accuracy she wished she had at Miller's Glen, she fired the snowball at him, catching him squarely on the side of the head. He staggered, stopped, then whipped around to look in the direction the missile had come from.

Grinning, she crouched behind a small spruce.

Leaning down, he scooped snow off a bench seat, quickly formed a ball, and arced it toward her.

"Missed," she called, taking aim with another snowball.

"On purpose," he returned, pelting her soundly.

Bolder now, she packed another ball and started toward him. Dancing to one side, he packed his own, and before long they were pelting one another with snow at a steady pace until they were within feet of one another.

As she scooped up a handful with the intent of dumping it down his collar, Gray leaped out and grabbed her around the waist, swinging her in a wide circle.

"Oh, no you don't," he warned, stuffing a handful of snow down her neck.

"Don't you dare!"

"Can't take it?"

"Not fair!" she cried. "You're bigger than I am."

"Didn't stop you from throwing that first snowball."

"Truce?"

"Too late," he said, shoving another wad of snow down her collar.

They were hidden from view of the stores by a line of shrubs that circled the center of the square.

"Gray!"

"Beg."

"Never."

His voice was warm against her cheek. "Beg," he whispered, pulling her closer until her body molded tightly to his.

"I never beg."

"Then surrender, or I'll kiss you, Miss Truitt. After all, it is the season."

"There's not any . . . mistletoe."

"Then we'll have to pretend, won't we?" he whispered. Turning her into his arms, he looked longingly into her eyes for what seemed an eternity before his lips descended on hers.

His eyes were cool from the snowball fight, then warm, then searing, sensual and devastating. He fitted her more closely, and she went willingly. She forgot the cold and the knowledge that they were kissing in a public place.

"Surrender?" he whispered huskily.

She came slowly back to her senses, realizing they were kissing in the middle of the town square—and not at all concerned by the impropriety. If Grandfather heard of her shameless conduct, would he be angry? Not when he discovered the man she was kissing was Gray.

"Never," she whispered, then rubbed a handful of snow around his neck.

He jumped as the wetness seeped down the back of his shirt, and she ran laughingly down the mall.

Licking her lips, she savored the taste of him, closing her eyes with ecstasy. Not looking where she was going, she ran straight into Willa Madden, bowling her off her feet.

Packages flew every which way as Willa spilled to the ground in a tangle of wildly flailing arms and legs.

Grinning, Gray dug snow out of his collar and watched April make apologies, then helped the woman to her feet while trying to gather the neatly wrapped gifts that were now a bit soggy.

He laughed to himself. April's mishaps warmed his heart. She wasn't prim and proper, constantly worried about the way society viewed her. She was refreshing. Exactly what he wanted after being crushed under Francesca's thumb for so long.

A second later April sprinted off, her bright red cap bobbing like a cork on a white lake.

April spent the rest of the day warring with her emotions. By the time supper was ready, she hadn't forgotten her earlier encounter with Gray.

But she had to. One experience with a fickle man was enough. The last thing she wanted was for Francesca to single her out for a duel. Of course, she was experienced now, but she doubted Gray would survive another assault. She smiled at the thought.

"What is the matter with you?" Riley demanded when April spent the first twenty minutes of supper moving her food about her plate.

"Just tired."

"Uh-huh. Pass the creamed corn."

April listlessly handed him the bowl.

"Have you seen Gray lately?"

April glanced up, wondering if he could read her mind.

"I . . . love him," she whispered.

Riley set the corn down with a loud thump. "What?!"

She hadn't realized she'd spoken the words out loud. Now that she had, why try to pretend any longer? "I love him."

"Does he know this?"

"No. He loves Francesca."

"Francesca," Riley mused. "The woman who's partial to purple?"

"The same." She sighed.

"Can't trust a woman who'd do that to a man's home," Riley said. "Now, peach, there's a color. Makes women look all soft and pretty."

Toying with her peas, April only half listened. "What about men?"

"Charcoal. Charcoal is a manly color."

Riley took a bite of chicken, keeping his eyes on his plate. "You and Gray been seeing each other?"

"No," she admitted. "You know he's engaged to Francesca."

"But you're in love with him."

"Yes." She sighed again.

"Pretty foolish of you, isn't it? Falling in love with a man who's already spoken for?"

"Yes."

"Then I'd suggest you two stop kissing in the public square." He took another bite of chicken.

Her head snapped up. "You know about that?"

"I've known about it *all*, April."

It didn't surprise her. She knew her luck would run out someday. "Was it Gray who told you I was working with Mrs. Pinkham?"

"No, Midge Shoeman told me. Why?"

"Midge told you?"

"Yes, why?"

"No reason." Wrong again. She went back to stirring her peas.

"Gray told me about the duel."

"Oh, for heaven's sake!" April threw her fork on the table. Was nothing sacred in this town?

"Now, that was stupid." He reached for a biscuit. "If you ever get it in your mind to do something that foolish again, you just get it right out again. Do you hear me, April Delane?"

"I wasn't shot!"

"You darn near killed the doctor!"

"I didn't even come close."

"From now on, I don't want to hear of you packing a gun. You hear me?"

"Yes, sir."

"And what's this rot going around about Pinkham's tonic being able to cure male impotency! I've never heard such drivel—you aren't responsible for that, are you? Charley Black is downright scary lately!"

"No," she said honestly. "I'm not responsible for that."

Porky was.

"Selling Pinkham's poison, fighting a *pistol* duel over Henry Long," he muttered, slathering the biscuit with butter he shouldn't have. "What next? Set your hair on fire and run buck naked through the town square?"

The rapid-fire staccato knocking drew April from the kitchen at a run the next morning. Expecting to find a messenger with a dire emergency, she was relieved to see Porky, who rushed in before April could get the door all the way open.

"Where's the fire?"

"Raymond asked me!"

April blinked as if she didn't know. "Asked you what?"

Porky was dancing in place as if she didn't know what to do with herself. "Asked me to marry him!"

"To marry him!" She grabbed Porky's arms, and they danced around the kitchen together, laughing and crying at the same time.

"When?" April asked when they were finally able to talk.

"Christmas!"

"Christmas?!"

"Well, the twentieth. Close enough."

"Just before the town Christmas party."

"Two days before. I still can't believe it!"

April's mind was racing. She was deliriously happy for Porky, but it was obvious she had to take control of the situation. Porky was so excited, she wouldn't be a bit of help.

"You need a dress."

"Yes, and I don't have time to have one made! What will I do?"

"Let's not panic." April paced the foyer, trying to formulate plans. "Datha can help. She's very good with a needle and, since she's not able to do much around the house, she'd be happy to sew your dress. Now, we've got to talk to Pastor Dobbins, reserve the church, see about flowers, bridesmaids. . . . We can use holly and lots of candles for decorations—"

"You'll be my maid of honor. You can wear the green dress you wore at Thanksgiving."

"But I've worn it!"

"Only once. It'll be perfect. Raymond is going to ask Gray to be his best man."

"He is?"

"Uh-huh. Oh, my gosh!" Grabbing April's waist, Porky swung her around the room. "*I'm* getting married!"

The following ten days were a flurry of activity as Datha cut and sewed an ivory silk dress with an empire waist and lace insets. April busied herself in wedding plans and preparations, purposely filling every minute so she wouldn't think about how unfair it was that Gray was

going to marry Francesca, even when he didn't love—
She stopped, her sewing needle paused in midair.

Even when he didn't love her.

Of course, that's what was bothering her. Gray *didn't*
love Francesca, any more than he loved the plague. The
blinding revelation was exhilarating!

Every act, every inflection, every nuance confirmed
her suspicions. That's why he spent so little time with
her, why she was always coming to Dignity to see him.
He didn't love her. She had no idea why he was engaged
to marry Francesca, but he didn't love her.

She'd stake Porky's wedding on it.

She bumped into Gray twice during the next week,
once when he was rushing down the stairs from his
rooms and dashing off toward the livery and another time
unlocking the door to his office. Both times she wanted
to laugh, throw her arms around him and assure him that
as soon as he figured out he didn't love Francesca
DuBois, who made his life miserable, she would be
waiting for him.

Of course, she didn't.

It was up to him to figure that out.

"I'm going to Boston," she told Riley that evening. "I
want a new dress for Porky's wedding."

"Thought she said you could wear the green one."

"She did, but I want something new. After all, I'm
maid of honor, and I want everything to be perfect."

"Hogwash. You're buying a new dress to impress
Gray Fuller."

"Guilty," she admitted, "for what good it will do me."

"Don't count yourself out," he advised.

"He still thinks he's going to marry Francesca."

"Well, where was she at Thanksgiving?"

"He didn't say." Patting his shoulder, she said good night. "I'm going to bed."

"Before you give up, don't you think you should let Gray know how you feel? The man's not a mind reader."

April paused, her hand on the stair railing. "No, that wouldn't be proper." She hurried on up the stairs.

Scratching his head, Riley grunted. "Since when did that make any difference?"

The clock downstairs chimed three. April lay awake, thinking. She was happy for Porky, there was no question of that. It was just that . . . she was jealous. That was it, though she hated to say it. Jealous.

She wanted Gray. More than anything she'd ever wanted in her life, she wanted the good doctor. She wanted to marry him, be the mother of his children, grow old, and die with Gray Fuller.

And a mere dress wasn't going to accomplish her goal.

She could buy a hundred dresses and never catch his eye. What good was a dress when a woman in Boston gave him the entire wardrobe?

What she needed was a plan, not a dress. A plan to make him see he didn't love Francesca, he was merely infatuated with her.

Smiling, she wiggled deeper beneath the covers, suddenly very sleepy.

Life was so much simpler when you figured out the basics.

Morning dawned with sunshine glinting off heavy snow. April hitched up the carriage and added a couple of heavy blankets to keep her warm on the ride to Boston.

Driving through town, she saw Gray coming out of his office. She pulled the carriage to a halt and waved at him. "Good morning, Dr. Fuller!"

"Where are you off to this morning?" he asked, coming over to the buggy.

"Boston. To buy a new dress for Porky's wedding."

"I was just going to the hotel for coffee. Care to join me?"

"I can't stop for coffee, but I woke up this morning with a rash. Can you look at it?"

He frowned. "A rash?"

Unable to meet his eye, she handed him the reins. He tethered the horse, then lifted her down as if she weighed no more than a feather.

Their eyes met, and she noticed he held her a bit longer than necessary. Not that she was complaining. It fit well with her plan—

What was her plan? What was she doing? This was insane. She didn't have a rash. How was she going to explain that?

She wasn't the sort of woman to vamp an unsuspecting man. She needed to leave now, while she could, before he saw through her little sham.

Opening the door to his office, he allowed her to go first. She stood in the waiting area, unsure of her next move.

Gray walked straight through to the examining room. "May I take your cloak?"

"My cloak?"

"Yes, I need to examine your rash."

Her heart pounded. The rash.

"My rash, of course." She slowly removed her cloak and handed it to him.

He gestured toward the table that stood in the middle of the room. "Have a seat."

Her feet felt as if they were made of lead. Buckets of it. Her shoes were new, and slick. She had to be careful on the wooden floor or she would fall and make a bigger fool of herself.

She took tiny steps across the room, watching as Gray's tall frame bent over and picked up a stool. She loved the way he moved.

"You'll need this to reach the table." He positioned the stool at the bottom of her feet.

"Thank you."

"You're welcome."

April was mesmerized by his presence. "Thank you," she repeated, barely above a whisper.

Gray abruptly turned away, and she wondered what had gone through his mind to make him react that way to her. Maybe she wasn't pretty enough for him. She certainly didn't have Francesca's exquisite beauty.

Lifting her skirt, she stepped on the wooden footstool and lost her footing. A scream escaped her throat, then darkness momentarily overtook her. She woke in Gray's arms.

Concern eclipsed his eyes. "Are you all right?"

Her sight was blurred slightly. "I must have bumped my head."

"Yes, you did. Can you stand up?"

"I think so." Excruciating pain shot through her when she tried to stand. She leaned against him, grabbing her leg. "My foot!"

The power behind his strong arms, as he easily lifted her off the floor, amazed her. Seizing the moment, her arms went around his neck.

Laying her gently on top of the examining table, his gaze never left hers. He was close, so close she could feel the warmth of his breath fan her cheek and that luscious aroma that belonged only to him. She wanted him to kiss her. She longed to feel his lips pressed tightly against hers, soft . . . warm.

He backed away, his breathing uneven. "I'm sorry, did the stool trip you?"

The heat building within her was overwhelming. Henry had never affected her this way. "I think it's my shoes. They're new."

Clearing his throat, he moved to the end of the table. "Let's take a look at that bump on your head."

"I have a bump on my head?"

"I don't see how you could escape it."

Loosening the hairpins allowed her silken tresses to fall free, their tips almost caressing the table. He eased his fingers through her hair in a search for the bump.

She closed her eyes and enjoyed his innocent touch. Did her imagination play tricks on her, or did his motions have a hint of sensuality?

"Do you feel anything?"

She experienced a myriad of emotions: excitement, fear—guilt. But why? She hadn't done anything. His touch was causing her confusion. His mere presence brought out feelings she had never experienced.

"April?"

Her eyes fluttered open to find his face only inches from hers. Moistening her lips, her gaze lingered on his inviting mouth then lifted to blaze a trail across his masculine features. Their eyes locked. Something elemental showed in his eyes, so intense it reached deep into her soul. The slightest whimper of wanting passed her lips when the space between them became shorter and shorter. Her heart skipped a beat. She closed her eyes in searing anticipation. She could almost taste his mouth.

Kiss me. Kiss me the way you kiss her. . . . Then the warmth of his body was suddenly gone.

Before he looked away, she caught a glimpse of the scarlet color his face had acquired. He reached into a cabinet and removed a bandage.

She watched his back, and wondered why his stance shifted several times before he turned back toward her.

"Yes, well, we better take a look at that ankle."

Sitting her up on the table, his eyes avoided hers as he eased her dress up enough to release her garter. As he talked, he drew the stocking down over her knee, then her shapely calf.

"Are you in any pain?"

Oh, she was in a lot of pain. But it was impossible to explain where. She felt warm all over, then hot. Light-headed. And her heart felt as big as a watermelon pounding against her ribcage. His practiced hand was professional, but the feelings he aroused in her were anything but businesslike.

Taking her slender ankle in his hands, he gently rotated it. "Hurt?"

Unable to find her voice, she just nodded.

"I'll wrap it. It doesn't appear to be broken." He left her for a moment, and she released the breath she was holding in a silent *whoosh*. The next time she had a plan, she was going to forget it.

"It's hard to believe Christmas is just around the corner."

"I love the holidays. They're my favorite time of year."

"Yes, almost everyone feels that way. They don't hold that much meaning for me, other than the birth of Christ."

"You sound as if your Christmas memories aren't happy ones."

Perching on the end of the table, he bandaged her ankle. "Mother died when I was eight, and my father brooded a great deal. He never got over losing her."

"I'm sorry. Do you have brothers or sisters?"

"No . . . just me."

"Is your father alive?"

"He died while I was in medical school."

Finished, he rolled her stocking back into place with the informality of a man who'd done it before. Many times. "There, it should be healed in plenty of time to wear your pretty new dress."

Taking her hand, he helped her off the table. "Now, if you'll excuse me, I have a patient due in a few minutes."

Her knees were still quivering from the medical attention.

As she opened the door to leave, Gray said softly. "About that rash."

Turning around slowly, her gaze met his. Painfully.

"Oh . . . the rash."

"Bathe in oatmeal water. That should take care of the problem."

"Thank you. I will."

Closing the door, she leaned against it weakly. So much for plans.

Chapter 21

Porky's wedding day dawned cold and overcast.

April got to the church two hours early, certain she'd forgotten something. Something so colossal, so enormously important, it would make Porky's happiest day of her life tantamount to the burning of Atlanta.

She stood in the middle of the center aisle, critically studying the altar profusely banked with bushels of greenery and two dozen candles waiting to be lit. The spicy scent of cedar hung in the air, embodied by heat from the big wood stove at the back of the room.

Two hours. *Two hours and Porky and Raymond will walk down the aisle and pledge themselves to one another.*

"I wish it was me," she whispered.

Then feeling as if the selfish wish would rob Porky of some of her glory, she amended. "No, I wish it was me, too."

She wanted Porky to be happy. She truly did. But the man she loved was going to marry another. A rich, beautiful woman who had an influential father in the medical community.

It was the ideal marriage for Gray, and she should be happy for him. Wasn't that the measure of true love? To love something or someone so deeply that you had only his best interest at heart. But was it his best interest. She was sure he didn't love Francesca.

Listen to her. All this mooning over a man she couldn't have had to stop. There were men in Dignity looking for a wife. Keith Williams, Zack Myers, Logan Booker . . . oh, who was she trying to fool. She didn't like any of those men, and Christmas would come on the Fourth of July before she would ever marry one of them.

Porky arrived with a bundle of nerves.

"I can't do this," she said for the tenth time. "Mama is so nervous, she can't help me with anything. She and Papa are pacing in the foyer. My stomach feels like a volcano about to erupt."

"Well, whatever you do, don't let it erupt right now," April murmured around the hairpins in her mouth. "You're going to have to stand still so I can finish your hair and get this veil on."

Porky tried, and failed. She was as fidgety as a first grader needing the chamber pot.

"Can you believe it? *I'm* getting married. And to a perfectly marvelous man who thinks I'm perfect. Me. Perfect." Frowning, her round face filled with hysteria. "Do you think there's something wrong with Raymond—like maybe he's blind and just hasn't said anything?"

"No, I don't think Raymond's blind. Now, stand still."

Porky stared in the looking glass, dismayed. "I look—"

"Perfectly marvelous," April said. "And if you don't stand still, your veil is going to fall off when you walk down the aisle, trip poor Raymond, and he'll be laid up with a broken leg on the honeymoon. And while you're nursing him back to health, instead of enjoying the magic of the wedding bed, you'll be absolutely sick you didn't listen to me."

Porky stood still long enough for April to finish pinning the last curl and position the long veil on top.

"There. Now, aren't you pretty?"

"Oh, April," Porky cried softly, her hands covering the lower half of her face. "I never thought—I really don't look so awful, do I?"

"Buelah Ludwig, you look ravishing." April hugged her, knowing that after today things would never be quite the same between them. Porky would have a husband to look after, and she . . . well, she would go on taking care of Grandpa for as long as he needed her. Bittersweet tears stung her eyes as she clung tightly to Porky, desperately wanting to hold on to the past, but knowing that she was losing a part of her best friend.

"Thank you," Porky whispered.

"For what? You're the best friend a girl ever had."

"Dash . . . I promised myself I wouldn't cry." But cry Porky did. Tears rolled down her cheeks, blending with April's.

"I know, I told myself the same thing."

"It won't be so bad. . . ."

"No, of course not. You're not dying, you're just getting married."

"Sure. I'm not dying, I'm just getting married."

They rocked in each other's arms, reluctant to let go, knowing that when they did, they would never come back to this hour, this precious moment, when they said good-bye to their youth.

"I love you."

"I love you, too, silly. Go, be happy."

The small chapel was overflowing. April waited in the coat closet with Porky, the only place in the church a bride could dress for her wedding, until the pastor knocked lightly on the door.

"Ready, girls?"

"Girls?" they mouthed, breaking into giggles.

"Someone needs to tell him we're women," Porky whispered. "He still thinks of us as six-year-olds!"

They giggled again.

"We're ready, Pastor Dobbins." Opening the door, April gave her friend a look of assurance and slipped out.

Gray was waiting in the chapel doorway for her. His commanding appearance took her breath away. He was dressed simply in a charcoal-gray suit with a snow-white shirt and black tie. His hair, still a shade too long, was brushed off his face in soft curls lying against his shirt collar. She had the absurd urge to smooth it back over his ears like a hovering mother.

He offered his arm as she approached.

"You look beautiful."

She couldn't meet his eyes. "Thank you. You look very nice yourself."

"How is the bride holding up?"

"Nervous as a long-tailed cat in a room full of rocking chairs."

He smiled. "The groom paced off half his shoe leather and quoted me the price of every piece of equipment and pharmaceutical product available on the eastern coast. That's nothing compared to the Ludwigs. I thought I was going to have to use smelling salts on them."

April managed to laugh, wondering if he really thought she was beautiful or if it was just something to say. Did she look pretty? Did her hair, drawn up into a loose nest of curls atop her head and fastened with a ribbon that matched her holly green dress, look all right? Was the single pearl strung on a delicate gold chain around her neck appropriate?

As she took his arm, she realized she was trembling.

"Don't worry, no one's going to bite—unless he's invited to."

She looked at him with something very fragile in her eyes. "I think I'm going to be sick."

He patted the hand that wasn't trying to control a quivering sprig of holly.

"Not now, Miss Truitt. Right now we are going to get Porky and Raymond married."

A smiling Pastor Dobbins waited at the altar as April walked slowly down the aisle holding tight to Gray's arm. Wedding bells pealed overhead from the steeple as Edna Folsom played the "Wedding March." Edna wasn't very good on the organ, but she was dedicated. The strains of the music, though not perfect, brought tears to the eye.

As they parted at the altar, Gray lightly squeezed April's hand before stepping to Raymond's side.

The guests rose, waiting expectantly as Porky and her father stood framed in the doorway.

Porky was radiant. Smiling, her eyes were focused on Raymond as she started down the aisle. Datha had done a wonderful job in such short time on the ivory silk wedding dress. It flared and nipped and tucked exactly in the places it should. A strand of pearls, a gift from her groom, nestled around her neck. Her dark hair was lifted back and up from her face into a swirl, capped by a crown of lace cascading into a floor-length veil.

She carried a bouquet of mistletoe and holly Datha had fashioned with bits of lace and ribbon.

Candlelight bathed the altar in golden flickers. As Porky approached, the glow surrounded her in a heavenly light that brought tears to April's eyes. It was as if God looked down—and smiled his approval.

As the bride reached the groom's side, April looked at Gray and their gazes joined. With a dazzling leap of imagination, she pictured Gray slipping a wedding ring on her finger, then dashing down the aisle to begin a life together. The thought sent delightful sensations to every part of her body.

The ceremony was brief but poignant. Vows were made and exchanged in hushed reverence. Porky and Raymond pledged their love with emotion-filled voices.

Then, the moment they'd all been waiting for: Pastor Dobbins pronounced Porky and Raymond husband and wife, and a trembling bridegroom lifted the veil of his new wife and kissed her.

April closed her eyes and felt Gray's lips on hers.

Coming out of her reverie she saw the newlyweds, red-faced and grinning as they turned to smile at the congregation.

The pastor announced, "Ladies and Gentlemen, I present to you, Mr. and Mrs. Raymond Grimes."

Applause accompanied Porky and Raymond up the aisle. Someone had shoveled the walk, and guests poured from the church to rain rice down upon the happy couple. Raymond hurried Porky into a carriage liberally decorated with bright red ribbons, and everyone followed to the town hall where the reception would take place.

Menson's Bakery had volunteered the wedding cake. An elaborate, three-tiered confection that caused many an ahhh. Addy Menson had insisted on overseeing the reception, and nearly every woman in town had helped with the decorations. The new Porky Grimes was well loved by her neighbors, as was evident by the joy that shone in their faces.

Almost as soon as Porky and Raymond arrived, couples were dancing to the tunes of three fiddlers. After two dances, the couple cut the cake and accepted best wishes.

The day was indeed perfect for all in attendance.

"Miss Truitt? I believe this is our dance."

April turned at the sound of Gray's husky, liquid voice. She told herself one dance wouldn't hurt as she went quietly into his arms.

Their gazes held as he guided her gracefully around the floor. She remembered the night she'd watched him dance with Francesca this way, the envy she'd felt.

"I trust you're enjoying the festivities?" They swirled beneath the festive lights, their steps blending perfectly to the music.

"I'm having a wonderful time, Dr. Fuller. And you?"

"It's a lovely wedding."

Severn and Mary Rader danced by, smiling. "Perfect wedding, eh, Doc?"

Smiling, Gray acknowledged Severn's greeting.

As they turned around the floor, April said, "Gray, I'm sorry Francesca couldn't come—we sent an invitation. I hope she isn't ill."

His eyes turned distant, reserved. "Francesca is fine."

"She sent a lovely gift. It's an elephant . . . something."

Throwing his head back, he laughed. She decided it was the nicest laugh she'd ever heard.

"Ivory tusks, no doubt?"

"Porky and I couldn't decide." She grinned. "But they're expensive, whatever they are."

The music changed tempo, and they slowed to a lovely waltz. Conversation was easy now.

"Perhaps you could help me with a question," he began.

"Of course. What is the question, Dr. Fuller?"

"Why is it that all brides are beautiful?"

Gratefulness glowed in April's eyes. Immense gratitude that he appreciated the woman, regardless of her physical shortcomings. "That's simple. Because she's never again as happy as she is on her wedding day."

Their eyes met, and she was caught by the candidness she saw in his, the simple honesty. "A woman's wedding day should be just the beginning of her happiness."

April was stricken by the irony of it all. Francesca had all the happiness she wanted. Money, position, and most of all, him.

It was the "him" she envied the most.

"That's a noble sentiment, Dr. Fuller."

"Not so noble, Miss Truitt." His eyes caressed her lightly. "If a man loves a woman, he wants to give everything her heart desires."

April gazed back at him, the unspoken feelings hanging between them. The music faded, and there was only him now. Fool that she was, she wanted him to know—needed him to know she loved him. "When all she desires is her husband's heart?"

She could barely breathe now. His gaze confirmed what she knew. They were talking about more now, more than a silly schoolgirl crush. They were speaking of love—deep and enduring love between a man and a woman.

He said softly, "Perhaps you can help me with the most perplexing problem of all?"

"I'll try."

"How does a man choose between what he wants, and what he feels is his obligation?"

"That's harder," she admitted.

"But you know the answer?"

Yes, she knew the answer. "He follows his heart."

"May I cut in?"

April glanced up, her spirits sinking when she saw Henry Long. How does he have the nerve to ask her to dance?

Smiling, Henry bowed mockingly, offering his arm. "Miss Truitt?"

Glancing at Gray, she shrugged. She didn't want to cause a scene. Gray seemed to understand and reluctantly gave her over to Henry. She felt bereft as she left Gray's arms.

Taking her hand, Henry swept her onto the dance floor as she continued to look over her shoulder at Gray, who was threading his way toward the front of the reception hall.

"You look ravishing, my love."

April kept her distance from him. When he tried to pull her closer, she resisted, keeping him at arm's length.

"Dancing like this brings back a lot of memories, doesn't it?"

"Not any I care to think about."

Arching his brows into triangles, he frowned. "April, darling, I thought I had allowed you enough time to pout. Come now, let's settle our little misunderstanding and get on with it. Men will be men, my love. You know this."

"I didn't know it, but I do now."

"What have I done so wrong? One tiny little indiscretion, and you're ready to draw and quarter me. Grace means nothing to me; she was a mere diversion to pass the time. I was lonely, love, working long, hard hours to secure our future. Surely you don't deny me a few trivial moments of relaxation."

"I expected more of you, Henry. I believed you when you said you loved me, and we had a future together."

"More?" He looked puzzled. "What haven't I given you?"

"Devotion, respect—you, Henry. You didn't give me you."

His brow pulled into an affronted frown. "I must say, April, this is a side I've never seen of you—and frankly, I don't like it. You're still angry. What must I do to win back your favor? Tell me—I'll do anything. You know you're the only woman I truly love."

"Move on with your life, Henry, and let me move on with mine."

He looked contrite, shocked at her insensibility. "You don't mean that. Have you no idea how much I regret my faux pas? Grace had *no* right to confront you like that—"

"Henry, please. This is Porky's day. Let's not ruin it by dredging up unpleasant memories."

Henry was silent for a long moment.

"Well, I must say, Porky didn't look as fat as usual today."

"What?"

"Porky. She actually looked very nice—" He grinned. "For a hog."

Disgusted, scene or no scene, April pulled her hand back and slapped him square across his cheek, then walked off the dance floor, leaving him red-faced, trying to look as if the parting was mutual.

It was late when April swept the last grain of rice out of the town hall. After storing the broom in the closet, she blew out each candle and lamp.

Closing the door behind her, she locked it, then walked slowly home in the dark, thoughts of dancing in Gray's arms vivid in her mind.

The cold crept into her bones as she walked with her hands stuffed inside a fur mitt. The sky was clear. A full moon glistened off newly fallen snow. She was reminded of the snow fight she had with Gray and his kiss. Yes, his kiss.

Porky's wedding night couldn't have been more perfect. She tried to picture Porky in the marriage bed but ended up giggling. She supposed Porky would figure it out before Ray, but then Raymond Grimes might surprise her.

Though it was late, the lights were still on in Flora Lee's cabin when April arrived home. Worried that she might have eaten too much wedding cake, April made her way down the snow-covered path to the cabin and knocked softly on the door. Datha opened it, grinning when she saw who it was.

"Miss April?"

"I was just wondering if you were all right. I saw the light on in the window . . ."

Datha smiled widely. "Nothing's wrong. Come in."

April stepped inside, letting her muff hang loosely from its string around her neck. "I thought Flora Lee might have eaten too much wedding cake."

"Flora Lee's just fine," the old woman cackled from the fireside.

Surprised, April saw Jacel sitting next to Flora Lee. "Oh . . . I'm sorry I've intruded—"

"You could never do that," Datha said, closing the door.

"Come, warm yourself," Flora Lee invited.

"Thank you." She chafed her hands together, then held them out to the warm flame. "I guess Porky and Raymond are on their way to Boston."

"Yes, I suppose they are. Is it true he won't tell her where he's taking her on the honeymoon?"

"No, he wants to surprise her. They're sailing for 'somewhere' late tomorrow afternoon."

"Isn't that romantic?" Datha said, smiling at Jacel. "Mama and Jace and I have been talking."

"Thank goodness," April breathed. "I've been afraid—"

"I'd take a broom to Jacel?" Flora Lee laughed, waving a hand good-naturedly.

Seeing the grins on each of their faces, April started to smile. "What is going on here?"

Datha rested a hand on Jacel's shoulder, smiling at him lovingly. "Mama's found out that Jacel isn't the devil himself."

"Never thought he was," Flora Lee scoffed.

"And," Datha said, "we've come to an agreement."

"Oh?" The news was almost too good to be true, but April was glad they had apparently settled their differences. It was good to know that some things worked out for the best.

Holding Jacel's hand tightly, Datha said, "We, Jacel and me, made a mistake. One that almost cost me my life."

Jacel took Datha's other hand between his large ones and the adoration in his eyes was nearly blinding.

"We're not going to talk about that," Flora Lee said. "That's all in the past, and you've learned your mistake."

"What Datha's trying to say," Jacel said, "is that we're going to wait until I'm out of school before we get married, but we're not going to, well—"

"I understand," April said softly. "You're not going to take the chance of ruining your future again."

"That's right," Datha said. "What we did was foolish— what I did was wrong. I'll never forgive myself for . . ."

"It was my fault," Jacel said.

"It's past," Flora Lee said. "God's going to give us a better day tomorrow."

"Yes," Datha whispered. "A brand-new day."

Reaching for Datha's hand, Jacel said softly, "What we have will last a lifetime. Once we're married, we're going to have babies, lots of babies, and we're going to thank God every night that he forgives our mistakes."

"Everyone makes mistakes, Jacel." Somewhere in her mind April heard her mother's voice: "How can we appreciate the good, if we don't know the bad?"

"Yes, ma'am."

When April saw Flora Lee was getting tired, she quietly excused herself. "It's late. I'll go and let you get to bed."

"You want me to walk you back to the house?" Jacel asked.

"No, I'm fine. It's just a few steps."

"You take care, Miss April."

April stuffed her hands back into the muff as she stepped off the cabin porch and walked toward the back of the mortuary. This was a night of celebration, victory for everyone but her. It only made her feelings for Gray more intense and the fact she couldn't have him more regretful.

Riley had already gone to bed. The house was quiet when she let herself in the back way. Only the snap of dying embers in the kitchen stove disturbed the silence.

She made her way upstairs to her room and softly closed the door. Poking at the coals in the hearth, she added kindling and coaxed a small flame before removing her cloak. Shadows danced on the wall as the fire took hold.

Pulling off her mittens, she removed her hat and tossed it onto the chair in front of her vanity. The image of her reflection caught her, and she stopped to look. Her hair was coming loose from its pins, and she took them out to let it fall over her shoulders. Her cheeks were rosy from the cold, and her image looked back at her with . . . what? Sadness? No. She was happy for Porky—and for Datha.

Surprise? Perhaps. She'd been surprised that seeing Henry had brought not one twinge of regret.

Then what? She wasn't sure why she felt she was staring at a stranger.

Unhooking her dress, she let it fall in a pool at her feet.

"Where did you go, Gray? Was Francesca waiting for you? Is she too good to come to Porky's wedding, choosing instead to wait for you in your bed, between silken lavender sheets, smelling of expensive French perfume?"

Shame on you, Gray Fuller, for taking the easy way out. For choosing obligation over love. For trapping yourself in a velvet-coated, money-and-prestige-oriented prison.

For refusing to follow your heart.

Sliding into bed, she drew the covers up to her chin, trying to get warm. A coldness settled around her heart and refused to budge. The room was growing warm, but she still felt cold.

Incredibly cold and empty inside.

Chapter 22

The DuBois house was lit up like a Christmas tree. Light spilled from every window as Gray rode up. A footman took charge of his horse, and he climbed the steps to the front door.

Louis DuBois and his daughter were in the middle of another holiday party. Music and loud laughter filtered from behind the closed doors.

"Good evening, Dr. Fuller," the butler greeted as he took Gray's overcoat and hat. "I'll inform Miss DuBois you have arrived."

Gowns of red and blue and gold formed a colorful maze on the ballroom floor as couples waltzed beneath elaborate crystal chandeliers. A large ensemble of musicians played from the alcove.

Glass clinked against glass as guests took refreshments from four long tables heavily laden with food and drink. As usual, the room was too warm. Gray's gaze moved over the crowd, searching for Francesca.

He was able to single her out from among the swirling array of lavish women's finery. She was dancing with a tall, older man wearing a black suit and red cape. Her clear, tinkling laughter came to him as he stood in the doorway, watching.

Spotting Louis chatting with a group of men, he moved in the doctor's direction, threading his way across the crowded room.

When Louis spotted him, he paused in midconversation, smiling. "Gray! I wasn't expecting you! Francesca said you wouldn't be attending this evening."

No, he wouldn't be expecting him. Gray had sent apologies by messenger earlier this week, saying he would be unable to attend tonight's gathering. Louis had no reason to believe he'd changed his mind.

"Good evening, Louis. May I have a word in private, if you have a moment?"

Louis glanced at the group of men standing around him. "Now?"

"Now."

Making his apologies, Louis quietly excused himself from his associates.

The two men threaded their way across the dance floor to Louis's study. As he closed the heavy double doors, Louis turned, smiling. "Should I ask Francesca to join us?"

"That isn't necessary, Louis."

"Ah, well, she is dancing with a dear friend of mine—Count Evelyn, from England. Have you met?"

"No, I don't believe we have."

"Well, no matter." Louis crossed the room to pour drinks from a crystal decanter. "You know, Gray, at one time I thought Count Evelyn would be a perfect match for Francesca, but she set her cap for a very promising young doctor." He smiled, handing Gray a glass. "You. I have to say, my daughter is very astute. The greatest Christmas gift you could give my daughter is to tell her you've decided to join me in my clinics." As Gray's expression turned solemn, Louis's smile faded. "No, that would not be why you're here this evening."

"No, it isn't."

Walking to the fire, Louis stared into the burning embers. The silence in the room was suddenly deafening.

"So, what brings you to Boston on such a cold night? Francesca isn't expecting you."

Removing an envelope from the inside pocket of his jacket, Gray laid it on the table.

Turning, Louis spared the missive a fleeting glance. "What is it?"

"The final payment on the financial debt I owe you."

Louis looked at the envelope as if he wouldn't take it. "I've told you before, this isn't necessary," he began.

"Louis, I want you to know how much I appreciate your faith and confidence in me. Without you, I would not have been able to achieve my dream of becoming a doctor."

"Nonsense, you're a brilliant man. I can assure you, if I hadn't taken you under my mentorship, someone else would have. You give me far too much credit."

"You will always have my gratitude. The kind of faith you've shown in me can never be repaid."

"I don't expect it to be repaid. When you marry my daughter—"

"Please," Gray stopped him. "Hear me out, Louis."

"Of course." Louis circled the large mahogany desk and sat down.

"It is precisely that gratitude that makes what I have to say so difficult."

Louis studied him, a frown forming on his distinguished features.

"I don't love your daughter."

The words were like a shotgun blast, reverberating off the richly paneled walls.

Louis didn't flinch, but his eyes mirrored his great disappointment.

"I'm sorry, Louis. You have my deepest respect, but I don't love Francesca. I would only hurt her if I were to marry her."

Leaning back in his chair, Louis closed his eyes, his fingers gently massaging his temples. He looked old, weary.

"I can't say that I saw this coming."

"Francesca deserves someone who will love her, Louis. I don't love her. I've tried, God knows I've tried, but I don't. I see no purpose in going on with the engagement."

A deep sigh escaped Louis as he straightened and poured another drink. "This seems rather sudden—are you certain you've given this proper thought, son?"

"It isn't sudden, Louis." Moving to the study window, Gray looked out. Snow was falling again. Whispery light puffs that swirled around the gaslights, coating the branches of the trees. His decision wasn't sudden. He'd thought of nothing else since the day he moved to Dignity. "I've thought about it for months."

"Does Francesca know?"

Gray was silent for a moment. He'd tried to tell her in a hundred—a thousand different ways, but she wouldn't accept what he knew to be true. Whatever attraction she'd once held for him was gone.

He could go on as if nothing was wrong, go through with the marriage, insist she move to Dignity, struggle to build a marriage, try to live a lie, take Louis's money and live the life of a king, but he wouldn't.

Life was a precious commodity. Who knew that better than he and Louis, men who dealt with life and death every day. He didn't plan on wasting his in a meaningless marriage to a woman he didn't love.

"No, I plan to tell her tonight."

Kneading his temples, Louis said softly, "Of course, I'll see to it you'll never practice in Boston again."

"Would you do that for me, Louis? I'd deeply appreciate it." Threats didn't faze him, although he had expected more from Louis. But Francesca was his daughter, and she would be embarrassed and hurt by his decision.

"I see my power and prestige holds no meaning for you."

"On the contrary, I respect you, Louis. You're my mentor, a man whose talents I respect immensely. That won't change, but I can't marry your daughter."

Staring unseeing into the bottom of his brandy, Louis nodded. "I ask that you be gentle with her."

"I have deep affection for your daughter, Louis. I don't want to hurt her, but I'll hurt her more by marrying her. Dignity is where I belong, Louis, not in Boston, where Francesca wants me to be."

He knew now what he had only suspected until recently. He had changed. He had gone to Dignity in search of a practice; instead, he found a family, a real home.

"Surely there is a way you and Francesca can reach a compromise," Louis said softly.

Gray studied the painting of Francesca hanging over the imported mantel. "Look at her, Louis. She's young, beautiful, spoiled. She's known nothing but the finest things in life. She would wither away in Dignity."

Louis was silent for a long time. Then: "She is a difficult young woman. As my only child, I indulged her far too much. Perhaps if I had been less lenient . . ."

Gray's relief was almost tangible. He hadn't dared hope Louis would understand, and in his own way, support his decision.

"Thank you."

"Don't thank me." Louis reached for the decanter to pour another drink. "My parents chose a girl for me back in France, but she was not the girl of my own choosing. I refused to marry her, and they never forgave me." Taking a sip of Scotch, he looked thoughtful. "Like you, I could not bear to marry a woman I did not love."

The fire crackled in the grate as the two men shared an easy silence.

"Is there another woman?"

"Yes," Gray admitted. "But she doesn't know it. I only knew for certain recently myself."

"I was afraid of that."

Getting up slowly, he extended his hand to Gray. "Of course, you now become the no-good bastard who deserted my daughter." He flashed a tired grin.

Smiling, Gray accepted his hand. "I know, Louis."

"You are a good man, Gray Fuller. An honorable man. You have my best wishes for your future."

"Thank you, sir."

Louis grew sober. "Be assured, should you ever need my help, my advice, or my service, I will be available. Now, let us join the celebration. You and Francesca can talk at the end of the evening. It will be . . . simpler, yes?"

"Yes," Gray said. "It will be simpler."

Picking up a Lalique vase, Francesca hurled it against the study wall. "You cad! You despicable womanizer!"

Gray was indifferent to her wrath. "Damn it, it's over, Francesca. Let it go."

Striding across the room, she drew her hand back to slap him, but he thwarted her efforts. Their eyes locked in silent duel.

"Don't push me, Francesca. You have a right to be

angry, but if I married you it would be the worst mistake of our lives."

"You *bastard*."

Letting go of her hands, he turned away. "You need to learn humility, Francesca. The world isn't your bowl of cherries."

"It's April Truitt, isn't it? The little trollop. She's been after you from the first day she laid eyes on you—"

Turning, Gray pinned her with a hard look. "Leave April out of this."

"The bitch—has she been gracing your bed? Is that it? Is that why you haven't made love to me in weeks? Is she more experienced between the sheets than I?"

Gray had never lifted a hand to a woman, but she was sorely tempting him.

Francesca reverted to tears. "Can't you see what she wants? She smells money, Gray. Power. She's using her grandfather's ill health as a ploy to entrap you. She can never love you the way I do. Don't be swayed by sweet innocence!"

"April is a woman of integrity, Francesca."

Her brows lifted with resentment. "And I'm not?"

Gray smiled in the calm strength of knowledge.

"Consider what I've done for you, Gray. The things I bought—the things *father's* done for you. How can you think of throwing it all away on that little tramp—"

"Enough!" His tone took on a dangerous edge. "Not another word about April."

Stunned, Francesca stared at him. "You actually love her."

"Yes, I actually love her."

"Well," she said in biting desperation. "Why should I care? It was only a matter of time before I broke off our relationship." Her eyes took on a look of superiority.

"You fool. I never loved you. You were merely a diversion, couldn't you see that? Do you honestly think I would marry a picayune doctor like you?"

"No," Gray admitted. "I couldn't see that, Francesca. That's why I'm breaking the engagement."

Picking up a crystal goblet, she heatedly flung it at him.

It was snowing again.

April stared out the window of the mortuary, wondering if it would ever stop. Snow was piled high along the sides of the road. Only a few lone travelers braved the inclement weather.

Shivering, she let the curtain drop into place and moved to the fire. She missed Porky. There was no one to pour her heart out to, no one to share her melancholy, no one who understood her love for a man she couldn't have, like Porky did.

Suddenly the walls seemed to be closing in on her. Grabbing her cloak and muffler, she ran down the stairs, calling to Riley as she passed the smoking room, "I'm going for a walk, Grandpa!"

"At this hour?"

"I won't be gone long."

"Can I eat the last piece of the sweet potato pie?"

"Sure, enjoy yourself." He had been so good about his diet and walking, she didn't have the heart to tell him he couldn't.

Besides, there was only half of a piece left; she'd eaten the other half earlier.

The wind was moaning through the trees as she stepped out of the house, wrapping her muffler tightly around her throat. It was a horrible night for a walk, but she was getting used to adversity.

If Porky were here, she'd tell her to buck up and stop feeling sorry for herself.

No, she wouldn't. She'd say, "Dash it all, April, if you love Gray Fuller, stop mooning around and do something about it!"

Well, she loved Gray Fuller, but she didn't know what to do about it. Her one attempt to vamp him hadn't worked. She'd left his office that day feeling as if he'd seduced her when she'd gone there in hopes of seducing him.

No, she had tried her hand at seduction. Now she had to back away gracefully, prove that she was mature enough to know when she was beaten.

The cold night air wrapped itself around her, snatching her breath. Blowing snow nearly obscured the gaslights lining the square. A few were dark, unable to stand the onslaught of Old Man Winter. She circled the square twice, hoping to make herself so tired that she'd fall into bed, exhausted. Her breath came in thick, vaporous puffs as she started on her third round.

Snow was falling in heavy sheets. Icy crystals formed on the tip of her nose, and the cold air hurt her lungs.

Where was Gray?

With Frenchie?

Maybe not.

Maybe yes.

He'd been in such an all-fired hurry to leave the wedding reception. To get to her? Most likely. Where were they at this moment, snuggled somewhere in a hotel room in Boston, making love—

She wouldn't think about it.

She couldn't.

She would dissolve in tears in a crumpled heap and lose her composure.

Her footsteps slowed as she realized she was standing

in front of his office. Wouldn't you know it? She wasn't going to let it rest. She started to cry. Foolish, wasted tears that would result in nothing more than a miserable chapped face.

Silent weeping turned into deep, heartrending sobs as she realized that Gray would never be hers. Never. And it hurt. Worse than her mother's death, and the long hours she'd spent holding Datha's hand, praying she would live.

Leaning against the building, she tried to hold it in, but that only made it worse.

Why? Why had Gray come into her life, only to be denied to her? Why couldn't he have come to Dignity completely unattached.

From out of nowhere, a handkerchief appeared. A nice, snowy-white handkerchief.

Unconsciously accepting it, she blew her nose, trying to stem the tide of salty weeping.

Suddenly she looked up. Where did that handkerchief come from?

Trying to focus on the blurry apparition blocking her path, she whispered softly, "Gray?"

Taking her into his arms, he started waltzing with her. Right there in the middle of the sidewalk in a blowing snowstorm. He danced with her as if it were as natural as breathing. Moving her gracefully about the snowy side-walk, he held her closely, his gaze locked with hers. "Now, where were we when Henry so rudely interrupted us?"

"Gray?" she repeated, stunned by his almost ghostly appearance. His overcoat was covered in snow, as if he'd been out in the weather for some time.

Whirling her lightly, he caught her by the waist and lifted her off the sidewalk, setting her down in the middle of the street.

As they began waltzing again, his gaze held hers in the snowy gaslight.

"Did I get around to telling you how beautiful you looked today?"

Regaining her composure, she turned angry. How dare he dance with her in the snow, hold her indecently close, and gaze at her as if they were destined to be lovers, and how *dare* he make her want him more than anything she'd ever wanted in her life.

When she opened her mouth to "how dare you," he kissed her. Kissed her so long, so hard, so thoroughly, so completely, he rendered her speechless.

As their lips parted many long moments later, he whispered, "Merry Christmas."

Laughter bubbled up inside her. Kissing him left her giddy, feeling as carefree as a child. "It's not Christmas yet."

"No?" He frowned. "Are you certain? I have a gift for you."

"You do?"

He reached into his pocket. "I believe—yes, here it is." He opened his hand, displaying a small blue velvet box resting in its palm.

She wouldn't let herself think— No, she wouldn't let herself hope. But strange as he was acting, there was no reason to hope he was here to— He'd imbibed too much this evening. A patient had insisted he celebrate the season, and he was drunk—no, he'd gotten her a small token for appearance sake. She felt foolish; she hadn't gotten him anything—except for the outrageously expensive gold tie tack that had taken all her money, hidden away in the bottom of her armoire.

Taking her hand, he closed it around the box. "Aren't you going to open it?"

"No." She looked away, refusing to be disappointed.

What right did he have to be giving her gifts when he was engaged to another woman.

"Coward."

"Gray . . ." She was tired of playing games. "Unless that's an engagement ring, I don't want it." There. She'd said it. Let him have a good laugh, then run back to Frenchie.

His brows lifted in surprise. "Engagement ring? You want an engagement ring from me?"

Well, now she did feel stupid. How could she have blurted that out—an engagement ring. Why hadn't she said a . . . diamond tiara or, better yet, a stupid old Ming vase!

Gray reached out and brushed a strand of hair the wind had blown from beneath her cloak. "If I gave you an engagement ring, that would mean I wasn't engaged to Francesca any longer."

"Well . . . would that be so bad?" She gazed up at him, willing him to say the words she wanted to hear.

He pretended to think about it.

She didn't find that funny.

"Given that I hate purple, no, that wouldn't be so bad." Pulling her to him, his lips brushed hers, exquisitely teased, then kissed her again. "Perhaps that's why I find myself no longer engaged to marry Francesca DuBois."

"Oh, Gray!" Her words were issued on a rush of disbelief. Joy started to grow inside her. "Do you mean it? I thought you were in love with her."

"That's odd, because I thought the same thing for a while." He gazed at her with such love, such perfect devotion, she started to cry again. Opening the box, he displayed a tiny sparkling diamond. "From the first day I met you, April, I knew I didn't love Francesca."

"Then why did you stay engaged to her?"

His face sobered. "I think it had something to do with gratitude, but I'm not certain. When I'm able to sort through it, I'll tell you. Right now, I want to be with you, April, just you. I want to hold you in my arms, make love to you, whisper all the things that have been in my heart for so long now."

"But you didn't like me at first, and I didn't like you. We disagreed, Gray. A lot."

"Never about us."

No, that was true. Over the Pinkham tonic, the duel, her impetuous nature, but they hadn't fought over that in a while . . . actually, they hadn't fought about anything lately.

Really, she loved him exactly the way he was.

"And if disagreeing worries you, get over it. We'll do that a lot in the next fifty years."

Suddenly, he lifted her off her feet and started carrying her to the outside staircase.

"Put me down! Where are you taking me?" she laughed.

"Remember when you came to my office complaining of a trumped-up rash, trying to seduce me?"

"Oh." She grinned, touching cold noses with him. "Was I that obvious?"

He looked at her, mocking her feigned innocence. Snowflakes covered his long, dark lashes.

"Guess so, huh?"

He kissed her. "Guess so."

"So, where are we going?" she asked as he began to climb the stairs. She didn't care where. It could be to the moon, as long as he took her.

"To finish what you started." Pausing, his mouth caught hers again in an unrestrained, ravenous kiss. She was trembling when it was over.

"You're going to let me, shamelessly, and without the slightest hint of remorse, seduce you?" she teased.

His mouth silenced her.

Yes, she thought—her last coherent one for many hours.

That was precisely what he was about to do.

Live the

romance of

Lori Copeland's

historic

America!

*And don't miss these
romantic adventures!*

SOMEONE TO LOVE

Maggie Fletcher did not think life could get much
worse after she took one look at the haunted, tumble-
down mine nicknamed the Hellhole that she had
come thousands of miles to inherit. Then she met
T. J. Manning, a man with a past who found a crew
of female ex-convicts to work in the Hellhole. Now
Maggie is wondering if the treasure she is seeking is
inside a cave or in the burly arms of a man who
promises a lifetime of riches.

BRIDAL LACE AND BUCKSKIN

When Beth Baylor announces her engagement to gorgeous rancher Adam Baldwin, seamstress Vonnie
Taylor would rather choke than make the wedding
dress. What Beth does not know is that Vonnie and
Adam eloped as childhood sweethearts but then
could not face their feuding fathers. Seven long years
have passed, but old passions and present dangers
have combined to throw these star-crossed lovers
together again. Vonnie discovers that love may take
its time, but it is never too late.

Lori Copeland

brings to life the adventure, passion, and beauty of the Old West with the authentic detail and charming characters sure to captivate your imagination—and capture your heart.

Published by Fawcett Books.
Available in your local bookstore.